ISENVEE

KER?

DELLING

FJERDA

AVFALLE

ELBJEN

DJERHOLM

HALMHEND   PERMAFROST

ARKESK   ULENSK   CHERNAST

TSIBEYA

THE
UNSEA   PETRAZOI   RAVKA

NOVO-
KRIBIRSK   RYEVOST

KRIBIRSK   BALAKIREV

OS
KERVO   OS ALTA

KERAMZIN   POLIZNAYA

SIKURSK

TSEMNA   DVA
        CARYEVA   STOLBA   SIKURZOI

KOBA

BHEZ JU   SHU HAN

AHMRAT JEN

Before

The boy and the girl had once dreamed of ships, long ago, before they'd ever seen the True Sea. They were the vessels of stories, magic ships with masts hewn from sweet cedar and sails spun by maidens from thread of pure gold. Their crews were white mice who sang songs and scrubbed the decks with their pink tails.

The *Verrhader* was not a magic ship. It was a Kerch trader, its hold bursting with millet and molasses. It stank of unwashed bodies and the raw onions the sailors claimed would prevent scurvy. Its crew spat and swore and gambled for rum rations. The bread the boy and the girl were given spilled weevils, and their cabin was a cramped closet they were forced to share with two other passengers and a barrel of salt cod.

They didn't mind. They grew used to the clang of bells sounding the hour, the cry of the gulls, the unintelligible gabble of Kerch. The ship was their kingdom, and the sea a vast moat that kept their enemies at bay.

The boy took to life aboard ship as easily as he took to everything else. He learned to tie knots and mend sails, and as his wounds healed, he worked the lines beside the crew. He abandoned his shoes and climbed barefoot and fearless in the rigging. The sailors marvelled at the way he spotted dolphins, schools of rays, brightly striped tigerfish, the way he sensed the place a whale would breach the moment before its broad, pebbled back broke the waves. They claimed they'd be rich if they just had a bit of his luck.

The girl made them nervous.

Three days out to sea, the captain asked her to remain belowdecks as much as possible. He blamed it on the crew's superstition, claimed that they thought women aboard ship would bring ill winds. This was true, but the sailors might have welcomed a laughing, happy girl, a girl who told jokes or tried her hand at the tin whistle.

This girl stood quiet and unmoving by the rail, clutching her scarf around her neck, frozen like a figurehead carved from white wood. This girl screamed in her sleep and woke the men dozing in the foretop.

So the girl spent her days haunting the dark belly of the ship. She counted barrels of molasses, studied the captain's charts. At night, she slipped into the shelter of the boy's arms as they stood together on deck, picking out constellations from the vast spill of stars: the Hunter, the Scholar, the Three Foolish Sons, the bright spokes of the Spinning Wheel, the Southern Palace with its six crooked spires.

She kept him there as long as she could, telling stories, asking questions. Because she knew when she slept, she would dream. Sometimes she dreamed of broken skiffs with black sails and decks slick with blood, of people crying out in the darkness. But worse were the dreams of a pale prince who pressed his lips to her neck, who placed his hands on the collar that circled her throat and called forth her power in a blaze of bright sunlight.

When she dreamed of him, she woke shaking, the

echo of her power still vibrating through her, the feeling of the light still warm on her skin.

The boy held her tighter, murmured soft words to lull her to sleep.

"It's only a nightmare," he whispered. "The dreams will stop."

He didn't understand. The dreams were the only place it was safe to use her power now, and she longed for them.

On the day the *Verrhader* made land, the boy and girl stood at the rail together, watching as the coast of Novyi Zem drew closer.

They drifted into harbour through an orchard of weathered masts and bound sails. There were sleek sloops and little junks from the rocky coasts of the Shu Han, armed warships and pleasure schooners, fat merchantmen and Fjerdan whalers. A bloated prison galley bound for the southern colonies flew the red-tipped banner that warned there were murderers aboard. As they floated by, the girl could have sworn she heard the clink of chains.

The *Verrhader* found its berth. The gangway was lowered. The dockworkers and crew shouted their greetings, tied off ropes, prepared the cargo.

The boy and the girl scanned the docks, searching for a flash of Heartrender crimson or Summoner blue, for the glint of sunlight off Ravkan guns.

It was time. The boy slid his hand into hers. His palm was rough and calloused from the days he'd spent working the lines. When their feet hit the planks of the quay, the ground seemed to buck and roll beneath them.

The sailors laughed. "*Vaarwel, fentomen!*" they cried.

The boy and girl walked forward, and took their first rolling steps in the new world.

Please, the girl prayed silently to any Saints who might be listening, *let us be safe here. Let us be home.*

CHAPTER 1

Two weeks we'd been in Cofton, and I was still getting lost. The town lay inland, west of the Novyi Zem coast, miles from the harbour where we'd landed. Soon we would go further, deep into the wilds of the Zemeni frontier. Maybe then we'd begin to feel safe.

I checked the little map I'd drawn for myself and retraced my steps. Mal and I met every day after work to walk back to the boarding house together, but today I'd got completely lost when I'd detoured to buy our dinner. The calf and collard pies were stuffed in my satchel and giving off a very peculiar smell. The shopkeeper had claimed they were a Zemeni delicacy, though I had my doubts. It didn't much matter. Everything tasted like ashes to me lately.

Mal and I had come to Cofton to find work that would finance our trip west. It was the centre of the *jurda* trade, surrounded by fields of the little orange flowers that people chewed by the bushel. The stimulant was considered a luxury in Ravka, but some of the sailors aboard the *Verrhader* had used it to stay awake on long watches. Zemeni men liked to tuck the dried blooms between lip and gum, and even the women carried them in embroidered pouches that dangled from their wrists. Each store window I passed advertised different brands:

Brightleaf, Shade, Dhoka, the Burly. I saw a beautifully dressed girl in petticoats lean over and spit a stream of rust-coloured juice right into one of the brass spittoons that sat outside every shop door. I stifled a gag. That was one Zemeni custom I didn't think I could get used to.

With a sigh of relief, I turned onto the city's main thoroughfare. At least now I knew where I was. Cofton still didn't feel quite real to me. There was something raw and unfinished about it. Most of the streets were unpaved, and I always felt as if the flat-roofed buildings with their flimsy wooden walls might tip over at any minute. And yet they all had glass windows. The women dressed in velvet and lace. The shop displays overflowed with sweets and baubles and all manner of finery instead of rifles, knives, and tin cookpots. Here, even the beggars wore shoes. This was what a country looked like when it wasn't under siege.

As I passed a gin shop, I caught a flash of crimson out of the corner of my eye. *Corporalki.* Instantly, I drew back, pressing myself into the shadowy space between two buildings, heart hammering, my hand already reaching for the pistol at my hip.

Dagger first, I reminded myself, sliding the blade from my sleeve. *Try not to draw attention. Pistol if you must. Power as a last resort.* Not for the first time, I missed the Fabrikator-made gloves that I'd had to leave behind in Ravka. They'd been lined with mirrors that gave me an easy way to blind opponents in a hand-to-hand fight – and a nice alternative to slicing someone in half with the Cut. But if I'd been spotted by a Corporalnik Heartrender, I might not have a choice in the matter. They were the Darkling's favoured soldiers and could stop my heart or crush my lungs without ever landing a blow.

I waited, my grip slippery on the dagger's handle, then finally dared to peek around the wall. I saw a cart piled high with barrels. The driver had stopped to talk to a woman whose daughter danced impatiently beside her, fluttering and twirling in her dark red skirt.

Just a little girl. Not a Corporalnik in sight. I sank against the building and took a deep breath, trying to calm down.

It won't always be this way, I told myself. *The longer you're free, the easier it will get.*

One day I would wake from a sleep free of nightmares, walk down a street unafraid. Until then, I kept my flimsy dagger close and wished for the sure heft of Grisha steel in my palm.

I pushed my way back into the bustling thoroughfare and clutched at the scarf around my neck, drawing it tighter. It had become a nervous habit. Beneath it lay Morozova's collar, the most powerful amplifier ever known, as well as the only means of identifying me. Without it, I was just another dirty, underfed, Ravkan refugee.

I wasn't sure what I would do when the weather turned. I couldn't very well walk around in scarves and high-necked coats when summer came. But by then, hopefully, Mal and I would be far from crowded towns and unwanted questions. We'd be on our own for the first time since we'd fled Ravka. The thought sent a nervous flutter through me.

I crossed the street, dodging wagons and horses, still scanning the crowd, sure that at any moment I would see a troop of Grisha or *oprichniki* descending on me. Or maybe it would be Shu Han mercenaries, or Fjerdan assassins, or the soldiers of the Ravkan King, or even the

Darkling himself. So many people might be hunting us. *Hunting me*, I amended. If it weren't for me, Mal would still be a tracker in the First Army, not a deserter running for his life.

A memory rose unbidden in my mind: black hair, slate eyes, the Darkling's face exultant in victory as he unleashed the power of the Fold. Then I'd snatched that victory away.

News was easy to come by in Novyi Zem, but none of it was good. Rumours had surfaced that the Darkling had somehow survived the battle on the Fold, that he had gone to ground to gather his forces before making another attempt on the Ravkan throne. I didn't want to believe it was possible, but I knew better than to underestimate him. The other stories were just as disturbing: that the Fold had begun to overflow its shores, driving refugees east and west; that a cult had risen up around a Saint who could summon the sun. I didn't want to think about it. Mal and I had a new life now. We'd left Ravka behind.

I hurried my steps, and soon I was in the square where Mal and I met every evening. I spotted him leaning against the lip of a fountain, talking with a Zemeni friend he'd met working at the warehouse. I couldn't remember his name . . . Jep, maybe? Jef?

Fed by four huge spigots, the fountain was less decorative than useful, a large basin where girls and house servants came to wash clothes. None of the washerwomen were paying much attention to the laundry, though. They were all gawking at Mal. It was hard not to. His hair had grown out of its short military cut and was starting to curl at the nape of his neck. The spray from the fountain had left his shirt damp and it clung to skin bronzed by long days at sea. He threw his head back, laughing at something his friend had said, seemingly oblivious to the sly smiles thrown his way.

He's probably so used to it, he doesn't even notice any more, I thought irritably.

When he caught sight of me, his face broke into a grin and he waved. The washerwomen turned to look and then exchanged glances of disbelief. I knew what they saw: a scrawny girl with stringy, dull brown hair and sallow cheeks, fingers stained orange from packing *jurda*. I'd never been much to look at, and weeks of not using my power had taken their toll. I wasn't eating or sleeping well, and the nightmares didn't help. The women's faces all said the same thing: What was a boy like Mal doing with a girl like me?

I straightened and tried to ignore them as Mal threw his arm around me and drew me close. "Where were you?" he asked. "I was getting worried."

"I was waylaid by a gang of angry bears," I murmured into his shoulder.

"You got lost again?"

"I don't know where you get these ideas."

"You remember Jes, right?" he said, nodding to his friend.

"How do you go?" Jes asked in broken Ravkan, offering me his hand. His expression seemed unduly grave.

"Very well, thank you," I replied in Zemeni. He didn't return my smile, but gently patted my hand. Jes was definitely an odd one.

We chatted a short while longer, but I knew Mal could see I was getting anxious. I didn't like to be out in the open for too long. We said our goodbyes, and before

Jes left, he shot me another grim look and leaned in to whisper something to Mal.

"What did he say?" I asked as we watched him stroll away across the square.

"Hmm? Oh, nothing. Did you know you have pollen in your eyebrows?" He reached out to gently brush it away.

"Maybe I wanted it there."

"My mistake."

As we pushed off from the fountain, one of the washerwomen leaned forward, practically spilling out of her dress.

"If you ever get tired of skin and bones," she called to Mal, "I've got something to tempt you."

I stiffened. Mal glanced over his shoulder. Slowly, he looked her up and down. "No," he said flatly. "You don't."

The girl's face flushed an ugly red as the others jeered and cackled, splashing her with water. I tried for a haughtily arched brow, but it was hard to restrain the goofy grin pulling at the corners of my mouth.

"Thanks," I mumbled as we crossed the square, heading towards our boarding house.

"For what?"

I rolled my eyes. "For defending my honour, you dullard."

He yanked me beneath a shadowed awning. I had a moment's panic when I thought he'd spotted trouble, but then his arms were around me and his lips were pressed to mine.

When he finally drew away, my cheeks were warm and my legs had gone wobbly.

"Just to be clear," he said, "I'm not really interested in defending your honour."

"Understood," I managed, hoping I didn't sound too ridiculously breathless.

"Besides," he said, "I need to steal every minute I can before we're back at the Pit."

The Pit was what Mal called our boarding house. It was crowded and filthy and afforded us no privacy at all, but it was cheap. He grinned, cocky as ever, and pulled me back into the flow of people on the street. Despite my exhaustion, my steps felt decidedly lighter. I still wasn't used to the idea of us together. Another flutter passed through me. On the frontier there would be no curious boarders or unwanted interruptions. My pulse gave a little jump – whether from nerves or excitement, I wasn't sure.

"So what did Jes say?" I asked again, when my brain felt a bit less scrambled.

"He said I should take good care of you."

"That's all?"

Mal cleared his throat. "And . . . he said he would pray to the God of Work to heal your affliction."

"My *what*?"

"I may have told him that you have a goiter."

I stumbled. "I beg your pardon?"

"Well, I had to explain why you were always clinging to that scarf."

I dropped my hand. I'd been doing it again without even realising.

"So you told him I had a goiter?" I whispered incredulously.

"I had to say something. And it makes you quite a tragic figure. Pretty girl, giant growth, you know."

I punched him hard in the arm.

"Ow! Hey, in some countries, goiters are considered very fashionable."

"Do they like eunuchs, too? Because I can arrange that."

"So bloodthirsty!"

"My goiter makes me cranky."

Mal laughed, but I noticed that he kept his hand on his pistol. The Pit was located in one of the less savoury parts of Cofton, and we were carrying a lot of coin, the wages we'd saved for the start of our new life. Just a few more days, and we'd have enough to leave Cofton behind – the noise, the pollen-filled air, the constant fear. We'd be safe in a place where nobody cared what happened to Ravka, where Grisha were scarce and no one had ever heard of a Sun Summoner.

And no one has any use for one. The thought soured my mood, but it had come to me more and more lately. What was I good for in this strange country? Mal could hunt, track, handle a gun. The only thing I'd ever been good at was being a Grisha. I missed summoning light, and each day I didn't use my power, I grew more weak and sickly. Just walking beside Mal left me out of breath, and I struggled beneath the weight of my satchel. I was so frail and clumsy that I'd barely managed to keep my job packing *jurda* at one of the fieldhouses. It brought in mere pennies, but I'd insisted on working, on trying to help. I felt like I had when we were kids: capable Mal and useless Alina.

I pushed the thought away. I might not be the Sun Summoner any more, but I wasn't that sad little girl either. I'd find a way to be useful.

The sight of our boarding house didn't exactly lift my spirits. It was two storeys high and in desperate need of a fresh coat of paint. The sign in the window advertised hot baths and tick-free beds in five different languages. Having sampled the bath and the bed, I knew the sign lied no matter how you translated it. Still, with Mal beside me, it didn't seem so bad.

We climbed the steps of the sagging porch and entered the tavern that took up most of the lower floor of the house. It was cool and quiet after the dusty clamour of the street. At this hour, there were usually a few workers at the pockmarked tables drinking away their day's wages, but today it was empty, save for the surly-looking landlord standing behind the bar.

He was a Kerch immigrant, and I had the distinct impression he didn't like Ravkans. Or maybe he just thought we were thieves. We'd shown up two weeks ago, ragged and grubby, with no baggage and no way to pay for lodging except a single golden hairpin that he probably thought we'd stolen. But that hadn't stopped him from snapping it up in exchange for a narrow bed in a room that we shared with six other boarders.

As we approached the bar, he slapped the room key on the counter and shoved it across to us without being asked. It was tied to a carved piece of chicken bone. Another charming touch.

In the stilted Kerch he'd picked up aboard the *Verrhader*, Mal requested a pitcher of hot water for washing.

"Extra," the landlord grunted. He was a heavy-set man with thinning hair and the orange-stained teeth that came from chewing *jurda*. He was sweating, I noticed. Though the day wasn't particularly warm, beads of perspiration had broken out over his upper lip.

I glanced back at him as we headed for the staircase

on the other side of the deserted tavern. He was still watching us, his arms crossed over his chest, his beady eyes narrowed. There was something about his expression that set my nerves jangling.

I hesitated at the base of the steps. "That guy really doesn't like us," I said.

Mal was already headed up the stairs. "No, but he likes our money just fine. And we'll be out of here in a few days."

I shook off my nervousness. I'd been jumpy all afternoon.

"Fine," I grumbled as I followed after Mal. "But just so I'm prepared, how do you say 'you're an ass' in Kerch?"

"*Jer ven azel.*"

"Really?"

Mal laughed. "The first thing sailors teach you is how to swear."

The second floor of the boarding house was in considerably worse shape than the public rooms below. The carpet was faded and threadbare, and the dim corridor stank of cabbage and tobacco. The doors to the private rooms were all closed, and not a sound came from behind them as we passed. The quiet was eerie. Maybe everyone was out for the day.

The only light came from a single grimy window at the end of the hall. As Mal fumbled with the key, I looked down through the smudged glass to the carts and carriages rumbling by below. Across the street, a man stood beneath a balcony, peering up at the boarding house. He pulled at his collar and his sleeves, as if his clothes were new and didn't quite fit right. His eyes met mine through the window, then darted quickly away.

I felt a sudden pang of fear.

"Mal," I whispered, reaching out to him.

But it was too late. The door flew open.

"No!" I shouted. I threw up my hands and light burst through the corridor in a blinding cascade. Rough hands seized me, pinning my arms behind my back. I was dragged inside the room, kicking and thrashing.

"Easy now," said a cool voice from somewhere in the corner. "I'd hate to have to gut your friend so soon."

Time seemed to slow. I saw the shabby, low-ceilinged room, the cracked washbasin sitting on the battered table, dust motes swirling in a slender beam of sunlight, the bright edge of the blade pressed to Mal's throat. The man holding him wore a familiar sneer. *Ivan.* There were others, men and women. All wore the fitted coats and breeches of Zemeni merchants and labourers, but I recognised some of their faces from my time with the Second Army. They were Grisha.

Behind them, shrouded in shadow, lounging in a rickety chair as if it were a throne, was the Darkling.

For a moment, everything in the room was silent and still. I could hear Mal's breathing, the shuffle of feet. I heard a man calling a hello down on the street. I couldn't seem to stop staring at the Darkling's hands – his long white fingers resting casually on the arms of the chair. I had the foolish thought that I'd never seen him in ordinary clothes.

Then reality crashed in on me. *This* was how it ended? Without a fight? Without so much as a shot fired or a voice raised? A sob of pure rage and frustration tore free from my chest.

"Take her pistol, and search her for other weapons," the Darkling said softly. I felt the comforting weight of my firearm lifted from my hip, the dagger pulled from its sheath at my wrist. "I'm going to tell them to let you go," he said when they were done, "with the knowledge that if you so much as raise your hands, Ivan will end the tracker. Show me that you understand."

I gave a single stiff nod.

He raised a finger, and the men holding me let go. I stumbled forward and then stood frozen in the centre of the room, my hands balled into fists.

I could cut the Darkling in two with my power. I could crack this whole saintsforsaken building right down the middle. But not before Ivan opened Mal's throat.

"How did you find us?" I rasped.

"You leave a very expensive trail," he said, and lazily tossed something onto the table. It landed with a *plink* beside the washbasin. It was one of the golden pins Genya had woven into my hair so many weeks ago. We'd used them to pay for passage across the True Sea, the wagon to Cofton, our miserable, not-quite-tick-free bed.

The Darkling rose, and a strange trepidation crackled through the room. It was as if every Grisha had taken a breath and was holding it, waiting. I could feel the fear coming off them, and that sent a spike of alarm through me. The Darkling's underlings had always treated him with awe and respect, but this was something new. Even Ivan looked a little ill.

The Darkling stepped into the light, and I saw a faint tracery of scars over his face. They'd been healed by a Corporalnik, but they were still visible. So the volcra had left their mark. *Good*, I thought with petty satisfaction. It was small comfort, but at least he wasn't quite as perfect as he had been.

He paused, studying me. "How are you finding life in hiding, Alina? You don't look well."

"Neither do you," I said. It wasn't just the scars. He wore his weariness like an elegant cloak, but it was still there. Faint smudges showed beneath his eyes, and the hollows of his sharp cheekbones cut a little deeper.

"A small price to pay," he said, his lips quirking in a half smile.

A chill snaked up my spine. *For what?*

He reached out, and it took everything in me not to flinch backwards. But all he did was take hold of one end of my scarf. He tugged gently and the rough wool slipped free, gliding over my neck and fluttering to the ground.

"Back to pretending to be less than you are, I see. The sham doesn't suit you."

A twinge of unease passed through me. Hadn't I had a similar thought just minutes ago? "Thanks for your concern," I muttered.

He let his fingers trail over the collar. "It's mine as much as yours, Alina."

I batted his hand away and an anxious murmur rose from the Grisha. "Then you shouldn't have put it around my neck," I snapped. "What do you want?"

Of course, I already knew. He wanted everything – Ravka, the world, the power of the Fold. His answer didn't matter. I just needed to keep him talking. I'd known this moment might come, and I'd prepared for it. I wasn't going to let him take me again. I glanced at Mal, hoping he understood what I intended.

"I want to thank you," the Darkling said.

Now, that I hadn't expected. "Thank me?"

"For the gift you gave me."

My eyes flicked to the scars on his pale cheek.

"No," he said with a small smile, "not these. But they do make a good reminder."

"Of what?" I asked, curious despite myself.

His gaze was grey flint. "That all men can be made fools. No, Alina, the gift you've given me is so much greater."

He turned away. I darted another glance at Mal.

"Unlike you," the Darkling said, "I understand gratitude and I wish to express it."

He raised his hands. Darkness tumbled through the room.

"Now!" I shouted.

Mal drove his elbow into Ivan's side. At the same moment, I threw up my hands and light blazed out, blinding the men around us. I focused my power, honing it to a scythe of pure light. I had only one goal. I wasn't going to leave the Darkling standing. I peered into the seething blackness, trying to find my target. But something was wrong.

I'd seen the Darkling use his power countless times before. This was different. The shadows whirled and skittered around the circle of my light, spinning faster, a writhing mass that clicked and whirred like a fog of hungry insects. I pushed against them with my power, but they twisted and wriggled, drawing ever nearer.

Mal was beside me. Somehow he'd got hold of Ivan's knife.

"Stay close," I said. Better to take my chances and open a hole in the floor than to just stand there doing nothing. I concentrated and felt the power of the Cut vibrate through me. I raised my arm . . . and something stepped out of the darkness.

It's a trick, I thought as the thing came towards us. *It has to be some kind of illusion.*

It was a creature wrought from shadow, its face blank and devoid of features. Its body seemed to tremble and blur, then form again: arms, legs, long hands ending in the dim suggestion of claws, a broad back crested by wings that roiled and shifted as they unfurled like a black stain. It was almost like a volcra, though its shape was more human. And it did not fear the light. It did not fear me.

It's a trick, my panicked mind insisted. *It isn't possible.* It was a violation of everything I knew about Grisha power. We couldn't make matter. We couldn't create life. But the creature was coming for us, and the Darkling's Grisha were cringing against the walls in very real terror. This was what had so frightened them.

I pushed down my horror and refocused my power. I swung my arm, bringing it down in a shining, unforgiving arc. The light sliced through the creature. For a moment, I thought it might just keep coming. Then it wavered, glowing like a cloud lit by lightning, and blew apart into nothing. I had time for the barest surge of relief before the Darkling lifted his hand and another monster took its place, followed by another, and another.

"This is the gift you gave me," said the Darkling. "The gift I earned on the Fold." His face was alive with power and a kind of terrible joy. But I could see strain there too. Whatever he was doing, it was costing him.

Mal and I backed towards the door as the creatures stalked closer. Suddenly, one of them shot forward with astonishing speed. Mal slashed with his knife. The thing paused, wavered slightly, then grabbed him and tossed him aside like a child's doll. This was no illusion.

"Mal!" I cried.

I lashed out with the Cut and the creature burned away to nothing, but the next monster was on me in seconds. It seized me and revulsion shuddered through my body. Its grip was like a thousand crawling insects swarming over my arms.

It lifted me off my feet, and I saw how very wrong I'd been. It *did* have a mouth, a yawning, twisting hole that spread open to reveal row upon row of teeth. I felt them all as the thing bit deeply into my shoulder.

The pain was like nothing I'd ever known. It echoed inside me, multiplying on itself, cracking me open and scraping at the bone. From a distance, I heard Mal call my name. I heard myself scream.

The creature released me. I dropped to the floor in a limp heap. I was on my back, the pain still reverberating through me in endless waves. I could see the water-stained ceiling, the shadow creature looming high above, Mal's pale face as he knelt beside me. I saw his lips form the shape of my name, but I couldn't hear him. I was already slipping away.

The last thing I heard was the Darkling's voice – so clear, as if he was lying right next to me, his lips pressed against my ear, whispering so that only I could hear: *Thank you*.

CHAPTER 2

Darkness again. Something seething inside me. I look for the light, but it's out of my reach.

"Drink."

I open my eyes. Ivan's scowling face comes into focus. "You do it," he grumbles to someone.

Then Genya leans over me, more beautiful than ever, even in a bedraggled red *kefta. Am I dreaming?*

She presses something against my lips. "Drink, Alina."

I try to knock the cup away, but I can't move my hands.

My nose is pinched shut, my mouth forced open. Some kind of broth slides down my throat. I cough and sputter.

"Where am I?" I try to say.

Another voice, cold and pure: "Put her back under."

I am in the pony cart, riding back from the village with Ana Kuya. Her bony elbow jabs into my rib as we jounce up the road that will take us home to Keramzin. Mal is on her other side, laughing and pointing at everything we see.

The fat little pony plods along, twitching its shaggy mane as we climb the last hill. Halfway up, we pass a man and a woman on the side of the road. He is whistling as they go, waving his walking stick in time with the music. The woman trudges along, head bent, a block of salt strapped to her back.

"Are they very poor?" I ask Ana Kuya.

"Not so poor as others."

"Then why doesn't he buy a donkey?"

"He doesn't need a donkey," says Ana Kuya. "He has a wife."

"I'm going to marry Alina," Mal says.

The cart rolls past. The man doffs his cap and calls a jolly greeting.

Mal shouts back gleefully, waving and smiling, nearly bouncing from his seat.

I look back over my shoulder, craning my neck to watch the woman slogging along behind her husband. She's just a girl, really, but her eyes are old and worn.

Ana Kuya misses nothing. "That's what happens to peasant girls who do not have the benefit of the Duke's kindness. That is why you must be grateful and keep him every night in your prayers."

The clink of chains.

Genya's worried face. "It isn't safe to keep doing this to her."

"Don't tell me how to do my job," Ivan snaps.

The Darkling, in black, standing in the shadows. The rhythm of the sea beneath me. The realisation hits me like a blow: We're on a ship.

Please let me be dreaming.

I'm on the road to Keramzin again, watching the pony's bent neck as he labours up the hill. When I look back, the girl struggling beneath the weight of the salt block has my face. Baghra sits beside me in the cart, "The ox feels the yoke," she says, "but does the bird feel the weight of its wings?"

Her eyes are black jet. Be grateful, they say. Be grateful. She snaps the reins.

"Drink." More broth. I don't fight it now. I don't want to choke again. I fall back, let my lids drop, drifting away, too weak to struggle.

A hand on my cheek.

"Mal," I manage to croak.

The hand is withdrawn.

Nothingness.

"Wake up." This time, I don't recognise the voice. "Bring her out of it."

My lids flutter open. Am I still dreaming? A boy leans over me: ruddy hair, a broken nose. He reminds me of the too-clever fox, another of Ana Kuya's stories, smart enough to get out of one trap, but too foolish to realise he won't escape a second. There's another boy standing behind him, but this one is a giant, one of the largest people I've ever seen. His golden eyes have the Shu tilt.

"Alina," says the fox. How does he know my name?

The door opens, and I see another stranger's face, a girl with short dark hair and the same golden gaze as the giant.

"They're coming," she says.

The fox curses. "Put her back down." The giant comes closer. Darkness bleeds back in.

"No, please—"

It's too late. The dark has me.

I am a girl, trudging up a hill. My boots squelch in the mud and my back aches from the weight of the salt upon it. When I think I cannot take another step, I feel myself lifted off the ground. The salt slips from my shoulders, and I watch it shatter on the road. I float higher, higher. Below me, I can see a pony cart, the three passengers looking up at me, their mouths open in surprise. I can see my shadow pass over them, pass over the road and the barren winter fields, the black shape of a girl, borne high by her own unfurling wings.

The first thing I knew was real was the rocking of the ship – the creak of the rigging, the slap of water on the hull.

When I tried to turn over, a shard of pain sliced through my shoulder. I gasped and jolted upright, my eyes flying open, heart racing, fully awake. A wave of nausea rolled through me, and I had to blink back the stars that floated across my vision. I was in a ship's cabin, lying on a narrow bunk. Daylight spilled through the sidescuttle.

Genya sat at the edge of my bed. So I hadn't dreamed her. Or was I dreaming now? I tried to shake the cobwebs from my mind and was rewarded with another surge of nausea. The unpleasant smell in the air wasn't helping to settle my stomach. I forced myself to take a long, shaky breath.

Genya wore a red *kefta* embroidered in blue, a combination I'd never seen on any other Grisha. The garment was dirty and a bit worn, but her hair was arranged in flawless curls, and she looked more lovely than any queen. She held a tin cup to my lips.

"Drink," she said.

"What is it?" I asked warily.

"Just water."

I tried to take the cup from her and realised my wrists were in irons. I lifted my hands awkwardly. The water had a flat metallic tang, but I was parched. I sipped, coughed, then drank greedily.

"Slowly," she said, her hand smoothing the hair back from my face, "or you'll make yourself sick."

"How long?" I asked, glancing at Ivan, who was leaning against the door watching me. "How long have I been out?"

"A little over a week," Genya said.

"A *week*?"

Panic seized me. A week of Ivan slowing my heart rate to keep me unconscious.

I shoved myself to my feet and blood rushed to my head. I would have fallen if Genya hadn't reached out to steady me. I willed the dizziness away, shook her off, then stumbled to the sidescuttle and peered through the foggy circle of glass. Nothing. Nothing but blue sea. No harbour. No coast. Novyi Zem was long gone. I fought the tears that rose behind my eyes.

"Where's Mal?" I asked. When no one answered, I turned around. "Where's Mal?" I demanded of Ivan.

"The Darkling wants to see you," he said. "Are you strong enough to walk, or do I have to carry you?"

"Give her a minute," said Genya. "Let her eat, wash her face at least."

"No. Take me to him."

Genya frowned.

"I'm fine," I insisted. Actually, I felt weak and woozy and terrified. But I wasn't about to lie back down on that bunk, and I needed answers, not food.

As we left the cabin, we were engulfed in a wall of stench – not the usual ship smells of bilge and fish and bodies that I remembered from our voyage aboard the *Verrhader*, but something far worse. I gagged and clamped my mouth shut. I was suddenly glad I hadn't eaten.

"What is that?"

"Blood, bone, rendered blubber," said Ivan. We were aboard a whaler. "You get used to it," he said.

"*You* get used to it," retorted Genya, wrinkling her nose.

They brought me to a hatch that led to the deck above. Ivan clambered up the ladder, and I scrambled hastily after him, eager to be out of the dark bowels of the ship and free of that rotting stench. It was hard climbing with my hands in irons, and Ivan quickly lost patience. He hooked my wrists to haul me the last few feet. I took in great gulps of cold air and blinked in the bright light.

The whaler was lumbering along at full sail, driven forward by three Grisha Squallers who stood by the masts with arms raised, their blue *kefta* flapping around their legs. Etherealki, the Order of Summoners. Just a few short months ago, I'd been one of them.

The ship's crew wore roughspun, and many were barefoot, the better to grip the ship's slippery deck. *No uniforms*, I noted. So they weren't military, and the ship flew no colours that I could see.

The rest of the Darkling's Grisha were easy to pick out among the crew, not just because of their brightly coloured *kefta*, but because they stood idly at the railings, gazing out at the sea or talking while the sailors worked. I even saw a Fabrikator in her purple *kefta*, propped up against a coil of rope, reading.

As we passed by two massive cast-iron kettles set into the deck, I got a fierce whiff of the stink that had been so powerful below.

"The try-pots," Genya said. "Where they render the oil. They haven't been used on this voyage, but the smell never fades."

Grisha and crewmen alike turned to stare as we walked the length of the ship. When we passed beneath the mizzenmast, I looked up and saw the dark-haired boy and girl from my dream perched high above us. They hung from the rigging like two birds of prey, watching us with matching golden eyes.

So it hadn't been a dream at all. They'd been in my cabin.

Ivan led me to the prow of the ship, where the Darkling was waiting. He stood with his back to us, staring out over the bowsprit to the blue horizon beyond, his black *kefta* billowing around him like an inky banner of war.

Genya and Ivan made their bows and left us.

"Where's Mal?" I rasped, my throat still rusty.

The Darkling didn't turn, but shook his head and said, "You're predictable, at least."

"Sorry to bore you. Where is he?"

"How do you know he isn't dead?"

My stomach lurched. "Because I know you," I said with more confidence than I felt.

"And if he were? Would you throw yourself into the sea?"

"Not unless I could take you with me. Where is he?"

"Look behind you."

I whirled. Far down the stretch of the main deck, through the tangle of rope and rigging, I saw Mal. He was flanked by Corporalki guards, but his focus was trained on me. He'd been watching, waiting for me to turn. I stepped forward. The Darkling seized my arm.

"No further," he said.

"Let me talk to him," I begged. I hated the desperation in my voice.

"Not a chance. You two have a bad habit of acting like fools and calling it heroic."

The Darkling lifted his hand, and Mal's guards started to lead him away. "Alina!" he yelled, and then grunted as a guard cuffed him hard across the face.

"Mal!" I shouted as they dragged him, struggling, belowdecks. "Mal!"

I flinched out of the Darkling's grip, my throat choked with rage. "If you hurt him—"

"I'm not going to hurt him," he said. "At least not while he can be of use to me."

"I don't want him harmed."

"He's safe for now, Alina. But don't test me. If one of you steps out of line, the other will suffer. I've told him the same."

I shut my eyes, trying to push back the fury and

LEIGH BARDUGO is a #1 *New York Times*–bestselling author of fantasy novels and the creator of the Grishaverse. With over one million copies sold, her Grishaverse spans the Shadow and Bone Trilogy, the Six of Crows Duology, and *The Language of Thorns*—with more to come. Her short stories can be found in multiple anthologies, including *Some of the Best from Tor.com* and *The Best American Science Fiction and Fantasy 2017*. Her other works include *Wonder Woman: Warbringer* and the forthcoming *Ninth House*. Leigh was born in Jerusalem, grew up in Los Angeles, graduated from Yale University, and has worked in advertising, journalism, and even makeup and special effects. These days, she lives and writes in Hollywood, where she can occasionally be heard singing with her band.

LEIGHBARDUGO.COM

GRISHAVERSE.COM

DON'T MISS THE BRAND-NEW, BREATHTAKING
GRISHAVERSE ADVENTURE FROM
LEIGH BARDUGO

KING
OF
SCARS

COMING 29TH JANUARY 2019

hopelessness I felt. We were right back where we'd started. I nodded once.

Again, the Darkling shook his head. "You two make it so easy. I prick him, you bleed."

"And you can't begin to understand that, can you?"

He reached out and tapped Morozova's collar, letting his fingers graze the skin of my throat. Even that faint touch opened the connection between us, and a rush of power vibrated through me like a bell being struck.

"I understand enough," he said softly.

"I want to see him," I managed. "Every day. I want to know he's safe."

"Of course. I'm not cruel, Alina. Just cautious."

I almost laughed. "Is that why you had one of your monsters bite me?"

"That's not why," he said, his gaze steady. He glanced at my shoulder. "Does it hurt?"

"No," I lied.

The barest hint of a smile touched his lips. "It will get better," he said. "But the wound can never be fully healed. Not even by Grisha."

"Those creatures—"

"The *nichevo'ya*."

Nothings. I shuddered, remembering the skittering, clicking sounds they'd made, the gaping holes of their mouths. My shoulder throbbed. "What are they?"

His lips tilted. The faint scars on his face were barely visible, like the ghost of a map. One ran perilously close to his right eye. He'd almost lost it. He cupped my cheek with his hand, and when he spoke, his voice was almost tender.

"They're just the beginning," he whispered.

He left me standing on the foredeck, my skin still alive with the touch of his fingers, my head swimming with questions.

Before I could begin to sort through them, Ivan appeared and began yanking me back across the main deck. "Slow down," I protested, but he just gave another jerk on my sleeve. I lost my footing and pitched forward. My knees banged painfully on the deck, and I barely had time to put out my shackled palms to break my fall. I winced as a splinter dug into my flesh.

"Move," Ivan ordered. I struggled to my knees. He nudged me with the toe of his boot, and my knee slipped out from beneath me, sending me back down to the deck with a loud thud. "I said *move*."

Then a large hand scooped me up and gently set me on my feet. When I turned, I was surprised to see the giant and the dark-haired girl.

"Are you all right?" she asked.

"This is none of your concern," Ivan said angrily.

"She's Sturmhond's prisoner," replied the girl. "She should be treated accordingly."

Sturmhond. The name was familiar. Was this his ship, then? And his crew? There'd been talk of him aboard the *Verrhader*. He was a Ravkan privateer and a smuggler, infamous for breaking the Fjerdan blockade and for the fortune he'd made capturing enemy ships. But he wasn't flying the double eagle flag.

"She's the *Darkling's* prisoner," said Ivan, "and a traitor."

"Maybe on land," the girl shot back.

Ivan gabbled something in Shu that I didn't understand. The giant just laughed.

"You speak Shu like a tourist," he said.

"And we don't take orders from you in any language," the girl added.

Ivan smirked. "Don't you?" His hand twitched, and the girl grabbed at her chest, buckling to one knee.

Before I could blink, the giant had a wickedly curved blade in his hand and was lunging at Ivan. Lazily, Ivan flicked his other hand out, and the giant grimaced. Still, he kept coming.

"Leave them alone," I protested, tugging helplessly at my irons. I could summon light with my wrists bound, but I had no way to focus it.

Ivan ignored me. His hand tightened into a fist. The giant stopped in his tracks, and the sword fell from his fingers. Sweat broke out on his brow as Ivan squeezed the life from his heart.

"Let's not get out of line, *ye zho*," Ivan chided.

"You're killing him!" I said, panicked now. I rammed my shoulder into Ivan's side, trying to knock him down.

At that moment, a loud double *click* sounded.

Ivan froze, his smirk evaporating. Behind him stood a tall boy around my age, maybe a few years older – ruddy hair, a broken nose. The too-clever fox.

He had a cocked pistol in his hand, the barrel pressed against Ivan's neck.

"I'm a gracious host, bloodletter. But every house has rules."

Host. So this must be Sturmhond. He looked too young to be a captain of anything.

Ivan dropped his hands.

The giant sucked in air. The girl rose to her feet, still clutching her chest. They were both breathing hard, and their eyes burned with hate.

"That's a good fellow," Sturmhond said to Ivan. "Now, I'll take the prisoner back to her quarters, and you can run off and do . . . whatever it is you do when everyone else is working."

Ivan scowled. "I don't think—"

"Clearly. Why start now?"

Ivan's face flushed in anger. "You don't—"

Sturmhond leaned in close, the laughter gone from his voice, his easy demeanour replaced by something with a sword's edge. "I don't care who you are on land. On this ship, you're nothing but ballast. Unless I put you over the side, in which case you're shark bait. I like shark. Cooks up tough, but it makes for a little variety. Remember that the next time you have a mind to threaten anyone aboard this vessel." He stepped back, his jolly manner restored. "Go on now, shark bait. Scurry back to your master."

"I won't forget this, Sturmhond," Ivan spat.

The captain rolled his eyes. "That's the idea."

Ivan turned on his heel and stomped off.

Sturmhond holstered his weapon and smiled pleasantly. "Amazing how quickly a ship feels crowded, no?" He reached out and gave the giant and the girl each a pat on the shoulder. "You did well," he said quietly.

Their attention was still on Ivan. The girl's fists were clenched.

"I don't want trouble," the captain warned. "Understood?"

They exchanged a glance, then nodded grudgingly.

"Good," said Sturmhond. "Get back to work. I'll take her belowdecks." They nodded again. Then, to my surprise, they each sketched a quick bow to me before they departed.

"Are they related?" I asked, watching them go.

"Twins," he said. "Tolya and Tamar."

"And you're Sturmhond."

"On my good days," he replied. He wore leather breeches, a brace of pistols at his hips, and a bright teal frock coat with gaudy gold buttons and enormous cuffs. It belonged in a ballroom or on an opera stage, not on the deck of a ship.

"What's a pirate doing on a whaler?" I asked.

"Privateer," he corrected. "I have several ships. The Darkling wanted a whaler, so I got him one."

"You mean you stole it."

"Acquired it."

"You were in my cabin."

"Many women dream of me," he said lightly as he steered me down the deck.

"I saw you when I woke up," I insisted. "I need—"

He held up a hand. "Don't waste your breath, lovely."

"You don't even know what I was going to say."

"You were about to plead your case, tell me you need my help, you can't pay me but your heart is true, the usual thing."

I blinked. That was exactly what I'd been about to do. "But—"

"Waste of breath, waste of time, waste of a fine afternoon," he said. "I don't like to see prisoners mistreated, but that's as far as my interest goes."

"You—"

He shook his head. "And I'm notoriously immune to tales of woe. So unless your story involves a talking dog, I don't want to hear it. Does it?"

"Does it what?"

"Involve a talking dog."

"No," I snapped. "It involves the future of a kingdom and everyone in it."

"A pity," he said, and took me by the arm, leading me to the aft hatch.

"I thought you worked for Ravka," I said angrily.

"I work for the fattest purse."

"So you'd sell your country to the Darkling for a little gold?"

"No, for a *lot* of gold," he said. "I assure you, I don't come cheap." He gestured to the hatch. "After you."

With Sturmhond's help, I made it back to my cabin, where two Grisha guards were waiting to lock me inside. The captain bowed and left me without another word.

I sat down on my bunk, resting my head in my hands. Sturmhond could play the fool all he wanted. I knew he'd been in here, and there had to be a reason. Or maybe I was just grasping at any little bit of hope.

When Genya brought me my dinner tray, she found me curled up on my bunk, facing the wall.

"You should eat," she said.

"Leave me alone."

"Sulking gives you wrinkles."

"Well, lying gives you warts," I said sourly. She laughed, then entered and set down the tray. She crossed to the sidescuttle and glanced at her reflection in the glass. "Maybe I should go blond," she said. "Corporalki red clashes horribly with my hair."

I cast a glance over my shoulder. "You know you could wear baked mud and outshine every girl on two continents."

"True," she said with a grin.

I didn't return her smile. She sighed and studied the toes of her boots. "I missed you," she said.

I was surprised at how much those words hurt. I'd missed her too. And I'd felt like a fool for it.

"Were you ever my friend?" I asked.

She sat down at the edge of the bunk. "Would it make a difference?"

"I like to know just how stupid I've been."

"I loved being your friend, Alina. But I'm not sorry for what I did."

"And what the Darkling did? Are you sorry for that?"

"I know you think he's a monster, but he's trying to do what's right for Ravka, for all of us."

I shoved up to my elbows. I'd lived with the knowledge of the Darkling's lies so long that it was easy to forget how few people knew what he really was. "Genya, he created the Fold."

"The Black Heretic—"

"There is no Black Heretic," I said, revealing the truth that Baghra had laid out before me months ago at the Little Palace. "He blamed his ancestor for the Fold, but there's only ever been one Darkling, and all he cares about is power."

"That's impossible. The Darkling has spent his life trying to free Ravka from the Fold."

"How can you say that after what he did to Novo-kribirsk?" The Darkling had used the power of the Unsea to destroy an entire town, a show of strength meant to cow his enemies and mark the start of his rule. And I'd made it possible.

"I know there was . . . an incident."

"An incident? He killed hundreds of people, maybe thousands."

"And what about the people on the skiff?" she said quietly.

I drew in a sharp breath and lay back. For a long

moment, I studied the planks above me. I didn't want to ask, but I knew I was going to. The question had haunted me over long weeks and miles of ocean. "Were there . . . were there other survivors?"

"Besides Ivan and the Darkling?"

I nodded, waiting.

"Two Inferni who helped them escape," she said. "A few soldiers from the First Army made it back, and a Squaller named Nathalia got out, but she died of her injuries a few days later."

I closed my eyes. How many people had been aboard that sandskiff? Thirty? Forty? I felt sick. I could hear the screams, the howls of the volcra. I could smell the gunpowder and blood. I'd sacrificed those people for Mal's life, for my freedom, and in the end, they'd died for nothing. We were back in the Darkling's grasp, and he was more powerful than ever.

Genya laid her hand over mine. "You did what you had to, Alina."

I let out a harsh bark of laughter and pulled my hand away. "Is that what the Darkling tells you, Genya? Does that make it easier?"

"Not really, no." She looked down at her lap, pleating and unpleating the folds of her *kefta*. "He freed me, Alina," she said. "What am I supposed to do? Run back to the palace? Back to the King?" She gave a fierce shake of her head. "No. I made my choice."

"What about the other Grisha?" I asked. "They can't all have sided with the Darkling. How many of them stayed in Ravka?"

Genya stiffened. "I don't think I'm supposed to talk about that with you."

"Genya—"

"Eat, Alina. Try to get some rest. We'll be in the ice soon."

The ice. Then we weren't headed back to Ravka. We must be travelling north.

She stood up and brushed the dust off her *kefta*. She might joke about the colour, but I knew how much it meant to her. It proved she was really a Grisha – protected, favoured, a servant no more. I remembered the mysterious illness that had weakened the King just before the Darkling's coup. Genya had been one of the few Grisha with access to the royal family. She'd used that access to earn the right to wear red.

"Genya," I said as she reached the door. "One more question."

She paused, her hand on the latch.

It seemed so unimportant, so silly to mention it after all this time. But it was something that had bothered me for a long while. "The letters I wrote to Mal back at the Little Palace. He said he never got them."

She didn't turn back to me, but I saw her shoulders sag.

"They were never sent," she whispered. "The Darkling said you needed to leave your old life behind."

She closed the door, and I heard the bolt click home.

All those hours spent talking and laughing with Genya, drinking tea and trying on dresses. She'd been lying to me the whole time. The worst part about it was that the Darkling had been right. If I'd kept clinging to Mal and the memory of the love I had for him, I might never have mastered my power. But Genya didn't know that. She had just followed orders and let my heart break. I didn't know what that was, but it wasn't friendship.

I turned onto my side, feeling the gentle roll of the ship beneath me. Was this what it was like to be rocked to sleep in a mother's arms? I couldn't remember. Ana Kuya used to hum sometimes, under her breath, as she went about turning down the lamps and closing up the dormitories at Keramzin for the night. That was the closest Mal and I had ever come to a lullaby.

Somewhere above, I heard a sailor shout something over the wind. The bell rang to signal the change of the watch. *We're alive*, I reminded myself. *We escaped from him before. We can do it again.* But it was no good, and finally, I gave in and let the tears come. Sturmhond was bought and paid for. Genya had chosen the Darkling. Mal and I were alone as we'd always been, without friends or allies, surrounded by nothing but pitiless sea. This time, even if we escaped, there was nowhere to run.

CHAPTER 3

Less than a week later, I spotted the first ice floes. We were far north, where the sea darkened and ice bloomed from its depths in perilous spikes. Though it was early summer, the wind bit into our skin. In the morning, the ropes were hard with frost.

I spent hours pacing my cabin and staring out at the endless sea. Each morning, I was brought above deck, where I was given a chance to stretch my legs and see Mal from afar. Always, the Darkling stood by the railing, scanning the horizon, searching for something. Sturmhond and his crew kept their distance.

On the seventh day, we passed between two slate stone islands that I recognised from my time as a mapmaker: Jelka and Vilki, the Fork and Knife. We had entered the Bone Road, the long stretch of black water where countless ships had wrecked on the nameless islands that appeared and disappeared in its mists. On maps, it was marked by sailors' skulls, wide-mouthed monsters, mermaids with ice-white hair and the deep black eyes of seals. Only the most experienced Fjerdan hunters came here, seeking skins and furs, chancing death to claim rich prizes. But what prize did we seek?

Sturmhond ordered the sails trimmed, and our pace slowed as we drifted through the mist. An uneasy silence blanketed the ship. I studied the whaler's longboats, the racks of harpoons tipped in Grisha steel. It wasn't hard to guess what they were for. The Darkling was after some kind of amplifier. I surveyed the ranks of Grisha and wondered who might be singled out for another of the Darkling's "gifts". But a terrible suspicion had taken root inside me.

It's madness, I told myself. *He wouldn't dare attempt it.* The thought brought me little comfort. He always dared.

Next day, the Darkling ordered me brought to him.

"Who is it for?" I asked as Ivan deposited me by the starboard rail.

The Darkling just stared out into the waves. I considered shoving him over the railing. Sure, he was hundreds of years old, but could he swim?

"Tell me you're not contemplating what I think you are," I said. "Tell me the amplifier is for some other stupid, gullible girl."

"Someone less stubborn? Less selfish? Less hungry for the life of a mouse? Believe me," he said. "I wish I could."

I felt sick. "A Grisha can have only one amplifier. You told me that yourself."

"Morozova's amplifiers are different."

I gaped at him. "There's another like the stag?"

"They were meant to be used together, Alina. They are unique, just as we are."

I thought of the books I'd read on Grisha theory. Every one of them had said the same thing: Grisha power was not meant to be limitless; it had to be held in check.

"No," I said. "I don't want this. I want—"

"You *want*," the Darkling mocked. "I want to watch your tracker die slowly with my knife in his heart. I want to let the sea swallow you both. But our fates are entwined now, Alina, and there's nothing either of us can do about that."

"You're mad."

"I know it pleases you to think so," he said. "But the amplifiers must be brought together. If we have any hope of controlling the Fold—"

"You can't *control* the Fold. It has to be destroyed."

"Careful, Alina," he said with a slight smile. "I've had the same thought about you." He gestured to Ivan, who was waiting a respectful distance away. "Bring me the boy."

My heart leapt into my throat. "Wait," I said. "You told me you wouldn't hurt him."

He ignored me. Like a fool, I looked around. As if anyone on this saintsforsaken ship would hear my appeal. Sturmhond stood by the wheel, watching us, his face impassive.

I snatched at the Darkling's sleeve. "We had a deal. I haven't done anything. You said—"

The Darkling looked at me with cool quartz eyes and the words died on my lips.

A moment later, Ivan appeared with Mal in tow and steered him over to the rail. He stood before us, squinting in the sunlight, hands bound. It was the closest we'd been in weeks. Though he looked tired and pale, he appeared unharmed. I saw the question in his wary expression, but I had no answer.

"All right, tracker," the Darkling said. "Track."

Mal glanced from the Darkling to me and back again. "Track what? We're in the middle of the ocean."

"Alina once told me that you could make rabbits out of rocks. I questioned the crew of the *Verrhader* myself and they claim that you're just as capable at sea. They seemed to think you could make some lucky captain very rich with your expertise."

Mal frowned. "You want me to hunt whales?"

"No," said the Darkling. "I want you to hunt the sea whip."

We stared at him in shock. I almost laughed.

"You're looking for a dragon?" Mal said incredulously.

"The ice dragon," said the Darkling. "Rusalye."

Rusalye. In the stories, the sea whip was a cursed prince, forced to take the form of a sea serpent and guard the frigid waters of the Bone Road. That was Morozova's second amplifier?

"It's a fairy tale," Mal said, voicing my own thoughts. "A children's story. It doesn't actually exist."

"There have been sightings of the sea whip in these waters for years," said the Darkling.

"Along with mermaids and white selkies. It's a myth."

The Darkling arched a brow. "Like the stag?"

Mal glanced at me. I gave an infinitesimal shake of my head. Whatever the Darkling was doing, we weren't going to help.

Mal peered out at the waves. "I wouldn't even know where to start."

"For her sake, I hope that's not true." The Darkling pulled a slender knife from the folds of his *kefta*. "Because every day we don't find the sea whip, I'll peel away a piece of her skin. Slowly. Then Ivan will heal her, and the next day, we'll do it all over again."

I felt the blood drain from my face.

"You won't hurt her," Mal said, but I could hear the fear in his voice.

"I don't *want* to hurt her," said the Darkling. "I want you to do as I ask."

"It took me months to find the stag," Mal said desperately. "I still don't know how we did it."

Sturmhond stepped forward. I'd been so focused on Mal and the Darkling, I'd nearly forgotten him. "I won't have a girl tortured on my ship," he said.

The Darkling turned his cold gaze on the privateer. "You work for me, Sturmhond. You'll do your job or getting paid will be the least of your worries."

An ugly ripple of disquiet passed over the ship. Sturmhond's crew were sizing up the Grisha, and their expressions were not friendly. Genya had a hand pressed over her mouth, but she did not say a word.

"Give the tracker some time," Sturmhond said quietly. "A week. At least a few days."

The Darkling slid his fingers up my arm, pushing back my sleeve to reveal bare white flesh. "Shall I start with her arm?" he asked. He dropped the sleeve, then brushed his knuckles over my cheek. "Or with her face?" He nodded to Ivan. "Hold her."

Ivan clasped the back of my head. The Darkling lifted the knife. I saw it glittering from the corner of my eye. I tried to cringe back, but Ivan held me in place. The blade met my cheek. I sucked in a frightened breath.

"Stop!" Mal shouted.

The Darkling waited.

"I . . . I can do it."

"Mal, no," I said with more courage than I felt.

Mal swallowed and said, "Tack south-west. Back the way we came."

I stayed very still. Had he seen something? Or was he just trying to keep me from getting hurt?

The Darkling cocked his head to one side and studied him. "I think you know better than to play games with me, tracker."

Mal gave a sharp nod. "I can do it. I can find it. Just . . . just give me time."

The Darkling sheathed his knife. I exhaled slowly and tried to suppress a shiver.

"You have a week," he said, turning away and disappearing into the hatch. "Bring her," he called to Ivan.

"Mal—" I began as Ivan grasped my arm.

Mal lifted his bound hands, reaching for me. His fingers grazed mine briefly, then Ivan was hauling me back towards the hatch.

My mind was racing as we descended into the dank belly of the ship. I stumbled along behind Ivan, trying to make sense of everything that had just happened. The Darkling had said that he wouldn't harm Mal as long as he needed him. I'd assumed he just meant to use him to keep me in line, but now it was clear there was more to it than that. Did Mal really think he could find the sea whip or was he stalling for time? I wasn't sure what I wanted to be true. I didn't savour the idea of being tortured, but what if we did find the ice dragon? What would a second amplifier mean?

Ivan pulled me into a spacious cabin that looked like the captain's quarters. Sturmhond must have been squeezed in with the rest of his crew. A bed was pushed into one corner, and the deeply curved aft wall was studded with a row of thick-paned windows. They shed watery light on a desk behind which the Darkling seated himself.

Ivan bowed and darted from the room, closing the door behind him.

"He can't wait to get away from you," I said, hovering by the door. "He's afraid of what you've become. They all are."

"Do you fear me, Alina?"

"That's what you want, isn't it?"

The Darkling shrugged. "Fear is a powerful ally," he said. "And loyal."

He was watching me in that cold, assessing way that always made me feel as if he were reading me like words on a page, his fingers moving over the text, gleaning some secret knowledge that I could only guess at. I tried not to fidget, but the irons at my wrists chafed.

"I'd like to free you," he said quietly.

"Free me, flay me. So many options." I could still feel the press of his knife at my cheek.

He sighed. "It was a threat, Alina. It accomplished what it needed to."

"So you wouldn't have cut me?"

"I didn't say that." His voice was pleasant and matter-of-fact, as always. He might have been threatening to carve me up or ordering his dinner.

In the dim light, I could just make out the fine traces of his scars. I knew I should stay quiet, force him to speak first, but my curiosity was too great.

"How did you survive?"

He ran his hand over the sharp line of his jaw. "It seems the volcra did not care for the taste of my flesh," he said, almost idly. "Have you ever noticed that they do not feed on each other?"

I shuddered. They were his creations, just like the thing that had buried its teeth in my shoulder. The skin there still pulsed. "Like calls to like."

"It's not an experience I'd care to repeat. I've had my fill of the volcra's mercy. And yours."

I crossed the room, coming to stand before the desk. "Then why give me a second amplifier?" I asked desperately, grasping for an argument that would somehow make him see sense. "In case you've forgotten, I tried to kill you."

"And failed."

"Here's to second chances. Why make me stronger?"

Again, he shrugged. "Without Morozova's amplifiers, Ravka is lost. You were meant to have them, just as I was meant to rule. It can be no other way."

"How convenient for you."

He leaned back and folded his arms. "You have been anything but convenient, Alina."

"You can't combine amplifiers. All the books say the same thing—"

"Not *all* the books."

I wanted to scream in frustration. "Baghra warned me. She said you were arrogant, blinded by ambition."

"Did she now?" His voice was ice. "And what other treason did she whisper in your ear?"

"That she loved you," I said angrily. "That she believed you could be redeemed."

He looked away then, but not before I saw the flash of

pain on his face. What had he done to her? And what had it cost him?

"Redemption," he murmured. "Salvation. Penance. My mother's quaint ideas. Perhaps I should have paid closer attention." He reached into the desk and drew out a slender red volume. As he held it up, light glinted off the gold lettering on its cover: *Istorii Sankt'ya*. "Do you know what this is?"

I frowned. *The Lives of Saints*. A dim memory came back to me. The Apparat had given me a copy months ago at the Little Palace. I'd thrown it into the drawer of my dressing table and never spared it another thought.

"It's a children's book," I said.

"Have you read it?"

"No," I admitted, suddenly wishing I had. The Darkling was watching me too closely. What could be so important about an old collection of religious drawings?

"Superstition," he said glancing down at the cover. "Peasant propaganda. Or so I thought. Morozova was a strange man. He was a bit like you, drawn to the ordinary and the weak."

"Mal isn't weak."

"He's gifted, I grant you, but no Grisha. He can never be your equal."

"He's my equal and more," I spat.

The Darkling shook his head. If I hadn't known better, I might have mistaken the look on his face for pity. "You think you've found a family with him. You think you've found a future. But you will grow powerful, and he will grow old. He will live his short *otkazat'sya* life, and you will watch him die."

"Shut up."

He smiled. "Go on, stamp your foot, fight your true nature. All the while, your country suffers."

"Because of you!"

"Because I put my trust in a girl who cannot stand the thought of her own potential." He rose and rounded the desk. Despite my anger, I took a step back, banging into the chair behind me.

"I know what you feel when you're with the tracker," he said.

"I doubt that."

He gave a dismissive wave. "No, not the absurd pining you've yet to outgrow. I know the truth in your heart. The loneliness. The growing knowledge of your own difference." He leaned in closer. "The ache of it."

I tried to hide the shock of recognition that went through me. "I don't know what you're talking about," I said, but the words sounded false to my ears.

"It will never fade, Alina. It will only grow worse, no matter how many scarves you hide behind or what lies you tell, no matter how far or how fast you run."

I tried to turn away, but he reached out and took hold of my chin, forcing me to look at him. He was so close I could feel his breath. "There are no others like us, Alina," he whispered. "And there never will be."

I lurched away from him, knocking the chair over, nearly losing my balance. I pounded on the door with my iron-bound fists, calling out to Ivan as the Darkling looked on. He didn't come until the Darkling gave the order.

Dimly, I registered Ivan's hand at my back, the stench of the corridor, a sailor letting us pass, then the quiet of my narrow cabin, the door locking behind me, the bunk, the scratch of rough fabric as I pressed my face into the covers, trembling, trying to drive the Darkling's words from my head. Mal's death. The long life before me. The pain of otherness that would never ease. Each fear sank into me, a barbed talon burrowing deep into my heart.

I knew he was a practised liar. He could fake any emotion, play on any human failing. But I couldn't deny what I'd felt in Novyi Zem or the truth of what the Darkling had shown me: my own sadness, my own longing, reflected back to me in his bleak grey eyes.

The mood had changed aboard the whaler. The crew had grown restless and watchful, the slight to their captain still fresh in their minds. The Grisha muttered among themselves, their nerves worn thin by our slow progress through the waters of the Bone Road.

Each day, the Darkling had me brought above deck to stand beside him at the prow. Mal was kept well guarded at the other end of the ship. Sometimes I heard him call out bearings to Sturmhond or saw him gesture to what looked like deep scratches just above the waterline on the large ice shelves we passed.

I peered at the rough grooves. They might be claw marks. They might be nothing at all. Still, I'd seen what Mal was capable of in Tsibeya. When we were tracking the stag, he had shown me broken branches, trampled grass, signs that seemed obvious once he pointed them out but that had been invisible moments before. The crewmen seemed skeptical. The Grisha were outright contemptuous.

At dusk, when another day had come and gone, the Darkling would parade me across the deck and down through the hatch directly in front of Mal. We weren't permitted to speak. I tried to hold his gaze, to tell him silently that I was all right, but I could see his fury and desperation growing, and I was powerless to reassure him.

Once, when I stumbled by the hatch, the Darkling caught me up against himself. He might have let me go, but he lingered, and before I could pull away, he let his hand graze the small of my back.

Mal surged forward, and it was only the grip of his Grisha guards that kept him from charging the Darkling.

"Three more days, tracker."

"Leave her alone," Mal snarled.

"I've kept my end of the bargain. She's still unharmed. But perhaps that isn't what you fear?"

Mal looked frayed to the point of snapping. His face was pale, his mouth a taut line, the muscles of his forearms knotted as he strained against his bonds. I couldn't bear it.

"I'm fine," I said softly, risking the Darkling's knife. "He can't hurt me." It was a lie, but it felt good on my lips.

The Darkling looked from me to Mal, and I glimpsed that bleak, yawning fissure within him. "Don't worry, tracker. You'll know when our deal is up." He shoved me belowdecks, but not before I heard his parting words to Mal – "I'll be certain you hear it when I make her scream."

The week wore on, and on the sixth day, Genya woke me early. As I gathered my wits, I saw it was barely dawn.

Fear sliced through me. Maybe the Darkling had decided to cut short my reprieve and make good on this threats.

But Genya was beaming.

"He found something!" she crowed, bouncing on the soles of her feet, practically dancing as she helped me from the bunk. "The tracker says we're close!"

"His name is Mal," I muttered, pulling away from her. I ignored her stricken look.

Can it be true? I wondered as Genya led me above. Or did Mal simply hope to buy me more time?

We emerged into the dim grey light of dawn. The deck was crowded with Grisha gazing out at the water while the Squallers worked the winds, and Sturmhond's crew managed the sails above.

The mist was heavier than the day before. It clung thick against the water and crawled in damp tendrils over the ship's hull. The silence was broken only by Mal's directions and the orders Sturmhond called.

When we entered a wide, open stretch of sea, Mal turned to the Darkling and said, "I think we're close."

"You *think*?"

Mal gave a single nod.

The Darkling considered. If Mal was stalling, his efforts were doomed to be short-lived and the price would be high.

After what felt like an eternity, the Darkling nodded to Sturmhond.

"Trim the sails," commanded the privateer, and the topmen moved to obey.

Ivan tapped the Darkling's shoulder and gestured to the southern horizon. "A ship, *moi soverenyi*."

I squinted at the tiny smudge.

"Are they flying colours?" the Darkling asked Sturmhond.

"Probably fishermen," Sturmhond said. "We'll keep an eye on her just in case." He signalled to one of his crewmen, who went scurrying up the main royal with a long glass in hand.

The longboats were prepared and in minutes they were being lowered over the starboard side, loaded with Sturmhond's men and bristling with harpoons. The Darkling's Grisha crowded by the rail to view the boats' progress. The mist seemed to magnify the steady slap of their oars against the waves.

I took a step closer to Mal. Everyone's attention was focused on the men in the water. Only Genya was watching me. She hesitated, then deliberately turned and joined the others at the railing.

Mal and I faced forwards, but we were close enough that our shoulders touched.

"Tell me you're all right," he murmured, his voice raw.

I nodded, swallowing the lump in my throat. "I'm fine," I said softly. "Is it out there?"

"I don't know. Maybe. There were times when I was tracking the stag that I thought we were close and . . . Alina, if I'm wrong—"

I turned then, not caring who saw us or what punishment I might receive. The mist was rising off the water now, creeping along the deck. I looked up at him, taking in every detail of his face: the bright blue of his irises, the curve of his lip, the scar that ran the length of his jaw. Behind him, I glimpsed Tamar scampering up the rigging, a lantern in her hands.

"None of this is your fault, Mal. None of it."

He lowered his head, setting his forehead against mine. "I won't let him hurt you."

We both knew he was powerless to stop it, but the truth of that was too painful, so I just said, "I know."

"You're humouring me," he said with the hint of a grin.

"You require a lot of coddling."

He pressed his lips to the top of my head. "We'll find a way out of this, Alina. We always do."

I rested my ironbound hands against his chest and closed my eyes. We were alone on an icy sea, prisoners of a man who could literally make monsters, and yet somehow I believed. I leaned into him, and for the first time in days, I let myself hope.

A cry rang out: "Two points off the starboard bow!"

As one, our heads turned, and I stilled. Something was moving in the mist, a shimmering, undulating white shape.

"Saints," Mal breathed.

At that moment, the creature's back breached the waves, its body cutting through the water in a sinuous arch, rainbows sparking off the iridescent scales on its back.

Rusalye.

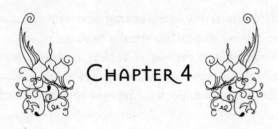

CHAPTER 4

Rusalye was a folk story, a fairy tale, a creature of dreams that lived on the edges of maps. But there could be no doubt. The ice dragon was real and Mal had found it, just as he had found the stag. It felt wrong, as if everything was happening too quickly, as if we were rushing towards something we didn't understand.

A shout from the longboats drew my attention. A man on the boat nearest the sea whip stood up, a harpoon in his hand, taking aim. But the dragon's white tail lashed through the sea, split the waves, and came down with a slap, sending a rolling wall of water up against the boat's hull. The man with the harpoon sat down hard as the longboat tipped precariously, then righted itself at the last moment.

Good, I thought. *Fight them.*

Then the other boat let fly their harpoons. The first went wide and splashed harmlessly in the water. The second lodged in the sea whip's hide.

It bucked, tail whipping back and forth, then reared up like a snake, hurling its body out of the water. For a moment, it hung suspended in the air: translucent winglike fins, gleaming scales, and wrathful red eyes. Beads of water flew from its mane and its massive jaws opened, revealing a pink tongue and rows of gleaming teeth. It came down on the nearest boat with a loud crash of splintering wood. The slender craft split in two, and men poured into the sea. The dragon's maw snapped closed over a sailor's legs and he vanished, screaming, beneath the waves. With furious strokes, the rest of the crewmen swam through the bloodstained water, making for the remaining longboat, where they were hauled over the side.

I glanced back up to the whaler's rigging. The tops of the masts were shrouded in mist now, but I could still make out the light of Tamar's lantern burning steadily atop the main royal.

Another harpoon found its target and the sea whip began to sing, a sound more lovely than anything I'd ever heard, a choir of voices lifted in a plaintive, wordless song. *No*, I realised, *not a song*. The sea whip was crying out, writhing and rolling in the waves as the longboats gave chase, struggling to shake the hooked tips of the harpoons free. *Fight*, I pleaded silently. *Once he has you, he'll never let you go.*

I could already see the dragon slowing, its movements growing sluggish as its cries wavered, mournful now, their music bleak and fading.

Part of me wished the Darkling would just end it. Why didn't he? Why not use the Cut on the sea whip and bind me to him as he had done with the stag?

"Nets!" shouted Sturmhond. The mist had grown so thick that I couldn't quite tell where his voice was coming from. I heard a series of thunks from somewhere near the starboard rail.

"Clear the mist," ordered the Darkling. "We're losing the longboat."

I heard the Grisha calling to one another and then felt the billow of Squaller winds tugging at the hem of my coat.

The mist lifted and my jaw dropped. The Darkling and his Grisha still stood on the starboard side, attention focused on the longboat that now seemed to be rowing away from the whaler. But on the port side, another ship had appeared as if from nowhere, a sleek schooner with gleaming masts and colours flying: a red dog on a teal field – and below it, in pale blue and gold, the Ravkan double eagle.

I heard another series of thunks and saw steel claws studding the whaler's portside rail. *Grappling hooks.*

And then everything seemed to happen at once. A howl went up from somewhere, like a wolf baying at the moon. Men swarmed over the rail onto the whaler's deck, pistols strapped to their chests, cutlasses in their hands, yowling and barking like a pack of wild dogs. I saw the Darkling turn, confusion and rage on his face.

"What the hell is going on?" Mal said, stepping in front of me as we edged towards the meagre protection of the mizzenmast.

"I don't know," I replied. "Something very good or something very, very bad."

We stood back-to-back, my hands still trapped in irons, his still bound, powerless to defend ourselves as the deck erupted into fighting. Pistol shots rang out. The air came alive with Inferni fire. "To me, hounds!" Sturmhond shouted, and plunged into the action, a sabre in his hands.

Barking, yipping, snarling men were descending on the Darkling's Grisha from all sides – not just from the railing of the schooner but from the rigging of the whaler as well. *Sturmhond*'s men. Sturmhond was turning against the Darkling.

The privateer had clearly lost his mind. Yes, the Grisha were outnumbered, but numbers didn't matter in a fight with the Darkling.

"Look!" Mal shouted.

Down in the water, the men in the remaining longboat had the struggling sea whip in tow. They had raised a sail and a brisk wind was driving them, not towards the whaler but directly towards the schooner instead. The stiff breeze that carried them seemed to come from nowhere. I looked closer. A crewman was standing in the longboat, arms raised. There was no mistaking it: Sturmhond had a Squaller working for him.

Suddenly, an arm seized me around the waist and I was lifted off my feet. The world seemed to upend itself, and I shrieked as I was thrown over a huge shoulder.

I lifted my head, struggling against the arm that held me like a steel band, and saw Tamar rushing at Mal, a knife gleaming in her grasp. "No!" I screamed. "Mal!"

He put up his hands to defend himself, but all she did was slice through his bonds. "Go!" she shouted, tossing him the knife and drawing a sword from the scabbard at her hip.

Tolya clutched me tighter as he sprinted over the deck. Tamar and Mal were close behind.

"What are you doing?" I squawked, my head jouncing against the giant's back.

"Just run!" Tamar replied, slashing at a Corporalnik who threw himself into her path.

"I can't run," I shouted back. "Your idiot brother has me slung over his shoulder like a ham!"

"Do you want to be rescued or not?"

I didn't have time to answer.

"Hold tight," Tolya said. "We're going over."

I squeezed my eyes shut, preparing to tumble into the icy water. But Tolya hadn't gone more than a few steps when he gave a sudden grunt and fell to one knee, losing his grip on me. I toppled to the deck and rolled clumsily onto my side. When I looked up, I saw Ivan and a blue-robed Inferni standing over us.

Ivan's hand was outstretched. He was crushing Tolya's heart, and this time, Sturmhond wasn't there to stop him.

The Inferni advanced on Tamar and Mal, flint in hand, arm already moving in an arc of flame. *Over before it began*, I thought miserably. But in the next moment, the Inferni stopped and gasped. His flames died on the air.

"What are you waiting for?" Ivan snarled.

The Inferni's only response was a choked hiss. His eyes bulged. He clawed at his throat.

Tamar held her sword in her right hand, but her left fist was clenched.

"Good trick," she said, swatting away the paralysed Inferni's flint. "I know a good trick, too." She raised her blade, and as the Inferni stood helpless, desperate for air, she ran him through with one vicious thrust.

The Inferni crumpled to the deck. Ivan stared in confusion at Tamar standing over the lifeless body, her sword dripping blood. His concentration must have wavered, because in that moment, Tolya came up from his knee with a terrifying roar.

Ivan clenched his fist, refocusing his efforts. Tolya grimaced, but he did not fall. Then the giant's hand shot out, and Ivan's face spasmed in pain and bewilderment.

I looked from Tolya to Tamar, realisation dawning.

They were Grisha. Heartrenders.

"Do you like that, little man?" Tolya asked as he stalked towards Ivan. Desperately, Ivan cast out another hand. He was shaking, and I could see he was struggling for breath.

Tolya wobbled slightly but kept coming. "Now we learn who has the stronger heart," he growled.

He strode slowly forward, as though he was walking against a strong wind, his face beaded with sweat, his teeth bared in feral glee. I wondered if he and Ivan would both just fall down dead.

Then the fingers of Tolya's outstretched hand curled into a fist. Ivan convulsed. His eyes rolled up in his head. A bubble of blood blossomed and burst on his lips. He collapsed onto the deck.

Dimly, I was aware of the chaos raging around me. Tamar was struggling with a Squaller. Two other Grisha had leapt onto Tolya. I heard a gunshot and realised Mal had managed to get hold of a pistol. But all I could see was Ivan's lifeless body.

He was dead. The Darkling's right hand. One of the most powerful Heartrenders in the Second Army. He'd survived the Fold and the volcra, and now he was dead.

A tiny sob drew me out of my reverie. Genya stood gazing down at Ivan, her hands over her mouth.

"Genya—" I said.

"Stop them!" The shout came from across the deck. I turned and saw the Darkling grappling with an armed sailor.

Genya was shaking. She reached into the pocket of her *kefta* and drew out a pistol. Tolya lunged at her.

"No!" I said, stepping between them. I wasn't going to watch him kill Genya.

The heavy pistol trembled in her hand.

"Genya," I said quietly, "are you really going to shoot me?" She looked around wildly, unsure where to aim. I laid a hand on her sleeve. She flinched and turned the barrel on me.

A crack like thunder rent the air, and I knew the Darkling had broken free. I looked back and saw a wave of darkness tumbling in our direction. *It's over*, I thought. *We're done for.* But in the next instant, I glimpsed a bright flash and a shot rang out. The swell of darkness blew away to nothing, and I saw the Darkling clutching his arm, his face contorted in fury and pain. In disbelief, I realised he'd been shot.

Sturmhond was racing towards us, pistols in hand. "Run!" he shouted.

"Come on, Alina!" Mal cried, reaching for my arm.

"Genya," I said desperately, "come with us."

Her hand was shaking so badly I thought the pistol might fly from her grip. Tears spilled over her cheeks.

"I can't," she sobbed brokenly. She lowered her weapon. "Go, Alina," she said. "Just go."

In the next instant, Tolya had tossed me over his shoulder again. I beat uselessly on his broad back. "No!" I yelled. "Wait!"

No one paid me any attention. Tolya took a running leap and vaulted over the railing. I screamed as we plummeted towards the icy water, bracing for the impact. Instead, we were scooped up by what could only have been a Squaller wind and deposited on the attacking schooner's deck with a bone-jarring thud. Tamar and Mal followed, with Sturmhond close behind.

"Give the signal," Sturmhond shouted, springing to his feet.

A piercing whistle blew.

"Privyet," he called to a crewman I didn't recognise, "how many do we have?"

"Eight men down," replied Privyet. "Four remaining on the whaler. Cargo on its way up."

"Saints," Sturmhond swore. He looked back to the whaler, struggling with himself. "Musketeers!" he shouted to the men on the schooner's maintop. "Lend them cover!"

The musketeers began firing their rifles down onto the deck of the whaler. Tolya tossed Mal a rifle, then slung another over his back. He leapt into the rigging and began to climb. Tamar drew a pistol from her hip. I was still sprawled on the deck in an undignified tangle, my hands held useless in irons.

"Sea whip is secured, *kapitan*!" shouted Privyet.

Two more of Sturmhond's men hurdled over the whaler's railing and flew through the air, arms pinwheeling wildly, to crash in a heap on the schooner's deck. One was bleeding badly from a wound to his arm.

Then it came again, the boom of thunder.

"He's up!" called Tamar.

Blackness engulfed the schooner, blotting out everything in its path.

"Free me!" I pleaded. "Let me help!"

Sturmhond threw Tamar the keys and shouted, "Do it!"

Tamar reached for my wrists, fumbling with the key as darkness rolled over us.

We were blind. I heard someone scream. Then the lock clicked free. The irons fell from my wrists and hit the deck with a dull *clang*.

I raised my hands, and light blazed through the dark,

pushing the blackness back over the whaler. A cheer went up from Sturmhond's crew, but it withered on their lips as another sound filled the air – a grating shriek, piercing in its wrongness, the creak of a door swinging open, a door that should have remained forever shut. The wound in my shoulder gave a sharp throb. *Nichevo'ya.*

I turned to Sturmhond. "We have to get out of here," I said. "*Now.*"

He hesitated, battling himself. Two of his men were still aboard the whaler. His expression hardened. "Topmen make sail!" he shouted. "Squallers due east!"

I saw a row of sailors standing by the masts raise their arms and heard a *whump* as the canvas above us swelled with a hard-driving wind. Just how many Grisha did the privateer have in his crew?

But the Darkling's Squallers had arranged themselves on the whaler's deck and were sending their own winds to buffet us. The schooner rocked unsteadily.

"Portside guns!" roared Sturmhond. "Rolling broadside. On my signal!"

I heard two shrill whistle blasts. A deafening *boom* shook the ship, then another and another, as the schooner's guns opened up a gaping hole in the whaler's hull. A panicked shout went up from the Darkling's ship. Sturmhond's Squallers seized the advantage, and the schooner surged free.

As the smoke from the cannons cleared, I saw a figure in black step up to the railing of the disabled whaler. Another wave of darkness rushed towards us, but this one was different. It writhed over the water as if it were clawing its way forward, and with it came the eerie clicking of a thousand angry insects.

The darkness frothed and foamed, like a wave breaking over a boulder, and began to separate itself into shapes. Beside me, Mal muttered a prayer and lifted his rifle to his shoulder. I focused my power and slashed out with the Cut, burning through the black cloud, trying to destroy the *nichevo'ya* before they could take their full form. I couldn't stop them all. They came on in a moaning horde of black teeth and claws.

Sturmhond's crew opened fire.

The *nichevo'ya* reached the masts of the schooner, whirling around the sails, plucking sailors from the rigging like fruit. Then they were skittering down onto the deck. Mal fired again and again as the crewmen drew their sabres, but bullets and blades seemed only to slow the monsters. Their shadow bodies wavered and re-formed, and they just kept coming.

The schooner was still moving ahead, widening the distance between itself and the whaler. Not fast enough. I heard that shrieking moan, and another wave of shifting, slithering dark was headed for us, already separating into winged bodies, reinforcements for the shadow soldiers.

Sturmhond saw it too. He pointed to one of the Squallers still summoning wind to the sails. "Lightning," he shouted.

I flinched. He couldn't mean it. Squallers were never permitted to draw lightning. It was too unpredictable, too dangerous—and on open seas? With wooden ships? But Sturmhond's Grisha didn't hesitate. The Squallers clapped their hands together, rubbing their palms back and forth. My ears popped as the pressure plummeted. The air crackled with current.

We had just enough time to hurl ourselves to the deck

as jagged bolts of lightning zigzagged across the sky. The new wave of *nichevo'ya* scattered in momentary confusion.

"Go!" Sturmhond bellowed. "Squallers at full!" Mal and I were thrown against the railing as the schooner shot forward. The sleek ship seemed to fly over the waves.

I saw another black swell billow out from the side of the whaler. I lurched to my feet and braced myself, gathering my strength for another onslaught.

But it did not come. It seemed there was a limit to the Darkling's power. We'd edged out of his range.

I leaned over the railing. The wind and sea spray stung my skin as the Darkling's ship and his monsters disappeared from view. Something between a laugh and a sob racked my chest.

Mal threw his arms around me and I held tight, feeling the wet press of his shirt against my cheek, listening to the pounding of his heart, clinging to the unbelievable truth that we were still alive.

Then, despite the blood they'd shed and the friends they'd lost, the schooner's crew broke into cheers. They whooped and hollered and barked and growled. In the rigging, Tolya lifted his rifle with one hand and threw his head back, releasing a howl of triumph that lifted the hair on my arms.

Mal and I drew apart, gazing at the crewmen yipping and laughing around us. I knew we were both thinking the same thing: Just what had we got ourselves into?

CHAPTER 5

We slumped against the railing and scooted down until we were sitting next to each other, exhausted and dazed. We'd escaped the Darkling, but we were on a strange ship, surrounded by a bunch of crazed Grisha dressed as sailors and howling like mad dogs.

"You all right?" Mal asked.

I nodded. The wound in my shoulder felt like it was on fire, but I was unhurt and my whole body was thrumming from using my power again.

"You?" I asked.

"Not a scratch on me," Mal said in disbelief.

The ship rode the waves at seemingly impossible speed, driven forward by Squallers and what I knew must be Tidemakers. As the terror and thrill of the battle receded, I realised I was soaking wet. My teeth began to chatter. Mal put his arm around me, and at some point, one of the crew dropped a blanket over us.

Finally, Sturmhond called a halt and ordered the sails trimmed. The Squallers and Tidemakers dropped their arms and fell against each other, completely spent. Their power had left their faces glowing, their eyes alight.

The schooner slowed until it rocked gently in what suddenly seemed an overwhelming silence.

"Keep a watch," Sturmhond commanded, and Privyet

sent a sailor up into the shrouds with a long glass. Mal and I slowly got to our feet.

Sturmhond walked along the row of exhausted Etherealki, clapping Squallers and Tidemakers on the back and saying quiet words to a few of them. I saw him directing injured sailors belowdecks, where I assumed they'd be seen by a ship's surgeon or maybe a Corporalki Healer. The privateer seemed to have every kind of Grisha in his employ.

Then Sturmhond strode towards me, pulling a knife from his belt. My hands went up, and Mal stepped in front of me, levelling his rifle at Sturmhond's chest. Instantly, I heard swords being drawn and pistols cocking all around us as the crew drew their weapons.

"Easy, Oretsev," Sturmhond said, his steps slowing. "I've just gone to a lot of trouble and expense to put you on my ship. Be a shame to fill you full of holes now." He flipped the knife over, offering the hilt to me. "This is for the beast."

The sea whip. In the excitement of the battle, I'd almost forgotten.

Mal hesitated, then cautiously lowered his rifle.

"Stand down," Sturmhond instructed his crew. They holstered their pistols and put up their swords.

Sturmhond nodded to Tamar. "Haul it in."

On Tamar's orders, a group of sailors leaned over the starboard rail and unlashed a complex webbing of ropes. They heaved, and slowly raised the sea whip's body over the schooner's side. It thumped to the deck, struggling weakly in the silvery confines of the net. It gave a vicious thrash, its huge teeth snapping. We all jumped back.

"As I understand it, you have to be the one," said

Sturmhond, holding the knife out to me once more. I eyed the privateer, wondering how much he might know about amplifiers, and this amplifier in particular.

"Go on," he said. "We need to get moving. The Darkling's ship is disabled, but it won't stay that way."

The blade in Sturmhond's hand gleamed dully in the sun. Grisha steel. Somehow I wasn't surprised.

Still, I hesitated.

"I just lost thirteen good men," Sturmhond said quietly. "Don't tell me it was for nothing."

I looked at the sea whip. It lay twitching on the deck, air fluttering through its gills, its red eyes cloudy, but still full of rage. I remembered the stag's dark, steady gaze, the quiet panic of its final moments.

The stag had lived so long in my imagination that, when it had finally stepped from the trees and into the snowy glade, it had been almost familiar to me. The sea whip was a stranger, more myth than reality, despite the sad and solid truth of its broken body.

"Either way, it won't survive," the privateer said.

I grasped the knife's hilt. It felt heavy in my hand. *Is this mercy?* It certainly wasn't the same mercy I had shown Morozova's stag.

Rusalye. The cursed prince, guardian of the Bone Road. In the stories, he lured lonely maidens onto his back and carried them, laughing, over the waves, until they were too far from shore to cry for help. Then he dove down, dragging them beneath the surface to his underwater palace. The girls wasted away, for there was nothing to eat there but coral and pearls. Rusalye wept and sang his mournful song over their bodies, then returned to the surface to claim another queen.

Just stories, I told myself. *It's not a prince, just an animal in pain.*

The sea whip's sides heaved. It snapped its jaws uselessly in the air. Two harpoons extended from its back, watery blood trickling from the wounds. I held up the knife, unsure of what to do, where to put the blade. My arms shook. The sea whip gave a wheezing, pitiful sigh, a weak echo of that magical choir.

Mal stepped forward. "End it, Alina," he said hoarsely. "For Saints' sake."

He pulled the knife from my grip and dropped it to the deck. He took hold of my hands and closed them over the shaft of one of the harpoons. With one clean thrust, we drove it home.

The sea whip shuddered and then went still, its blood pooling on the deck.

Mal looked down at his hands, then wiped them on his torn shirt and turned away.

Tolya and Tamar came forward. My stomach churned. I knew what had to come next. *That isn't true*, said a voice in my head. *You can walk away. Leave it be.* Again, I had the sense that things were moving too fast. But I couldn't just throw an amplifier like this back into the sea. The dragon had already given up its life. And taking the amplifier didn't necessarily mean that I would use it.

The sea whip's scales were an iridescent white that shimmered with soft rainbows, except for a single strip that began between its large eyes and ran over the ridge of its skull into its soft mane – those were edged in gold.

Tamar slid a dagger from her belt and, with Tolya's help, worked the scales free. I didn't let myself look away.

When they were done, they handed me seven perfect scales, still wet with blood.

"Let us bow our heads for the men lost today," Sturmhond said. "Good sailors. Good soldiers. Let the sea carry them to safe harbour, and may the Saints receive them on a brighter shore."

He repeated the Sailor's Prayer in Kerch, then Tamar murmured the words in Shu. For a moment, we stood on the rocking ship, heads bent. A lump rose in my throat.

More men dead and another magical, ancient creature gone, its body desecrated by Grisha steel. I laid my hand on the sea whip's shimmering hide. It was cool and slick beneath my fingers. Its red eyes were cloudy and blank. I gripped the golden scales in my palm, feeling their edges dig into my flesh. What Saints waited for creatures like this?

A long minute passed and then Sturmhond murmured, "Saints receive them."

"Saints receive them," replied the crew.

"We need to move," Sturmhond said quietly. "The whaler's hull was cracked, but the Darkling has Squallers and a Fabrikator or two, and for all I know, those monsters of his can be trained to use a hammer and nails. Let's not take any chances." He turned to Privyet. "Give the Squallers a few minutes to rest and get me a damage report, then make sail."

"*Da, kapitan,*" Privyet responded crisply. He hesitated. "*Kapitan* . . . could be people will pay good money for dragon scales, no matter the colour."

Sturmhond frowned, but then gave a terse nod. "Take what you want, then clear the deck and get us moving. You have our coordinates."

Several of the crew fell on the sea whip's body to cut away its scales. This I couldn't watch. I turned my back on them, my gut in knots.

Sturmhond came up beside me.

"Don't judge them too harshly," he said, glancing over his shoulder.

"It's not them I'm judging," I said. "You're the captain."

"And they have purses to fill, parents and siblings to feed. We just lost nearly half our crew and took no rich prize to ease the sting. Not that you aren't fetching."

"What am I doing here?" I asked. "Why did you help us?"

"Are you so sure I have?"

"Answer the question, Sturmhond," said Mal, joining us. "Why hunt the sea whip if you only meant to turn it over to Alina?"

"I wasn't hunting the sea whip. I was hunting you."

"That's why you raised a mutiny against the Darkling?" I asked. "To get at me?"

"You can't very well *mutiny* on your own ship."

"Call it what you like," I said, exasperated. "Just explain yourself."

Sturmhond leaned back and rested his elbows on the rail, surveying the deck. "As I would have explained to the Darkling had he bothered to ask – which, thankfully, he didn't – the problem with hiring a man who sells his honour is that you can always be outbid."

I gaped at him. "You betrayed the Darkling for *money*?"

"'Betrayed' seems a strong word. I hardly know the fellow."

"You're mad," I said. "You know what he can do. No prize is worth that."

70

Sturmhond grinned. "That remains to be seen."

"The Darkling will hunt you for the rest of your days."

"Then you and I will have something in common, won't we? Besides, I like to have powerful enemies. Makes me feel important."

Mal crossed his arms and considered the privateer. "I can't decide if you're crazy or stupid."

"I have so many good qualities," Sturmhond said. "It can be hard to choose."

I shook my head. The privateer was out of his mind. "If the Darkling was outbid, then who hired you? Where are you taking us?"

"First answer a question for me," Sturmhond said, reaching into his frock coat. He drew a little red volume from his pocket and tossed it to me. "Why was the Darkling carrying this around with him? He doesn't strike me as the religious type."

I caught it and turned it over, but I already knew what it was. Its gold lettering sparkled in the sun.

"You stole it?" I asked.

"And a number of other documents from his cabin. Although, again, since it was technically *my* cabin, I'm not sure you can call it theft."

"*Technically*," I observed in irritation, "the cabin belongs to the whaling captain you stole the ship from."

"Fair enough," admitted Sturmhond. "If this whole Sun Summoner thing doesn't work out, you might consider a career as a barrister. You seem to have the carping disposition. But I should point out that this actually belongs to you."

He reached out and flipped the book open. My name was inscribed inside the cover: *Alina Starkov.*

I tried to keep my face blank, but my mind was suddenly racing. This was my *Istorii Sankt'ya*, the very copy the Apparat had given to me months ago in the library of the Little Palace. The Darkling would have had my room searched after I fled Os Alta, but why take this book? And why had he been so concerned that I might have read it?

I thumbed through the pages. The volume was beautifully illustrated, though given that it was meant for children, it was awfully gruesome. Some of the Saints were depicted performing miracles or acts of charity: Sankt Feliks among the apple boughs. Sankta Anastasia ridding Arkesk of the wasting plague. But most of the pages showed the Saints in their martyrdoms: Sankta Lizabeta being drawn and quartered, the beheading of Sankt Lubov, Sankt Ilya in Chains. I froze. This time I could not disguise my reaction.

"Interesting, no?" said Sturmhond. He tapped the page with one long finger. "Unless I'm very much mistaken, that's the creature we just captured."

There was no hiding it: Behind Sankt Ilya, splashing around in the waves of a lake or an ocean, was the distinctive shape of the sea whip. And that wasn't all. Somehow, I kept my hand from straying to the collar at my neck.

I shut the book and shrugged. "Just another story."

Mal shot me a baffled look. I didn't know if he'd seen what was on that page.

I didn't want to return the *Istorii Sankt'ya* to Sturmhond, but he was already suspicious enough. I made myself hold it out to him, hoping he couldn't see the tremor in my hand.

Sturmhond studied me, then levered himself up and shook out his cuffs. "Keep it. It *is* yours, after all. As I'm sure you've noticed, I have a deep respect for personal property. Besides, you'll need something to keep you occupied until we get to Os Kervo."

Mal and I both gave a start.

"You're taking us to West Ravka?" I asked.

"I'm taking you to meet my client, and that's really all I can tell you."

"Who is he? What does he want from me?"

"Are you so sure it's a he? Maybe I'm delivering you to the Fjerdan Queen."

"Are you?"

"No. But it's always wise to keep an open mind."

I blew out a frustrated breath. "Do you ever answer a question directly?"

"Hard to say. Ah, there, I've done it again."

I turned to Mal, fists clenched. "I'm going to kill him."

"Answer the question, Sturmhond," Mal growled.

Sturmhond lifted a brow. "Two things you should know," he said, and this time I heard that hint of steel in his voice. "One, captains don't like taking orders on their own ships. Two, I'm going to offer you a deal."

Mal snorted. "Why would we ever trust you?"

"You don't have much choice," Sturmhond said pleasantly. "I'm well aware that you could sink this ship and consign us all to the watery deep, but I hope you'll take your chances with my client. Listen to what he has to say. If you don't like what he proposes, I swear to help you make your escape. Take you anywhere in the world."

I couldn't believe what I was hearing. "So you crossed

the Darkling, and now you're going to turn right around and betray your new client, too?"

"Not at all," said Sturmhond, genuinely affronted. "My client paid me to *get* you to Ravka, not to *keep* you there. That would be extra."

I looked at Mal. He lifted a shoulder and said, "He's a liar and probably insane, but he's also right. We don't have much choice."

I rubbed my temples. I felt a headache coming on. I was tired and confused, and Sturmhond had a way of talking that made me want to shoot someone. Preferably him. But he'd freed us from the Darkling, and once Mal and I were off his ship, we might find our own way to escape. For now, I couldn't think much beyond that.

"All right," I said.

He smiled. "So good to know you won't be drowning us all." He beckoned a deckhand who had been hovering nearby. "Fetch Tamar and tell her she'll be sharing her quarters with the Summoner," he instructed. Then he pointed to Mal. "He can stay with Tolya."

Before Mal could open his mouth to protest, Sturmhond forestalled him. "That's the way of things on this ship. I'm giving you both free run of the *Volkvolny* until we reach Ravka, but I beg you not to trifle with my generous nature. The ship has rules and I have limits."

"You and me both," Mal said through gritted teeth.

I laid my hand on Mal's arm. I would have felt safer staying together, but this wasn't the time to quibble with the privateer. "Let it go," I said. "I'll be fine."

Mal scowled, then turned on his heel and strode across the deck, disappearing into the ordered chaos of rope and sail. I took a step after him.

"Might want to leave him alone," Sturmhond said. "That type needs plenty of time for brooding and self-recrimination. Otherwise they get cranky."

"Do you take anything seriously?"

"Not if I can help it. Makes life so tedious."

I shook my head. "This client—"

"Don't bother asking. Needless to say, I've had plenty of bidders. You're in very high demand since you disappeared from the Fold. Of course, most people think you're dead. Tends to drive the price down. Try not to take it personally."

I looked across the deck to where the crew were hefting the sea whip's body over the ship's rail. With a straining heave, they rolled it over the side of the schooner. It struck the water with a loud splash. That quickly, Rusalye was gone, swallowed by the sea.

A long whistle blew. The crewmen scattered to their stations, and the Squallers took their places. Seconds later, the sails bloomed like great white flowers – the schooner was once more on its way, tacking southeast to Ravka, to home.

"What are you going to do with those scales?" Sturmhond asked.

"I don't know."

"Don't you? Despite my dazzling good looks, I'm not quite the pretty fool I appear to be. The Darkling intended for you to wear the sea whip's scales."

So why didn't he kill it? When the Darkling had murdered the stag and placed Morozova's collar around my neck, he'd bound us forever. I shivered, remembering the way he had reached across that connection, seizing hold of my power as I stood by, helpless. Would the dragon's scales have given him the same control? And if so, why not take it?

"I already have an amplifier," I said.

"A powerful one, if the stories are true."

The most powerful amplifier the world had ever known. So the Darkling had told me, and so I'd believed. But what if there was more to it? What if I'd only touched the beginnings of the stag's power? I shook my head. That was madness.

"Amplifiers can't be combined."

"I saw the book," he replied. "It certainly looks like they can."

I felt the weight of the *Istorii Sankt'ya* in my pocket. Had the Darkling feared I might learn Morozova's secrets from the pages of a children's book?

"You don't understand what you're saying," I told Sturmhond. "No Grisha has ever taken a second amplifier. The risks—"

"Now, that's a word best not used around me. I tend to be overfond of risk."

"Not this kind," I said grimly.

"Pity," he murmured. "If the Darkling catches up with us, I doubt this ship or this crew will survive another battle. A second amplifier might even the odds. Better yet, give us an edge. I do so hate a fair fight."

"Or it could kill me or sink the ship or create another Shadow Fold, or worse."

"You certainly have a flare for the dire."

My fingers snaked into my pocket, seeking out the damp edges of the scales. I had so little information, and my knowledge of Grisha theory was sketchy at best. But this rule had always seemed fairly clear: one Grisha, one amplifier. I remembered the words from one of the convoluted philosophy texts I'd been required to read: "*Why can a Grisha possess but one amplifier? I will answer this question instead: What is infinite? The universe and the greed of men.*" I needed time to think.

"Will you keep your word?" I said at last. "Will you help us escape?" I didn't know why I bothered asking. If he intended to betray us, he certainly wouldn't say so.

I expected him to reply with some kind of joke, so I was surprised when he said, "Are you so eager to leave your country behind once again?"

I stilled. *All the while, your country suffers.* The Darkling had accused me of abandoning Ravka. He was wrong about a lot of things, but I couldn't help feeling that he was right about that. I'd left my country to the mercy of the Shadow Fold, to a weak king and grasping tyrants like the Darkling and the Apparat. Now, if the rumours could be believed, the Fold was expanding and Ravka was falling apart. Because of the Darkling. Because of the collar. Because of me.

I lifted my face to the sun, feeling the rush of sea air over my skin, and said, "I'm eager to be free."

"As long as the Darkling lives, you'll never be free. And neither will your country. You know that."

I'd considered the possibility that Sturmhond was greedy or stupid, but it hadn't occurred to me that he might actually be a patriot. He was Ravkan, after all, and even if his exploits had lined his own pockets, they'd probably done more to help his country than all of the feeble Ravkan navy.

"I want the choice," I said.

"You'll have it," he replied. "On my word as a liar and

cutthroat." He set off across the deck but then turned back to me. "You are right about one thing, Summoner. The Darkling is a powerful enemy. You might want to think about making some powerful friends."

I wanted nothing more than to pull the copy of the *Istorii Sankt'ya* from my pocket and spend an hour studying the illustration of Sankt Ilya, but Tamar was already waiting to escort me to her quarters.

Sturmhond's schooner wasn't at all like the sturdy merchant ship that had carried Mal and me to Novyi Zem or the clunky whaler we'd just left behind. It was sleek, heavily armed, and beautifully built. Tamar told me that Sturmhond had captured the schooner from a Zemeni pirate who was picking off Ravkan ships near the ports of the southern coast. He had liked the vessel so much that he'd taken it for his own flagship and renamed it *Volkvolny*, Wolf of the Waves.

Wolves. Storm hound. The red dog on the ship's flag. At least I knew why the crew were always howling and yapping.

Every inch of space on the schooner was put to use. The crew slept on the gun deck. In case of engagement, their hammocks could be quickly stowed and the cannon slotted into place. I'd been right about the fact that, with Corporalki on board, there was no need for an *otkazat'sya* surgeon. The doctor's quarters and supply room had been turned into Tamar's berth. The cabin was tiny, with barely enough room for two hammocks and a chest. The walls were lined with cupboards full of unused ointments and salves, arsenic powder, tincture of lead antimony.

I balanced carefully in one of the hammocks, my feet resting on the floor, acutely conscious of the red book tucked inside my coat as I watched Tamar throw open the lid of her trunk and begin divesting herself of weapons: the brace of pistols that crossed her chest, two slender axes from her belt, a dagger from her boot, and another from the sheath secured around her thigh. She was a walking armoury.

"I feel sorry for your friend," she said as she pulled what looked like a sock full of ball bearings from one of her pockets. It hit the bottom of the chest with a loud *thunk*.

"Why?" I asked, making a circle on the planks with the toe of my boot.

"My brother snores like a drunk bear."

I laughed. "Mal snores too."

"Then they can perform a duet." She disappeared and then returned a moment later with a bucket. "The Tidemakers filled the rain barrels," she said. "Feel free to wash if you like."

Fresh water was usually a luxury aboard ship, but I supposed that with Grisha in the crew, there would be no need to ration it.

She dunked her head in the bucket and ruffled her short dark hair. "He's handsome, the tracker."

I rolled my eyes. "You don't say."

"Not my type, but handsome."

My brows shot up. In my experience, Mal was just about everyone's type. But I wasn't going to start asking Tamar personal questions. If Sturmhond couldn't be trusted, then neither could his crew, and I didn't need to grow attached to any of them. I'd learned my lesson with Genya, and one shattered friendship was enough. Instead, I said, "There are Kerch in Sturmhond's crew. Aren't they superstitious about having a girl onboard?"

"Sturmhond does things his own way."

"And they don't . . . bother you?"

Tamar grinned, her white teeth flashing against her bronze skin. She tapped the gleaming shark's tooth hanging around her neck, and I realised it was an amplifier. "No," she said simply.

"Ah."

Faster than I could blink, she pulled yet another knife from her sleeve. "This comes in handy, too," she said.

"However do you choose?" I breathed faintly.

"Depends on my mood." She flipped the knife over in her hand and offered it to me. "Sturmhond's given orders that you're to be left alone, but just in case someone gets drunk and forgetful . . . you do know how to take care of yourself?"

I nodded. I didn't walk around with thirty knives hidden about my person, but I wasn't completely incompetent.

She dunked her head again, then said, "They're throwing dice above deck, and I'm ready for my ration. You can come if you like."

I didn't care much for gambling or rum, but I was still tempted. My whole body was crackling with the feeling of using my power against the *nichevo'ya*. I was restless and positively famished for the first time in weeks. I shook my head. "No thanks."

"Suit yourself. I have debts to collect. Privyet wagered we wouldn't be coming back. I swear he looked like a mourner at a funeral when we came over that rail."

"He bet you'd be killed?" I said, aghast.

She laughed. "I don't blame him. To go up against the Darkling and his Grisha? Everyone knew it was suicide. The crew ended up drawing straws to see who got stuck with the honour."

"And you and your brother are just unlucky?"

"Us?" Tamar paused in the doorway. Her hair was damp, and the lamplight glinted off her Heartrender's grin. "We didn't draw anything," she said as she stepped through the door. "We volunteered."

I didn't have a chance to talk to Mal alone until late that night. We'd been invited to dine with Sturmhond in his quarters, and it had been a strange supper. The meal was served by the steward, a servant of impeccable manners, who was several years older than anyone else on the ship. We ate better than we had in weeks: fresh bread, roasted haddock, pickled radishes, and a sweet iced wine that set my head spinning after just a few sips.

My appetite was fierce, as it always was after I'd used my power, but Mal ate little and said less until Sturmhond mentioned the shipment of arms he was bringing back to Ravka. Then he seemed to perk up and they spent the rest of the meal talking about guns, grenades, and exciting ways to make things explode. I couldn't seem to pay attention. As they yammered on about the repeating rifles used on the Zemeni frontier, all I could think about were the scales in my pocket and what I intended to do with them.

Did I dare claim a second amplifier for myself? I had

taken the sea whip's life – that meant its power belonged to me. And if the scales functioned like Morozova's collar, then the dragon's power was also mine to bestow. I could give the scales to one of Sturmhond's Heartrenders, maybe even Tolya, try to take control of him the way the Darkling had once taken control of me. I might be able to force the privateer to sail us back to Novyi Zem. But I had to admit that wasn't what I wanted.

I took another sip of wine. I needed to talk to Mal.

To distract myself, I catalogued the trappings of Sturmhond's cabin. Everything was gleaming wood and polished brass. The desk was littered with charts, the pieces of a dismembered sextant, and strange drawings of what looked like the hinged wing of a mechanical bird. The table glittered with Kerch porcelain and crystal. The wines bore labels in a language I didn't recognise. *All plunder*, I realised. Sturmhond had done well for himself.

As for the captain, I took the opportunity to really look at him for the first time. He was probably four or five years older than I was, and there was something very odd about his face. His chin was overly pointy. His eyes were a muddy green, his hair a peculiar shade of red. His nose looked like it had been broken and badly set several times. At one point, he caught me studying him, and I could have sworn he turned his face away from the light.

When we finally left Sturmhond's cabin, it was past midnight. I herded Mal above deck to a secluded spot by the ship's prow. I knew there were men on watch in the foretop above us, but I didn't know when I'd have another chance to get him alone.

"I like him," Mal was saying, a little unsteady on his feet from the wine. "I mean, he talks too much, and he'd probably steal the buttons from your boots, but he's not a bad guy, and he seems to know a lot about—"

"Would you shut up?" I whispered. "I want to show you something."

Mal peered at me blearily. "No need to be rude."

I ignored him and pulled the red book out of my pocket. "Look," I said, holding the page open and casting a glow over Sankt Ilya's exultant face.

Mal went still. "The stag," he said. "And Rusalye." I watched him examine the illustration and saw the moment that realisation struck. "Saints," he breathed. "There's a third."

CHAPTER 6

Sankt Ilya stood barefoot on the shore of a dark sea. He wore the ragged remnants of a purple robe, his arms outstretched, his palms turned upward. His face had the blissful, placid expression Saints always seemed to wear in paintings, usually before they were murdered in some horrific way. Around his neck he wore an iron collar that had once been connected to the heavy fetters around his wrists by thick chains. Now the chains hung broken by his sides.

Behind Sankt Ilya, a sinuous white serpent splashed in the waves.

A white stag lay at his feet, gazing out at us with dark, steady eyes.

But neither of these creatures held our attention. Mountains crowded the background behind the Saint's left shoulder, and there, barely visible in the distance, a bird circled a towering stone arch.

Mal's finger traced its long tailfeathers, rendered in white and the same pale gold that illuminated Sankt Ilya's halo. "It can't be," he said.

"The stag was real. So was the sea whip."

"But this is . . . different."

He was right. The firebird didn't belong to one story, but to a thousand. It was at the heart of every Ravkan myth, the inspiration for countless plays and ballads, novels and operas. Ravka's borders were said to have been sketched by the firebird's flight. Its rivers ran with the firebird's tears. Its capital was said to have been founded where a firebird's feather fell to earth. A young warrior had picked up that feather and carried it into battle. No army had been able to stand against him, and he became the first king of Ravka. Or so the legend went.

The firebird *was* Ravka. It was not meant to be brought down by a tracker's arrow, its bones worn for the greater glory of some upstart orphan.

"Sankt Ilya," Mal said.

"Ilya Morozova."

"A Grisha Saint?"

I touched the tip of my finger to the page, to the collar, to the two fetters on Morozova's wrists. "Three amplifiers. Three creatures. And we have two of them."

Mal gave his head a firm shake, probably trying to clear away the haze of wine. Abruptly, he shut the book. For a second, I thought he might throw it into the sea, but then he handed it back to me.

"What are we supposed to do with this?" he said. He sounded almost angry.

I'd thought about that all afternoon, all evening, throughout that interminable dinner, my fingers straying to the sea whip's scales again and again, as if anxious for the feel of them.

"Mal, Sturmhond has Fabrikators in his crew. He thinks I should use the scales . . . and I think he might be right."

Mal's head snapped around. "What?"

I swallowed nervously and plunged ahead. "The stag's

power isn't enough. Not to fight the Darkling. Not to destroy the Fold."

"And your answer is a second amplifier?"

"For now."

"*For now?*" He ran a hand through his hair. "Saints," he swore. "You want all three. You want to hunt the firebird."

I felt suddenly foolish, greedy, even a little ridiculous. "The illustration—"

"It's just a picture, Alina," he whispered furiously. "It's a drawing by some dead monk."

"But what if it's more? The Darkling said Morozova's amplifiers were different, that they were meant to be used together."

"So now you're taking advice from murderers?"

"No, but—"

"Did you make any other plans with the Darkling while you were holed up together belowdecks?"

"We weren't holed up together," I said sharply. "He was just trying to get under your skin."

"Well, it worked." He gripped the ship's railing, his knuckles flexing white. "Someday I'm going to put an arrow through that bastard's neck."

I heard the echo of the Darkling's voice. *There are no others like us.* I pushed it aside and reached out to lay my hand on Mal's arm. "You found the stag, and you found the sea whip. Maybe you were meant to find the firebird too."

He laughed outright, a rueful sound, but I was relieved to hear the bitter edge was gone. "I'm a good tracker, Alina, but I'm not that good. We need somewhere to start. The firebird could be anywhere in the world."

"You can do it. I know you can."

Finally, he sighed and covered my hand with his own. "I don't remember anything about Sankt Ilya."

That was no surprise. There were hundreds of Saints, one for every tiny village and backwater in Ravka. Besides, at Keramzin, religion was considered a peasant preoccupation. We'd gone to church only once or twice a year. My thoughts strayed to the Apparat. He had given me the *Istorii Sankt'ya*, but I had no way of knowing what he intended by it, or if he even knew the secret it contained.

"Me neither," I said. "But that arch must mean something."

"Do you recognise it?"

When I'd first glanced at the illustration, the arch had seemed almost familiar. But I'd looked at countless books of maps during my training as a cartographer. My memory was a blur of valleys and monuments from Ravka and beyond. I shook my head. "No."

"Of course not. That would be too easy." He released a long breath, then drew me closer, studying my face in the moonlight. He touched the collar at my neck. "Alina," he said, "how do we know what these things will do to you?"

"We don't," I admitted.

"But you want them anyway. The stag. The sea whip. The firebird."

I thought of the surge of exultation that had come from using my power in the battle against the Darkling's horde, the way my body fizzed and thrummed when I wielded the Cut. What might it feel like to have that power doubled? Trebled? The thought made me dizzy.

I looked up at the star-filled sky. The night was

velvety black and strewn with jewels. The hunger struck me suddenly. *I want them*, I thought. All that light, all that power. *I want it all.*

A restless shiver moved over me. I ran my thumb down the spine of the *Istorii Sankt'ya*. Was my greed making me see what I wanted to see? Maybe it was the same greed that had driven the Darkling so many years ago, the greed that had turned him into the Black Heretic and torn Ravka in two. And yet I couldn't escape the truth that without the amplifiers, I was no match for him. Mal and I were low on options.

"We need them," I said. "All three. If we ever want to stop running. If we ever want to be free."

Mal traced the line of my throat, the curve of my cheek, and all the while, he held my gaze. I felt like he was looking for an answer there, but when he finally spoke, he just said, "All right."

He kissed me once, gently, and though I tried to ignore it, there was something mournful in the brush of his lips.

I didn't know if I was eager or simply afraid I'd lose my nerve, but we ignored the late hour and went to Sturmhond that night. The privateer greeted our request with his usual good cheer, and Mal and I returned to the deck to wait beneath the mizzenmast. A few minutes later, the captain appeared, a Materialnik in tow. With her hair in braids and yawning like a sleepy child, she didn't look very impressive, but if Sturmhond said she was his best Fabrikator, I had to take him at his word.

Tolya and Tamar trailed behind, carrying lanterns to help the Fabrikator at her work. If we survived whatever came next, everyone aboard the *Volkvolny* would know about the second amplifier. I didn't like it, but there was nothing to be done about it.

"Evening, all," said Sturmhond, slapping his hands together, seemingly oblivious to our sombre mood. "Perfect night for tearing a hole in the universe, no?"

I scowled at him and slipped the scales from my pocket. I'd rinsed them in a bucket of seawater, and they gleamed golden in the lamplight.

"Do you know what to do?" I asked the Fabrikator.

She had me turn and show her the back of the collar. I'd only ever glimpsed it in mirrors, but I knew the surface must be near perfect. Certainly my fingers had never been able to detect any seam where David had joined the two pieces of antler together.

I handed the scales to Mal, who held one out to the Fabrikator.

"Are you sure this is a good idea?" she asked. She was gnawing on her lip so agressively, I thought she might draw blood.

"Of course not," said Sturmhond. "Anything worth doing always starts as a bad idea."

The Fabrikator plucked the scale from Mal's fingers and rested it against my wrist, then held out her hand for another. She bent to her work.

I felt the heat first, radiating from the scales as their edges began to come apart and then re-form. One after another, they melded together, fusing into an overlapping row as the fetter grew around my wrist. The Fabrikator worked in silence, her hands moving infinitesimal degrees.

Tolya and Tamar kept the lamps steady, their faces so still and solemn they might have been icons themselves. Even Sturmhond had gone quiet.

Finally, the two ends of the cuff were nearly touching and only one scale remained. Mal stared down at it, cupped in his palm.

"Mal?" I said.

He didn't look at me, but touched one finger to the bare skin of my wrist, the place where my pulse beat, where the fetter would close. Then he handed the last scale to the Fabrikator.

In moments, it was done.

Sturmhond peered at the glittering cuff of scales. "Huh," he murmured. "I thought the end of the world would be more exciting."

"Stand back," I said.

The group shuffled over to the rail.

"You too," I told Mal. Reluctantly, he complied. I saw Privyet peering at us from his place by the wheel. Above, the ropes creaked as the men on watch craned their necks to get a better view.

I took a deep breath. I had to be careful. No heat. Just light. I wiped my damp palms on my coat and spread my arms. Almost before I'd formed the call, the light was rushing towards me.

It came from every direction, from a million stars, from a sun still hidden below the horizon. It came with relentless speed and furious intent.

"Oh, Saints," I had time to whisper. Then the light was blazing through me and the night came apart. The sky exploded into brilliant gold. The surface of the water glittered like a massive diamond, reflecting piercing white shards of sunlight. Despite my best intentions, the air shimmered with heat.

I closed my eyes against the brightness, trying to focus, to regain control. I heard Baghra's harsh voice in my head, demanding that I trust my power: *It isn't an animal that shies away from you or chooses whether or not to come when you call it.* But this was like nothing I'd felt before. It *was* an animal, a creature of infinite fire that breathed with the stag's strength and the sea whip's wrath. It coursed through me, stealing my breath, breaking me up, dissolving my edges, until all I knew was light.

Too much, I thought in desperation. And at the same time, all I could think was, *More*.

From somewhere far away, I heard voices shouting. I felt the heat billowing around me, lifting my coat, singeing the hair on my arms. I didn't care.

"Alina!"

I felt the ship rocking as the sea began to crackle and hiss.

"Alina!" Suddenly Mal's arms were around me, pulling me back. He held me in a crushing grip, his eyes shut tight against the blaze around us. I smelled sea salt and sweat and, beneath it, his familiar scent – Keramzin, meadow grass, the dark green heart of the woods.

I remembered my arms, my legs, the press of my ribs, as he held me tighter, piecing me back together. I recognised my lips, my teeth, my tongue, my heart, and these new things that were a part of me: collar and fetter. They were bone and breath, muscle and flesh. They were mine.

Does the bird feel the weight of its wings?

I inhaled, felt sense return. I didn't have to take hold

of the power. It clung to me, as if it were grateful to be home. In a single glorious burst, I released the light. The bright sky fractured, letting the night back in, and all around us, sparks fell like fading fireworks, a dream of shining petals blown loose from a thousand flowers.

The heat relented. The sea calmed. I drew the last scraps of light together and wove them into a soft sheen that pulsed over the deck of the ship.

Sturmhond and the others were crouched by the railing, their mouths open in what might have been awe or fear. Mal had me crushed to his chest, his faced pressed to my hair, his breath coming in harsh gasps.

"Mal," I said quietly. He clutched me tighter. I squeaked. "Mal, I can't breathe."

Slowly, he opened his eyes and looked down at me. I dropped my hands, and the light disappeared entirely. Only then did he ease his grip.

Tolya lit a lamp, and the others got to their feet. Sturmhond dusted off the gaudy folds of his teal coat. The Fabrikator looked as if she was going to be sick, but it was harder to read the twins' faces. Their golden eyes were alight with something I couldn't name.

"Well, Summoner," said Sturmhond, a slight wobble to his voice, "you certainly know how to put on a show."

Mal bracketed my face with his hands. He kissed my brow, my nose, my lips, my hair, then drew me tight against him once again.

"You're all right?" he asked. His voice was rough.

"Yes," I replied.

That wasn't quite true. I felt the collar at my throat, the pressure of the fetter at my wrist. My other arm felt naked. I was incomplete.

Sturmhond roused his crew, and we were well on our way as dawn broke. We couldn't be sure how far the light I'd created might have stretched, but there was a good chance I'd given away our location. We needed to move fast.

Every crewman wanted a look at the second amplifier. Some were wary, others just curious. Mal was the one I was worried about. He watched me constantly, as if he was afraid that at any moment, I might lose control. When dusk fell and we went belowdecks, I cornered him in one of the narrow passageways.

"I'm fine," I said. "Really."

"How do you know?"

"I just do. I can feel it."

"You didn't see what I saw. It was—"

"It got away from me. I didn't know what to expect."

He shook his head. "You were like a stranger, Alina. Beautiful," he said. "Terrible."

"It won't happen again. The fetter is a part of me now, like my lungs or my heart."

"Your heart," he said flatly.

I took his hand in mine and pressed it against my chest. "It's still the same heart, Mal. It's still yours."

I lifted my other hand and cast a soft tide of sunlight over his face. He flinched. *He can never understand your power, and if he does, he will only come to fear you.* I pushed the Darkling's voice from my mind. Mal had every right to be afraid.

"I can do this," I said gently.

He shut his eyes and turned his face to the sunlight that radiated from my hand. Then he tilted his head, resting his cheek against my palm. The light glowed warm against his skin.

We stood that way, in silence, until the watch bell rang.

CHAPTER 7

The winds warmed, and the waters turned from grey to blue as the *Volkvolny* carried us south-east to Ravka. Sturmhond's crew was made up of sailors and rogue Grisha who worked together to keep the ship running smoothly. Despite the stories that had spread about the power of the second amplifier, they didn't pay Mal or me much attention, though they occasionally came to watch me practise at the schooner's stern. I was careful, never pushing too hard, always summoning at noon, when the sun was high in the sky and there was no chance of my efforts being spotted. Mal was still wary, but I'd spoken the truth: the sea whip's power was a part of me now. It thrilled me. It buoyed me. I didn't fear it.

I was fascinated by the rogues. They all had different stories. One had an aunt who had spirited him away rather than let him be turned over to the Darkling. Another had deserted the Second Army. Another had been hidden in a root cellar when the Grisha Examiners arrived to test her.

"My mother told them I'd been killed by the fever that had swept through our village the previous spring," the Tidemaker said. "The neighbours cut my hair and passed me off as their dead *otkazat'sya* son until I was old enough to leave."

Tolya and Tamar's mother had been a Grisha stationed on Ravka's southern border when she met their father, a Shu Han mercenary.

"When she died," Tamar explained, "she made my father promise not to let us be drafted into the Second Army. We left for Novyi Zem the next day."

Most rogue Grisha ended up in Novyi Zem. Aside from Ravka, it was the only place where they didn't have to fear being experimented on by Shu doctors or burned by Fjerdan witchhunters. Even so, they had to be cautious about displaying their power. Grisha were valued slaves, and less scrupulous Kerch traders were known to round them up and sell them in secret auctions.

These were the very threats that had led so many Grisha to take refuge in Ravka and join the Second Army in the first place. But the rogues thought differently. For them, a life spent looking over their shoulders and moving from one place to the next to avoid discovery was preferable to a life in service to the Darkling and the Ravkan King. It was a choice I understood.

After a few monotonous days on the schooner, Mal and I asked Tamar if she would show us some Zemeni combat techniques. It helped ease the tedium of shipboard life and the awful anxiety of returning to West Ravka.

Sturmhond's crew had confirmed the disturbing rumours we'd picked up in Novyi Zem. Crossings of the Fold had all but ceased, and refugees were fleeing its expanding shores. The First Army was close to revolt, and the Second Army was in tatters. I was most frightened by the news that the Apparat's cult of the Sun Saint was growing. No one knew how he'd managed to escape the Grand Palace after the Darkling's failed coup, but he had resurfaced somewhere in the network of monasteries spread across Ravka.

He was circulating the story that I'd died on the Fold and been resurrected as a Saint. Part of me wanted to laugh, but turning through the bloody pages of the *Istorii Sankt'ya* late at night, I couldn't summon so much as a chuckle. I remembered the Apparat's smell, that unpleasant combination of incense and mildew, and pulled my coat tighter around me. He had given me the red book. I had to wonder why.

Despite the bruises and bumps, my practices with Tamar helped to dull the edge of my constant worry. Girls were drafted right along with boys into the King's Army when they came of age, so I'd seen plenty of girls fight and had trained alongside them. But I'd never seen anyone, male or female, fight the way Tamar did. She had a dancer's grace and a seemingly unerring instinct for what her opponent would do next. Her weapons of choice were two double-bit axes that she wielded in tandem, the blades flashing like light off water, and she was nearly as dangerous with a sabre, a pistol, or her bare hands. Only Tolya could match her, and when they sparred, all the crew stopped to watch.

The giant spoke little and spent most of his time working the lines or standing around looking intimidating. Occasionally, he stepped in to help with our lessons. He wasn't much of a teacher. "Move faster" was about all we could get out of him. Tamar was a far better instructor, although my lessons became less challenging after Sturmhond caught us practising on the foredeck.

"Tamar," Sturmhond chided, "please don't damage the cargo."

Immediately, Tamar snapped to attention and gave a crisp, "*Da, kapitan.*"

I shot him a sour look. "I'm not a package you're delivering, Sturmhond."

"More's the pity," he said, sauntering past. "Packages don't talk, and they stay where you put them."

But when Tamar started us on rapiers and sabres, even Sturmhond joined in. Mal improved daily, though Sturmhond still beat him easily every time. And yet, Mal didn't seem to mind. He took his thumpings with a kind of good humour I never seemed able to muster. Losing made me irritable; Mal just laughed it off.

"How did you and Tolya learn to use your powers?" I asked Tamar one afternoon as we watched Mal and Sturmhond sparring with dulled swords on deck. She'd found me a marlinspike, and when she wasn't pummeling me, she was trying to teach me knots and splices.

"Keep your elbows in!" Sturmhond berated Mal. "Stop flapping them like some kind of chicken."

Mal let out a disturbingly convincing cluck.

Tamar raised a brow. "Your friend seems to be enjoying himself."

I shrugged. "Mal's always been like that. You could drop him in a camp full of Fjerdan assassins, and he'd come out carried on their shoulders. He just blooms wherever he's planted."

"And you?"

"I'm more of a weed," I said drily.

Tamar grinned. In combat, she was cold and silent fire, but when she wasn't fighting, her smiles came easily. "I like weeds," she said, pushing herself off from the railing and gathering her scattered lengths of rope. "They're survivors."

I caught myself returning her smile and quickly went back to working on the knot I was trying to tie. The problem was that I liked being aboard Sturmhond's ship. I liked Tolya and Tamar and the rest of the crew. I liked sitting at meals with them, and the sound of Privyet's lilting tenor. I liked the afternoons when we took target practice, lining up empty wine bottles to shoot off the fantail, and making harmless wagers.

It was a bit like being at the Little Palace, but with none of the messy politics and constant jockeying for status. The crew had an easy, open way with each other. They were all young and poor, and had spent most of their lives in hiding. On this ship, they'd found a home, and they welcomed Mal and me into it with little fuss.

I didn't know what was waiting for us in West Ravka, and I felt fairly sure it was madness to be going back at all. But aboard the *Volkvolny*, with the wind blowing and the white canvas cutting crisp lines across a broad blue sky, I could forget the future and my fear.

And I had to admit, I liked Sturmhond too. He was cocky and brash, and always used ten words when two would do, but I was impressed with the way he led his crew. He didn't bother with any of the tricks I'd seen the Darkling employ, yet they followed him without hesitation. He had their respect, not their fear.

"What's Sturmhond's real name?" I asked Tamar. "His Ravkan name?"

"No idea."

"You've never asked?"

"Why would I?"

"But where in Ravka is he from?"

She squinted up at the sky. "Do you want to go

another round with sabres?" she asked. "We should have time before my watch starts."

She always changed the subject when I brought up Sturmhond. "He didn't just drop out of the sky onto a ship, Tamar. Don't you care where he came from?"

Tamar picked up the swords and handed them over to Tolya, who served as the ship's Master of Arms. "Not particularly. He lets us sail, and he lets us fight."

"And he doesn't make us dress up in red silk and play lapdog," said Tolya, unlocking the rack with the key he wore around his thick neck.

"A sorry lapdog you'd make." Tamar laughed.

"Anything's better than following orders from some puffed-up cully in black," Tolya grumbled.

"You follow Sturmhond's orders," I pointed out.

"Only when he feels like it."

I jumped. Sturmhond was standing right behind me.

"You try telling that ox what to do and see what happens," the privateer said.

Tamar snorted, and she and Tolya began stowing the rest of the weapons.

Sturmhond leaned in and murmured, "If you want to know something about me, lovely, all you need to do is ask."

"I was just wondering where you're from," I said defensively. "That's all."

"Where are *you* from?"

"Keramzin. You know that."

"But where are you from?"

A few dim memories flashed through my mind. A shallow dish of cooked beets, the slippery feel of them between my fingers as they stained my hands red. The smell of egg porridge. Riding on someone's shoulders

– maybe my father's – down a dusty road. At Keramzin, even mentioning our parents had been considered a betrayal of the Duke's kindness and a sign of ingratitude. We'd been taught never to speak of our lives before we arrived at the estate, and eventually most of the memories just disappeared.

"Nowhere," I said. "The village I was born in was too small to be worth a name. Now, what about you, Sturmhond? Where did you come from?"

The privateer grinned. Again I was struck by the thought that there was something off about his features.

"My mother was an oyster," he said with a wink. "And I'm the pearl."

He strolled away, whistling an off-key tune.

Two nights later, I woke to find Tamar looming over me, shaking my good shoulder.

"Time to go," she said.

"Now?" I asked blearily. "What time is it?"

"Coming on three bells."

"In the morning?" I yawned and threw my legs over the side of my hammock. "Where are we?"

"Fifteen miles off the coast of West Ravka. Come on, Sturmhond is waiting." She was dressed and had her canvas ditty bag slung over her shoulder.

I had no belongings to gather, so I pulled on my boots, patted the inner pocket of my coat to make sure I had the red book, and followed her out of the door.

On deck, Mal stood by the ship's starboard rail with a small group of crewmen. I had a moment of confusion when I realised Privyet was wearing Sturmhond's garish teal frock coat. I wouldn't have recognised Sturmhond himself if he hadn't been giving orders. He was swaddled in a voluminous greatcoat, the collar turned up, a wool hat pulled low over his ears.

A cold wind was blowing. The stars were bright in the sky, and a sickle moon sat low on the horizon. I peered across the moonlit waves, listening to the steady sigh of the sea. If land was nearby, I couldn't see it.

Mal tried to rub some warmth into my arms.

"What's happening?" I asked.

"We're going ashore." I could hear the wariness in his voice.

"In the middle of the night?"

"The *Volkvolny* will raise my colours near the Fjerdan coast," said Sturmhond. "The Darkling doesn't need to know that you're back on Ravkan soil just yet."

As Sturmhond bent his head in conversation with Privyet, Mal drew me over to the portside rail. "Are you sure about this?"

"Not at all," I admitted.

He rested his hands on my shoulders and said, "There's a good chance I'll be arrested if we're found, Alina. You may be the Sun Summoner, but I'm just a soldier who defied orders."

"The Darkling's orders."

"That may not matter."

"I'll make it matter. Besides, we're not going to be found. We're going to get into West Ravka, meet Sturmhond's client, and decide what we want to do."

Mal pulled me closer. "Were you always this much trouble?"

"I like to think of myself as delightfully complex."

As he bent to kiss me, Sturmhond's voice cut through the dark. "Can we get to the cuddling later? I want us ashore before dawn."

Mal sighed. "Eventually, I'm going to punch him."

"I will support you in that endeavour."

He took my hand, and we returned to the group.

Sturmhond gave Privyet an envelope sealed with a blob of pale blue wax, then clapped him on the back. Maybe it was the moonlight, but the first mate looked as if he might cry. Tolya and Tamar slipped over the railing, holding tight to the weighted ladder secured to the schooner.

I peered over the side. I'd expected to see an ordinary longboat, so I was surprised at the little craft I saw bobbing alongside the *Volkvolny*. It was like no boat I'd ever seen. Its two hulls looked like a pair of hollowed-out shoes, and they were held together by a deck with a giant hole in its centre.

Mal and I followed, stepping gingerly onto one of the craft's curved hulls. We picked our way across it and descended to the central deck, where a sunken cockpit was nestled between two masts. Sturmhond leapt down after us, then swung up onto a raised platform behind the cockpit and took his place at the ship's wheel.

"What is this thing?" I asked.

"I call her the *Hummingbird*," he said, consulting some kind of chart that I couldn't see. "I'm thinking of renaming her the *Firebird* though." I drew in a sharp breath, but Sturmhond just grinned and ordered, "Cut anchor and release!"

Tamar and Tolya unhitched the knots of the grapples

that held us to the *Volkvolny*. I saw the anchor line slither like a live snake over the *Hummingbird*'s stern, the end slipping silently into the sea. I would have thought we'd need an anchor when we made port, but I supposed Sturmhond knew what he was doing.

"Make sail," called Sturmhond.

The sails unfurled. Though the *Hummingbird*'s masts were considerably shorter than those aboard the schooner, its double sails were huge, rectangular things, and required two crewmen each to maneuver them into position.

A light breeze caught the canvas, and we pulled further from the *Volkvolny*. I looked up and saw Sturmhond watching the schooner slip away. I couldn't see his face, but I had the distinct sense that he was saying goodbye. He shook himself, then called out, "Squallers!"

A Grisha was positioned in each hull. They raised their arms, and wind billowed around us, filling the sails. Sturmhond adjusted our course and called for more speed. The Squallers obliged, and the strange little boat leapt forward.

"Take these," said Sturmhond. He dropped a pair of goggles into my lap and tossed another pair to Mal. They looked similar to those worn by Fabrikators in the workshops of the Little Palace. I glanced around. All of the crew seemed to be wearing them, along with Sturmhond. We pulled them over our heads.

I was grateful for them seconds later, when Sturmhond called for yet more speed. The sails rattled in the rigging above us, and I felt a twinge of nervousness. Why was he in such a hurry?

The *Hummingbird* sped over the water, its shallow double hulls skating from wave to wave, barely seeming to touch the surface of the sea. I held tight to my seat, my stomach floating upwards with every jounce.

"All right, Squallers," commanded Sturmhond, "take us up. Sailors to wings, on my count."

I turned to Mal. "What does that mean, 'take us up'?"

"Five!" shouted Sturmhond.

The crewmen started to move counterclockwise, pulling on the lines.

"Four!"

The Squallers spread their hands wider.

"Three!"

A boom lifted between the two masts, the sails gliding along its length.

"Two!"

"Heave!" cried the sailors. The Squallers lifted their arms in a massive swoop.

"One!" yelled Sturmhond.

The sails billowed up and out, snapping into place high above the deck like two gigantic wings. My stomach lurched, and the unthinkable happened: The *Hummingbird* took flight.

I gripped my seat, mumbling old prayers under my breath, squeezing my eyes shut as the wind buffeted my face and we rose into the night sky.

Sturmhond was laughing like a loon. The Squallers were calling out to each other in a volley, making sure they kept the updraft steady. I thought my heart would pound right through my chest.

Oh, Saints, I thought queasily. *This can't be happening.*

"Alina," Mal yelled over the rush of the wind.

"What?" I forced the word through tightly clenched lips.

"Alina, open your eyes. You've got to see this."

I gave a terse shake of my head. That was exactly what I did *not* need to do.

Mal's hand slid into mine, taking hold of my frozen fingers. "Just try it."

I took a trembling breath and forced my lids open. We were surrounded by stars. Above us, white canvas stretched in two broad arcs, like the taut curves of an archer's bow.

I knew I shouldn't, but I couldn't stop myself from craning my neck over the cockpit's edge. The roar of the wind was deafening. Below – far below – the moonlit waves rippled like the bright scales of a slow-moving serpent. If we fell, I knew we would shatter on its back.

A little laugh, somewhere between elation and hysteria, burbled out of me. We were flying. *Flying.*

Mal squeezed my hand and gave an exultant shout.

"This is impossible!" I yelled.

Sturmhond whooped. "When people say impossible, they usually mean improbable." With the moonlight gleaming off the lenses of his goggles and his greatcoat billowing around him, he looked like a complete madman.

I tried to breathe. The wind was holding steady. The Squallers and the crew seemed focused, but calm. Slowly, very slowly, the knot in my chest loosened, and I began to relax.

"Where did this thing come from?" I shouted up to Sturmhond.

"I designed her. I built her. And I crashed a few prototypes."

I swallowed hard. *Crash* was the last word I wanted to hear.

Mal leaned over the lip of the cockpit, trying to get a better view of the gigantic guns positioned at the foremost points of the hulls.

"Those guns," he said. "They have multiple barrels."

"And they're gravity fed. No need to stop to reload. They fire two hundred rounds per minute."

"That's—"

"Impossible? The only problem is overheating, but it isn't so bad on this model. I have a Zemeni gunsmith trying to work out the flaws. The aft seats rotate so you can shoot from any angle."

"And fire down on the enemy," Mal shouted almost giddily. "If Ravka had a fleet of these—"

"Quite an advantage, no? But the First and Second Armies would have to work together."

I thought of what the Darkling had said to me so long ago. *The age of Grisha power is coming to an end.* His answer had been to turn the Fold into a weapon. But what if Grisha power could be transformed by men like Sturmhond? I looked over the deck of the *Hummingbird*, at the sailors and Squallers working side by side, at Tolya and Tamar seated behind those frightening guns. It wasn't impossible.

He's a privateer, I reminded myself. *And he'd stoop to war profiteer in a second.* Sturmhond's weapons could give Ravka an advantage, but those guns could just as easily be used by Ravka's enemies.

I was pulled from my thoughts by a bright light shining off the port bow. The great lighthouse at Alkhem Bay. We were close now. If I craned my neck, I could just make out the glittering towers of Os Kervo's harbour.

Sturmhond did not make directly for it but tacked

south-west. I assumed we'd set down somewhere offshore. The thought of landing made me queasy. I decided to keep my eyes shut for that, no matter what Mal said.

Soon I lost sight of the lighthouse beam. Just how far south did Sturmhond intend to take us? He'd said he wanted to reach the coast before dawn, and that couldn't be more than an hour or two away.

My thoughts drifted, lost to the stars around us and the clouds scudding across the wide sky. The night wind bit into my cheeks and seemed to cut right through the thin fabric of my coat.

I glanced down and gulped back a scream. We weren't over the water any more. We were over land – solid, unforgiving land.

I tugged on Mal's sleeve and gestured frantically to the countryside below us, painted in moonlit shades of black and silver.

"Sturmhond!" I shouted in a panic. "What are you doing?"

"You said you were taking us to Os Kervo—" Mal yelled.

"I said I was taking you to meet my client."

"Forget that," I wailed. "Where are we going to land?"

"Not to worry," said Sturmhond. "I have a lovely little lake in mind."

"How little?" I squeaked. But then I saw that Mal was climbing out of the cockpit, his face furious. "Mal, sit down!"

"You lying, thieving—"

"I'd stay where you are. I don't think you want to be jostling around when we enter the Fold."

Mal froze. Sturmhond began to whistle that same off-key little tune. It was snatched away by the wind.

"You can't be serious," I said.

"Not on a regular basis, no," said Sturmhond. "There's a rifle secured beneath your seat, Oretsev. You may want to grab it. Just in case."

"You can't take this thing into the Fold!" Mal bellowed.

"Why not? From what I understand, I'm travelling with the one person who can guarantee safe passage."

I clenched my fists, rage suddenly driving fear from my mind. "Maybe I'll just let the volcra have you and your crew for a late-night snack!"

Sturmhond kept one hand on the wheel and consulted his timepiece. "More of an early breakfast. We really are behind schedule. Besides," he said, "it's a long way down. Even for a Sun Summoner."

I glanced at Mal and knew his fury must be mirrored on my own face.

The landscape was unrolling beneath us at a terrifying pace. I stood up, trying to get a sense for where we were.

"Saints," I swore.

Behind us lay stars, moonlight, the living world. Ahead of us, there was nothing. He was really going to do it. He was taking us into the Fold.

"Gunners, at your stations," Sturmhond called. "Squallers, hold steady."

"Sturmhond, I'm going to kill you!" I shouted. "Turn this thing around right now!"

"Wish I could oblige. I'm afraid if you want to kill me, you'll just have to wait until we land. Ready?"

"No!" I shrieked.

But the next moment, we were in darkness. It was

like no night ever known – a perfect, deep, unnatural blackness that seemed to close around us in a suffocating grip. We were in the Fold.

CHAPTER 8

The moment we entered the Unsea, I knew something had changed.

Hurriedly, I braced my feet against the deck and threw up my hands, casting a wide golden swathe of sunlight around the *Hummingbird*. As angry as I was with Sturmhond, I wasn't going to let a flock of volcra bring us down only to prove a point.

With the power of both amplifiers, I barely had to think to summon the light. I tested its edges carefully, sensing none of the wild disruption that had overcome me the first time I'd used the fetter. But something was very wrong. The Fold *felt* different. I told myself it was just imagination, but it seemed as if the darkness had a texture. I could almost feel it moving over my skin. The edges of the wound at my shoulder began to itch and pull, as if the flesh were restless.

I'd been on the Unsea twice before, and both times I'd felt like a stranger, like a vulnerable interloper in a dangerous, unnatural world that did not want me there. Now it was as if the Fold was reaching out to me, welcoming me. I knew it made no sense. The Fold was a dead and empty place, not a living thing.

It knows me, I thought. *Like calls to like.*

I was being ridiculous. I cleared my head and thrust

the light out further, letting the power pulse warm and reassuring around me. *This* was what I was. Not the darkness.

"They're coming," Mal said beside me. "Listen."

Over the rush of the wind, I heard a cry echo through the Fold, and then the steady pounding of volcra wings. They'd found us quickly, drawn by the smell of human prey.

Their wings beat the air around the circle of light I'd created, pushing the darkness back at us in fluttering ripples. With crossings of the Fold at a standstill, they'd been too long without food. Appetite made them bold.

I spread my arms, letting the light bloom brighter, driving them back.

"No," said Sturmhond. "Bring them closer."

"What? Why?" I asked. The volcra were pure predators. They weren't to be toyed with.

"They hunt us," he said, raising his voice so everyone could hear him. "Maybe it's time we hunted them."

A warlike whoop went up from the crew, followed by a series of barks and howls.

"Pull back the light," Sturmhond told me.

"He's out of his mind," I said to Mal. "Tell him he's out of his mind."

Mal hesitated. "Well . . ."

"Well *what*?" I asked, incredulously. "In case you've forgotten, one of those things tried to eat you!"

He shrugged, and a grin touched his lips. "Maybe that's why I'd like to see what those guns can do."

I shook my head. I didn't like this. Any of it.

"Just for a moment," pressed Sturmhond. "Indulge me."

Indulge him. Like he was asking for another slice of cake.

The crew was waiting. Tolya and Tamar were hunched over the protruding barrels of their guns. They looked like leather-backed insects.

"All right," I said. "But don't say I didn't warn you."

Mal lifted his rifle to his shoulder.

"Here we go," I muttered. I curled my fingers. The circle of light contracted, shrinking around the ship.

The volcra shrieked in excitement.

"All the way!" commanded Sturmhond.

I gritted my teeth in frustration, then did as he asked. The Fold went dark.

I heard a rustle of wings. The volcra dove.

"Now, Alina!" Sturmhond shouted. "Throw it wide!"

I didn't stop to think. I cast the light out in a blazing wave. It showed the horror surrounding us in the harsh, unforgiving light of a noonday sun. There were volcra everywhere, suspended in the air around the ship, a mass of grey, winged, writhing bodies, milky, sightless eyes, and jaws crowded with teeth. Their resemblance to the *nichevo'ya* was unmistakable, and yet they were so much more grotesque, so much more clumsy.

"Fire!" Sturmhond cried.

Tolya and Tamar opened fire. It was a sound like I'd never heard, a relentless, skull-shattering thunder that shook the air around us and rattled my bones.

It was a massacre. The volcra plummeted from the skies around us, chests blown open, wings torn from their bodies. The spent cartridges pinged to the deck of the ship. The sharp burn of gunpowder filled the air.

Two hundred rounds per minute. So this was what a modern army could do.

The monsters didn't seem to know what was happening. They whirled and beat the air, driven into a tizzy of bloodlust, hunger, and fear, tearing at each other in their confusion and desire to escape. Their screams . . . Baghra had once told me the volcra's ancestors were human. I could have sworn I heard it in their cries.

The gunfire died away. My ears rang. I looked up and saw smears of black blood and bits of flesh on the canvas sails. A cold sweat had broken out over my brow. I thought I might be ill.

The quiet lasted only moments before Tolya threw back his head and gave a triumphant howl. The rest of the crew joined in, barking and yapping. I wanted to scream at all of them to shut up.

"Do you think we can draw another flock?" one of the Squallers asked.

"Maybe," Sturmhond said. "But we should probably head east. It's almost dawn and I don't want us to be spotted."

Yes, I thought. *Let's head east. Let's get out of here.* My hands shook. The wound at my shoulder burned and throbbed. What was wrong with me? The volcra were monsters. They would have torn us apart without a thought. I knew that. And yet, I could still hear their cries.

"There are more of them," Mal said suddenly. "A lot more."

"How do you know?" asked Sturmhond.

"I just do."

Sturmhond hesitated. Between the goggles, his hat, and the high collar, it was impossible to read his expression. "Where?" he said finally.

"Just a little north," Mal said. "That way." He pointed

into the dark, and I had the urge to slap his hand. Just because he *could* track the volcra didn't mean he had to.

Sturmhond called the bearing. My heart sank.

The *Hummingbird* dipped its wings and turned as Mal called out directions and Sturmhond corrected our course. I tried to focus on the light, on the comforting presence of my power, tried to ignore the sick feeling in my gut.

Sturmhond took us lower. My light shimmered over the Fold's colourless sand and touched the shadowy bulk of a wrecked sandskiff.

A tremor passed through me as we drew closer. The skiff had been broken in half. One of its masts had snapped in two, and I could just make out the remnants of three ragged black sails. Mal had led us to the ruins of the Darkling's skiff.

The little bit of calm I'd managed to pull together vanished.

The *Hummingbird* sank lower. Our shadow passed over the splintered deck.

I felt the tiniest bit of relief. Illogical as it was, I'd expected to see the bodies of the Grisha I'd left behind spread out on the deck, the skeletons of the King's emissary and the foreign ambassadors huddled in a corner. But of course they were long gone, food for the volcra, their bones scattered over the barren reaches of the Fold.

The *Hummingbird* banked starboard. My light pierced the murky depths of the broken hull. The screams began.

"Saints," Mal swore, and raised his rifle.

Three large volcra cringed beneath the skiff's hull, their backs to us, their wings spread wide. But it was what they were trying to shield with their bodies that sent a spike of fear and revulsion quaking through me: a sea of wriggling, twisted shapes, tiny, glistening arms, little backs split by the transparent membranes of barely formed wings. They mewled and whimpered, slithering over each other, trying to get away from the light.

We'd uncovered a nest.

The crew had gone silent. There was no barking or yapping now.

Sturmhond brought the ship around in another low arc. Then he shouted, "Tolya, Tamar, *grenatki*."

The twins rolled out two cast-iron shells and hefted them to the edge of the rail.

Another wave of dread washed over me. *They're volcra*, I reminded myself. *Look at them. They're monsters.*

"Squallers, on my signal," Sturmhond said grimly. "Fuses!" he shouted, then "Gunners, drop heavy!"

The instant the shells were released, Sturmhond roared, "Now!" and cut the ship's wheel hard to the right.

The Squallers threw up their arms, and the *Hummingbird* shot skyward.

A silent second passed, then a massive *boom* sounded beneath us. The heat and force of the explosion struck the *Hummingbird* in a powerful gust.

"Steady!" Sturmhond bellowed.

The little craft foundered wildly, swinging like a pendulum beneath its canvas wings. Mal planted a hand to either side of me, shielding my body with his as I fought to keep my balance and hold the light alive around us.

Finally, the ship stopped swaying and settled into a smooth arc, tracing a wide circle high above the burning wreckage of the skiff.

I was shaking hard. The air stank of charred flesh. My lungs felt singed, and each breath seared my chest. Sturmhond's crew were howling and barking again. Mal joined in, raising his rifle in the air in triumph. Above the cheering, I could hear the volcra's screams, helpless and human to my ears, the keening of mothers mourning their young.

I closed my eyes. It was all I could do to keep from clamping my hands to my ears and crumpling to the deck.

"Enough," I whispered. No one seemed to hear me. "Please," I rasped. "Mal—"

"You've become quite the killer, Alina."

That cool voice. My eyes flew open.

The Darkling stood before me, his black *kefta* rippling over the *Hummingbird*'s deck. I gasped and stepped back, staring wildly around me, but no one was watching. They were whooping and shouting, gazing down at the flames.

"Don't worry," the Darkling said gently. "It gets easier with time. Here, I'll show you."

He slid a knife from the sleeve of his *kefta*, and before I could cry out, he slashed towards my face. I threw my hands up to defend myself, a scream tearing loose from my throat. The light vanished, and the ship was plunged into darkness. I fell to my knees, huddling on the deck, ready to feel the piercing sting of Grisha steel.

It didn't come. People were yelling in the darkness around me. Sturmhond was shouting my name. I heard the echoing shriek of a volcra. *Close. Too close.*

Someone wailed, and the ship listed sharply. I heard the thump of boots as the crew scrambled to keep their footing.

"Alina!" Mal's voice this time.

I felt him fumbling towards me in the dark. Some bit of sense returned. I threw the light back up in a shining cascade.

The volcra that had descended upon us yowled and wheeled back into darkness, but one of the Squallers lay bleeding on the deck, his arm nearly torn from its socket. The sail above him flapped uselessly. The *Hummingbird* tilted, listing hard to starboard, rapidly losing altitude.

"Tamar, help him!" Sturmhond ordered. The twins were already scrambling over the hulls towards the downed Squaller.

The other Squaller had both hands raised, her face rigid with strain as she tried to summon a strong enough current to keep us aloft. The ship bobbled and wavered. Sturmhond held fast to the wheel, yelling orders to the crewmen working the sails.

My heart hammered. I looked frantically over the deck, torn between terror and confusion. I'd seen the Darkling. I'd *seen* him.

"Are you all right?" Mal was asking beside me. "Are you hurt?"

I couldn't look at him. I shook so badly that I thought I might fly apart. I focused all my effort on keeping the light blazing around us.

"Is she injured?" shouted Sturmhond.

"Just get us out of here!" Mal replied.

"Oh, is *that* what I should be trying to do?" Sturmhond barked back.

The volcra were shrieking and whirling, beating at the circle of light. Monsters they might be, but I wondered if they understood vengeance. The *Hummingbird* rocked and shuddered. I looked down and saw grey sands rushing up to meet us.

And then suddenly we were out of the darkness, bursting through the last black wisps of the Fold as we shot into the blue light of early dawn.

The ground loomed terrifyingly close beneath us.

"Lights out!" Sturmhond commanded.

I dropped my hands and took desperate hold of the cockpit's rail. I could see a long stretch of road, a town's lights glowing in the distance, and there, beyond a low rise of hills, a slender blue lake, morning light glinting off its surface.

"Just a little further!" cried Sturmhond.

The Squaller let out a sob of effort, her arms trembling. The sails dipped. The *Hummingbird* continued to fall. Branches scraped the hull as we skimmed the treetops.

"Everyone get low and hold on tight!" shouted Sturmhond. Mal and I hunkered down into the cockpit, arms and legs braced against the sides, hands clasped. The little ship rattled and shook.

"We aren't going to make it," I rasped.

He said nothing, just squeezed my fingers tighter.

"Get ready!" Sturmhond roared.

At the last second, he hurled himself into the cockpit in a tangle of limbs. He just had time to say, "This is cozy," before we struck land with a bone-shattering jolt.

Mal and I were thrown into the nose of the cockpit as the ship tore into the ground, clattering and banging, its hull splintering apart. There was a loud splash, and suddenly we were skimming across the water. I heard a terrible wrenching sound and knew that one of the hulls had broken free. We bounced roughly over the surface and then, miraculously, shuddered to a halt.

I tried to get my bearings. I was on my back, pressed

up against the side of the cockpit. Someone was breathing hard beside me.

I shifted gingerly. I'd taken a hard knock to the head and cut open both of my palms, but I seemed to be in one piece.

Water was flooding in through the cockpit's floor. I heard splashing, people calling to one another.

"Mal?" I ventured, my voice a quavery squeak.

"I'm okay," he replied. He was somewhere to my left. "We need to get out of here."

I peered around. Sturmhond was nowhere to be seen.

As we clambered out of the cockpit, the broken ship began to tilt alarmingly. We heard a creaking sigh, and one of the masts gave way, collapsing into the lake beneath the weight of its sails.

We threw ourselves into the water, kicking hard as the lake tried to swallow us along with the ship.

One of the crewmen was tangled in the ropes. Mal dove down to help extricate him, and I nearly wept with relief when they both broke the surface.

I saw Tolya and Tamar paddling free, followed by the other crewmen. Tolya had the wounded Squaller in tow. Sturmhond swam behind, supporting an unconscious sailor beneath his arm. We made for the shore.

My bruised limbs felt heavy, weighted down by my sodden clothes, but finally we reached the shallows. We hauled ourselves out of the water, slogging through patches of slimy reeds, and threw our bodies on to the wide crescent of beach.

I lay there panting, listening to the oddly ordinary sounds of early morning: crickets in the grass, birds calling from somewhere in the woods, a frog's low, tentative croak. Tolya was ministering to the injured Squaller, finishing the business of healing his arm, instructing him to flex his fingers, bend his elbow. I heard Sturmhond come ashore and hand the last sailor into Tamar's care.

"He's not breathing," Sturmhond said, "and I don't feel a pulse."

I forced myself to sit up. The sun was rising behind us, warming my back, gilding the lake and the edges of the trees. Tamar had her hands pressed to the sailor's chest, using her power to draw the water from his lungs and drive life back into his heart. The minutes seemed to stretch as the sailor lay motionless on the sand. Then he gasped. His eyes fluttered open, and he spewed lake water over his shirt.

I heaved a sigh of relief. One less death on my conscience.

Another crewman was clutching his side, testing to see if he'd broken any ribs. Mal had a nasty gash across his forehead. But we were all there. We'd made it.

Sturmhond waded back into the water. He stood knee deep in it, contemplating the smooth surface of the lake, his greatcoat pooling out behind him. Other than a torn-up stretch of earth along the shore, there was no sign that the *Hummingbird* had ever been.

The uninjured Squaller turned on me. "What happened back there?" she spat. "Kovu was almost killed. We all were!"

"I don't know," I said, resting my head against my knees.

Mal drew his arm around me, but I didn't want comfort. I wanted an explanation for what I'd seen.

"You don't know?" she said incredulously.

"I don't know," I repeated, surprised at the surge of

anger that came with the words. "I didn't ask to be shoved into the Fold. I'm not the one who went looking for a fight with the volcra. Why don't you ask your captain what happened?"

"She's right," Sturmhond said, trudging out of the water and up the shore towards us as he stripped off his ruined gloves. "I should have given her more warning, and I shouldn't have gone after the nest."

Somehow the fact that he was agreeing with me just made me angrier. Then Sturmhond removed his hat and goggles, and my rage disappeared, replaced by complete and utter bewilderment.

Mal was on his feet in an instant. "What the hell is this?" he said, his voice low and dangerous.

I sat paralysed, my pain and exhaustion eclipsed by the bizarre sight before me. I didn't know what I was looking at, but I was glad Mal saw it too. After what had happened on the Fold, I didn't trust myself.

Sturmhond sighed and ran a hand over his face – a stranger's face.

His chin had lost its pronounced point. His nose was still slightly crooked, but nothing like the busted lump it had been. His hair was no longer ruddy brown but dark gold, neatly cut to military length, and those strange, muddy green eyes were now a clear, bright hazel. He looked completely different, but he was unmistakably Sturmhond.

And he's handsome, I thought with a baffling jab of resentment.

Mal and I were the only ones staring. None of Sturmhond's crew seemed remotely surprised.

"You have a Tailor," I said.

Sturmhond winced.

"I am *not* a Tailor," Tolya said angrily.

"No, Tolya, your gifts lie elsewhere," Sturmhond said soothingly. "Mostly in the celebrated fields of killing and maiming."

"Why would you do this?" I asked, still trying to adapt to the jarring experience of Sturmhond's voice coming from a different person's mouth.

"It was essential that the Darkling not recognise me. He hasn't seen me since I was fourteen, but it wasn't something I wanted to chance."

"Who are you?" Mal asked furiously.

"That's a complicated question."

"Actually, it's pretty straightforward," I said, springing to my feet. "But it does require telling the truth. Something you seem thoroughly incapable of."

"Oh, I can do it," Sturmhond said, shaking water from one of his boots. "I'm just not very good at it."

"Sturmhond," Mal snarled, advancing on him. "You have exactly ten seconds to explain yourself, or Tolya's going to have to make you a whole new face."

Then Tamar leapt to her feet. "Someone's coming."

We all quieted, listening. The sounds came from beyond the wood surrounding the lake: hoofbeats – lots of them, the snap and rustle of broken branches as men moved towards us through the trees.

Sturmhond groaned. "I knew we'd been sighted. We spent too long on the Fold." He heaved a ragged sigh. "A wrecked ship and a crew that looks like a bunch of drowned possums. This is not what I had in mind."

I wanted to know exactly what he did have in mind, but there was no time to ask.

The trees parted, and a group of mounted men charged onto the beach. Ten . . . twenty . . . thirty soldiers of the First Army. King's men, heavily armed. Where had they all come from?

After the slaughter of the volcra and the crash, I didn't think I had any fear left, but I was wrong. Panic shot through me as I remembered what Mal had said about deserting his post. Were we about to be arrested as traitors? My fingers twitched. I wasn't going to be taken prisoner again.

"Easy, Summoner," the privateer whispered. "Let me handle this."

"Since you've handled everything else so well, Sturmhond?"

"It might be wise if you didn't call me that for a while."

"And why is that?" I bit out.

"Because it's not my name."

The soldiers cantered to a halt in front of us, the morning light glittering off their rifles and sabres. A young captain drew his blade. "In the name of the King of Ravka, throw down your arms."

Sturmhond stepped forward, placing himself between the enemy and his wounded crew. He raised his hands in a gesture of surrender. "Our weapons are at the bottom of the lake. We are unarmed."

Knowing what I did of both Sturmhond and the twins, I seriously doubted that.

"State your name and business here," commanded the young captain.

Slowly, Sturmhond peeled his sodden greatcoat from his shoulders and handed it to Tolya.

An uneasy stir went through the line of soldiers.

Sturmhond wore Ravkan military dress. He was soaked through to the skin, but there was no mistaking the olive drab and brass buttons of the Ravkan First Army – or the golden double eagle that indicated an officer's rank. What game was the privateer playing?

An older man broke through the lines, wheeling his horse around to confront Sturmhond. With a start, I recognised Colonel Raevsky, the commander of the military encampment at Kribirsk. Had we crashed so close to town? Was that how the soldiers had got here so quickly?

"Explain yourself, boy!" the colonel commanded. "State your name and business before I have you stripped of that uniform and strung up from a high tree."

Sturmhond seemed unconcerned. When he spoke, his voice had a quality I'd never heard in it before. "I am Nikolai Lantsov, Major of the Twenty-Second Regiment, Soldier of the King's Army, Grand Duke of Udova, and second son to His Most Royal Majesty, King Alexander the Third, Ruler of the Double Eagle Throne, may his life and reign be long."

My jaw dropped. Shock passed like a wave through the row of soldiers. A nervous titter rose from somewhere in the ranks. I didn't know what joke this madman thought he was making, but Raevsky did not look amused. He leapt from his horse, tossing the reins to a soldier.

"You listen to me, you disrespectful whelp," he said, his hand already on the hilt of his sword, his weathered features set in lines of fury as he strode directly up to Sturmhond. "Nikolai Lantsov served under me on the northern border and . . ."

His voice faded away. He was nose to nose with the

privateer now, but Sturmhond did not blink. The colonel opened his mouth, then closed it. He took a step back and scanned Sturmhond's face. I watched his expression change from scorn to disbelief to what could only be recognition.

Abruptly, he dropped to one knee and bent his head.

"Forgive me, *moi tsarevich*," he said, gaze trained on the ground before him. "Welcome home."

The soldiers exchanged confused glances.

Sturmhond turned a cold and expectant eye on them. He radiated command. A pulse seemed to pass through the ranks. Then, one by one, they slipped from their horses and dropped to their knees, heads bent.

Oh, Saints.

"You've got to be kidding me," Mal muttered.

I'd hunted a magical stag. I wore the scales of a slain ice dragon around my wrist. I'd seen an entire city swallowed by darkness. But this was the strangest thing I'd ever witnessed. It had to be another one of Sturmhond's deceptions, one that was sure to get us all killed.

I stared at the privateer. Was it even possible? I couldn't seem to get my mind to work. I was too exhausted, too drained from fear and panic. I scoured my memory for the little bit I knew about the Ravkan King's two sons. I'd met the eldest briefly at the Little Palace, but the younger son hadn't been seen at court in years. He was supposed to be off somewhere apprenticing with a gunsmith or studying shipbuilding.

Or maybe he had done both.

I felt dizzy. *Sobachka*, Genya had called the prince. Puppy. *He insisted on doing his military service in the infantry.*

Sturmhond. Storm hound. Wolf of the Waves.

Sobachka. It couldn't be. It just couldn't.

"Rise," commanded Sturmhond – or whoever he was. His whole bearing seemed to have changed.

The soldiers got to their feet and stood at attention.

"It's been too long since I was home," boomed the privateer. "But I did not return empty-handed."

He stepped to the side, then threw his arm out, gesturing to me. Every face turned, waiting, expectant.

"Brothers," he said, "I have brought the Sun Summoner back to Ravka."

I couldn't help myself. I hauled off and punched him in the face.

Chapter 9

"**Y**ou're lucky you didn't get shot," Mal said angrily. He was pacing back and forth in a simply furnished tent, one of the few that remained in the Grisha camp next to Kribirsk. The Darkling's glorious black silk pavillion had been pulled down. All that survived was a broad swathe of dead grass littered with bent nails and the broken remnants of what had once been a polished wood floor.

I took a seat at the rough-hewn table and glanced outside to where Tolya and Tamar flanked the entrance. Whether they were guarding us or keeping us from escaping, I couldn't be sure.

"It was worth it," I replied. "Besides, no one's going to shoot the Sun Summoner."

"You just punched a prince, Alina. I guess we can add one more act of treason to our list."

I shook out my sore hand. My knuckles smarted. "First of all, are we so sure he really *is* a prince? And second, you're just jealous."

"Of course I'm jealous. I thought *I* was going to get to punch him. That isn't the point."

Chaos had erupted after my outburst, and only some fast talking by Sturmhond and some very aggressive crowd control by Tolya had kept me from being taken away in chains or worse.

Sturmhond had escorted us through Kribirsk to the military encampment. When he left us at the tent, he'd said quietly, "All I ask is that you stay long enough to let me explain. If you don't like what you hear, you're free to go."

"Just like that?" I scoffed.

"Trust me."

"Every time you say 'trust me', I trust you a little less," I hissed.

Mal and I did stay though, unsure what our next move might be. Sturmhond hadn't bound us or put us under heavy guard. He'd provided us with clean, dry clothes. If we wanted to, we could try to slip past Tolya and Tamar and escape back across the Fold. It wasn't as if anyone could follow us. We could emerge anywhere we liked along its western shore. But where would we go after that? Sturmhond had changed; our situation hadn't. We had no money, no allies, and we were still being hunted by the Darkling. And I wasn't eager to return to the Fold, not after what had happened aboard the *Hummingbird*.

I pushed down a bleak bubble of laughter. If I was actually thinking of taking refuge on the Unsea, things were very bad indeed.

A servant entered with a large tray. He set down a pitcher of water, a bottle of *kvas* and glasses, and several small plates of *zakuski*. Each of the dishes was bordered in gold and emblazoned with a double eagle.

I considered the food: smoked sprats on black bread, marinated beets, stuffed eggs. We hadn't had a meal since the previous night, aboard the *Volkvolny*, and using my power had left me famished, but I was too nervous to eat.

"What happened back there?" Mal asked as soon as the servant departed.

I shook out my knuckles again. "I lost my temper."

"That's not what I meant. What happened on the Fold?"

I studied a little pot of herbed butter, turning the dish in my hands. *I saw him.*

"I was just tired," I said lightly.

"You used a lot more of your power when we escaped from the *nichevo'ya*, and you never faltered. Is it the fetter?"

"The fetter makes me stronger," I said, tugging the edge of my sleeve over the sea whip's scales. Besides, I'd been wearing it for weeks. There was nothing wrong with my power, but there might be something wrong with me. I traced an invisible pattern on the tabletop. "When we were fighting the volcra, did they sound different to you?" I asked.

"Different how?"

"More . . . human?"

Mal frowned. "No, they sounded pretty much like they always do. Like monsters who want to eat us." He laid his hand over mine. "What happened, Alina?"

I saw him. "I told you: I was tired. I lost focus."

He drew back. "If you want to lie to me, go ahead. But I'm not going to pretend to believe you."

"Why not?" asked Sturmhond, stepping into the tent. "It's only common courtesy."

Instantly, we were on our feet, ready to fight.

Sturmhond stopped short and lifted his hands in a gesture of peace. He'd changed into a dry uniform. A bruise was beginning to form on his cheek. Cautiously, he removed his sword and hung it on a post by the tent flap.

"I'm just here to talk," he said.

"So talk," Mal retorted. "Who are you, and what are you playing at?"

"Nikolai Lantsov. Please don't make me recite my titles again. It's no fun for anybody, and the only important one is 'prince'. "

"And what about Sturmhond?" I asked.

"I'm also Sturmhond, commander of the *Volkvolny*, scourge of the True Sea."

"Scourge?"

"Well, I'm vexing at the very least."

I shook my head. "Impossible."

"Improbable."

"This is *not* the time to try to be entertaining."

"Please," he said in a conciliatory tone. "Sit. I don't know about you, but I find everything much more understandable when seated. Something about circulation, I suspect. Reclining is, of course, preferable, but I don't think we're on those kinds of terms yet."

I didn't budge. Mal crossed his arms.

"All right, well, I'm going to sit. I find playing the returning hero a most wearying task, and I'm positively worn out." He crossed to the table, poured himself a glass of *kvas*, and settled into a chair with a contented sigh. He took a sip and grimaced. "Awful stuff," he said. "Never could stomach it."

"Then order some brandy, *Your Highness*," I said irritably. "I'm sure they'll bring you all you want."

His face brightened. "True enough. I suppose I could bathe in a tub of it. I may just."

Mal threw up his hands in exasperation and walked to the flap of the tent to look out at the camp.

"You can't honestly expect us to believe any of this," I said.

Sturmhond wiggled his fingers to better display his ring. "I do have the royal seal."

I snorted. "You probably stole it from the real Prince Nikolai."

"I served with Raevsky. He knows me."

"Maybe you stole the prince's face too."

He sighed. "You have to understand, the only place I could safely reveal my identity was here in Ravka. Only the most trusted members of my crew knew who I really was – Tolya, Tamar, Privyet, a few of the Etherealki. The rest . . . well, they're good men, but they're also mercenaries and pirates."

"So you deceived your own crew?" I asked.

"On the seas, Nikolai Lantsov is more valuable as a hostage than as a captain. Hard to command a ship when you're constantly worrying about being bashed on the head late at night and then ransomed to your royal papa."

I shook my head. "None of this makes any sense. Prince Nikolai is supposed to be off somewhere studying boats or—"

"I did apprentice with a Fjerdan shipbuilder. And a Zemeni gunsmith. And a civil engineer from the Han Province of Bolh. Tried my hand at poetry for a while. The results were . . . unfortunate. These days, being Sturmhond requires most of my attention."

Mal leaned against the tent post, arms crossed. "So one day you decided to cast off your life of luxury and try your hand at playing pirate?"

"Privateer," he said. "And I wasn't *playing* at anything.

I knew I could do more for Ravka as Sturmhond than lazing about at court."

"And just where do the King and Queen think you are?" I asked.

"The university at Ketterdam," he replied. "Lovely place. Very lofty. There's an extremely well-compensated shipping clerk sitting through my philosophy classes as we speak. Gets passable grades, answers to Nikolai, drinks copiously and often so no one gets suspicious."

Was there no end to this? "Why?"

"I tried, I really did. But I've never been good at sitting still. Drove my nanny to distraction. Well, nannies. There was quite an army of them, as I recall."

I should have hit him harder. "I mean, why go through this whole charade?"

"I'm second in line for the Ravkan throne. I nearly had to run away to do my military service. I don't think my parents would approve of my picking off Zemeni pirates and breaking Fjerdan blockades. They're rather fond of Sturmhond, though."

"Fine," said Mal from the doorway. "You're a prince. You're a privateer. You're a prat. What do you want with us?"

Sturmhond took another tentative sip of *kvas* and shuddered. "Your help," he said. "The game has changed. The Fold is expanding. The First Army is close to outright revolt. The Darkling's coup may have failed, but it shattered the Second Army, and Ravka is on the brink of collapse."

I felt a sinking sensation. "And let me guess: you're just the one to put things right?"

Sturmhond leaned forward. "Did you meet my

brother, Vasily, when you were at court? He cares more about horses and his next drink of whiskey than his people. My father never had more than a passing interest in governing Ravka, and reports are he's lost even that. This country is coming apart. Someone needs to put it back together before it's too late."

"Vasily is the heir," I observed.

"I think he can be convinced to step aside."

"That's why you dragged us back here?" I said in disgust. "Because you want to be King?"

"I dragged you back here because the Apparat has practically turned you into a living Saint and the people love you. I dragged you back here because your power is the key to Ravka's survival."

I banged my hands down on the table. "You dragged me back here so you could make a grand entrance with the Sun Summoner and steal your brother's throne!"

Sturmhond leaned back. "I'm not going to apologise for being ambitious. It doesn't change the fact that I'm the best man for the job."

"Of course you are."

"Come back to Os Alta with me."

"Why? So you can show me off like some kind of prize goat?"

"I know you don't trust me. You have no reason to. But I'll abide by what I promised you aboard the *Volkvolny*. Listen to what I have to offer. If you're still not interested, Sturmhond's ships will take you anywhere in the world. I think you'll stay. I think I can give you something no one else can."

"This ought to be good," muttered Mal.

"I can give you the chance to change Ravka," said

Sturmhond. "I can give you the chance to bring your people hope."

"Oh, is that all?" I said sourly. "And just how am I supposed to do that?"

"By helping me unite the First and Second Armies. By becoming my Queen."

Before I could blink, Mal had shoved the table aside and closed in on Sturmhond, lifting him off his feet and slamming him into the tent post. Sturmhond winced but made no move to fight back.

"Easy, now. Mustn't get blood on the uniform. Let me explain—"

"Try explaining with my fist in your mouth."

Sturmhond twisted, and in a flash, he'd slipped from Mal's grip. A knife was in his hand, pulled from somewhere up his sleeve.

"Step back, Oretsev. I'm keeping my temper for her sake, but I'd just as soon gut you like a carp."

"Try it," Mal snarled.

"Enough!" I threw out a bright shard of light that blinded them both. They put up their hands against the glare, momentarily distracted. "Sturmhond, sheathe that weapon or you'll be the one who gets gutted. Mal, stand down."

I waited until Sturmhond tucked away his knife, then slowly let the light fade.

Mal dropped his hands, his fists still clenched. They eyed each other warily. Just a few hours ago, they'd been friends. Of course, Sturmhond had been a completely different person then.

Sturmhond straightened the sleeves of his uniform. "I'm not proposing a love match, you heartsick oaf, just a political alliance. If you'd stop and think for a minute, you'd see it makes good sense for the country."

Mal let out a harsh bark of laughter. "You mean it makes good sense for you."

"Can't both things be true? I've served in the military. I understand warfare, and I understand weaponry. I know the First Army will follow me. I may be second in line, but I have a blood right to the throne."

Mal jabbed his finger in Sturmhond's face. "You don't have a right to her."

Some of Sturmhond's composure seemed to leave him. "What did you think was going to happen? Did you think you could just carry off one of the most powerful Grisha in the world like some peasant girl you tumbled in a barn? Is that how you think this story ends? I'm trying to keep a country from falling apart, not steal your best girl."

"That's enough," I said quietly.

"You can stay at the palace," Nikolai continued. "Perhaps as the captain of her personal guard? It wouldn't be the first such arrangement."

A muscle jumped in Mal's jaw. "You make me sick."

Sturmhond gave a dismissive wave. "I'm a depraved monster, I know. Just think about what I'm saying for a moment."

"I don't need to think about it," Mal shouted. "And neither does she. It isn't going to happen."

"It would be a marriage in name only," Sturmhond insisted. Then, as if he couldn't help himself, he flashed Mal a taunting grin. "Except for the matter of producing heirs."

Mal surged forward, and Sturmhond reached for his

knife, but I saw what was coming and stepped between them.

"Stop!" I shouted. "Just stop it. And stop talking about me as if I'm not here!"

Mal released a frustrated growl and began pacing back and forth again. Sturmhond picked up a chair that had toppled and reseated himself, making a great show of stretching out his legs and pouring himself another glass of *kvas*.

I took a breath. "Your Highness—"

"Nikolai," he corrected. "But I've also been known to answer to 'sweetheart' or 'handsome'. "

Mal whirled, but I silenced him with a pleading look.

"You need to stop that right now, *Nikolai*," I said. "Or I'll knock those princely teeth out myself."

Nikolai rubbed his darkening bruise. "I know you're good for it."

"I am," I said firmly. "And I'm not going to marry you."

Mal released a breath, and some of the stiffness went out of his shoulders. It bothered me that he had thought there was any possibility I might accept Nikolai's offer, and I knew he wasn't going to like what I had to say next.

I steeled myself and said, "But I will return to Os Alta with you."

Mal's head jerked up. "Alina—"

"Mal, we always said we'd find a way to come back to Ravka, that we'd find a way to help. If we don't do something, there may not be a Ravka to come back to." He shook his head. I turned to Nikolai and plunged on. "I'll return to Os Alta with you, and I'll consider helping you make a bid for the throne." I took a deep breath. "But I want the Second Army."

The tent got very quiet. They were looking at me like I was mad. And, truth be told, I didn't feel entirely sane. But I was sick of being shuffled across the True Sea and half of Ravka by people trying to use me and my power.

Nikolai gave a nervous laugh. "The people love you, Alina, but I was thinking of a more symbolic title—"

"I'm not a symbol," I snapped. "And I'm tired of being a pawn."

"No," Mal said. "It's too dangerous. It would be like painting a target on your back."

"I already have a target on my back," I said. "And neither of us will ever be safe until the Darkling is defeated."

"Have you even held a command?" Nikolai asked.

I'd once led a seminar of junior mapmakers, but I didn't think that was what he meant.

"No," I admitted.

"You have no experience, no precedent, and no claim," he said. "The Second Army has been led by Darklings since it was founded."

By one Darkling, though this wasn't the time to explain that.

"Age and birthright don't matter to the Grisha. All they care about is power. I'm the only Grisha to ever wear two amplifiers. And I'm the only Grisha alive powerful enough to take on the Darkling or his shadow soldiers. No one else can do what I can."

I tried to put confidence in my voice, even though I wasn't sure what had come over me. I just knew I was tired of living in fear. I was tired of running. And if Mal and I were to have any hope of locating the firebird, we needed answers. The Little Palace might be the only place to find them.

For a long moment, the three of us just stood there.

"Well," Nikolai said. "Well."

He drummed his fingers on the tabletop, considering. Then he rose and offered me his hand.

"All right, Summoner," he said. "Help me win the people and the Grisha are yours."

"Really?" I blurted.

Nikolai laughed. "If you plan to lead an army, you'd better learn to act the part. The proper response is, 'I knew you'd see sense.'"

I took his hand. It was roughly calloused. The hand of a pirate, not a prince. We shook.

"As for my proposal," he began.

"Don't push your luck," I said, snatching my hand back. "I said I'd go with you to Os Alta, and that's it."

"And where will I go?" Mal said quietly.

He stood with his arms crossed, watching us with steady blue eyes. There was blood on his brow from the crash of the *Hummingbird*. He looked tired and very, very far away.

"I . . . I thought you'd come with me," I stammered.

"As what?" he asked. "The captain of your personal guard?"

I flushed.

Nikolai cleared his throat. "As much as I'd love to see how this plays out, I do have some arrangements to make. Unless, of course—"

"Get out," Mal ordered.

"Right, then. I'll leave you to it." He hastened away, stopping only to retrieve his sword.

The silence in the tent seemed to stretch and expand.

"Where is all this going, Alina?" Mal asked. "We

fought our way out of this saintsforsaken place, and now we're sinking right back into the swamp."

I lowered myself to the cot and rested my head in my hands. I was exhausted, and every bone in my body ached.

"What am I supposed to do?" I pleaded. "What's happening here, what's happening to Ravka – part of the blame belongs to me."

"That isn't true."

I gave a hollow laugh. "Oh yes it is. If it weren't for me, the Fold wouldn't be growing. Novokribirsk would still be standing."

"Alina," Mal said, crouching down in front of me and laying his hands on my knees, "even with all the Grisha and a thousand of Sturmhond's guns, you aren't strong enough to stop him."

"If we had the third amplifier—"

"But we don't!"

I gripped his hands. "We will."

He held my gaze. "Did it ever occur to you that I might say no?"

My stomach dropped. It hadn't. It had never entered my mind that Mal might refuse, and I felt suddenly ashamed. He had given up everything to be with me, but that didn't mean he was happy about it. Maybe he'd had enough of fighting and fear and uncertainty. Maybe he'd had enough of me.

"I thought . . . I thought we both wanted to help Ravka."

"Is that what we both wanted?" he asked.

He stood up and turned his back on me. I swallowed hard, forcing down the sudden ache in my throat.

"Then you won't go to Os Alta?"

He paused at the entrance of the tent. "You wanted to

wear the second amplifier. You have it. You want to go to Os Alta? Fine, we'll go. You say you need the firebird. I'll find a way to get it for you. But when all this is over, Alina, I wonder if you'll still want me."

I shot to my feet. "Of course I will! Mal—"

Whatever I might have said, he didn't wait to hear it. He stepped out into the sunlight and was gone.

I pressed the heels of my hands against my eyes, trying to push down the tears that threatened. What was I doing? I wasn't a queen. I wasn't a saint. And I certainly didn't know how to lead an army.

I caught a glimpse of myself in a soldier's shaving mirror that had been propped on the bedside table. I pulled my coat and shirt to the side, baring the wound at my shoulder. The puncture marks from the *nichevo'ya* stood out, puckered and black against my skin. The Darkling had said they would never heal completely.

What wound couldn't be healed by Grisha power? One made by something that never should have existed in the first place.

I saw him. The Darkling's face, pale and beautiful, the slash of the knife. It had been so real. What had happened on the Fold?

Going back to Os Alta, taking control of the Second Army, was as good as a declaration of war. The Darkling would know where to find me, and when he was strong enough, he'd come looking. Ready or not, we'd have no choice but to make a stand. It was a terrifying thought, but I was surprised to find that it also brought me some relief.

I would face him. And one way or another, this would end.

Chapter 10

We didn't leave for Os Alta straightaway. Instead we spent the next three days transporting shipments of goods across the Fold. We operated out of what was left of the military encampment at Kribirsk. Most of the troops had been pulled back when the Fold started expanding. A new watchtower had been erected to monitor the black shores of the Unsea, and only a skeleton crew stayed on to operate the drydocks.

Not a single Grisha remained at the encampment. After the Darkling's attempted coup and the destruction of Novokribirsk, a wave of anti-Grisha sentiment had swept through Ravka and the ranks of the First Army. I wasn't surprised. An entire town was gone, its people food for monsters. Ravka wouldn't soon forget. Neither could I.

Some Grisha had fled to Os Alta to seek the protection of the King. Others had gone into hiding. Nikolai suspected that most of them had sought out the Darkling and defected to his side. But with the help of Nikolai's rogue Squallers, we managed two trips across the Fold on the first day, three on the second, and four on the last. Sandskiffs journeyed to West Ravka empty and returned with huge cargos of Zemeni rifles, crates full of ammunition, parts for repeating guns similar to those

Nikolai had used aboard the *Hummingbird*, and a few tons of sugar and *jurda* – all courtesy of Sturmhond's smuggling.

"Bribes," Mal said as we watched giddy soldiers tear into a shipment being unloaded on the dock, hooting and marvelling over the glittering array of weaponry.

"Gifts," Nikolai corrected. "You'll find the bullets work, regardless of my motives." He turned to me. "I think we can fit in one more trip today. Game?"

I wasn't, but I nodded.

He smiled and clapped me on the back. "I'll give the orders."

I could feel Mal watching me as I turned to look into the shifting darkness of the Fold. There hadn't been a recurrence of the incident aboard the *Hummingbird*. Whatever I'd seen that day – vision, hallucination, I couldn't name it – it hadn't happened again. Still, I spent each moment on the Unsea alert and wary, trying to hide just how frightened I really was.

Nikolai wanted to use the crossings to hunt volcra, but I refused. I told him that I still felt weak and that I wasn't sure enough about my power to guarantee our safety. My fear was real, but the rest was a lie. My power was stronger than ever. It flowed from me in pure and vibrant waves, radiant with the strength of the stag and the scales. I just couldn't bear the thought of hearing those screams again. I kept the light in a wide, glowing dome around the skiffs, and though the volcra shrieked and beat their wings, they kept their distance.

Mal accompanied us on all the crossings, staying close by my side, rifle at the ready. I knew he sensed my anxiousness, but he didn't press me for an explanation.

In fact, he hadn't said much at all since our argument in the tent. I was afraid that when he did start talking, I wouldn't like what he had to say. I hadn't changed my mind about returning to Os Alta, but I was worried that he might.

The morning we decamped for the capital, I searched the crowd for him, terrified that he might just decide not to show up. I said a little prayer of thanks when I glimpsed him, straight-backed and silent in his saddle, waiting to join the column of riders.

We set out before dawn, a twisting procession of horses and wagons that wended its way out of camp on the broad road known as the Vy. Nikolai had obtained a plain blue *kefta* for me, but it was tucked away in the luggage. Until he had more of his own men in place to guard me, I was just another soldier in the prince's retinue.

As the sun crested the horizon, I felt a small flutter of hope. The idea of trying to take the Darkling's place, of attempting to reassemble the Grisha and command the Second Army, felt impossibly daunting. But at least I was doing something instead of just fleeing from the Darkling or waiting for him to snatch me up. I had two of Morozova's amplifiers, and I was heading to a place where I might find answers that would lead me to the third. Mal was unhappy, but watching the morning light break over the treetops, I felt sure I could bring him around.

My mood didn't survive the journey through Kribirsk. We'd passed through the ramshackle port town after the crash on the lake, but I'd been too shaken and distracted to really take note of the way the place had changed. This time, it was unavoidable.

Though Kribirsk had never had much beauty to recommend it, its sidewalks had always teemed with travellers and merchants, King's men and dockworkers. Its bustling streets had been lined with busy stores ready to outfit expeditions into the Fold, along with bars and brothels that catered to the soldiers at the encampment. Today its streets were quiet and nearly empty. Most of the inns and shops had been boarded up.

The real revelation came when we reached the church. I remembered it as a tidy building capped with bright blue domes. Now the whitewashed walls were covered in writing, row after row of names written in red paint that had dried to the colour of blood. The steps were littered with heaps of withered flowers, small painted icons, the melted stubs of prayer candles. I saw bottles of *kvas*, piles of candy, the abandoned body of a child's doll. Gifts for the dead.

I scanned the names:

Stepan Ruschkin, 57
Anya Sirenka, 13
Mikah Lasky, 45
Rebeka Lasky, 44
Petyr Ozerov, 22
Marina Koska, 19
Valentin Yomki, 72
Sasha Penkin, 8 months

They went on and on. My fingers tightened on the reins as a cold fist closed over my heart. Memories came back to me unbidden: a mother running with a child in her arms, a man stumbling as the darkness caught him, his mouth open in a scream, an old woman, confused and frightened, swallowed by the panicked crowd. I'd seen it all. I'd made it possible.

These were the people of Novokribirsk, the city that had once stood directly across from Kribirsk on the other side of the Fold. A sister city full of relatives, friends, business partners. People who had worked the docks and manned the skiffs, some who must have survived multiple crossings. They'd lived on the edge of a horror, thinking they were safe in their own homes, walking the streets of their little port town. And now they were gone because I'd failed to stop the Darkling.

Mal brought his horse up beside mine.

"Alina," he said softly. "Come away."

I shook my head. I wanted to remember. *Tasha Stol, Andrei Bazin, Shura Rychenko.* As many as I could. They'd been murdered by the Darkling. Did they haunt his sleep the way they haunted mine?

"We have to stop him, Mal," I said hoarsely. "We have to find a way."

I don't know what I hoped he would say, but he remained silent. I wasn't sure Mal wanted to make me any more promises.

Eventually, he rode on, but I forced myself to read every single name, and only then did I turn to go, guiding my horse back into the deserted street.

A bit of life seemed to return to Kribirsk as we moved further away from the Fold. A few shops were open, and there were still merchants hawking their wares on the stretch of the Vy known as Peddlers' Way. Rickety tables lined the road, their surfaces covered in brightly coloured cloth and spread with a jumble of merchandise: boots and prayer shawls, wooden toys, shoddy knives in hand-tooled sheaths. Many of the tables were littered with what looked like bits of rock and chicken bones.

"*Provin'ye osti!*" the peddlers shouted. "*Autchen'ye osti!*" Real bone. Genuine bone.

As I leaned over my horse's head to get a better look, an old man called out, "Alina!"

I looked up in surprise. Did he know me?

Nikolai was suddenly beside me. He nudged his horse close to mine and snatched my reins, giving them a hard yank to draw me away from the table.

"*Net, spasibo,*" he said to the old man.

"Alina!" the peddler cried. "*Autchen'ye* Alina!"

"Wait," I said, twisting in my saddle, trying to get a better look at the old man's face. He was tidying the display on his table. Without the possibility of a sale, he seemed to have lost all interest in us.

"*Wait,*" I insisted. "He knew me."

"No he didn't."

"He knew my name," I said, angrily grabbing the reins back from him.

"He was trying to sell you relics. Finger bones. Genuine Sankta Alina."

I froze, a deep chill stealing over me. My oblivious horse kept steadily on.

"Genuine Alina," I repeated numbly.

Nikolai shifted uneasily. "There are rumours that you died on the Fold. People have been selling off parts of you all over Ravka and West Ravka for months. You're quite the good luck charm."

"Those are supposed to be *my fingers*?"

"Knuckles, toes, fragments of rib."

I felt sick. I looked around, hoping to spot Mal, needing to see something familiar.

"Of course," Nikolai continued, "if half of those were

really your toes, you'd have about a hundred feet. But superstition is a powerful thing."

"So is faith," said a voice behind me, and when I turned, I was surprised to see Tolya there, mounted on a huge black war horse, his broad face solemn.

It was too much. The optimism I'd felt only an hour ago had vanished. It suddenly seemed as if the sky were pressing down on me, closing in like a trap. I kicked my horse into a canter. I'd always been a clumsy rider, but I held on tight and did not stop until Kribirsk was far behind me and I no longer heard the rattling of bones.

That night we stayed at an inn in the little village of Vernost, where we were joined by a heavily armed group of soldiers from the First Army. I soon learned that many of them were from the Twenty-Second, the regiment Nikolai had served with and eventually helped lead in the northern campaign. Apparently, the prince wanted to be surrounded by friends when he entered Os Alta. I couldn't blame him.

He seemed to relax in their presence and, once again, I noticed his demeanour change. He'd transitioned effortlessly from the role of glib adventurer to arrogant prince, and now he became a beloved commander, a soldier who laughed easily with his companions and knew each commoner's name.

The soldiers had a lavish coach in tow. It was lacquered in pale Ravkan blue and emblazoned with the King's double eagle on one side. Nikolai had ordered a golden sunburst added to the other, and it was drawn by a matched team of six white horses. As the glittering contraption rumbled into the inn's courtyard, I had to roll my eyes, remembering the excesses of the Grand Palace. Maybe bad taste was inherited.

I had hoped to eat dinner alone with Mal in my room, but Nikolai insisted that we dine together in the inn's common room. So instead of relaxing by the fire in peace, we were jammed elbow to elbow at a noisy table packed with officers. Mal hadn't said a word throughout the entire meal, but Nikolai talked enough for all three of us.

As he dug into a dish of braised oxtail, he ran through a seemingly endless list of places he intended to stop on the way to Os Alta. Just listening to him wore me out.

"I didn't realise 'winning the people' meant meeting every single one of them," I grumbled. "Aren't we in a hurry?"

"Ravka needs to know its Sun Summoner has returned."

"And its wayward prince?"

"Him too. Gossip will do more than royal pronouncements. And that reminds me," he said, lowering his voice. "From here on out, you need to behave as if someone is watching every minute." He gestured between me and Mal with his fork. "What you do in private is your own affair. Just be discreet."

I nearly choked on my wine. "What?" I sputtered.

"It's one thing for you to be linked with a royal prince, quite another for people to think you're tumbling a peasant."

"I'm not – it's nobody's business!" I whispered furiously. I darted a glance at Mal. His teeth were clenched, and he was gripping his knife a little too tightly.

"Power is alliance," said Nikolai. "It's everyone's business." He took another sip of wine as I glared at him in disbelief. "And you should be wearing your own colours."

I shook my head, thrown by the change of subject. "Now you're choosing my clothes?" I was wearing the blue *kefta*, but clearly Nikolai wasn't satisfied.

"If you intend to lead the Second Army and take the Darkling's place, then you need to look the part."

"Summoners wear blue," I said.

"Don't underestimate the power of the grand gesture, Alina. The people like spectacle. The Darkling understood that."

"I'll think about it."

"Might I suggest gold?" Nikolai went on. "Very regal, very appropriate—"

"Very tacky?"

"Gold and black would be best. Perfect symbolism and—"

"No black," Mal said. He pushed back from the table and, without another word, disappeared into the crowded room.

I set down my fork. "I can't tell if you're deliberately making trouble or if you're just an ass."

The prince took another bite of his dinner. "He doesn't like black?"

"It's the colour of the man who tried to kill him and regularly takes me hostage. My sworn enemy?"

"All the more reason to claim that colour as your own."

I craned my neck to see where Mal had gone. Through the doorway, I watched him take a seat by himself at the bar.

"No," I said. "No black."

"As you like," Nikolai replied. "But choose something for yourself and your guards."

I sighed. "Do I really need guards?"

Nikolai leaned back in his chair and studied me, his face suddenly serious. "Do you know how I got the name Sturmhond?" he asked.

"I thought it was some kind of joke, a play on Sobachka."

"No," he said. "It's a name I earned. The first enemy ship I ever boarded was a Fjerdan trader out of Djerholm. When I told the captain to lay down his sword, he laughed in my face and told me to run home to my mother. He said Fjerdan men make bread from the bones of skinny Ravkan boys."

"So you killed him?"

"No. I told him foolish old captains weren't fit meat for Ravkan men. Then I cut off his fingers and fed them to my dog while he watched."

"You . . . what?"

The room was packed with rowdy soldiers singing, shouting, telling stories, but it all fell away as I stared at Nikolai in stunned silence. It was as if I was watching him transform again, as if the charming mask had shifted to reveal a very dangerous man.

"You heard me. My enemies understood brutality. And so did my crew. After it was over, I drank with my men and divvied up the spoils. Then I went back to my cabin, vomited up the very fine dinner my steward had prepared and cried myself to sleep. But that was the day I became a real privateer, and that was the day Sturmhond was born."

"So much for 'puppy'," I said, feeling a bit nauseated myself.

"I was a boy trying to lead an undisciplined crew of thieves and rogues against enemies who were older, wiser and tougher. I needed them to fear me. All of them. And if they hadn't, more people would have died."

I pushed my plate away. "Just whose fingers are you telling me to cut off?"

"I'm telling you that if you want to be a leader, it's time you started thinking and acting like one."

"I've heard this before, you know, from the Darkling and his supporters. Be brutal. Be cruel. More lives will be saved in the long run."

"Do you think I'm like the Darkling?"

I studied him – the golden hair, the sharp uniform, those too-clever hazel eyes.

"No," I said slowly. "I don't think you are." I rose to go and join Mal. "But I've been wrong before."

The journey to Os Alta was less a march than a slow, excruciating parade. We stopped at every town along the Vy, at farms, schools, churches, and dairies. We greeted local dignitaries and walked the wards of hospitals. We dined with war veterans and applauded girls' choirs.

It was hard not to notice that the villages were mostly populated by the very young and the very old. Every able body had been drafted to serve in the King's Army and fight in Ravka's endless wars. The graveyards were as big as the towns.

Nikolai handed out gold coins and sacks of sugar. He

accepted handshakes from merchants and kisses on the cheek from wrinkled matrons who called him Sobachka, and charmed anyone who came within two feet of him. He never seemed to tire, never seemed to flag. No matter how many miles we'd ridden or people we'd met, he was ready to meet another.

He always seemed to know what people wanted from him, when to be the laughing boy, the golden prince, the weary soldier. I supposed it was the training that came with being born a royal and raised at court, but it was still unnerving to watch.

He hadn't been kidding about spectacle. He always tried to time our arrivals at dawn or dusk, or he'd stop our procession in the deep shadows of a church or town square – all the better to show off the Sun Summoner.

When he caught me rolling my eyes, he just winked and said, "Everyone thinks you're dead, lovely. It's important to make a good showing."

So I held up my end of the bargain and acted my part. I smiled graciously and called the light to shine over rooftops and steeples and bathe every awestruck face in warmth. People wept. Mothers brought me their babies to kiss, and old men bowed over my hand, their cheeks damp with tears. I felt like a complete fraud, and I said as much to Nikolai.

"What do you mean?" he asked, genuinely puzzled. "The people love you."

"You mean they love your prize goat," I grumbled as we rode out of one town.

"Have you actually won any prizes?"

"This isn't funny," I whispered angrily. "You've seen what the Darkling can do. These people will be sending their sons and daughters off to fight *nichevo'ya*, and I won't be able to save them. You're feeding them a lie."

"We're giving them hope. That's better than nothing."

"Spoken like a man who's never had nothing," I said, and wheeled my horse away.

Ravka in summer was at its most lovely, its fields thick with gold and green, the air balmy and sweet with the scent of warm hay. Despite Nikolai's protests, I insisted on forgoing the comforts of the coach. My bottom was sore, and my thighs complained loudly when I eased from the saddle every night, but sitting my own horse meant fresh air and the chance to seek out Mal on each day's ride. He didn't talk much, but he seemed to be thawing a bit.

Nikolai had circulated the story of how the Darkling had tried to execute Mal on the Fold. It had earned Mal instant trust among the soldiers, even a small measure of celebrity. Occasionally, he scouted with the trackers in the unit, and he was trying to teach Tolya how to hunt, though the big Grisha wasn't much for stalking silently through the woods.

On the road out of Sala, we were passing through a stand of white elms when Mal cleared his throat and said, "I was thinking . . ."

I sat up straight and gave him my full attention. It was the first time he'd initiated a conversation since we'd left Kribirsk.

He shifted in his saddle, not meeting my eye. "I was thinking of who we could get to round out the guard."

I frowned. "The guard?"

He cleared his throat. "For you. A few of Nikolai's men seem all right, and I think Tolya and Tamar should be considered. They're Shu, but they're Grisha, so it shouldn't be a problem. And there's . . . well, me."

I didn't think I'd ever actually seen Mal blush.

I grinned. "Are you saying you want to be the captain of my personal guard?"

Mal glanced at me, his lips quirking in a smile. "Do I get to wear a fancy hat?"

"The fanciest," I said. "And possibly a cape."

"Will there be plumes?"

"Oh, yes. Several."

"Then I'm in."

I wanted to leave it at that, but I couldn't seem to help myself. "I thought . . . I thought you might want to go back to your unit, to be a tracker again."

Mal studied the knot in his reins. "I can't go back. Hopefully, Nikolai can keep me from being hanged—"

"Hopefully?" I squeaked.

"I deserted my post, Alina. Not even the King can make me a tracker again."

Mal's voice was steady, untroubled.

He adapts, I thought. But I knew some part of him would always grieve for the life he'd been meant to have, the life he would have had without me.

He nodded up ahead to where Nikolai's back was barely visible in the column of riders. "And there's no way I'm leaving you alone with Prince Perfect."

"So you don't trust me to resist his charms?"

"I don't even trust myself. I've never seen anyone work a crowd the way he does. I'm pretty sure the rocks and trees are getting ready to swear fealty to him."

I laughed and leaned back, felt the sun warming my skin through the dappled shade of the tree boughs overhead. I touched my fingers to the sea whip's fetter, safely hidden by my sleeve. For now, I wanted to keep the second amplifier a secret. Nikolai's Grisha had been sworn to silence, and I could only hope they'd hold their tongues.

My thoughts strayed to the firebird. Some part of me still couldn't quite believe it was real. Would it look the way it had in the pages of the red book, its feathers wrought in white and gold? Or would its wings be tipped with fire? And what kind of monster would nock an arrow and bring it down?

I had refused to take the stag's life, and countless people had died because of it – the citizens of Novokribirsk, the Grisha and soldiers I'd abandoned on the Darkling's skiff. I thought of those high church walls covered in the names of the dead.

Morozova's stag. Rusalye. The firebird. Legends come to life before my eyes, just to die in front of me. I remembered the sea whip's heaving sides, the thready whistle of its last breaths. It had been on the brink of death, and still I'd hesitated.

I don't want to be a killer. But mercy might not be a gift the Sun Summoner could afford. I gave myself a shake. First we had to find the firebird. Until then, all our hopes rested on the shoulders of one untrustworthy prince.

The next day, the first pilgrims appeared. They looked like any other townspeople, waiting by the road to see the royal procession roll past, but they wore armbands and carried banners emblazoned with a rising sun. Dirty from long days of travel, they hefted satchels and sacks stuffed with their few belongings, and when they caught sight of me in my blue *kefta*, the stag's collar around my neck, they swarmed around my horse, murmuring *Sankta, Sankta*, and trying to grab my sleeve or my hem. Sometimes they fell to their knees and I had to be careful or risk my horse trampling one of them.

I thought I'd grown used to all the attention, even being pawed at by strangers, but this felt different. I didn't like being called "Saint", and there was something hungry in their faces that set my nerves on edge.

As we pushed deeper into Ravka's interior, the crowds grew. They came from every direction, from cities, towns, and ports. They clustered in village squares and by the side of the Vy, men and women, old and young, some on foot, some astride donkeys or crowded into haycarts. Wherever we went, they cried out to me.

Sometimes I was Sankta Alina, sometimes Alina the Just or the Bright or the Merciful. Daughter of Keramzin, they shouted, Daughter of Ravka. Daughter of the Fold. Rebe Dva Stolba, they called me, Daughter of Two Mills, after the valley that was home to the nameless settlement of my birth. I had the vaguest memory of the ruins the valley was named after, two rocky spindles by the side of a dusty road. The Apparat had been busy breaking open my past, sifting through the rubble to build the story of a Saint.

The pilgrims' expectations terrified me. As far as they were concerned, I'd come to liberate Ravka from its enemies, from the Shadow Fold, from the Darkling, from poverty, from hunger, from sore feet and mosquitos and anything else that might trouble them. They begged for me to bless them, to cure them, but I could only summon light, wave, let them touch my hand. It was all part of Nikolai's show.

The pilgrims had come not just to see me but to follow me. They attached themselves to the royal processional, and their ragged band swelled with every passing day. They trailed us from town to town, camping in fallow fields, holding dawn vigils to pray for my safety and the salvation of Ravka. They were close to outnumbering Nikolai's soldiers.

"This is the Apparat's doing," I complained to Tamar one night at dinner.

We were lodged at a roadhouse for the evening. Through the windows I could see the lights of the pilgrims' cookfires, hear them singing peasant songs.

"These people should be home, working their fields and caring for their children, not following some false Saint."

Tamar pushed a piece of overcooked potato around on her plate and said, "My mother told me that Grisha power is a divine gift."

"And you believed her?"

"I don't have a better explanation."

I set my fork down. "Tamar, we don't have a divine gift. Grisha power is just something you're born with, like having big feet or a good singing voice."

"That's what the Shu believe. That it's something physical, buried in your heart or your spleen, something that can be isolated and dissected." She glanced out the window to the pilgrims' camp. "I don't think those people would agree."

"Please don't tell me you think I'm a Saint."

"It doesn't matter what you are. It matters what you can do."

"Tamar—"

"Those people think you can save Ravka," she said. "Obviously you do too, or you wouldn't be going to Os Alta."

"I'm going to Os Alta to rebuild the Second Army."

"And find the third amplifier?"

I nearly dropped my fork. "Keep your voice down," I sputtered.

"We saw the *Istorii Sankt'ya*."

So Sturmhond hadn't kept the book a secret. "Who else knows?" I asked, trying to regain my composure.

"We're not going to tell anyone, Alina. We know what's at risk." Tamar's glass had left a damp circle on the table. She traced it with her finger and said, "You know, some people believe that all the first Saints were Grisha."

I frowned. "Which people?"

Tamar shrugged. "Enough that their leaders were excommunicated. Some were even burned at the stake."

"I've never heard that."

"It was a long time ago. I don't understand why that idea makes people so angry. Even if the Saints were Grisha, that doesn't make what they did any less miraculous."

I squirmed in my chair. "I don't want to be a Saint, Tamar. I'm not trying to save the world. I just want to find a way to defeat the Darkling."

"Rebuild the Second Army. Defeat the Darkling. Destroy the Fold. Free Ravka. Call it what you like, but that all sounds suspiciously like saving the world."

Well, when she put it that way, it did seem a little

ambitious. I took a sip of wine. It was sour stuff compared with the vintages aboard the *Volkvolny*.

"Mal is going to ask you and Tolya to be members of my personal guard."

Tamar's face broke into a beautiful grin. "Really?"

"You're practically doing the job now, anyway. But if you're going to be guarding me morning and night, you need to promise me something."

"Anything," she said, beaming.

"No more talk of Saints."

CHAPTER 11

As the crowds of pilgrims grew, they became harder to control, and soon I was forced to ride in the coach. Some days Mal accompanied me, but usually he chose to ride outside, guarding the vehicle with Tolya and Tamar. As eager as I was for his company, I knew it was for the best. Being stuck in the lacquered little jewel box always seemed to put him in a bad mood.

Nikolai only joined me on our way into or out of every village, so that we would be seen arriving or departing together. He talked constantly. He was always thinking of some new thing to build – a contraption for paving roads, a new irrigation system, a boat that could row itself. He sketched on any piece of paper he could find, and each day he seemed to have a new way to improve the next version of the *Hummingbird*.

As nervous as it made me, he was also eager to talk about the third amplifier and the Darkling. He didn't recognise the stone arch in the illustration either, and no matter how long we squinted at the page, Sankt Ilya wasn't giving up his secrets. But that didn't stop Nikolai from speculating endlessly on possible places to start hunting the firebird, or questioning me about the Darkling's new power.

"We're about to go to war together," he said. "In case

you've forgotten, the Darkling's not particularly fond of me. I'd like us to have every advantage we can get."

There was so little for me to tell. I barely understood what the Darkling was doing myself.

"Grisha can only use and alter what already exists. True creation is a different kind of power. Baghra called it 'the making at the heart of the world'."

"And you think that's what the Darkling is after?"

"Maybe. I don't know. We all have limits, and when we push them, we tire. But in the long term, using our power makes us stronger. It's different when the Darkling calls the *nichevo'ya*. I think it costs him." I described the strain that had shown on the Darkling's face, his fatigue. "The power isn't feeding him. It's feeding *on* him."

"Well, that explains it," Nikolai said, his fingers beating a tattoo against his thigh, his mind already churning with possibilities.

"Explains what?"

"That we're still alive, that my father is still sitting on the throne. If the Darkling could just raise a shadow army, he'd have marched on us already. This is good," he said decisively. "It buys us time."

The question was how much. I thought back to the desire I'd felt looking up at the stars aboard the *Volkvolny*. Hunger for power had corrupted the Darkling. For all I knew, it might well have corrupted Morozova, too. Bringing the amplifiers together might unleash misery of a kind the world had never seen.

I rubbed my arms, trying to shake the chill that had dropped over me. I couldn't speak these doubts to Nikolai, and Mal was already reluctant enough about the course we'd chosen.

"You know what we're up against," I said. "Time may not be enough."

"Os Alta is heavily fortified. It's close to the base at Poliznaya, and more importantly, it's far from both the northern and southern borders."

"Does that help us?"

"The Darkling's range is limited. When we disabled his ship, he wasn't able to send the *nichevo'ya* to pursue us. That means he'll have to enter Ravka with his monsters. The mountains to the east are impassable, and he can't cross the Fold without you, so he'll have to come at us from Fjerda or Shu Han. Either way, we'll have plenty of warning."

"And the King and Queen will stay?"

"If my father left the capital, it would be as good as handing the country over to the Darkling now. Besides, I don't know that he's strong enough to travel."

I thought of Genya's red *kefta*. "He hasn't recovered?"

"They've kept the worst of it from the gossips, but no, he hasn't, and I doubt he will." He crossed his arms and cocked his head to the side. "Your friend is stunning. For a poisoner."

"She isn't my friend," I said, though the words sounded childish to my ears and felt like a betrayal. I blamed Genya for a lot of things, but not for what she'd done to the King. Nikolai seemed to have spies everywhere. I wondered if he knew what kind of a man his father really was. "And I doubt she used poison."

"She did something to him. None of his doctors can find a cure, and my mother won't let a Corporalki Healer anywhere near him." After a moment, Nikolai said, "It was a clever move, really."

My brows shot up. "Trying to kill your father?"

"The Darkling could have murdered my father easily enough, but he would have risked outright rebellion from the peasants and the First Army. With the King alive and kept in isolation, no one knew quite what was happening. The Apparat was there, playing the trusted adviser, issuing commands. Vasily was off somewhere acquiring horses and whores." He paused, looked out of the window, ran his finger along its gilded edge. "I was at sea. I didn't hear the news until weeks after it was all over."

I waited, unsure if I should speak. His eyes were trained on the passing scenery, but his expression was distant.

"When word of the massacre in Novokribirsk and the Darkling's disappearance got out, all hell broke loose. A group of royal ministers and the palace guard forced their way into the Grand Palace and demanded to see the King. Do you know what they found? My mother cowering in her parlour, clutching that snuffly little dog. And the King of Ravka, Alexander the Third, alone in his bedchamber, barely breathing, lying in his own filth. I let that happen."

"You couldn't have known what the Darkling was planning, Nikolai. No one did."

He didn't seem to hear me. "The Grisha and *oprichniki* who held the palace on the Darkling's orders were caught in the lower town, trying to escape. They were executed."

I tried to restrain a shudder. "What about the Apparat?" The priest had colluded with the Darkling and might be working with him still. But he'd tried to approach me before the coup, and I'd always thought he might be playing a deeper game.

"Escaped. No one knows how." His voice was hard. "He'll answer for it when the time comes."

Again I glimpsed the ruthless edge that lurked beneath the polished demeanour. Was that the real Nikolai Lantsov? Or just another disguise?

"You let Genya go," I said.

"She was a pawn. You were the prize. I had to stay focused." Then he grinned, his dark mood vanishing as if it had never been. "Besides," he said with a wink, "she was too pretty for the sharks."

Riding in the coach left me restless, frustrated with the pace Nikolai was setting, and eager to get to the Little Palace. Still, it gave him a chance to help prepare me for our arrival in Os Alta. Nikolai had a considerable stake in my success as the leader of the Second Army, and he always seemed to have some new bit of wisdom he wanted to impart. It was overwhelming, but I didn't feel I could afford to disregard his advice, and I started to feel like I was back at the Little Palace library, cramming my head full of Grisha theory.

The less you say, the more weight your words will carry.

Don't argue. Never deign to deny. Meet insults with laughter.

"You didn't laugh at the Fjerdan captain," I observed.

"That wasn't an insult. It was a challenge," he said. "Know the difference."

Weakness is a guise. Wear it when they need to know you're human, but never when you feel it.

Don't wish for bricks when you can build from stone. Use whatever or whoever is in front of you.

Being a leader means someone is always watching you.

Get them to follow the little orders, and they'll follow the big ones.

It's okay to flout expectations, but never disappoint them.

"How am I supposed to remember all of this?" I asked in exasperation.

"You don't think too much about it, you just do it."

"Easy for you to say. You've been groomed for this since the day you were born."

"I was groomed for lawn tennis and champagne parties," Nikolai said. "The rest came with practice."

"I don't have time for practice!"

"You'll do fine," he said. "Just calm down."

I let out a squawk of frustration. I wanted to throttle him so badly my fingers itched.

"Oh, and the easiest way to make someone furious is to tell her to calm down."

I didn't know whether to laugh or throw my shoe at him.

Outside the coach, Nikolai's behaviour was getting more and more unnerving. He knew better than to renew his marriage proposal, but it was clear that he wanted people to think there was something between us. With every stop, he grew more bold, standing too close, kissing my hand, pushing my hair back over my ear when it was caught by a breeze.

In Tashta, Nikolai waved to the massive crowd of villagers and pilgrims that had formed by a statue of the town's founder. As he was helping me back into the coach, he slipped his arm around my waist.

"Please don't punch me," he whispered. Then he yanked me hard against his chest and pressed his lips to mine.

The crowd exploded into wild cheers, their voices

crashing over us in an exultant roar. Before I could even react, Nikolai shoved me into the shadowy interior of the coach and slipped in after. He slammed the door behind him, but I could still hear the townspeople cheering outside. Mixed in with the cries of "Nikolai!" and "Sankta Alina!" was a new chant: *Sol Koroleva*, they shouted. Sun Queen.

I could just see Mal through the coach's window. He was on horseback, working the edge of the crowd, making sure they stayed out of the road. It was clear from his stormy expression that he'd seen everything.

I turned on Nikolai and kicked him hard in the shin. He yelped, but that wasn't nearly satisfying enough. I kicked him again.

"Feel better?" he asked.

"Next time you try something like that, I won't kick you," I said angrily. "I'll cut you in half."

He brushed a speck of lint from his trousers. "Not sure that would be wise. I'm afraid the people rather frown on regicide."

"You're not King yet, *Sobachka*," I said sharply. "So don't tempt me."

"I don't see why you're upset. The crowd loved it."

"*I* didn't love it."

He raised a brow. "You didn't hate it."

I kicked him again. This time his hand snaked out like a flash and captured my ankle. If it had been winter, I would have been wearing boots, but I was in summer slippers and his fingers closed over my bare leg. My cheeks blazed red.

"Promise not to kick me again, and I'll promise not to kiss you again," he said.

"I only kicked you because you kissed me!"

I tried to pull my leg back, but he kept a hard grip.

"Promise," he said.

"All right," I bit out. "I promise."

"Then we have a deal."

He dropped my foot, and I drew it back beneath my *kefta*, hoping he couldn't see my idiotic blush.

"Great," I said. "Now get out."

"It's my coach."

"The deal was only for kicking. It did not prohibit slapping, punching, biting, or *cutting you in half*."

He grinned. "Afraid Oretsev will wonder what we're up to?"

That was exactly what I was worried about. "I'm concerned that if I'm forced to spend another minute with you, I may vomit on my *kefta*."

"It's an act, Alina. The stronger our alliance, the better it will be for both of us. I'm sorry if it puts a burr in Mal's sock, but it's a necessity."

"That kiss wasn't a necessity."

"I was improvising," he said. "I got carried away."

"You *never* improvise," I said. "Everything you do is calculated. You change personalities the way other people change hats. And you know what? It's creepy. Aren't you ever just yourself?"

"I'm a prince, Alina. I can't afford to be myself."

I blew out an annoyed breath.

He was silent for a moment and then said, "I . . . you really think I'm creepy?"

It was the first time he'd sounded less than sure of himself. Despite what he'd done, I actually felt a little sorry for him.

"Occasionally," I admitted.

He scrubbed a hand over the back of his neck, looking distinctly uncomfortable. Then he sighed and shrugged. "I'm a younger son, most likely a bastard, and I've been away from court for almost seven years. I'm going to do everything I can to strengthen my chances for the throne, and if that means courting an entire nation or making moon eyes at you, then I'll do it."

I goggled at him. I hadn't really heard anything after the word "bastard". Genya had hinted that there were rumours about Nikolai's parentage, but I was shocked that he would acknowledge them.

He laughed. "You're never going to survive at court if you don't learn to hide what you're thinking a bit better. You look like you just sat in a bowl of cold porridge. Close your mouth."

I shut my mouth with a snap and tried to school my features into a pleasant expression. That just made Nikolai laugh harder. "Now you look like you've had too much wine."

I gave up and slouched back against the seat. "How can you joke about something like that?"

"I've heard the whispers since I was a child. It's not something I want repeated outside of this coach – and I'll deny it if you do – but I couldn't care less whether or not I have Lantsov blood. In fact, given all the royal inbreeding, being a bastard is probably a point in my favour."

I shook my head. He was completely baffling. It was hard to know what to take seriously when it came to Nikolai.

"Why is the crown so important to you?" I asked. "Why go through all of this?"

"Is it so hard to believe I might actually care what happens to this country?"

"Honestly? Yes."

He studied the toes of his polished boots. I could never figure out how he kept them so shiny.

"I guess I like fixing things," he said. "I always have."

It wasn't much of an answer, but somehow it rang true.

"You truly think your brother will step aside?"

"I hope so. He knows the First Army will follow me, and I don't think he has the stomach for civil war. Besides, Vasily inherited our father's aversion to hard work. Once he realises what it really takes to run a country, I doubt he'll be able to run from the capital fast enough."

"And if he doesn't give up so easily?"

"It's simply a question of finding the right incentive. Pauper or prince, every man can be bought."

More wisdom from the mouth of Nikolai Lantsov. I glanced out the coach's window. I could just see Mal sitting tall in his saddle as he kept pace with the coach.

"Not every man," I murmured.

Nikolai followed my gaze. "Yes, Alina, even your stalwart champion has his price." He turned back to me, his hazel eyes thoughtful. "And I suspect I'm looking at it right now."

I shifted uneasily in my seat. "You're so sure of everything," I said sourly. "Maybe I'll decide *I* want the throne and smother you in your sleep."

Nikolai just grinned. "Finally," he said, "you're thinking like a politician."

Eventually, Nikolai relented and vacated the coach, though it was hours before we stopped for the night. I didn't have to seek Mal out. When the coach door opened, he was there, offering his hand to help me down. The square was crowded with pilgrims and other travellers, all craning their necks to get a better look at the Sun Summoner, but I wasn't sure when I'd have another chance to talk to him.

"Are you angry?" I whispered as he led me across the cobblestones. I could see Nikolai on the other end of the square, already chatting with a group of local dignitaries.

"With you? No. But Nikolai and I are going to have words when he isn't surrounded by an armed guard."

"If it makes you feel any better, I kicked him."

Mal laughed. "You did?"

"Twice. Does that help?"

"Actually, yes."

"I'll stomp on his foot tonight at dinner." That fell well outside the kicking prohibition.

"So, no heart flutters or swooning, even in the arms of a royal prince?"

He was teasing, but I heard the uncertainty beneath his words.

"I seem to be immune," I replied. "And luckily, I know what a *real* kiss should feel like."

I left him standing in the middle of the square. I could get used to making Mal blush.

The night before we were to enter Os Alta, we stayed at the dacha of a minor nobleman who lived just a few miles from the city walls. It reminded me a bit of Keramzin – the grand iron gates, the long, straight path to the graceful house with its two wide wings of pale brick. Count Minkoff was apparently known for breeding dwarf fruit trees, and the hallways of the dacha were lined with clever little topiaries that filled the rooms with the sweet scent of peaches and plums.

I was provided with an elegant bedchamber on the second floor. Tamar took the adjoining room, and Tolya and Mal were boarded across the hall. A large box waited for me on my bed, and inside, I found the *kefta* I had finally broken down and requested the previous week. Nikolai had sent orders to the Little Palace, and I recognised the work of Grisha Fabrikators in the dark blue silk shot through with golden thread. I expected it to be heavy in my hands, but Materialki craft had rendered the fabric nearly weightless. When I slipped it over my head, it glimmered and shifted like light glimpsed through water. The clasps were small golden suns. It was beautiful and a bit showy. Nikolai would approve.

The lady of the house had sent a maid to do my hair. She sat me down at the dressing table, clucking and fussing over my tangles as she pinned my tresses into a loose knot. She had a far gentler hand than Genya, but the results weren't nearly so spectacular. I shoved the thought from my mind. I didn't like thinking of Genya, of what might have happened to her after we left the whaler, or of how lonely the Little Palace would feel without her.

I thanked the maid and, before I left my room, snapped up the black velvet pouch that had come in the box with my *kefta*. I slipped it into my pocket, checked to make sure the fetter was hidden by my sleeve, then headed downstairs.

Talk over dinner centred around the latest plays, the possible whereabouts of the Darkling, and happenings in Os Alta. The city had been swamped with refugees. Newcomers were being turned away at the gate, and there were rumours of food riots in the lower town. It seemed impossibly far away from this sparkling place.

The Count and his wife, a plump lady with greying curls and alarmingly displayed cleavage, set a lavish table. We ate cold soup from jewelled cups shaped like pumpkins, roasted lamb slathered with currant jelly, mushrooms baked in cream, and a dish I only picked at that I later learned was brandied cuckoo. Each plate and glass was edged in silver and bore the Minkoff crest. But most impressive was the centrepiece that ran the length of the table: a living miniature forest rendered in elaborate detail, complete with groves of tiny pines, a climbing trumpet vine with blossoms no bigger than a fingernail, and a little hut that hid the salt cellar.

I sat between Nikolai and Colonel Raevsky, listening as the noble guests laughed and chattered and raised toast after toast to the young prince's return and the Sun Summoner's health. I'd asked Mal to join us, but he'd refused, choosing instead to patrol the grounds with Tamar and Tolya. Hard as I tried to keep my mind on the conversation, I kept glancing at the terrace, hoping to catch sight of him.

Nikolai must have noticed, because he whispered, "You don't have to pay attention, but you do have to look as if you're paying attention."

I did my best, though I didn't have much to say. Even

dressed in a glittering *kefta* and seated beside a prince, I was still a peasant from a no-name town. I didn't belong with these people, and I didn't really want to. I gave a silent prayer of thanks that Ana Kuya had taught her orphans how to sit at table and which fork to use to eat snails.

After dinner, we were herded into a parlour where the Count and Countess sang a duet accompanied by their daughter on the harp. Dessert was laid on the side table: honey mousse, a walnut and melon compote, and a tower of pastries covered in clouds of spun sugar that wasn't meant to be eaten so much as ogled. There was more wine, more gossip. I was asked to summon light, and I cast a warm glow over the coffered ceiling to enthusiastic applause. When some of the guests sat down to play cards, I pleaded a headache and quietly made my escape.

Nikolai caught me at the doors to the terrace. "You should stay," he said. "This is good practice for the monotony of court."

"Saints need their rest."

"Are you planning to sleep under a rosebush?" he asked, glancing towards the garden.

"I've been a good little dancing bear, Nikolai. I've done all my tricks, and now it's time for me to say goodnight."

Nikolai sighed. "Maybe I just wish I could go with you. The Countess kept squeezing my knee under the table at dinner, and I hate playing cards."

"I thought you were the consummate politician."

"I told you I have trouble keeping still."

"Then you'll just have to ask the Countess to dance," I said with a grin, and slipped out into the night air.

As I descended the terrace steps, I looked back over

my shoulder. Nikolai still hovered in the doorway. He wore full military dress, a pale blue sash across his chest. The light from the parlour glinted off his medals and gilded the edges of his golden hair. He was playing the role of the polished prince tonight. But standing there, he just looked like a lonely boy who didn't want to return to a party by himself.

I turned and took the curving staircase down to the sunken garden.

It didn't take me long to find Mal. He was leaning against the trunk of a large oak, scanning the manicured grounds.

"Anyone lurking in the dark?" I asked.

"Just me."

I settled beside him against the trunk. "You should have joined us at dinner."

Mal snorted. "No thank you. From what I could see, you looked positively miserable, and Nikolai didn't look much happier. Besides," he added with a glance at my *kefta*, "whatever would I have worn?"

"Do you hate it?"

"It's lovely. A perfect addition to your trousseau." Before I could even roll my eyes, he snagged hold of my hand. "I didn't mean that," he said. "You look beautiful. I've been wanting to say so since I first saw you tonight."

I flushed. "Thanks. Using my power every day helps."

"You were beautiful back in Cofton with *jurda* pollen in your brows."

I tugged self-consciously at a strand of my hair. "This place reminds me of Keramzin," I said.

"A little. It's a lot fussier. What exactly is the point of teeny tiny fruit?"

"It's for people with teeny tiny hands. Makes them feel better about themselves."

He laughed, a real laugh. I reached into my pocket and fished around inside the black velvet pouch.

"I have something for you," I said.

"What is it?"

I held out my closed fist.

"Guess," I said. It was a game we'd played as children.

"Obviously, it's a sweater."

I shook my head.

"A show pony?"

"Nope."

He reached out and took my hand, turning it over and gently unfolding my fingers.

I waited for his reaction.

His mouth tugged up at one corner as he plucked the golden sunburst from my hand. The rough brush of his fingers against my palm sent a shiver up my back.

"For the captain of your personal guard?" he asked.

I cleared my throat nervously. "I . . . I didn't want uniforms. I didn't want anything that looked like the Darkling's *oprichniki*."

For a long moment, we stood in silence as Mal looked down at the sunburst. Then he handed it back to me. My heart plummeted, but I tried to hide my disappointment.

"Put it on me?" he asked.

I let my breath out in a relieved rush. I took the pin between my fingers and pressed it through the folds on the left side of his shirt. It took me a couple of tries to get it hooked. When I finished and made to step back, he took my hand and pressed it over the golden sun, over his heart.

"Is that all?" he said.

We were standing close together now, alone in the warm dark of the garden. It was the first moment we'd had to ourselves in weeks.

"All?" I repeated. My voice came out as little more than a breath.

"I believe I was promised a cape and a fancy hat."

"I'll make it up to you," I said.

"Are you flirting?"

"I'm bartering."

"Fine," he said. "I'll take my first payment now."

His tone was light, but when his lips met mine, there was nothing playful in his kiss. He tasted of heat and newly ripe pears from the Duke's garden. I sensed hunger in the hard slant of his mouth, an unfamiliar edge to his need that sent restless sparks burning through me.

I came up on my toes, circling my arms around his neck, feeling the length of my body melt into his. He had a soldier's strength, and I felt it in the hard bands of his arms, the pressure of his fingers as his fist bunched in the silk at the small of my back and he drew me against him. There was something fierce and almost desperate in the way he held me, as if he could not have me close enough.

My head was spinning, my thoughts had gone slow and liquid, but somewhere I heard footsteps. In the next moment, Tamar came charging up the path.

"We have company," she said.

Mal broke away from me and unslung his rifle in a single swift movement. "Who is it?"

"There's a group of people at the gate demanding entry. They want to see the Sun Summoner."

"Pilgrims?" I asked, trying to get my kiss-addled brain to function properly.

Tamar shook her head. "They claim to be Grisha."

"Here?"

Mal placed a hand on my arm. "Alina, wait inside, at least until we see what this is about."

I hesitated. Part of me bridled at being told to run off and hide my head, but I didn't want to be stupid either. A shout rose from somewhere near the gates.

"No," I said, pulling from Mal's grasp. "If they really are Grisha, you may need me."

Neither Tamar nor Mal looked pleased, but they took up positions on either side of me and we hurried down the gravel path.

A crowd had gathered at the dacha's iron gates. Tolya was easy to spot, towering above everyone else. Nikolai was in front, surrounded by soldiers with their weapons drawn, as well as armed footmen from the Count's household. A small group of people were gathered on the other side of the bars, but I couldn't see more than that. Someone gave the gate an angry rattle, and I heard a clamour of raised voices.

"Get me in there," I said. Tamar cast Mal a worried glance. I lifted my chin. If they were going to be my guards, they would have to follow my orders. "*Now.* I need to see what's happening before things get out of hand."

Tamar signalled to Tolya, and the giant stepped in front of us, easily shouldering his way through the crowd to the gates. I'd always been small. Packed between Mal and the twins, with antsy soldiers jostling us from every side, it suddenly felt very hard to breathe. I pushed down my panic, peering past bodies and backs to where

I could see Nikolai arguing with someone at the gate.

"If we wanted to talk to the King's lackey, we'd be at the doors to the Grand Palace," said an impatient voice. "We came for the Sun Summoner."

"Show some respect, bloodletter," barked a soldier I didn't recognise. "You're addressing a Prince of Ravka and an officer of the First Army."

This was not going well. I edged closer to the front of the crowd but halted when I saw the Corporalnik standing beyond the iron bars. "Fedyor?"

His long face broke into a grin, and he bowed deeply. "Alina Starkov," he said. "I could only hope the rumours were true."

I studied Fedyor warily. He was surrounded by a group of Grisha in dust-covered *kefta*, mostly Corporalki red, some in Etherealki blue, and a smattering of Materialki purple.

"You know him?" Nikolai asked.

"Yes," I said. "He saved my life." Fedyor had once put himself between me and a swarm of Fjerdan assassins.

He bowed again. "It was my great honour."

Nikolai didn't look impressed. "Can he be trusted?"

"He's a deserter," said the soldier beside Nikolai.

There was grumbling on both sides of the gate.

Nikolai pointed to Tolya. "Move everyone back and make sure that none of those footmen get it in their heads to start shooting. I suspect they lack for excitement out here amid the fruit trees." He turned back to the gate. "Fedyor, is it? Give us a moment." He pulled me a short distance from the crowd and said quietly, "Well? Can he be trusted?"

"I don't know." The last time I'd seen Fedyor had

been at a party at the Grand Palace, just hours before I'd learned the Darkling's plans and fled in the back of a wagon. I racked my brain, trying to recall what he'd told me then. "I think he was stationed at the southern border. He was a high-ranking Heartrender, but not one of the Darkling's favourites."

"Nevsky is right," he said, nodding towards the angry soldier. "Grisha or not, their first loyalty should have been to the King. They left their posts. Technically, they're deserters."

"That doesn't make them traitors."

"The real question is whether they're spies."

"So what do we do with them?"

"We could arrest them, have them questioned."

I toyed with my sleeve, thinking.

"Talk to me," Nikolai said.

"Don't we want the Grisha to come back?" I asked. "If we arrest everyone who returns, I won't have much of an army to lead."

"Remember," he said, "you'll be eating with them, working with them, sleeping under the same roof."

"And they could all be working for the Darkling." I looked over my shoulder at Fedyor waiting patiently at the gate. "What do you think?"

"I don't think these Grisha are any more or less trustworthy than the ones waiting at the Little Palace."

"That's not encouraging."

"Once we're behind the palace walls, all communication will be closely monitored. It's hard to see how the Darkling can use his spies if he can't reach them."

I resisted the urge to touch the scars forming on my shoulder. I took a breath.

"All right," I said. "Open the gates. I'll speak to Fedyor and only him. The rest can camp outside the dacha tonight and join us on the way into Os Alta tomorrow."

"You're sure?"

"I doubt I'll be sure of anything ever again, but my army needs soldiers."

"Very good," Nikolai said with a short nod. "Just be careful who you trust."

I cast a pointed glance at him. "I will."

CHAPTER 12

Fedyor and I talked late into the night, though we were never left alone. Mal or Tolya or Tamar was always there, keeping watch.

Fedyor had been serving near Sikursk on the south-eastern border. When word of the destruction of Novokribirsk reached the outpost, the King's soldiers had turned on the Grisha, pulling them from their beds in the middle of the night and mounting sham trials to determine their loyalty. Fedyor had helped to lead an escape.

"We could have killed them all," he said. "Instead, we took our wounded and fled."

Some Grisha hadn't been so forgiving. There had been massacres at Chernast and Ulensk when the soldiers there had tried to attack members of the Second Army. Meanwhile, Mal and I had been aboard the *Verrhader*, sailing west, safe from the chaos we'd unleashed.

"A few weeks ago," he said, "the stories started circulating that you'd returned to Ravka. You can expect more Grisha to seek you out."

"How many?"

"There's no way of knowing."

Like Nikolai, Fedyor believed some Grisha had gone into hiding, waiting for order to be restored. But he suspected that most of them had sought out the Darkling.

"He's strength," said Fedyor. "He's safety. That's what they understand."

Or maybe they just think they've chosen the winning side, I thought bleakly. But I knew it was more than that. I'd felt the pull of the Darkling's power. Wasn't that why the pilgrims flocked to a false Saint? Why the First Army still marched for an incompetent king? Sometimes, it was just easier to follow.

When Fedyor finished his tale, I asked that he be brought dinner and advised him that he should be ready to travel to Os Alta at dawn.

"I don't know what kind of reception we can expect," I warned him.

"We'll be ready, *moi soverenyi*," he said, and bowed.

I started at the title. In my mind, it still belonged to the Darkling.

"Fedyor . . . " I began as I walked him to the door. Then I hesitated. I couldn't believe what I was about to say, but apparently Nikolai was getting through to me – for better or worse. "I realise you've been travelling, but tidy up a bit before tomorrow. It's important that we make a good impression."

He didn't even blink – just bowed again and replied, "*Da, soverenyi*," before disappearing into the night.

Great, I thought. *One order down, a few thousand more to go.*

Next morning, I dressed in my elaborate *kefta* and descended the dacha's steps with Mal and the twins. The gold sunbursts glittered from their chests, though they still wore peasant roughspun. Nikolai might not like it, but I wanted to erase the lines that had been drawn between the Grisha and the rest of Ravka's people.

Though we'd been warned that Os Alta was teeming with refugees and pilgrims, for once Nikolai didn't insist that I ride in the coach. He wanted me to be seen entering the city. But that didn't mean he wasn't going to put on a show. My guards and I were all seated on beautiful white horses, and men from his regiment flanked us on both sides, each bearing the Ravkan double eagle and flags emblazoned with golden suns.

"Subtle, as always," I sighed.

"Understatement is overrated," he replied as he mounted a dappled grey. "Now, shall we visit my quaint childhood home?"

It was a warm morning and the banners of our processional hung limp in the still air as we wended our way slowly along the Vy to the capital. Ordinarily, the royal family would have spent the hot months at their summer palace in the lake district. But Os Alta was more easily defended, and they'd chosen to hunker down behind its famous double walls.

My thoughts wandered as we rode. I hadn't got much sleep and, despite my nerves, the warmth of the morning combined with the steady sway of the horse and the low hum of insects made my chin droop. But when we crested the hill at the outskirts of the town, I came quickly awake.

In the distance, I saw Os Alta, the Dream City, its spires white and jagged against the cloudless sky. And between us and the capital, arrayed in perfect military formation, stood row after row of armed men. Hundreds of soldiers of the First Army, maybe a thousand – infantry, cavalry, officers, and grunts. Sunlight glittered off the hilts of their swords, and their backs bristled with rifles.

A man rode out before them. He wore an officer's coat covered with medals and sat atop one of the biggest horses I'd ever seen. It could have carried two Tolyas.

Nikolai watched the rider galloping back and forth across the lines and sighed. "Ah," he said. "It seems my brother has come to greet us."

Slowly, we descended the slope and halted in front of the masses of assembled men. Despite the white horses and glittering banners, our processional of wayward Grisha and ragged pilgrims no longer seemed quite so grand. Nikolai nudged his horse forward, and his brother cantered up to meet him.

I'd seen Vasily Lantsov a few times at Os Alta. He was handsome enough, though he'd had the bad luck to inherit his father's weak chin, and his eyes were so heavy-lidded that he always looked very bored or slightly drunk. But now he seemed to have roused himself from his perpetual stupor. He sat straight in his saddle, radiating arrogance and nobility. Next to him, Nikolai looked impossibly young.

I felt a prickle of fear. Nikolai always seemed so in control of every situation. It was easy to forget that he was just a few years older than Mal and I were, a boy captain who hoped to become a boy king.

It had been seven years since Nikolai had been at court, and I didn't think he'd seen Vasily in all that time. But there were no tears, no shouted greetings. The two princes simply dismounted and clasped each other in a brief embrace. Vasily surveyed our retinue, pausing meaningfully on me.

"So this is the girl you claim is the Sun Summoner?"

Nikolai raised his brows. His brother couldn't have given him a better opening. "It's a claim easy enough to prove." He nodded at me.

Understatement is overrated. I raised my hands and summoned a blazing wave of light that crashed over the assembled soldiers in a cascade of billowing heat. They threw up their hands, and several stepped back as the horses shied and whinnied. I let the light fade. Vasily sniffed.

"You've been busy, little brother."

"You have no idea, Vasya," replied Nikolai pleasantly. Vasily's mouth puckered at Nikolai's use of the diminutive. He looked almost prim. "I'm surprised to find you in Os Alta," Nikolai continued. "I thought you'd be in Caryeva for the races."

"I was," said Vasily. "My blue roan had an excellent showing. But when I heard you were returning home, I wanted to be here to greet you."

"Kind of you to go to all this trouble."

"The return of a royal prince is no small thing," Vasily said. "Even a younger son."

His emphasis was clear, and the fear inside me grew. Maybe Nikolai had underestimated Vasily's interest in retaining his place in the succession. I didn't want to imagine what his other mistakes or miscalculations might mean for us.

Nikolai just smiled. I remembered his advice: *Meet insults with with laughter.*

"We younger sons learn to appreciate what we can get," he said. Then he called to a soldier standing at attention down the line. "Sergeant Pechkin, I remember you from the Halmhend campaign. Leg must have healed well if you're able to stand there like a slab of stone."

The sergeant's face registered surprise. "*Da, moi tsarevich*," he said respectfully.

"'Sir' will do, sergeant. I'm an officer when I wear this uniform, not a prince." Vasily's lips twitched again. Like many noble sons, he had taken an honourary commission and done his military service in the comfort of the officers' tents, well away from enemy lines. Nikolai had served in the infantry. He'd earned his medals and rank.

"Yes, sir," said the sergeant. "Only bothers me when it rains."

"Then I imagine the Fjerdans pray daily for storms. You put quite a few of them out of their misery, if I recall."

"I seem to remember you doing the same, sir," said the soldier with a grin.

I almost laughed. In a single exchange, Nikolai had seized control of the field from his brother. Tonight, when the soldiers gathered in the taverns of Os Alta or played cards in their barracks, this was what they would be talking about: the prince who remembered an ordinary soldier's name, the prince who had fought side by side with them without concern for wealth or pedigree.

"Brother," Nikolai said to Vasily. "Let's get to the palace so we can dispense with our greetings. I have a case of Kerch whiskey that needs drinking, and I'd like to get your advice on a foal I spotted in Ketterdam. They tell me Dagrenner is his sire, but I have my doubts."

Vasily tried to disguise his interest, but it was as if he couldn't resist. "Dagrenner? Did they have papers?"

"Come have a look."

Though his face was still wary, Vasily spoke a few

words to one of the commanding officers and leapt into his saddle with practised ease. The brothers took their places at the head of the column and our procession was moving once again.

"Neatly done," Mal murmured to me as we passed between the rows of soldiers. "Nikolai's no fool."

"I hope not," I said. "For both our sakes."

As we drew closer to the capital, I saw what Count Minkoff's guests had been talking about. A city of tents had sprung up around the walls, and a long line of people waited at the gates. Several of them were arguing with the guards, no doubt petitioning for entry. Armed soldiers kept watch from the old battlements – a good precaution for a country at war, and a deadly reminder to the people below to keep things orderly.

Of course, the city gates sprang open for the princes of Ravka, and the procession continued through the crowd without pause.

Many of the tents and wagons were marked with crudely drawn suns, and as we rode through the makeshift camp, I heard the now-familiar cries of "Sankta Alina."

I felt foolish doing it, but forced myself to lift my hand and wave, determined to at least make an effort. The pilgrims cheered and waved back, many running to keep pace with us. But some of the other refugees stood silent by the side of the road, arms crossed, expressions skeptical and even blatantly hostile.

What do they see? I wondered. *Another privileged Grisha going to her safe, luxurious palace on the hill while they cook on open fires and sleep in the shadow of a city that refuses them sanctuary? Or something worse? A liar? A fraud? A girl who dares to style herself as a living Saint?*

I was grateful when we passed into the protection of the city walls.

Once inside, the procession slowed to a crawl. The lower town was full to bursting, the sidewalks crammed with people who spilled onto the street and halted traffic. The windows of the shops were plastered with signs declaring which goods were available, and long lines stretched out of every doorway. The stink of urine and garbage lay over everything. I wanted to bury my nose in my sleeve, but I had to settle for breathing through my mouth.

The crowds cheered and gawked here, but they were decidedly more subdued than those outside the gates.

"No pilgrims," I observed.

"They're not allowed within the city walls," said Tamar. "The King has had the Apparat declared an apostate and his followers banned from Os Alta."

The Apparat had conspired with the Darkling against the throne. Even if they'd since severed ties, there was no reason for the King to trust the priest and his cult. *Or you, for that matter*, I reminded myself. *You're just the one dumb enough to stroll into the Grand Palace and hope for clemency.*

We crossed the wide canal and left the noise and tumult of the lower town behind. I noticed that the bridge's gatehouse had been heavily fortified, but when we reached the far bank, it seemed that nothing in the upper town had changed. The broad boulevards were spotless and serene, the stately homes carefully maintained. We passed a park where fashionably turned out men and women strolled the manicured paths or took the air in open carriages. Children played at *babki*, watched over by their nannies, and a boy in a straw hat rode by on a pony with ribbons in its braided mane, the reins held by a uniformed servant.

They all turned to look as we passed, lifting their hats, whispering behind their hands, bowing and curtseying when they caught sight of Vasily and Nikolai. Were they really as calm and free of worry as they seemed? It was hard to fathom that they could be oblivious to the danger threatening Ravka or the turmoil on the other side of the bridge, but it was even harder for me to believe they trusted their King to keep them safe.

Sooner than I would have liked, we reached the golden gates of the Grand Palace. The sound of them clanging shut behind us sent a splinter of panic through me. The last time I'd passed through those gates, I'd been stowed away between pieces of scenery in a horse cart, fleeing from the Darkling, alone and on the run.

What if it's a trap? I thought suddenly. What if there was no pardon? What if Nikolai never intended for me to lead the Second Army? What if they clamped Mal and me in irons and tossed us into some dank cell?

Stop it, I chastised myself. *You're not some scared little girl any more, shaking in her army-issue boots. You're a Grisha, the Sun Summoner. They need you. And you could bring this whole palace down around them if you wanted to.* I straightened my spine and tried to steady my heart.

When we reached the double eagle fountain, Tolya helped me from my horse. I squinted up at the Grand Palace, its gleaming white terraces crammed with layer after layer of gold ornament and statuary. It was just as ugly and intimidating as I remembered.

Vasily handed the reins of his mount to a waiting

servant and headed up the marble steps without a backward glance.

Nikolai squared his shoulders. "Keep quiet and try to look penitent," he muttered to us. Then he bounded up the staircase to join his brother.

Mal's face was pale. I wiped my clammy hands on my *kefta*, and we followed the princes, leaving the rest of our party behind.

Inside, the halls of the palace were silent as we passed from room to glittering room. Our footfalls echoed on the polished parquet, and my anxiety grew with every step. At the doors to the throne room, I saw Nikolai take a deep breath. His uniform was immaculate, his handsome face cut in the lines of a fairy-tale prince. I suddenly missed Sturmhond's lumpy nose and muddy green eyes.

The doors were thrown open and the footman declared, "*Tsesarevich Vasily Lantsov and Grand Duke Nikolai Lantsov.*"

Nikolai had told us that we wouldn't be announced but that we should follow behind him and Vasily. With hesitating steps, we complied, keeping a respectful distance from the princes.

A long, pale blue carpet stretched the length of the room. At the end of it, a group of elegantly dressed courtiers and advisers milled around a raised dais. Above them all sat the King and Queen of Ravka, on matching golden thrones.

No priest, I noted as we drew closer. The Apparat had always seemed to be lurking somewhere behind the King, but now he was conspicuously absent. He did not seem to have been replaced with another spiritual adviser.

The King was far frailer and weaker than when I'd last seen him. His narrow chest looked like it had caved in on itself, and his drooping mustache was shot through with grey. The greatest change, though, had been wrought in the Queen. Without Genya there to tailor her face, she seemed to have aged twenty years in just a few months. Her skin had lost its creamy firmness. Deep furrows were beginning to form around her nose and mouth, and her too-bright irises had faded to a more natural but less arresting blue. Any pity I might have felt for her was eclipsed by my memory of the way she'd treated Genya. Maybe if she'd shown her servant a little less contempt, Genya wouldn't have felt compelled to throw her lot in with the Darkling. So many things might have been different.

When we reached the base of the dais, Nikolai bowed deeply. "*Moi tsar,*" he said. "*Moya tsaritsa.*"

For a long, anxious moment, the King and Queen gazed down at their son. Then some fragile thing seemed to snap in the Queen. She sprang from her throne and bounded down the steps in a flurry of silk and pearls.

"Nikolai!" she cried as she clutched him to her.

"*Madraya,*" he said with a smile, hugging her back.

There were murmurs from the watching courtiers and a smattering of applause. Tears overflowed the Queen's eyes. It was the first real emotion I'd ever seen her display.

The King got slowly to his feet, helped by a footman who scurried to his side and guided him down the steps of the dais. He really wasn't well. I was beginning to see that the succession might be an issue sooner than I'd thought.

"Come, Nikolai," said the King, holding his arm out to his son. "Come."

Nikolai offered his elbow to his father while his mother clung to his other arm and, without ever acknowledging us, they made their way out of the throne room. Vasily followed. His face was impassive, though I didn't miss the telltale purse of his lips.

Mal and I stood there, unsure what to do next. It was all very nice that the royal family had disappeared for a private reunion, but where did that leave us? We hadn't been dismissed, and we hadn't been told to stay. The King's advisers studied us with curiosity, while the courtiers tittered and whispered. I resisted the urge to fidget and kept what I hoped was a haughty tilt to my head.

The minutes crawled by. I was hungry and tired and fairly sure one of my feet had fallen asleep, but still we stood waiting. At one point I thought I heard shouting coming from the corridor. Maybe they were arguing about how long to leave us standing there.

Finally, after what must have been the better part of an hour, the royal family returned. The King was beaming. The Queen's face had gone pale. Vasily looked livid. But the most notable change was in Nikolai. He seemed more at ease and he'd regained the swagger I recognised from my time aboard the *Volkvolny*.

They know, I realised. *He's told them that he's Sturmhond.*

The King and Queen reseated themselves on their thrones. Vasily went to stand behind the King, while Nikolai took his place behind the Queen. She reached up, seeking his hand, and he laid it on her shoulder. *That's what a mother looks like with her child.* I was too old to be pining for parents I'd never known, but I was still touched by the gesture.

My sentimental thoughts were driven from my head when the King said, "You're very young to lead the Second Army."

He hadn't even addressed me. I bowed my head in acknowledgment. "Yes, *moi tsar*."

"I am tempted to put you to death immediately, but my son says that will only make you a martyr."

I stiffened. *The Apparat would love that*, I thought as fear coursed through me. *One more cheerful illustration for the red book: Sankta Alina on the Gallows.*

"He thinks you can be trusted," the King quavered. "I'm not so sure. Your escape from the Darkling seems a very unlikely story, though I cannot deny that Ravka does have need of your services."

He made it sound as if I was a groundskeeper or a county clerk. *Penitent*, I reminded myself, and bit back a sarcastic reply.

"It would be my greatest honour to serve the Ravkan King," I said.

Either the King loved flattery or Nikolai had done a remarkable job of pleading my case, because the King grunted and said, "Very well. At least temporarily, you will serve as the commander of the Grisha."

Could it possibly be that easy? "I . . . thank you, *moi tsar*," I stammered in baffled gratitude.

"But know this," he said, wagging a finger at me. "If I find any evidence that you are fomenting action against me or that you have had any contact with the apostate, I will have you hanged without plea or trial." His voice rose to a querulous wail. "The people say you are a Saint, but I think you are just another ragged refugee. Do you understand?"

Another ragged refugee and your best chance of keeping that shiny throne, I thought with a surprising surge of anger, but I swallowed my pride and bowed as deeply as I could manage. Was this how the Darkling had felt? Being forced to bend and scrape before a dissolute fool?

The King gave a vague wave of his blue-veined hand. We were being dismissed. I glanced at Mal.

Nikolai cleared his throat. "Father," he said, "there's the matter of the tracker."

"Hmm?" said the King, glancing up as if he'd been nodding off. "The . . . ? Ah, yes." He trained his rheumy stare on Mal and said in a bored tone, "You have deserted your post and directly disobeyed the orders of a commanding officer. That is a hanging offense."

I drew in a sharp breath. Beside me, Mal went very still. An ugly thought leapt into my head: If Nikolai wanted to get rid of Mal, this was certainly an easy way to do it.

An excited murmur rose from the crowd around the dais. What had I walked us into? I opened my mouth, but before I could say a word, Nikolai spoke.

"*Moi tsar*," he said humbly, "forgive me, but the tracker did aid the Sun Summoner in evading what would have been certain capture by an enemy of the Crown."

"*If* she was ever really in any danger."

"I saw him take up arms against the Darkling myself. He is a trusted friend, and I believe he acted in Ravka's best interest." The King's lower lip jutted out, but Nikolai pressed on. "I would feel better knowing that he is at the Little Palace."

The King frowned. *Probably already thinking of lunch and a nap*, I thought.

"What do you have to say for yourself, boy?" he asked.

"Only that I did what I thought was right," Mal replied evenly.

"My son seems to feel you had good reason."

"I imagine every man thinks his reasons are good," Mal said. "It was still desertion."

Nikolai raised his eyes heavenward, and I had the urge to give Mal a good shake. Couldn't he be a bit less flinty and forthright for once?

The King's frown deepened. We waited.

"Very well," he said at last. "What's one more viper in the nest? You will be dishonourably discharged."

"Dishonourably?" I blurted.

Mal just bowed and said, "Thank you, *moi tsar*."

The King lifted his hand in a lazy wave. "Go," he said petulantly.

I was tempted to stay and make an argument of it, but Nikolai was glaring a warning at me and Mal had already turned to leave. I had to scurry to catch up with him as he marched down the blue-carpeted aisle.

As soon as we left the throne room and the doors closed behind us, I said, "We'll talk to Nikolai. We'll get him to petition the King."

Mal didn't even break his stride. "There's no point," he said. "I knew it would be this way."

He said that, but I saw in the slump of his shoulders that some part of him had still hoped. I wanted to grab hold of his arm, make him stop, tell him I was sorry, that somehow we'd find a way to make things right. Instead, I hurried along beside him, struggling to keep up, keenly aware of the footmen watching us from every doorway.

We retraced our steps through the gleaming hallways of the palace and down the marble staircase. Fedyor and his Grisha were waiting by their horses. They'd cleaned up as best they could, but their brightly coloured *kefta* still seemed a bit bedraggled. Tamar and Tolya stood slightly apart from them, the golden sunbursts I'd given them sparkling on their roughspun tunics. I took a deep breath. Nikolai had done what he could. Now it was my turn.

CHAPTER 13

The winding white gravel path led us through the palace grounds, past the rolling lawns and follies, and the high walls of the hedge maze. Tolya, ordinarily so still and silent, squirmed in his saddle, his mouth set in a sullen line.

"Something wrong?" I asked.

I thought he might not answer, but then he said, "It smells like weakness here. Like people getting soft."

I shot a glance at the giant warrior. "Everyone is soft compared to you, Tolya."

Tamar could usually be counted upon to laugh off her brother's moods, but she surprised me by saying, "He's right. This place feels like it's dying."

They weren't helping to settle my nerves. Our audience in the throne room had left me jittery, and I was still a little taken aback by the anger I'd felt towards the King, though Saints knew he deserved it. He was a filthy old lech who liked to corner servant girls, to say nothing of the fact that he was a rotten leader and had threatened to execute both me and Mal in the space of a few minutes. Even thinking about it, I felt another jab of bitter resentment.

My heart beat faster as we entered the wooded tunnel. The trees pressed in on us and, above, the branches wove together in a canopy of green. The last time I'd seen them, they'd been bare.

We emerged into bright sunshine. Below us lay the Little Palace.

I missed it, I realised. I'd missed the shine of its golden domes, those strange walls carved with every manner of beast, real and imagined. I'd missed the blue lake gleaming like a slice of sky, the tiny island not quite at its centre, the white flecks of the Summoners' pavilions on its shore. It was a place like no other. I was surprised to discover how much it felt like home.

Not everything was as it had been. First Army soldiers were stationed around the grounds, rifles on their backs. I doubted they'd do much good against a force of determined Heartrenders, Squallers and Inferni, but the message was clear: the Grisha were not to be trusted.

A group of servants dressed in grey waited on the steps to take our horses.

"Ready?" Mal whispered as he helped me dismount.

"I wish people would stop asking me that. Don't I look ready?"

"You look like you did when I slipped a tadpole into your soup and you accidentally swallowed it."

I bit back a laugh, feeling some of my worry ease away. "Thanks for the reminder," I said. "I don't think I ever paid you back for that."

I paused to smoothe the folds of my *kefta*, taking my time in the hope that my legs would stop trembling. Then I climbed the steps, the others trailing behind me. The servants flung the doors open wide, and we stepped inside. We passed through the cool dark of the entry chamber and into the Hall of the Golden Dome.

The room was a giant hexagon with the proportions of a cathedral. Its carved walls were inlaid with mother-of-pearl and topped by a massive golden dome that seemed to float above us at an impossible height. There were four tables arranged in a square in the middle of the room, and that was where the Grisha waited. Despite their diminished numbers, they still kept to their Orders, sitting or standing in tightly clustered groups of red, purple and blue.

"They do love their pretty colours," grumbled Tolya.

"Don't give me any ideas," I whispered. "Maybe I'll decide my personal guard should wear bright yellow pantaloons."

For the first time, I saw an expression very much like fear cross his face.

We walked forward, and most of the Grisha rose. It was a young group, and with a twinge of unease, I realised that many of the older and more experienced Grisha had chosen to defect to the Darkling. Or maybe they'd just been wise enough to run.

I had anticipated that not many Corporalki would remain. They'd been the highest-ranking Grisha, the most valued fighters, and closest to the Darkling.

There were still several familiar faces. Sergei was one of the few Heartrenders who had decided to stay. Marie and Nadia stood with the Etherealki. I was surprised to see David slouching in his seat at the Materialki table. I knew he'd had qualms about the Darkling, but that hadn't stopped him from sealing the stag's collar around my neck. Maybe that was why he wouldn't look at me. Or maybe he was just eager to get back to his workshop.

The Darkling's ebony chair had been removed. His table sat vacant.

Sergei was the first to step forward. "Alina Starkov," he said tightly. "I'm pleased to welcome you back to the Little Palace." I noted that he didn't bow.

Tension swelled and pulsed in the room like a living thing. Part of me longed to shatter it. It would be easy. I could smile, laugh, embrace Marie and Nadia. Though I'd never quite belonged here, I'd made a decent show of it. It would be a relief to pretend that I was one of them again. But I remembered Nikolai's warnings and restrained myself. *Weakness is a guise.*

"Thank you, Sergei," I said, deliberately informal. "I'm glad to be here."

"There have been rumours of your return," he said. "And just as many of your death."

"As you can see, I'm alive and as well as can be expected after weeks of travel on the Vy."

"It's said you arrived in the company of the King's second son," said Sergei.

There it was. The first challenge.

"That's right," I said pleasantly. "He aided in my battle with the Darkling."

A stir went through the room.

"On the Fold?" Sergei asked in some confusion.

"On the True Sea," I corrected. A murmur rose from the crowd. I held up my hand and, to my relief, they fell silent. *Get them to follow the little orders, and they'll follow the big ones.* "I have plenty of stories to tell and information to impart," I said. "But that can wait. I've returned to Os Alta with a purpose."

"People are talking of a wedding," said Sergei.

Well, Nikolai would be thrilled.

"I didn't come back here to be a bride," I said. "I've

returned for a single reason." That wasn't entirely true, but I wasn't about to discuss the third amplifier in a room packed with Grisha of dubious loyalty. I took a breath. This was it. "I've returned to lead the Second Army."

Everyone began talking at once. There were a few cheers, some angry shouts. I saw Sergei exchange a glance with Marie. When the room quieted he said, "We expected as much."

"The King has agreed that I will hold command." *Temporarily*, I thought, but did not say.

Another wave of shouts and chatter broke out.

Sergei cleared his throat, "Alina, you are the Sun Summoner, and we're grateful for your safe return, but you aren't qualified to run a military campaign."

"Qualified or not, I have the King's blessing."

"Then we will petition the King. The Corporalki are the highest-ranking Grisha and should lead the Second Army."

"According to you, bloodletter."

As soon as I heard that silky voice, I knew who it belonged to, but my heart still lurched when I caught sight of her raven's wing hair. Zoya stepped through the crowd of Etherealki, her lithe form swathed in blue summer silk that made her eyes glow like gems – disgustingly long-lashed gems.

It took everything in me not to turn round and watch Mal's reaction. Zoya was the Grisha who had done all she could to make my life miserable at the Little Palace. She'd sneered at me, gossiped about me, and even broken two of my ribs. She was also the girl who had caught Mal's interest so long ago in Kribirsk. I wasn't sure what had happened between them, but I doubted it was just lively conversation.

"I speak for the Etherealki," said Zoya. "And we will follow the Sun Summoner."

I struggled not to show my surprise. She was the last person I'd expected to support me. What game might she be playing?

"Not all of us," Marie piped up weakly. I knew I shouldn't be surprised, but it still hurt.

Zoya gave a disdainful laugh. "Yes, we know you support Sergei in all his endeavours, Marie. But this isn't a late-night tryst by the *banya*. We're talking about the future of the Grisha and all of Ravka."

Snickers greeted Zoya's pronouncement, and Marie turned bright red.

"That's enough, Zoya," snapped Sergei.

An Etherealnik I didn't recognise stepped forward. He had dark skin and a faint scar high on his left cheek. He wore the embroidery of an Inferni.

"Marie is right," he said. "You don't speak for all of us, Zoya. I'd prefer to see an Etherealnik at the head of the Second Army, but it shouldn't be her." He pointed an accusatory finger at me. "She wasn't even raised here."

"That's right!" called out a Corporalnik. "She's been a Grisha less than a year!"

"Grisha are born, not made," growled Tolya.

Of course, I thought with an internal sigh. *He would choose now to come out of his shell.*

"And who are you?" asked Sergei, his natural arrogance emerging.

Tolya's hand went to his curved sword. "I am Tolya Yul-Baatar. I was raised far from this corpse of a palace, and I'd be happy to prove that I can stop your heart."

"You're Grisha?" Sergei asked incredulously.

"As much as you are," replied Tamar, her gold eyes flashing.

"And what about you?" Sergei asked Mal.

"I'm just a soldier," Mal replied, moving to stand beside me. "Her soldier."

"As are we all," added Fedyor. "We returned to Os Alta to serve the Sun Summoner, not some posturing boy."

Another Corporalnik got to his feet. "You're just one more coward who fled when the Darkling fell. You have no right to come here and insult us."

"And what about her?" cried another Squaller. "How do we know she isn't working with the Darkling? She helped him destroy Novokribirsk."

"And she shared his bed!" shouted another.

Never deign to deny, said Nikolai's voice in my head.

"Just what is your relationship with Nikolai Lantsov?" demanded a Fabrikator.

"What was your relationship with the Darkling?" came a shrill voice.

"Does it matter?" I asked coolly, but I could feel my control slipping.

"Of course it does," said Sergei. "How can we be sure of your loyalty?"

"You have no right to question her!" shouted one of the Summoners.

"Why?" retorted a Healer. "Because she's a living Saint?"

"Put her in a chapel where she belongs!" someone yelled. "Get her and her rabble out of the Little Palace."

Tolya reached for his sword. Tamar and Sergei both raised their hands. I saw Marie draw her flint and felt the swirl of Summoner winds lift the edges of my *kefta*. I thought I'd been ready to face them, but I wasn't prepared for the flood of rage that coursed through me. The wound in my shoulder throbbed, and something inside me broke free.

I looked at Sergei's sneering face, and my power rose up with clear and vicious purpose. I raised my arm. If they needed a lesson, I would give it to them. They could argue over the pieces of Sergei's body. My hand arced through the air, slicing towards him. The light was a blade honed sharp by my fury.

At the last second, some sliver of sanity pierced the buzzing haze of my anger. *No*, I thought in terror as I realised what I was about to do. My panicked mind reeled. I swerved and threw the Cut high.

A resounding *crack* shook the room. The Grisha screamed and backed away, crowding against the walls.

Daylight poured in through a jagged fissure above us. I'd split the Golden Dome open like a giant egg.

A deep silence followed as every Grisha turned to me in terrified disbelief. I swallowed, astonished by what I'd done, horrified by what I'd almost done. I thought of Nikolai's advice and hardened my heart. They mustn't see my fear.

"You think the Darkling is powerful?" I asked, startled by the icy clarity of my voice. "You have no idea what he is capable of. Only I have seen what he can do. Only I have faced him and lived to tell about it."

I sounded like a stranger to my own ears, but I felt the echo of my power vibrating through me and I pushed on. I turned slowly, meeting each stunned gaze.

"I don't care if you think I'm a Saint or a fool or the Darkling's whore. If you want to remain at the Little Palace, you will follow me. And if you don't like it, you will be gone by tonight, or I will have you in chains. I am a soldier. I am the Sun Summoner. And I'm the only chance you have."

I strode across the room and threw open the doors to the Darkling's chambers, giving silent thanks that they weren't locked.

I walked blindly down the hall, unsure of where I was going, but eager to get far from the domed hall before anyone saw that I was shaking.

By luck, I found my way to the war room. Mal entered behind me, and before he shut the door, I saw Tolya and Tamar taking up their posts. Fedyor and the others must have remained behind. Hopefully, they'd make their own peace with the rest of the Grisha. Or maybe they'd all just kill each other.

I paced back and forth in front of the ancient map of Ravka that ran the length of the far wall.

Mal cleared his throat. "I thought that went well."

A hysterical hiccup of laughter escaped my lips.

"Unless you intended to bring the whole ceiling down on our heads," he said. "Then I guess it was only a partial success."

I nibbled my thumb and continued pacing. "I had to get their attention."

"So you meant to do that?"

I almost killed someone. I wanted to kill someone. It was the dome or Sergei, and Sergei would have been a lot tougher to patch up.

"Not exactly," I admitted.

Suddenly, all the energy went out of me. I collapsed into a chair by the long table and rested my head in my hands. "They're all going to leave," I moaned.

"Maybe," Mal said, "but I doubt it."

I buried my face in my arms. "Who am I kidding? I can't do this. This is like some kind of bad joke."

"I didn't hear anyone laughing," Mal said. "For someone who has no idea what she's doing, I'd say you're managing pretty well."

I peered up at him. He was leaning against the table, arms crossed, the ghost of a smile playing over his lips.

"Mal, I put a *hole in the ceiling*."

"A very dramatic hole."

I let out a huff somewhere between a laugh and a sob. "What are we going to do when it rains?"

"What we always do," he said. "Keep dry."

A knock came at the door, and Tamar poked her head in. "One of the servants wants to know if you'll be sleeping in the Darkling's chambers."

I knew I would have to. I just wasn't looking forward to it. I rubbed my hands over my face and heaved myself out of the chair. Less than an hour at the Little Palace, and I was already exhausted. "Let's go and take a look."

The Darkling's quarters were just down the hall from the war room. A charcoal-clad servant led us into a large and rather formal common room furnished with a long table and a few uncomfortable-looking chairs. Each wall was set with a pair of double doors.

"These lead to a passage that will take you out of the Little Palace, *moi soverenyi*," the servant said, gesturing to the right. She pointed to the doors on the left and said, "Those lead to the guards' quarters."

The doors directly across from us needed no explanation. They stretched from floor to ceiling, and their ebony wood was carved with the Darkling's symbol, the sun in eclipse.

I didn't feel quite ready to face that, so I ambled over to the guards' quarters and peeked inside. Their common room was considerably cosier. It had a round table for playing cards, and several overstuffed chairs were set around a small tile oven for keeping warm in the winter. Through another door, I glimpsed rows of bunk beds.

"I guess the Darkling had more guards," said Tamar.

"Lots more," I replied.

"We could bring on some others."

"I thought about it," said Mal. "I don't know that it's necessary, and I'm not sure who we can trust."

I had to agree. I'd put a certain amount of faith in Tolya and Tamar, but the only person I really felt sure of was Mal.

"Maybe we should consider drawing from the pilgrims," suggested Tamar. "Some of them are former military. There must be a few good fighters among them, and they'd certainly lay down their lives for you."

"Not a chance," I replied. "The King would hear one whispered 'Sankta Alina' and have my neck in a noose. Besides, I'm not sure I want to put my life in the hands of someone who thinks I can rise from the dead."

"We'll make do," said Mal.

I nodded. "All right. And . . . can someone see about having the roof fixed?"

Matching grins broke out on Tolya's and Tamar's faces. "Can't we leave it that way for just a few days?"

"No," I laughed. "I don't want the whole thing caving in on us. Talk to the Fabrikators. They should know what to do." I ran my thumb over the raised ridge of flesh that ran the length of my palm. "But don't let them make it too perfect," I added. Scars made good reminders.

I returned to the main common room and addressed the servant hovering in the doorway. "We'll eat here tonight," I said. "Will you see about trays?"

The servant raised her brows, then bowed and scurried off. I winced. I was supposed to issue commands, not ask questions.

I left Mal and the twins discussing a schedule for the watch, and crossed to the ebony doors. The handles were two thin slivers of crescent moon made of what looked like bone. When I took hold of them and pulled, there was no creak or scrape of hinges. The doors slid open without a sound.

A servant had lit the lamps in the Darkling's chamber. I surveyed the room and let out a long breath. What had I been expecting? A dungeon? A pit? That the Darkling slept suspended from the branches of a tree?

The chamber was hexagonal, its dark wood walls carved into the illusion of a forest crowded with slender trees. Above the huge canopied bed, the domed ceiling was wrought in smooth black obsidian and spangled with chips of mother-of-pearl laid out in constellations. It was an unusual room and certainly luxurious, but it was still just a bedroom.

The shelves were empty of books. The desk and dressing table were bare. All his possessions must have been taken away, probably burned or smashed to bits. I supposed I should have been glad the King hadn't torn the entire Little Palace down.

I walked to the side of the bed and smoothed my hand over the cool fabric of the pillow. It was good to know that some part of him was still human, that he laid his head down to rest at night like everyone else. But could I really sleep in his bed, beneath his roof?

With a start, I realised that the room smelled like him. I had never even noticed that he had a scent. I shut my eyes and breathed deeply. What was it? The crisp edge of a winter wind. Bare branches. The smell of absence, the smell of night.

The wound at my shoulder prickled, and I opened my eyes. The doors to the chamber were shut. I hadn't heard them close.

"Alina."

I whirled. The Darkling was standing on the other side of the bed.

I clapped my hands over my mouth to stop my scream.

This isn't real, I told myself. *It's just another hallucination. Just like on the Fold.*

"My Alina," he said softly. His face was beautiful, unscarred. Perfect.

I will not scream, because this isn't real, and when they come running, there will be nothing to see.

He walked slowly round the bed. His footsteps made no sound.

I closed my eyes, pressed my palms against them, counted to three. But when I opened them again, he was standing right before me. *I will not scream.*

I took a step backwards, felt the press of the wall behind me. A choked sound squeaked free of my throat.

I will not scream.

He reached out. *He can't touch me*, I told myself. *His hand will just pass through me like a ghost. It's not real.*

"You cannot run from me," he whispered.

His fingers brushed my cheek. Solid. Real. I *felt* them.

Terror shot through me. I threw up my hands, and light blazed over the room in a brilliant wave that shimmered with heat. The Darkling vanished.

Footsteps clattered in the room outside. The doors were thrown open. Mal and the twins charged in, weapons in hand.

"What happened?" Tamar asked, scanning the empty room.

"Nothing," I said, forcing the word past my lips, hoping my voice sounded normal. I buried my hands in the folds of my *kefta* to hide their trembling. "Why?"

"We saw the light and—"

"Just a bit gloomy in here," I said. "All the black."

They stared at me for a long moment. Then Tamar looked around. "It is pretty grim. You may want to think about redecorating."

"Definitely on my list."

The twins took another glance around the room and then headed out the door, Tolya already grumbling to his sister about dinner. Mal stood in the doorway, waiting.

"You're shaking," he said.

I knew he wouldn't ask me to explain this time. He shouldn't have had to. I should have offered him the truth without having to be asked. But what could I say? That I was seeing things? That I was mad? That we would never be safe, no matter how far we ran? That I was as broken as the Golden Dome, but something far worse than daylight had crept inside of me?

I stayed silent.

Mal gave a single shake of his head, then simply walked away.

I stood alone in the Darkling's empty rooms.

Call to him, I thought desperately. *Tell him something. Tell him everything.*

Mal was just a few feet away, on the other side of that wall. I could say his name, bring him back, and tell it all – what had happened on the Fold, what I'd almost done to Sergei, what I'd seen just moments before. I opened my mouth, but the same words came to me again and again.

I will not scream. I will not scream. I will not scream.

CHAPTER 14

I woke the next day to the sound of angry voices. For a moment, I had no idea where I was. The darkness was near perfect, broken only by a thin crack of light from beneath the door.

Then reality returned. I sat up and fumbled for the lamp on the bedside wall. I turned up the flame and surveyed the dark silk bed hangings, the slate floor, the carved ebony walls. I really was going to have to make some changes. This room was just too depressing. It was strange to think that I was actually in the Darkling's chambers, that I'd spent the night in his bed. That I'd seen him standing in this very room.

Enough of that. I threw off the covers and swung my legs over the side of the bed. I didn't know whether the visions were a product of my imagination or some real attempt by the Darkling to manipulate me, but there had to be a rational explanation for them. Maybe the *nichevo'ya* bite had infected me with something. If that was the case, I'd just have to find a way to cure it. Or maybe the effects would wear off with time.

The argument outside my door grew louder. I thought I recognised Sergei's voice and Tolya's angry rumble. I threw on the embroidered dressing gown that had been left for me at the foot of the bed, checked to make sure the fetter on my wrist was hidden, and hurried out to the common room.

I almost ran straight into the twins. Tolya and Tamar were standing shoulder to shoulder, blocking a group of angry Grisha from entering my chamber. Tolya's arms were crossed, and Tamar was shaking her head as Sergei and Fedyor loudly made their case. I was distressed to see Zoya beside them, accompanied by the dark-skinned Inferni who had challenged me the previous day. Everyone seemed to be talking at once.

"What's going on?" I asked.

As soon as Sergei saw me, he strode forward, clutching a piece of paper in his hand. Tamar moved to block him, but I waved her off.

"It's all right," I said. "What's the problem?" But I thought I already knew. I recognised my own writing and the remnants of the gold sunburst seal that Nikolai had provided for me on the paper Sergei was now shaking in my face.

"This is unacceptable," Sergei huffed.

I'd sent out word the previous night that I would be convening a war council. Each Grisha Order was to elect two representatives to attend. I was pleased to see they'd chosen Fedyor as well as Sergei, though some of my good will wore off when the older Grisha chimed in.

"He's right," said Fedyor. "The Corporalki are the Grisha's first line of defense. We're the most experienced in military affairs and should be more fairly represented."

"We're just as valuable to the war effort," declared Zoya, her colour high. Even in a snit, she looked gorgeous. Though I'd suspected she would be chosen to represent the Etherealki, I certainly wasn't happy about it. "If there are going to be three Corporalki on the council," she said, "then there should be three Summoners, too."

Everyone started shouting again. I noted that the Materialki hadn't shown up to complain. As the lowest Grisha Order, they were probably just glad to be included, or possibly they were too caught up in their work to be bothered.

I still wasn't quite awake. I wanted my breakfast, not an argument. But I knew this had to be addressed. I intended to do things differently – and they might as well know just how differently or this effort would fall apart before it even began.

I held up my hand and they quieted instantly. Clearly, I had that trick down. Maybe they were afraid I was going to ruin another ceiling. "There will be two Grisha from each Order," I said. "No more, no less."

"But—" began Sergei.

"The Darkling has changed. If we have any hope of beating him, we need to change too. Two Grisha from each Order," I repeated. "And the Orders will no longer sit separately. You'll sit together, eat together, and fight together."

At least I'd got them to shut up. They just stood there, gaping.

"And the Fabrikators start combat training this week," I finished.

I took in their horrified expressions. They looked as if I'd told them we'd all be marching into battle naked. The Materialki weren't considered warriors, so no one had ever bothered to teach them to fight. It felt like a missed opportunity to me. *Use whatever or whoever is in front of you.*

"I can see you're all thrilled," I said with a small sigh.

Desperate for a glass of tea, I walked to the table where a breakfast tray had been laid with covered dishes. I lifted one of the lids: rye and herring. This morning was not getting off to a good start.

"But . . . but it's *always* been this way," sputtered Sergei.

"You can't just overturn hundreds of years of tradition," protested the Inferni.

"Are we really going to argue about this, too?" I asked irritably. "We're at war with an ancient power beyond reckoning, and you want to squabble over who sits next to you at lunch?"

"That's not the point," said Zoya. "There's an order to things, a way of doing them that—"

They all started gabbling again – about tradition, about the way things were done, about the need for structure and people knowing their places.

I set the cover back down on the dish with a loud *clang*.

"This is the way we're doing it," I said, rapidly losing patience. "No more Corporalki snobbery. No more Etherealki cliques. And no more herring."

Zoya opened her mouth, then thought better of it and shut it again.

"Now go," I barked. "I want to eat my breakfast in peace."

For a moment, they just stood there. Then Tamar and Tolya stepped forward, and to my continuing amazement, the Grisha did as they were told. Zoya looked peeved and Sergei's face was stormy, but they all shuffled meekly out of the room.

Seconds after they left, Nikolai appeared in the doorway, and I realised he'd been eavesdropping in the hall.

"Nicely done," he said. "Today shall be forever remembered as the date of the Great Herring Decree." He stepped inside and closed the door behind him. "Not the smoothest delivery though."

"I don't have your gift for 'amused and aloof', " I said, sitting down at the table and tearing eagerly into a roll. "But 'grouchy' seems to be working for me."

A servant rushed forward to bring me a cup of tea from the samovar. It was blissfully hot, and I loaded it with sugar. Nikolai took a chair and sat without being asked.

"You're really not going to eat these?" he said, already piling herring onto his plate.

"Revolting," I said succinctly.

Nikolai took a big bite. "You don't survive at sea if you can't stomach fish."

"Don't play the poor sailor with me. I ate on your ship, remember? Sturmhond's chef was hardly serving up salt cod and hardtack."

He gave a mournful sigh. "I wish I could have brought Burgos with me. The court kitchens seem to feel that a meal isn't complete if it isn't swimming in butter."

"Only a prince would complain about too much butter."

"Hmm," he said thoughtfully, patting his flat stomach. "Maybe a royal gut would lend me more authority."

I laughed and then nearly jumped as the door opened and Mal entered. He stopped when he saw Nikolai.

"I didn't realise you'd be dining at the Little Palace, *moi tsarevich*." He bowed stiffly to Nikolai and then to me.

"You don't have to do that," I said.

"Yes he does."

"You heard Prince Perfect," Mal said, and joined us at the table.

Nikolai grinned. "I've had a lot of nicknames, but that one is easily the most accurate."

"I didn't know you were awake," I said to Mal.

"I've been up for hours, roaming around, looking for something to do."

"Excellent," said Nikolai. "I've come to issue an invitation."

"Is it to a ball?" asked Mal, snagging the remaining bit of roll from my plate. "I do so hope it's to a ball."

"While I'm sure you dance a magnificent waltz, no. Boar have been spotted in the woods near Balakirev. There's a hunt leaving tomorrow, and I'd like you to go."

"Short on friends, Your Highness?"

"And long on enemies," replied Nikolai. "But I won't be there. My parents aren't quite ready to let me out of their sight. I've spoken to one of the generals, and he's agreed to have you as his guest."

Mal leaned back and crossed his arms. "I see. So I go gallivanting off to the woods for a few days and you stay here," he said with a meaningful glance at me.

I shifted in my chair. I didn't like the implication, but I did have to admit it seemed like an obvious ploy. Too obvious for Nikolai, really.

"You know, for two people with a love eternal, you're awfully insecure," Nikolai said. "Some of the highest-ranking members of the First Army will be in the hunting party, and so will my brother. He's an avid hunter, and I've seen for myself that you're the best tracker in Ravka."

"I thought I was supposed to be guarding Alina," Mal said. "Not running around with a bunch of pampered royals."

"Tolya and Tamar can manage while you're away. And this is a chance for you to make yourself useful."

Great, I thought as I watched Mal's eyes narrow. *Just perfect.*

"And what are you doing to be *useful*, Your Highness?"

"I'm a prince," said Nikolai. "Being useful isn't part of the job description. But," he added, "when I'm not lazing about being handsome, I'll be trying to better equip the First Army and gather intelligence on the Darkling's location. Word has it he's entered the Sikurzoi."

Mal and I both perked up at that. The Sikurzoi were the mountains that ran along much of the border between Ravka and the Shu Han.

"You think he's in the south?" I asked.

Nikolai popped another piece of herring into his mouth. "It's possible," he said. "I would have thought he'd be more likely to ally with the Fjerdans. The northern border is far more vulnerable. But the Sikurzoi are a good place to hide. If the reports are true, we need to move to forge an alliance with the Shu as fast as possible so that we can march on him from two fronts."

"You want to take the war to him?" I said, surprised.

"Better than waiting for him to be strong enough to bring it to us."

"I like it," Mal said with grudging admiration. "It's not something the Darkling would expect."

I was reminded that, while Mal and Nikolai had their differences, Mal and Sturmhond had been on the way to becoming friends.

Nikolai took a sip of tea and said, "There's also disturbing news coming out of the First Army. It seems a number of soldiers have found religion and deserted."

I frowned. "You don't mean—"

Nikolai nodded. "They're taking refuge in the monasteries, joining the Apparat's cult of the Sun Saint. The priest is claiming you've been taken prisoner by the corrupt monarchy."

"That's ridiculous," I said.

"Actually, it's completely plausible, and it makes for a very satisfying story. Needless to say, my father is not pleased. He flew into quite a rage last night, and he's doubled the price on the Apparat's head."

I groaned. "This is bad."

"It is," Nikolai admitted. "You can see why it might be wise for the captain of your personal guard to start forging alliances within the Grand Palace." He turned his keen gaze on Mal. "And that, Oretsev, is how you can be of use. As I recall, you rather charmed my crew, so perhaps you could pick up your bow and play the diplomat instead of the jealous lover."

"I'll think about it."

"Good boy," said Nikolai.

Oh, for Saints' sake. He just couldn't leave well enough alone, could he?

"Watch yourself, Nikolai," Mal said softly. "Princes bleed just like other men."

Nikolai plucked an invisible piece of dust from his sleeve. "Yes," he said. "They just do it in better clothes."

"Mal—"

Mal stood, his chair scraping the floor. "I need some air."

He strode out the door, all pretense of bowing and titles forgotten.

I threw down my napkin. "Why do you do that?" I

asked Nikolai angrily. "Why do you provoke him that way?"

"Did I?" Nikolai said, reaching for another roll. I thought about sticking a fork through his hand.

"Don't keep pushing him, Nikolai. Lose Mal and you'll lose me, too."

"He needs to learn what the rules are here. If he can't, then he becomes a liability. The stakes are too high for half measures."

I shivered and rubbed my hands over my arms. "I hate it when you talk like that. You sound just like the Darkling."

"If you ever have trouble telling us apart, look for the person who isn't torturing you or trying to kill Mal. That will be me."

"Are you so sure you wouldn't?" I shot back. "If it got you closer to what you want, to the throne and your big chance to save Ravka, are you sure you wouldn't walk me up the gallows steps yourself?"

I expected another of Nikolai's flip replies, but he looked like I'd punched him in the gut. He started to speak, stopped, then shook his head.

"Saints," he said, his tone somewhere between bewilderment and disgust. "I really don't know."

I slumped back in my chair. His admission should have made me furious, but instead I felt the anger drain out of me. Maybe it was his honesty. Or maybe it was because I'd begun to worry what I might be capable of myself.

We sat there in silence for a long minute. He rubbed his hand over the back of his neck and slowly got to his feet. At the doorway, he paused.

"I'm ambitious, Alina. I'm driven. But I hope . . . I hope

I still know the difference between right and wrong."
He hesitated. "I offered you freedom and I meant it. If
tomorrow you decided to run back to Novyi Zem with
Mal, I'd put you on a ship and let the sea take you." He
held my gaze, his hazel eyes steady. "But I'd be sorry to
see you go."

He vanished into the hall, his footsteps echoing over
the stone floors.

I sat there for a while, picking at my breakfast, mulling
over Nikolai's parting words. Then I gave myself a little
shake. I didn't have time to dissect his motives. In just a
few hours, the war council would meet to talk strategy
and how best to raise a defence against the Darkling. I
had plenty to do to prepare, but first I had a visit to pay.

As I fastened the sun-shaped buttons of my gold and blue
kefta, I gave a rueful shake of my head. Baghra would
waste no time mocking my new pretensions. I combed
my hair, then slipped out of the Little Palace through
the Darkling's entrance, and crossed the grounds to the
lake.

The servant I'd spoken to said that Baghra had taken
ill shortly after the winter fete and that, since then, she'd
stopped accepting students. Of course, I knew the truth.
The night of the party, Baghra had revealed the Darkling's
plans and helped me flee the Little Palace. Then she'd
sought to buy me time by concealing my absence. The
thought of his rage when he'd discovered her deception
sat like a stone in my stomach.

When I'd tried to press the jittery maid for details,

she'd bobbed a clumsy curtsey and gone scurrying from the room. Still, Baghra was alive, and she was here. The Darkling could destroy an entire town, but it seemed even he drew the line at murdering his own mother.

The path to Baghra's hut was overgrown with brambles, the summer wood tangled and pungent with the smell of leaves and damp earth. I hastened my steps, surprised at how eager I was to see her. She'd been a hard teacher and an unpleasant woman on her best days, but she'd tried to help me when no one else had, and I knew she was my best chance of solving the riddle of Morozova's third amplifier.

I climbed the three steps at the front of the hut and knocked. No one answered. I knocked again and then pushed the door open, wincing at the familiar blast of heat. Baghra always seemed to be cold, and entering her hut was like being stuffed into a cookstove.

The dark little room was just as I remembered it: sparsely furnished with only the barest necessities, a fire roaring in the tile oven, and Baghra huddled by it in her faded *kefta*. I was surprised to see that she wasn't alone. A servant sat beside her, a young boy dressed in grey. He got to his feet as I entered, peering at me through the gloom.

"No visitors," he said.

"By whose command?"

At the sound of my voice, Baghra looked up sharply.

She smacked her stick on the ground. "Leave, boy," she commanded.

"But—"

"Go!" she snarled.

Just as pleasant as ever, I thought warily.

The boy scurried across the room and out of the hut without another word.

The door had barely shut when Baghra said, "I wondered when you'd make your way back here, little Saint."

Trust Baghra to call me the one name I didn't want to hear.

I was already sweating and had no desire to step closer to the fire, but I did it anyway, and crossed the room to sit in the chair the servant had vacated.

She turned to the flames as I approached, showing me her back. She was in rare form today. I ignored the insult.

I sat silent for a moment, unsure of where to begin. "I was told you'd taken ill after I left."

"Hmph."

I didn't want to know, but I made myself ask. "What did he do to you?"

She gave a dry laugh. "Less than he might have. More than he should."

"Baghra—"

"You were meant to go to Novyi Zem. You were meant to disappear."

"I tried."

"No, you went hunting," she sneered with a smack of her stick on the ground. "And what did you find? A pretty necklace to wear for the rest of your life? Come closer," she said. "I want to know what I bought for my trouble."

Obligingly, I leaned in. When she turned to me, I gasped.

Baghra had aged a lifetime since I'd seen her last. Her black hair was sparse and greying. Her sharp features had blurred. The taut slash of her mouth looked sunken and soft.

But that was not why I recoiled. Baghra's eyes were gone. Where they should have been were two black pits, shadows writhing in their fathomless depths.

"Baghra," I choked out. I reached for her hand, but she flinched away from my touch.

"Spare me your pity, girl."

"What . . . what did he do to you?" My voice was little more than a whisper.

She gave another harsh laugh. "He left me in the dark."

Her voice was strong, but sitting by the fire, I realised it was the only part of her that had remained unchanged. She'd been lean and hard, with the knife-sharp posture of an acrobat. Now, there was a slight tremor in her ancient hands, and her formerly wiry body just looked gaunt and frail.

"Show me," she said, reaching out. I held still and let her run her hands over my face. The gnarled fingers moved like two white spiders, passing over my tears without interest, crawling down my jaw to the base of my throat, where they came to rest on the collar.

"Ah," she breathed, her fingertips tracing the rough pieces of antler at my neck, her voice soft, almost wistful. "I would have liked to see his stag."

I wanted to turn my head, to look away from the teeming black pools of her eyes. Instead, I pushed up my sleeve and grasped one of her hands. She tried to pull away, but I tightened my grip and laid her fingers over the fetter at my wrist. She went still.

"No," she said. "It cannot be."

She felt along the ridges of the sea whip's scales.

"*Rusalye*," she whispered. "What have you done, girl?"

Her words gave me hope. "You know about the other amplifiers."

I winced as her fingers dug into my wrist. "Is it true?" she asked abruptly. "What they say he can do, that he can give life to shadow?"

"Yes," I admitted.

Her hunched shoulders sagged even further. Then she cast my arm away as if it were something filthy. "Get out."

"Baghra, I need your help."

"I said, *get out.*"

"Please. I need to know where to find the firebird."

Her sunken mouth trembled slightly. "I betrayed my son once, little Saint. What makes you think I would do it again?"

"You wanted to stop him," I said hesitantly. "You—"

Baghra pounded the floor with her stick. "I wanted to keep him from becoming a monster! It's too late for that now, isn't it? Thanks to you, he is further from human than he's ever been. He's long past any redemption."

"Maybe," I admitted. "But Ravka isn't beyond saving."

"What do I care what happens to this wretched country? Is the world so very fine that you think it worth saving?"

"Yes," I said. "And I know you do too."

"You couldn't make a meat pie from what you know, girl."

"Fine!" I said, my desperation overwhelming my guilt. "I'm an idiot. I'm a fool. I'm hopeless. That's why I need your help."

"You cannot be helped. Your only hope was to run."

"Tell me what you know about Morozova," I begged. "Help me find the third amplifier."

"I couldn't begin to guess where to find the firebird, and I wouldn't tell you if I could. All I want now is a warm room and to be left alone to die."

"I could take away this room," I said angrily. "Your fire, your obedient servant. You might feel more like talking then."

The second the words were out of my mouth, I wanted to take them back. A wave of shame washed over me. Had I really just threatened a blind old woman?

Baghra laughed that rattling, vicious chuckle. "You're taking to power well, I see. As it grows, it will hunger for more. Like calls to like, girl."

Her words sent a spike of fear through me.

"I didn't mean it," I said weakly.

"You cannot violate the rules of this world without a price. Those amplifiers were never meant to be. No Grisha should have such power. Already you are changing. Seek the third, use it, and you will lose yourself completely, piece by piece. You want my help? You want to know what to do? Forget the firebird. Forget Morozova and his madness."

I shook my head. "I can't do that. I won't."

She turned back to the fire. "Then do what you like, girl. I'm done with this life, and I'm done with you."

What had I expected? That she would greet me as a daughter? Welcome me as a friend? She'd lost her son's love and sacrificed her sight, and in the end, I'd failed her. I wanted to dig in my heels and demand her help. I wanted to threaten her, cajole her, fall to my knees and beg forgiveness for everything she'd lost and every mistake I'd made. Instead, I did what she'd wanted me to do all along. I turned and ran.

I nearly lost my footing on the stairs as I stumbled from the hut, but the servant boy was waiting at the bottom of the steps. He reached out to steady me before I could fall.

I took grateful gulps of fresh air, feeling the sweat cool on my skin.

"Is it true?" he asked. "Are you really the Sun Summoner?"

I glanced at his hopeful face and felt the ache of tears in my throat. I nodded and tried to smile.

"My mother says you're a Saint."

What other fairy tales does she believe? I thought bitterly.

Before I could embarrass myself by breaking down in tears on his scrawny shoulder, I pushed past him and hurried down the narrow path.

When I reached the lakeshore, I made my way to one of the white stone Summoners' pavilions. They weren't really buildings, just domed shells where young Summoners could practise using their gifts without fear of blowing the roof off the school or setting fire to the Little Palace. I sat down in the shade of the pavilion's steps and buried my head in my hands, willing my tears away, trying to catch my breath. I'd been so sure that Baghra would know something about the firebird and so positive that she'd be willing to help. I hadn't realised just how much hope I'd invested in her until it was gone.

I smoothed the glittering folds of my *kefta* over my lap and had to choke back a sob. I'd thought Baghra would laugh at me, mock the little Saint all dressed up in her finery. Why had I ever believed the Darkling might show his mother mercy?

And why had I acted that way? How could I have

threatened to take away her few comforts? The ugliness of it made me feel ill. I could blame my desperation, but it didn't ease my shame. Or change the reality that some part of me wanted to march back to her hut and make good on those threats, haul her out into the sunlight and wrest answers from her sour, sunken mouth. What was wrong with me?

I took my copy of the *Istorii Sankt'ya* out of my pocket and ran my hands over the worn red leather cover. I'd looked at it so many times that it fell right open to the illustration of Sankt Ilya, though now the pages were waterlogged from the crash of the *Hummingbird*.

A Grisha Saint? Or another greedy fool who couldn't resist the temptation of power? A greedy fool like me. *Forget Morozova and his madness.* I ran my finger along the curve of the arch. It might be meaningless. It might be some reference to Ilya's past that had nothing to do with amplifiers, or just an artist's flourish. Even if we were right and it was some kind of signpost, it could be anywhere. Nikolai had travelled most of Ravka, and he'd never seen it. For all we knew, it had fallen into rubble hundreds of years ago.

A bell rang at the school across the lake, and a gaggle of Grisha children rushed from its doors, shouting, laughing, eager to be out in the summer sunshine. The school had continued to run, despite the disasters of the last months. If the Darkling was coming, I'd have to evacuate it. I didn't want children in the path of the *nichevo'ya*.

The ox feels the yoke, but does the bird feel the weight of its wings?

Had Baghra ever really spoken those words to me? Or had I only heard them in a dream?

I stood up and brushed the dust from my *kefta*. I wasn't sure what had shaken me more, Baghra's refusal to help or how broken she seemed. She wasn't just an old woman. She was a woman without hope, and I'd helped to take it from her.

Chapter 15

Despite its name, I loved the war room. The cartographer in me couldn't resist the old maps wrought in animal hide and embellished in whimsical detail: the gilded lighthouse at Os Kervo, the mountain temples of the Shu, the mermaids that swam at the edges of the seas.

I looked around the table at the faces of the Grisha, some familiar, some new. Any one of them could be a spy for the Darkling, the King, the Apparat. Any one of them could be looking for the chance to get me out of the way and assume power.

Tolya and Tamar stood outside, just a shout away in case of trouble, but it was Mal's presence that gave me comfort. He sat at my right in his roughspun clothes, the sunburst pinned above his heart. I hated to think that he might leave so soon for the hunt, though I had to admit a distraction could be a good thing. Mal had taken pride in being a soldier and, while he tried to hide it, I knew the King's ruling weighed heavily on him. That he'd guessed I was keeping something from him didn't help either.

Sergei sat to Mal's right, his arms crossed sullenly over his chest. He wasn't happy to be sitting next to an *otkazat'sya* guard, and he was even less pleased that I'd insisted on seating a Fabrikator directly to my left, in what was considered a position of honour. She was a Suli girl named Paja whom I'd never met before. She had dark hair and nearly black eyes, and the red embroidery at the cuffs of her purple *kefta* indicated that she was one of the Alkemi, Fabrikators who specialised in chemicals like blasting powders and poisons.

David sat further down the table, his cuffs emblazoned in grey. He worked in glass, steel, wood, stone – anything solid. David was a Durast, and I knew he was the best of them because the Darkling had chosen him to forge my collar. Then there was Fedyor, and Zoya beside him, gorgeous as always in Etherealki blue.

Across from Zoya sat Pavel, the dark-skinned Inferni who'd spoken so angrily against me the previous day. He had narrow features and a chipped tooth that whistled slightly when he talked.

The first part of the meeting was spent discussing the numbers of Grisha at the various outposts around Ravka and those who might be in hiding. Zoya suggested sending messengers to spread the news of my return and offer full and free pardon to those who swore their allegiance to the Sun Summoner. We spent close to an hour debating the terms and wording of the pardon. I knew I would have to take it to Nikolai for the King's approval and I wanted to step carefully. Finally, we agreed on "loyalty to the Ravkan throne and the Second Army". No one seemed happy with it, so I was pretty sure we'd got it right.

It was Fedyor who raised the issue of the Apparat. "It's troubling that he's evaded capture this long."

"Has he tried to contact you?" Pavel asked me.

"No," I said. I saw the skepticism on his face.

"He's been spotted in Kerskii and Ryevost," said Fedyor. "He shows up out of nowhere to preach, then disappears before the King's soldiers can close in."

"We should think about an assassination," said Sergei. "He's growing too powerful, and he could still be colluding with the Darkling."

"We'd have to find him first," observed Paja.

Zoya gave a graceful wave of her hand. "What would be the point? He seems bent on spreading word of the Sun Summoner and claiming she's a Saint. It's about time the people had some appreciation for the Grisha."

"Not the Grisha," said Pavel, jutting his chin truculently in my direction. "Her."

Zoya lifted one elegant shoulder. "It's better than them reviling us all as witches and traitors."

"Let the King do the dirty work," said Fedyor. "Let him find the Apparat and execute him *and* let him suffer the people's wrath."

I couldn't believe we were calmly debating a man's murder. And I wasn't sure I wanted the Apparat dead. The priest had plenty to answer for, but I wasn't convinced he was still working with the Darkling. Besides, he'd given me the *Istorii Sankt'ya*, and that meant he was a possible source of information. If he was captured, I could only hope the King would keep him alive long enough for questioning.

"Do you think he believes it?" asked Zoya, studying me. "That you're a Saint risen and back from the dead?"

"I'm not sure it makes a difference."

"It would help to know just how crazy he is."

"I'd rather fight a traitor than a zealot," Mal said quietly. It was the first time he'd spoken. "I may have some old contacts in the First Army who will still talk to me. There are rumours of soldiers defecting to join him, and if that's the case, they must know where he is."

I stole a glance at Zoya. She was gazing at Mal with those impossibly blue eyes. It seemed as if she'd spent half the meeting batting her lashes at him. Or maybe I was imagining things. She was a powerful Squaller and, potentially, a powerful ally. But she'd also been one of the Darkling's favourites, and that certainly made her difficult to trust.

I almost laughed out loud. Who was I kidding? I hated even sitting in the same room with her. *She* looked like a Saint. Delicate bones, glossy black hair, perfect skin. All she needed was a halo. Mal paid her no attention, though a twisting feeling in my gut made me think he was ignoring her a little too deliberately. I knew I had more important things to worry about than Zoya. I had an army to run and enemies on every side, but I couldn't seem to stop myself.

I took a breath and tried to focus. The hardest part of the meeting was still to come. As much as I just wanted to curl up somewhere quiet and dark, there were things that needed to be addressed.

I looked around the table and said, "You need to know what we're up against."

The room fell silent. It was as if a bell had rung, as if everything that had come before was mere playacting, and now the real meeting had begun.

Piece by piece, I laid out what I knew about the *nichevo'ya*, their strength and size, their near invulnerability to bullet and blade, and most important, the fact that they did not fear sunlight.

"But you escaped," Paja said tentatively, "so they must be mortal."

"My power can destroy them. It's the one thing they don't seem able to recover from. But it isn't easy. It requires the Cut, and I'm not sure how many I can handle at once." I didn't mention the second amplifier. Even with it, I knew I couldn't withstand the onslaught of a fully formed shadow army, and the fetter was a secret I intended to keep, at least for now. "We only escaped because Prince Nikolai got us outside the Darkling's range," I continued. "They seem to need to be close to their master."

"How close?" asked Pavel.

I looked to Mal.

"Hard to say," he replied. "A mile. Maybe two."

"So there's *some* limit to his power," Fedyor said, with no small amount of relief.

"Absolutely." I was glad to be able to relate something that wasn't completely dire. "He'll have to enter Ravka with his army to get to us. That means we'll have warning and that he'll be vulnerable. He can't summon them the way he summons darkness. The effort seems to cost him."

"Because it's not Grisha power," David said. "It's *merzost*."

In Ravkan, the word for magic and abomination was the same. Basic Grisha theory stated that matter couldn't just be created from nothing. But that was a tenet of the Small Science. *Merzost* was different, a corruption of the making at the heart of the world.

David fiddled with a loose thread at his sleeve. "That energy, that substance has to come from somewhere. It must be coming from him."

"But how is he doing it?" asked Zoya. "Has there ever been a Grisha with this kind of power?"

"The real question is how to fight them," said Fedyor.

Talk turned to defence of the Little Palace and the possible advantages of confronting the Darkling in the field. But I was watching David. When Zoya had asked about other Grisha, he'd looked directly at me for the first time since I'd arrived at the Little Palace. Well, not at *me* exactly, but at my collar. He'd gone right back to staring at the table, but if possible, he seemed even more uncomfortable than before. I wondered what he might know about Morozova. And I wanted an answer to Zoya's question too. I didn't know if I had the training or the nerve to attempt such a thing, but was there a way to summon soldiers of light to fight the Darkling's shadow army? Was that the power the three amplifiers might give me?

I meant to try to talk to David alone after the meeting, but as soon as we adjourned, he shot out of the door. Any thoughts I had of cornering him in the Materialki workshops that afternoon were squelched by the piles of paper waiting for me in my chambers. I spent hours preparing the Grisha pardon and signing countless documents guaranteeing funds and provisions for the outposts the Second Army hoped to reestablish on Ravka's borders. Sergei had tried to manage some of the Darkling's duties, but much of the work had simply gone unattended.

Everything seemed to be written in the most confusing way possible. I had to read and reread what should have been simple requests. By the time I'd made a small dent in the pile, I was late for dinner – my first meal in the domed hall. I would have preferred to take a tray in my room, but it was important that I assert my presence at the Little Palace. I also wanted to make sure my commands were being followed, and that the Grisha were actually mixing the Orders.

I sat at the Darkling's table. In an effort to get to know some of the unfamiliar Grisha and to avoid giving them any excuse to form a new elite, I'd decided that different people would dine with me every night. It was a nice idea, but I had none of Mal's easy way or Nikolai's charm. The conversation was stilted and pockmarked with awkward moments of silence.

The other tables didn't seem to be faring much better. The Grisha sat side by side in a jumble of red, purple, and blue, barely speaking. The clink of silverware echoed off the cracked dome – the Fabrikators had not yet begun their repairs.

I didn't know whether to laugh or scream. It was as if I'd asked them to take supper next to a volcra. At least Sergei and Marie seemed content, even if Nadia looked like she wanted to disappear into the butter dish as they cuddled and cooed beside her. I was happy for them, I supposed. And maybe a little jealous, too.

I made a silent count – forty Grisha, maybe fifty, most of them barely out of school. *Some army*, I thought with a sigh. My glorious reign was off to a miserable start.

Mal had agreed to join the hunting party, and I rose early the next morning to see him off. I was beginning to realise that we would have less privacy at the Little Palace than we'd had on the road. Between Tolya and Tamar and the constantly hovering servants, I'd started to think we might never get a moment alone.

I had lain awake the previous night in the Darkling's bed, remembering the way Mal had kissed me at the dacha, wondering if I might hear his knock at my door. I'd even debated crossing the common room and tapping at the guards' quarters, but I wasn't sure who was on duty, and the thought of Tolya or Tamar answering made me prickly with embarrassment. In the end, the fatigue of the day must have made the decision for me, because the next thing I knew, it was morning.

By the time I reached the double eagle fountain, the path to the palace gates was swarming with people and horses: Vasily and his aristocrat friends in their elaborate riding regalia, First Army officers in their sharp uniforms, and behind them, a legion of servants in white and gold.

I found Mal checking his saddle near a group of royal trackers. He was easy to pick out in his peasant roughspun. He had a gleaming new bow on his back and a quiver of arrows fletched in the pale blue and gold of the Ravkan King. The formal Ravkan hunt forbade the use of firearms, but I noticed that several of the servants had rifles on their backs, just in case the animals proved to be too much for their noble masters.

"Quite a show," I said, coming up beside him. "Just how many people does it take to bring down a few boar?"

Mal snorted. "This is nothing. Another group of servants left before dawn to set up the camp. Saints forbid a prince of Ravka should be kept waiting on a hot cup of tea."

A horn blew and the riders began to fall into place in

a clatter of hooves and clanking stirrups. Mal shook his head and gave a firm tug on the cinch. "Those boar had better be deaf," he grumbled.

I glanced around at the glittering uniforms and high-polished boots. "Maybe I should have outfitted you in something a little more . . . shiny."

"There's a reason peacocks aren't birds of prey," he said with a grin. It was an easy, open smile, the first I'd seen in a long time.

He's happy to be going, I thought. *He's grumbling about it, but he's glad.* I tried not to take it personally.

"And you're like a big brown hawk?" I asked.

"Exactly."

"Or an over-large pigeon?"

"Let's stick with hawk."

The others were mounting up, turning their horses to join the rest of the party as they headed down the gravel path.

"Let's go, Oretsev," called a tracker with sandy hair.

I felt suddenly awkward, keenly aware of the people surrounding us, of their inquisitive stares. I had probably breached some kind of protocol by even coming to say goodbye.

"Well," I said, patting his horse's flank, "have fun. Try not to shoot anyone."

"Got it. Wait, *don't* shoot anyone?"

I smiled, though it felt a bit forced.

We stood there a moment longer, the silence stretching out between us. I wanted to fling my arms around him, bury my face in his neck, and make him promise to be safe. But I didn't.

A rueful smile touched his lips. He bowed.

"*Moi soverenyi*," he said. My heart twisted in my chest.

He climbed into the saddle and kicked his horse forward, disappearing in the sea of riders flowing towards the golden gates.

I made the walk back to the Little Palace in low spirits. It was early, but the day was already growing warm. Tamar was waiting for me when I emerged from the wooded tunnel.

"He'll be back soon enough," she said. "No need to look so glum."

"I know," I replied, feeling foolish. I managed a laugh as we crossed the lawn down to the stables. "At Keramzin, I had a doll I made out of an old sock that I used to talk to whenever he was away hunting. Maybe that would make me feel better."

"You were an odd little girl."

"You have no idea. What did you and Tolya play with?"

"The skulls of our enemies."

I saw the glint in her eye, and we both burst out laughing.

Down at the training rooms, Tamar and I met briefly with Botkin, the instructor tasked with preparing Grisha for physical combat. The old mercenary was instantly enchanted with Tamar, and they yammered away at each other in Shu for nearly ten minutes before I managed to raise the issue of training the Fabrikators.

"Botkin can teach anyone to fight," he said in his thick accent. The dim light gave the ropy scar at his throat a pearly sheen. "Taught little girl to fight, no?"

"Yes," I agreed, wincing at the memory of Botkin's gruelling drills and the beatings I'd taken at his hands.

"But little girl is not so little any more," he said taking

in the gold of my *kefta*. "You come back to train with Botkin. I hit big girl same as little girl."

"That's very egalitarian of you," I said, and hurried Tamar out of the stables before Botkin decided to show me just how fair-minded he could be.

I went straight from the stables to another war council meeting, then I just had time to tidy my hair and brush off my *kefta* before heading back to the Grand Palace to join Nikolai as the King's advisers briefed him on Os Alta's defenses.

I felt a bit like we were children who had intruded on the adults. The advisers made it clear that they felt we were wasting their time. Nikolai seemed unfazed. He asked careful questions about armaments, the number of troops stationed around the city walls, the warning system that was in place in case of attack. Soon the advisers had lost their condescending air and were conversing with him in earnest, asking about the weaponry he'd brought with him from across the Fold and how it might be best deployed.

He had me give a short description of the *nichevo'ya* to help make the case for arming the Grisha with new weapons as well. The advisers were still deeply suspicious of the Second Army, but on the walk back to the Little Palace, Nikolai was unconcerned.

"They'll come around in time," he said. "That's why you need to be there, to reassure them and to help them understand that the Darkling isn't like other enemies."

"You think they don't know that?" I asked incredulously.

"They don't want to know it. If they can maintain the belief that the Darkling can be bargained with or brought to heel, then they don't have to face the reality of the situation."

"I can't say I blame them," I said gloomily. It was all

well and good to talk about troops and walls and warnings, but I doubted it would make much difference against the Darkling's shadow soldiers.

When we emerged from the tunnel, Nikolai said, "Walk with me down to the lake?"

I hesitated.

"I promise not to drop to one knee and start composing ballads to your beauty. I just want to show you something."

My cheeks went red and Nikolai grinned.

"You should see if the Corporalki can do something about that blush," he said, and strolled off around the side of the Little Palace to the lake.

I was tempted to follow just for the pleasure of pushing him in. Although . . . *could* the Corporalki fix my blushing? I shook the ridiculous thought from my head. The day I asked a Corporalnik to tend to my blushes was the day I'd be laughed out of the Little Palace.

Nikolai had stopped on the gravel path, halfway down to the lake, and I joined him there. He pointed to a strip of beach on the far shore, a short distance from the school. "I want to construct a pier there," he said.

"Why?"

"So I can rebuild the *Hummingbird*."

"You really can't keep still, can you? Don't you have enough on your plate?"

He squinted out at the glittering surface of the lake. "Alina, I'm hoping we can find a way to defeat the Darkling. But if we can't, we need a way to get you out."

I stared at him. "What about the rest of the Grisha?"

"There's nothing I can do for them."

I couldn't quite believe what he was suggesting. "I'm not going to run."

"I had a feeling you'd say that," he said with a sigh.

"And you?" I said angrily. "Are you just going to fly away and leave the rest of us to face the Darkling?"

"Come now," he said. "You know I've always wanted a hero's funeral." He looked back at the lake. "I'm happy to go down fighting, but I don't want my parents left to the Darkling's mercy. Will you give me two Squallers to train?"

"They're not gifts, Nikolai," I said, thinking of the way the Darkling had made a present of Genya to the Queen. "I'll ask for volunteers. Just don't tell them what it's for. I don't want the others to get discouraged." Or start vying for places aboard the craft. "And one more thing," I said. "I want you to make room for Baghra. She shouldn't have to face the Darkling again. She's been through enough."

"Of course," he said, then added, "I still believe we can win, Alina."

I'm glad someone does, I thought dismally, and turned to go inside.

Chapter 16

David had managed to slip away again after the last council meeting, and it was late the following evening before I had a free moment to corner him in the Fabrikator workrooms. I found him hunched over a pile of blueprints, his fingers stained with ink.

I settled myself on a stool beside him and cleared my throat. He looked up, blinking owlishly. He was so pale I could see the blue tracery of veins through his skin, and someone had given him a very bad haircut.

Probably did it himself, I thought with an inward shake of my head. It was hard to believe that this was the boy Genya had fallen so hard for.

His eyes flicked to the collar at my neck. He began to fidget with the items on his worktable, moving them around and arranging them in careful lines: a compass, graphite pencils, pens and pots of ink in different colours, pieces of clear and mirrored glass, a hard-boiled egg that I assumed was his dinner, and page after page of drawings and plans that I couldn't begin to make sense of.

"What are you working on?" I asked.

He blinked again. "Dishes."

"Ah."

"Reflective bowls," he said. "Based on a parabola."

"How . . . interesting?" I managed.

He scratched his nose, leaving a giant blue smudge along the ridge. "It might be a way to magnify your power."

"Like the mirrors in my gloves?" I'd asked that the Durasts remake them. With the power of two amplifiers, I probably didn't need them. But the mirrors allowed me to focus and pinpoint light, and there was something comforting in the control they gave me.

"Sort of," said David. "If I get it right, it will be a much bigger way to use the Cut."

"And if you get it wrong?"

"Either nothing will happen, or whoever's operating it will be blown to bits."

"Sounds promising."

"I thought so too," he said without a hint of humour, and bent back to his work.

"*David*," I said. He looked up, startled, as if he'd completely forgotten I was there. "I need to ask you something."

His gaze darted to the collar again, then back to his work table.

"What can you tell me about Ilya Morozova?"

David twitched, glancing around the nearly empty room. Most of the Fabrikators were still at dinner. He was clearly nervous, maybe even frightened.

He looked at the table, picked up his compass, put it down.

Finally, he whispered, "They called him the Bonesmith."

A quiver passed through me. I thought of the fingers and vertebrae lying on the peddlers' tables in Kribirsk. "Why?" I asked. "Because of the amplifiers he discovered?"

David looked up, surprised. "He didn't find them. He *made* them."

I didn't want to believe what I was hearing. "*Merzost*?"

He nodded. So that was why David had looked at Morozova's collar when Zoya asked if any Grisha had ever had such power. Morozova had been playing with the same forces as the Darkling. Magic. Abomination.

"How?" I asked.

"No one knows," David said, glancing over his shoulder again. "After the Black Heretic was killed in the accident that created the Fold, his son came out of hiding to take control of the Second Army. He had all of Morozova's journals destroyed."

His *son*? Again, I was faced with the knowledge of how few people knew the Darkling's secret. The Black Heretic had never died – there had only ever been one Darkling, a single powerful Grisha who had ruled the Second Army for generations, hiding his true identity. As far as I knew, he'd never had a son. And there was no way he would destroy something as valuable as Morozova's journals. Aboard the whaler, he'd said not all the books prohibited the combination of amplifiers. Maybe he'd been referring to Morozova's own writings.

"Why was his son in hiding?" I asked, curious as to how the Darkling had managed to frame such a deception.

This time David frowned as if the answer were obvious. "A Darkling and his heir never live at the Little Palace at the same time. The risk of assassination is too great."

"I see," I said. Plausible enough, and after hundreds of years, I doubted anyone would question such a story. The Grisha did love their traditions, and Genya couldn't have been the first Tailor the Darkling had kept in his employ. "Why would he have had the journals destroyed?"

"They documented Morozova's experiments with

amplifiers. The Black Heretic was trying to re-create those experiments when something went wrong."

The hair rose on my arms. "And the result was the Fold."

David nodded. "His son had all of Morozova's journals and papers burned. He said they were too dangerous, too much of a temptation to any Grisha. That's why I didn't say anything at the meeting. I shouldn't even know they ever existed."

"So how do you?"

David looked around the almost empty workshop again. "Morozova was a Fabrikator, maybe the first, certainly the most powerful. He did things that no one's ever dreamed of before or since." He gave a sheepish shrug. "To us, he's kind of a hero."

"Do you know anything else about the amplifiers he created?"

David shook his head. "There were rumours of others, but the stag was the only one I'd ever heard of."

It was possible David had never even seen the *Istorii Sankt'ya*. The Apparat had claimed that the book was once given to all Grisha children when they arrived at the Little Palace. But that was long ago. The Grisha put their faith in the Small Science, and I'd never known them to bother with religion. *Superstition*, the Darkling had called the red book. *Peasant propaganda*. Clearly David hadn't made the connection between Sankt Ilya and Ilya Morozova. Or he had something to hide.

"David," I said, "why are you here? You fashioned the collar. You must have known what he intended."

He swallowed. "I knew he would be able to control you, that the collar would allow him to use your power. I

247

never thought, I never believed . . . all those people . . ." He struggled to find the words. Finally, he held out his ink-stained hands and said, almost pleadingly. "I make things. I don't destroy them."

I wanted to believe that he had underestimated the Darkling's ruthlessness. I'd certainly made the same mistake. But he might be lying or he might just be weak. *Which is worse?* asked a harsh voice in my head. *If he can change sides once, he can do it again.* Was it Nikolai's voice? The Darkling's? Or was it just the part of me that had learned to trust no one?

"Good luck with the dishes," I said as I rose to leave.

David hunched over his papers. "I don't believe in luck."

Too bad, I thought. *We're going to need some.*

I went straight from the Fabrikator workrooms to the library and spent most of the night there. It was an exercise in frustration. The Grisha histories I searched had only the most basic information on Ilya Morozova, despite the fact that he was considered the greatest Fabrikator who ever lived. He had invented Grisha steel, a method of making unbreakable glass, and a compound for liquid fire so dangerous that he destroyed the formula just twelve hours after he created it. But any mentions of amplifiers or the Bonesmith had been expunged.

That didn't stop me from returning the next evening to bury myself in religious texts and any reference I could find to Sankt Ilya. Like most Saints' tales, the story of his martyrdom was depressingly brutal: one day, a plough had overturned in the fields behind his home. Hearing the screams, Ilya ran to help, only to find a man weeping over his dead son, the boy's body torn open by the blades, the ground soaked through with his blood. Ilya had brought the boy back to life – and the villagers had thanked him for it by clapping him in irons and tossing him into a river to sink beneath the weight of his chains.

The details were hopelessly muddy. Sometimes Ilya was a farmer, sometimes a mason or a woodworker. He had two daughters or one son or no children at all. A hundred different villages claimed to be the site of his martyrdom. Then, there was the small problem of the miracle he'd performed. I had no problem believing that Sankt Ilya might be a Corporalnik Healer, but Ilya Morozova was supposed to be a Fabrikator. What if they weren't the same person at all?

At night, the glass-domed room was lit by oil lamps, and the hush was so deep that I could hear myself breathe. Alone in the gloom, surrounded by books, it was hard not to feel overwhelmed. But the library seemed like my best hope, so I kept at it. Tolya found me there one evening, curled up in my favourite chair, struggling to make sense out of a text in ancient Ravkan.

"You shouldn't come here at night without one of us," he said grumpily.

I yawned and stretched. I was probably more in danger of a shelf falling on me than anything else, but I was too tired to argue. "Won't happen again," I said.

"What is that?" Tolya asked, lowering himself down to get a closer view of the book in my lap. He was so huge that it was a bit like having a bear join me for a study session.

"I'm not sure. I saw the name Ilya in the index, so I picked it up, but I can't make sense of it."

"It's a list of titles."

"You can read it?" I asked in surprise.

"We were raised in the church," he said, skimming the page.

I looked at him. Lots of children were raised in religious homes, but that didn't mean they could read liturgical Ravkan. "What does it say?"

He ran a finger down the words beneath Ilya's name. His huge hands were covered in scars. Beneath his roughspun sleeve, I could see the edge of a tattoo peeking out.

"Not much," he said. "Saint Ilya the Beloved, Saint Ilya the Treasured. There are a few towns listed, though, places where he's said to have performed miracles.

I sat up straighter. "That might be a place to start."

"You should explore the chapel. I think there are some books in the vestry."

I had walked past the royal chapel plenty of times, but I'd never been inside. I'd always thought of it as the Apparat's domain, and even with him gone, I wasn't sure I wanted to visit. "What's it like?"

Tolya lifted his huge shoulders. "Like any chapel."

"Tolya," I asked, suddenly curious, "did you ever even consider joining the Second Army?"

He looked offended. "I wasn't born to serve the Darkling." I wanted to ask what he *had* been born for, but he tapped the page and said, "I can translate this for you, if you like." He grinned. "Or maybe I'll just make Tamar do it."

"All right," I said. "Thanks."

He bent his head. It was just a bow, but he was still kneeling beside me, and there was something about his pose that sent a shiver up my spine.

I felt as if he were waiting for something. Tentatively, I reached out and laid a hand on his shoulder. As soon as my fingers came to rest, he let out a breath. It was almost a sigh.

We stayed there for a moment, silent in the halo of lamplight. Then he rose and bowed again.

"I'll be just outside the door," he said, and slipped away into the dark.

Mal returned from the hunt the next morning, and I was eager to tell him everything – what I'd learned from David, the plans for the new *Hummingbird*, my strange encounter with Tolya.

"He's an odd one," Mal agreed. "But it still couldn't hurt to check out the chapel."

We decided to walk over together, and on the way, I pressed him to tell me about the hunt.

"We spent more time every day playing cards and drinking *kvas* than doing anything else. And some duke got so drunk he passed out in the river. He almost drowned. His servants hauled him out by his boots, but he kept wading back in, slurring something about the best way to catch trout."

"Was it terrible?" I asked, laughing.

"It was fine." He kicked a pebble down the path with his boot. "There's a lot of curiosity about you."

"Why do I doubt I'm going to like any of this?"

"One of the royal trackers is sure your powers are fake."

"And just how would I manage that?"

"I believe there's an elaborate system of mirrors, pulleys, and possibly hypnotism involved. I got a little lost."

I started to giggle.

"It wasn't all funny, Alina. When they were in their cups, some of the nobles made it clear they think all of the Grisha should be rounded up and executed."

"Saints," I breathed.

"They're scared."

"That's no excuse," I said, feeling my anger rise. "We're Ravkans too. It's like they forget everything the Second Army has done for them."

Mal raised his hands. "I didn't say I agreed with them."

I sighed and swatted at an innocent tree branch. "I know."

"Anyway, I think I made a bit of progress."

"How did you manage that?"

"Well, they liked that you served in the First Army, and that you saved their prince's life."

"After he risked his own life rescuing us?"

"I may have taken some liberties with the details."

"Oh, Nikolai will love that. Is there more?"

"I told them you hate herring."

"Why?"

"And that you love plum cake. And that Ana Kuya took a switch to you when you ruined your spring slippers jumping in puddles."

I winced. "Why would you tell them all that?"

"I wanted to make you human," he said. "All they see when they look at you is the Sun Summoner. They see a threat, another powerful Grisha like the Darkling. I want them to see a daughter or a sister or a friend. I want them to see Alina."

I felt a lump rise in my throat. "Do you practise being wonderful?"

"Daily," he said with a grin. Then he winked. "But I prefer 'useful'."

The chapel was the only remaining building of a monastery that had once stood atop Os Alta, and it was said to be where the first kings of Ravka had been crowned. Compared to the other structures on the palace grounds, it was a humble building, with whitewashed walls and a single bright blue dome.

It was empty and looked like it could use a good cleaning. The pews were covered in dust, and there were pigeons roosting in the eaves. As we walked up the aisle, Mal took my hand, and my heart gave a funny little leap.

We didn't waste much time in the vestry. The few books on its shelves were a disappointment, just a bunch of old hymnals with crumbling, yellowed pages. The only thing of real interest in the chapel was the massive triptych behind the altar. A riot of colour, its three huge panels showed thirteen saints with benevolent faces. I recognised some of them from the *Istorii Sankt'ya*: Lizabeta with her bloody roses, Petyr with his still-burning arrows. And there was Sankt Ilya with his collar and fetters and broken chains.

"No animals," Mal observed.

"From what I've seen, he's never pictured with the amplifiers, just with the chains. Except in the *Istorii Sankt'ya*." I just didn't know why.

Most of the triptych was in fairly good condition, but

Ilya's panel had sustained bad water damage. The Saints' faces were barely visible under the mould, and the damp smell of mildew was nearly overpowering. I pressed my nose to my sleeve.

"There must be a leak somewhere," said Mal. "This place is a mess."

My eyes traced the shape of Ilya's face beneath the grime. Another dead end. I didn't like to admit it, but I'd got my hopes up. Again, I sensed that pull, that emptiness at my wrist. Where was the firebird?

"We can stand here all day," Mal said. "He's not going to start talking."

I knew he was teasing, but I felt a prickle of anger, though I wasn't sure if it was at him or myself.

We turned to go back down the aisle and I stopped short. The Darkling was waiting in the gloom by the entrance, seated in a shadowy pew.

"What is it?" Mal asked, following my gaze.

I waited, perfectly still. *See him*, I begged silently. *Please see him*.

"Alina? Is something wrong?"

I dug my fingers into my palm. "No," I said. "Do you think we should check the vestry again?"

"It didn't seem very promising."

I made myself smile and walk. "You're probably right. Wishful thinking."

As we passed by the Darkling, he turned his head to watch us. He pressed a finger to his lips, then bent his head in a mocking imitation of prayer.

I felt better when we were out in the fresh air, away from the mouldy smell of the chapel, but my mind was racing. It had happened again.

The Darkling's face had been unscarred. Mal hadn't seen him. That must mean it wasn't real, just some kind of vision.

But he'd touched me that night in his rooms. I'd felt his fingers on my cheek. What kind of hallucination could do that?

I shivered as we passed into the woods. Was this some manifestation of the Darkling's new powers? I was terrified by the prospect that he might have somehow found a way into my thoughts, but the other possibility was far worse.

You cannot violate the rules of this world without a price. I pressed my arm to my side, feeling the sea whip's scales chafe against my skin. *Forget Morozova and his madness.* Maybe this had nothing to do with the Darkling at all. Maybe I was just losing my mind.

"Mal," I began, not certain what I intended to say, "the third amp—"

He put a finger to his lips, and the gesture was so like the Darkling's that I nearly stumbled. In the next second, I heard rustling and Vasily emerged from the trees.

I wasn't used to seeing the prince anywhere except the Grand Palace, and for a moment, I just stood there. Then I recovered from my surprise and bowed.

Vasily acknowledged me with a nod, ignoring Mal completely.

"*Moi tsarevich*," I said in greeting.

"Alina Starkov," the prince replied with a smile. "I hope you will grant me a moment of your time."

"Of course," I replied.

"I'll be right down the path," Mal said, shooting Vasily a suspicious glare.

The prince watched him go. "The deserter hasn't quite learned his place, has he?"

I bit back my anger. "What can I do for you, *moi tsarevich*?"

"Please," he said, "I would prefer you call me Vasily, at least when we are in private."

I blinked. I'd never been alone with the prince before, and I didn't want to be now.

"How are you settling in at the Little Palace?" he asked.

"Very well, thank you, *moi tsarevich*."

"Vasily."

"I don't know that it's appropriate to speak to you so informally," I said primly.

"You call my brother by his given name."

"I met him under . . . unique circumstances."

"I know he can be very charming," Vasily said. "You should know that he's also very deceptive, and very clever."

That's certainly true, I thought, but all I said was, "He has an unusual mind."

Vasily chortled. "What a diplomat you've become! You've a most refreshing way about you. Given time, I have no doubt that, despite your humble antecedents, you will learn to conduct yourself with the restraint and elegance of a noblewoman."

"You mean I'll learn to shut up?"

Vasily gave a disapproving sniff. I needed to get out of this conversation before I really offended him. Vasily might seem a fool, but he was still a prince.

"Indeed no," he said with a stilted laugh. "You have a delightful candour."

"Thank you," I mumbled. "If you'll excuse me, Your Highness—"

Vasily stepped into my path. "I don't know what arrangement you've made with my brother, but you must realise that he's a second son. Whatever his ambitions, that's all he ever will be. Only I can make you Queen."

There it was. I heaved an internal sigh. "Only a king can make a queen," I reminded him.

Vasily waved this talk away. "My father won't live much longer. I as good as rule Ravka now."

Is that what you call it? I thought with a surge of irritation. I doubted Vasily would even be in Os Alta if Nikolai didn't present a threat to his crown, but this time I held my tongue.

"You've risen high for a Keramzin orphan," he went on, "and you might rise higher still."

"I can assure you, *moi tsarevich*," I said with complete honesty, "I have no such ambitions."

"Then what do you want, Sun Summoner?"

"Right now? I'd like to go and have my lunch."

His lower lip jutted out sulkily, and for a moment, he looked just like his father. Then he smiled.

"You're a smart girl," he said, "and I think you'll prove a useful one. I look forward to deepening our acquaintance."

"I would like nothing better," I lied.

He took my hand and pressed his moist mouth to my knuckles. "Until then, Alina Starkov."

I stifled a gag. As he strode off, I wiped my hand surreptitiously on my *kefta*.

Mal was waiting for me at the edge of the woods.

"What was that about?" he asked, his face worried.

"Oh, you know," I replied. "Another prince, another proposal."

"You can't be serious," Mal said with a disbelieving laugh. "He doesn't waste any time."

"Power is alliance," I intoned, imitating Nikolai.

"Should I offer my felicitations?" Mal asked, but there was no edge to his voice, only amusement. Apparently the heir to the throne of Ravka wasn't quite as threatening as an overconfident privateer.

"Do you think the Darkling had to deal with unwanted advances from wet-lipped royals?" I asked glumly.

Mal snickered.

"What's so funny?"

"I just pictured the Darkling being cornered by a sweaty duchess trying to have her way with him."

I snorted and then I started to laugh outright. Nikolai and Vasily were so different, it was hard to believe they shared any blood at all. Unbidden, I remembered Nikolai's kiss, the rough feel of his mouth on mine as he'd held me to him. I shook my head.

They may be different, I reminded myself as we headed into the palace, *but they both want to use you just the same*.

Chapter 17

Summer deepened, bringing waves of balmy heat to Os Alta. The only relief to be found was in the lake, or in the cold pools of the *banya* that lay in the dark shade of a birchwood grove beside the Little Palace. Whatever hostility the Ravkan court felt towards the Grisha, it didn't stop them from beckoning Squallers and Tidemakers to the Grand Palace to summon breezes and fashion massive blocks of ice to cool the stuffy rooms. It was hardly a worthy use of Grisha talent, but I was eager to keep the King and Queen happy, and I'd already deprived them of several much-valued Fabrikators, who were hard at work on David's mysterious mirrored dishes.

Every morning, I met with my Grisha council – sometimes for a few minutes, sometimes for hours – to discuss intelligence reports, troop movements, and what we were hearing from the northern and southern borders.

Nikolai still hoped to take the fight to the Darkling before he'd assembled the full strength of his shadow army, although so far Ravka's network of spies and informants had been unable to discover his location. It was looking more and more likely that we'd have to make our stand in Os Alta. Our only advantage was that the Darkling couldn't simply send the *nichevo'ya* against us. He had to stay close to his creatures, and that meant he would have to march to the capital with them. The big question was whether he would enter Ravka from Fjerda or from the Shu Han.

Standing in the war room before the Grisha council, Nikolai gestured to one of the massive maps along the wall. "We took back most of this territory in the last campaign," he said, pointing to Ravka's northern border with Fjerda. "It's dense forest, almost impossible to cross when the rivers aren't frozen, and all the access roads have been blockaded."

"Are there Grisha stationed there?" asked Zoya.

"No," Nikolai said. "But there are lots of scouts based out of Ulensk. If he comes that way, we'll have plenty of warning."

"And he would have to deal with the Petrazoi," said Paja. "Whether he goes over or around them, it will buy us more time." She'd come into her own over the last few weeks. Though David remained silent and fidgety, she actually seemed glad to have time away from the workrooms.

"I'm more concerned with the permafrost," Nikolai said, running his hand along the stretch of border that ran above Tsibeya. "It's heavily fortified. But that's a lot of territory to cover."

I nodded. Mal and I had once walked those wild lands together, and I remembered how vast they'd felt. I caught myself looking around the room, seeking him out, even though I knew he'd gone on another hunt, this time with a group of Kerch marksmen and Ravkan diplomats.

"And if he comes from the south?" asked Zoya.

Nikolai signalled to Fedyor, who rose and began to walk the Grisha through the weak points of the southern border. Because he'd been stationed at Sikursk, the Corporalnik knew the area well.

"It's almost impossible to patrol all the mountain passes coming out of the Sikurzoi," he observed grimly. "Shu raiding parties having been taking advantage of that fact for years. It would be easy enough for the Darkling to slip through."

"Then it's a straight march to Os Alta," said Sergei.

"Past the military base at Poliznaya," Nikolai noted. "That could work to our advantage. Either way, when he marches, we'll be ready."

"Ready?" Pavel snorted. "For an army of indestructible monsters?"

"They're not indestructible," Nikolai said, nodding to me. "And the Darkling isn't either. I know. I shot him."

Zoya's eyes widened. "You *shot* him?"

"Yes," he said. "Unfortunately, I didn't do a very good job of it, but I'm sure I'll improve with practice." He surveyed the Grisha, looking into each worried face before he spoke again. "The Darkling is powerful, but so are we. He's never faced the might of the First and Second Armies working in tandem, or the kinds of weapons I intend to supply. We face him. We flank him. We see which bullet gets lucky."

While the Darkling's shadow horde was focused on the Little Palace, he would be vulnerable. Small, heavily armed units of Grisha and soldiers would be stationed at two-mile intervals around the capital. Once the fighting began, they would close on the Darkling and unleash all the firepower that Nikolai could muster.

In a way, it was what the Darkling had always feared. Again, I remembered how he'd described the new weaponry being created beyond Ravka's borders, and what he'd said to me, so long ago, beneath the caved-in roof of an old barn: *The age of Grisha power is coming to an end.*

Paja cleared her throat. "Do we know what happens to the shadow soldiers when we kill the Darkling?"

I wanted to hug her. I didn't know what might happen to the *nichevo'ya* if we managed to put the Darkling down. They might vanish to nothing, or they might go into a mad frenzy or worse, but she'd said it: *When we kill the Darkling.* Tentative, frightened – it still sounded suspiciously like hope.

We focused the majority of our efforts on Os Alta's defence. The city had an ancient system of warning bells to alert the palace when an enemy was in sight. With his father's permission, Nikolai had installed heavy guns like those on the *Hummingbird* above the city and palace walls. Despite Grisha grumbling, I'd had several placed on the roof of the Little Palace. They might not stop the *nichevo'ya*, but they would slow them.

Tentatively, the other Grisha had begun to open up to the value of the Fabrikators. With help from the Inferni, the Materialki were trying to create *grenatki* that might produce a powerful enough flash of light to stall or stun the shadow soldiers. The problem was doing it without using blasting powders that would level everyone and everything around them. I sometimes worried that they might blow up the entire Little Palace and do the Darkling's work for him. More than once, I saw Grisha in the dining hall with burnt cuffs or singed brows. I encouraged them to try the more dangerous work by the lakeside with Tidemakers on hand in case of emergency.

Nikolai was intrigued enough by the project that he insisted on getting involved in the design. The Fabrikators tried to ignore him, then pretended to indulge him, but they quickly learned that Nikolai was more than a bored prince who liked to dabble. Not only did he understand David's ideas, he'd worked long enough with the rogue Grisha that he slipped easily into the language of the Small Science. Soon, they seemed to forget his rank and his *otkazat'sya* status, and he could often be found hunched over a table in the Materialki workshops.

I was most disturbed by the experiments taking place behind the red-lacquered doors of the Corporalki anatomy rooms, where they were collaborating with the Fabrikators to try to fuse Grisha steel with human bone. The idea was to make it possible for a soldier to withstand *nichevo'ya* attack. But the process was painful and imperfect, and often, the metal was simply rejected by the subject's body. The Healers did what they could, but the ragged screams of First Army volunteers could sometimes be heard echoing through the halls of the Little Palace.

Afternoons were taken up by endless meetings at the Grand Palace. The Sun Summoner's power was a valuable bartering chip in Ravka's attempts to forge alliances with other countries, and I was frequently asked to put in appearances at diplomatic gatherings to demonstrate my power and prove that I was, in fact, alive. The Queen hosted teas and dinners where I was paraded about to perform. Nikolai often dropped by to dole out compliments, flirt shamelessly, and hover protectively by my chair like a doting suitor.

But nothing was as tedious as the "strategy sessions" with the King's advisers and commanders. The King rarely attended. He preferred to spend his days hobbling after serving maids and sleeping in the sun like an old tomcat. In his absence, his counsellors talked in endless circles. They argued that we should make peace with the Darkling or that we should go to war with the Darkling. They argued for allying with the Shu, then for partnering with Fjerda. They argued every line of every budget, from quantities of ammunition to what the troops ate for breakfast. And yet it was rare that anything got done or decided.

When Vasily learned that Nikolai and I were attending the meetings, he put aside years of ignoring his duties as the Lantsov heir and insisted on being there as well. To my surprise, Nikolai welcomed him enthusiastically.

"What a relief," he said. "Please tell me you can make sense of these." He shoved a towering stack of ledgers across the table.

"What is this?" Vasily asked.

"A proposal for repairs to an aqueduct outside of Chernitsyn."

"All this for an aqueduct?"

"Don't worry," said Nikolai. "I'll have the rest delivered to your room."

"There's more? Can't one of the ministers—"

"You saw what happened when our father let others take over the business of ruling Ravka. We must remain vigilant."

Warily, Vasily lifted the topmost paper from the pile

as if he were picking up a soiled rag. It took everything in me not to burst out laughing.

"Vasily thinks he can lead as our father did," Nikolai confided to me later that afternoon, "throwing banquets, giving the occasional speech. I'm going to make sure he knows just what it means to rule without the Darkling or the Apparat there to take the reins."

It seemed like a good enough plan, but before long, I was cursing both princes beneath my breath. Vasily's presence ensured that meetings ran twice as long. He postured and preened, weighed in on every issue, held forth at length on patriotism, strategy, and the finer points of diplomacy.

"I've never met a man who can say so much without saying anything at all," I fumed as Nikolai walked me back to the Little Palace after a particularly wretched session. "There's got to be something you can do."

"Like what?"

"Get one of his prize ponies to kick him in the head."

"I'm sure they're frequently tempted," Nikolai said. "Vasily's lazy and vain, and he likes to take shortcuts, but there's no easy way to govern a country. Trust me, he'll tire of it soon enough."

"Maybe," I said. "But I'll probably die of boredom before he does."

Nikolai laughed. "Next time, bring a flask. Every time he changes his mind, take a sip."

I groaned. "I'd be passed out on the floor before the hour was up."

With Nikolai's help, I'd brought in armaments experts from Poliznaya to help familiarise the Grisha with modern weaponry and give them training in firearms. Though the sessions had started out tensely, they seemed to be going more smoothly now, and we hoped that a few friendships might be forming between the First and Second Armies. The units of Grisha and soldiers who had been assembled to hunt down the Darkling when he approached Os Alta made the fastest progress. They returned from training missions full of private jokes and new camaraderie. They even took to calling each other *nolniki*, zeroes, because they were no longer strictly First or Second Army.

I'd been worried about how Botkin might respond to all the changes. But the man seemed to have a gift for killing, no matter the method, and he delighted in any excuse to spend time talking weaponry with Tolya and Tamar.

Because the Shu had a bad habit of taking a scalpel to their Grisha, few survived to make it into the ranks of the Second Army. Botkin loved being able to speak in his native tongue; he also loved the twins' ferocity. They didn't rely only on their Corporalki abilities the way Grisha raised at the Little Palace tended to. Instead, Heartrending was just one more weapon in their impressive arsenal.

"Dangerous boy. Dangerous girl," Botkin commented, watching the twins spar with a group of Corporalki one morning while a clutch of nervous Summoners waited their turn. Marie and Sergei were there, Nadia trailing behind them as always.

"She'f worf than he if," complained Sergei. Tamar had split his lip open, and he was having trouble talking. "I feel forry for her hufband."

"Will not marry," said Botkin as Tamar threw a hapless Inferni to the ground.

"Why not?" I asked, surprised.

"Not her. Not brother either," said the mercenary. "They are like Botkin. Born for battle. Made for war."

Three Corporalki hurled themselves at Tolya. In moments, they were all moaning on the floor. I thought of what Tolya had said in the library, that he wasn't born to serve the Darkling. Like so many Shu, he'd taken the path of the soldier for hire, travelling the world as a mercenary and a privateer. But he'd ended up at the Little Palace anyway. How long would he and his sister stay?

"I like her," said Nadia, looking wistfully at Tamar. "She's fearless."

Botkin laughed. "*Fearless* is other word for *stupid*."

"I wouldn't fay that to her fafe," grumbled Sergei as Marie dabbed his lip with a damp cloth.

I found myself starting to smile and turned aside. I hadn't forgotten the way the three of them had welcomed me to the Little Palace. They hadn't been the ones to call me a whore or try to throw me out, but they certainly hadn't spoken up to defend me, and the idea of pretending friendship was just a little too much. Besides, I didn't quite know how to behave around them. We'd never been truly close, and now our difference in status felt like an unbridgeable gap.

Genya wouldn't care, I thought suddenly. Genya had known me. She'd laughed with me and confided in me, and no shiny *kefta* or title would have kept her from telling me exactly what she thought or slipping her arm through mine to share a bit of gossip. Despite the lies she'd told, I missed her.

As if in answer to my thoughts, I felt a tug on my sleeve, and a tremulous voice said, "*Moi soverenyi?*"

Nadia stood shifting from foot to foot. "I hoped . . ."

"What is it?"

She turned to a murky corner of the stables and gestured to a young boy in Etherealki blue whom I'd never seen before. A few Grisha had begun to trickle in after we'd sent out the pardon, but this boy looked too young to have served in the field. He approached nervously, fingers twisting in his *kefta*.

"This is Adrik," Nadia said, placing her arm around him. "My brother." The resemblance was there, though you had to look for it. "We heard that you plan to evacuate the school."

"That's right." I was sending the students to the one place I knew with dormitories and space enough to house them, a place far from the fighting: Keramzin. Botkin would go with them too. I hated to lose such a capable soldier, but this way the younger Grisha would still be able to learn from him – and he'd be able to keep an eye on them. Since Baghra wouldn't see me, I'd sent a servant to her with the same offer. She'd made no reply. Despite my best attempts to ignore her slights, the repeated rejections still stung.

"You're a student?" I asked Adrik, pushing thoughts of Baghra from my mind. He nodded once, and I noted the determined thrust to his chin.

"Adrik was wondering . . . *we* were wondering if—"

"I want to stay," he said fiercely.

My brows shot up. "How old are you?"

"Old enough to fight."

"He would have graduated this year," put in Nadia.

I frowned. He was only a couple of years younger

than I was, but he was all bony elbows and rumpled hair.

"Go with the others to Keramzin," I said. "If you still want to, you can join us in a year." *If we're still here.*

"I'm good," he said. "I'm a Squaller, and I'm as strong as Nadia, even without an amplifier."

"It's too dangerous—"

"This is my home. I'm not leaving."

"Adrik!" Nadia chastised.

"It's okay," I said. Adrik seemed almost feverish. His hands were balled into fists. I looked at Nadia. "You're sure you want him to stay?"

"I—" began Adrik.

"I'm talking to your sister. If you fall to the Darkling's army, she's the one who will have to mourn you." Nadia paled slightly at that, but Adrik didn't flinch. I had to admit he had mettle.

Nadia worried the inside of her lip, glancing from me to Adrik.

"If you're afraid to disappoint him, think what it will be like to bury him," I said. I knew I was being harsh, but I wanted them both to understand what they were asking.

She hesitated, then straightened her shoulders. "Let him fight," she said. "I say he stays. If you send him away, he'll just be back at the gates a week from now."

I sighed, then turned my attention back to Adrik, who was already grinning. "Not a word to the other students," I said. "I don't want them getting ideas." I jabbed a finger at Nadia. "And he's your responsibility."

"Thank you, *moi soverenyi*," said Adrik, bowing so low I thought he might tip over.

I was already regretting my decision. "Get him back to classes."

I watched them walk up the hill towards the lake, then dusted myself off and made my way to one of the smaller training rooms, where I found Mal sparring with Pavel. Mal had been at the Little Palace less and less lately. The invitations had started arriving the afternoon he returned from Balakirev – hunts, house parties, trout fishing, card games. Every nobleman and officer seemed to want Mal at his next event.

Sometimes he was just gone for an afternoon, sometimes for a few days. It reminded me of being back at Keramzin, when I would watch him ride away and then wait each day at the kitchen window for him to return. But if I was honest with myself, the days when he was gone were almost easier. When he was at the Little Palace, I felt guilty for not being able to spend more time with him, and I hated the way the Grisha ignored him or talked down to him like a servant. As much as I missed him, I encouraged him to go.

It's better this way, I told myself. Before he'd deserted to help me, Mal had been a tracker with a bright future, surrounded by friends and admirers. He didn't belong standing guard in doorways or lurking at the edges of rooms, playing the role of my dutiful shadow as I went from one meeting to the next.

"I could watch him all day," said a voice behind me. I stiffened. Zoya was standing there. Even in the heat, she never seemed to sweat.

"You don't think he stinks of Keramzin?" I asked, remembering the vicious words she had once spoken to me.

"I find the lower classes have a certain rough appeal. You will let me know when you're through with him, won't you?"

"I beg your pardon?"

"Oh, did I misunderstand? You two seem so . . . close. But I'm sure you're setting your sights higher these days."

I turned on her. "What are you doing here, Zoya?"

"I came for a training session."

"You know what I mean. What are you doing at the Little Palace?"

"I'm a soldier of the Second Army. This is where I belong."

I folded my arms. It was time Zoya and I had this out. "You don't like me, and you've never missed an opportunity to let me know it. Why follow me now?"

"What choice do I have?"

"I'm sure the Darkling would gladly welcome you back at his side."

"Are you ordering me to leave?" She was striving for her usual haughty tone, but I could tell she was scared. It gave me a guilty little thrill.

"I want to know why you're so determined to stay."

"Because I don't want to live in darkness," she said. "Because you're our best chance."

I shook my head. "Too easy."

She flushed. "Am I supposed to beg?"

Would she? I found I didn't mind the idea. "You're vain. You're ambitious. You would have done anything for the Darkling's attention. What changed?"

"What changed?" she choked out. Her lips thinned, and her fists clenched at her sides. "I had an aunt who lived in Novokribirsk. A niece. The Darkling could have told me what he meant to do. If I could have warned them—" Her voice broke, and I was instantly ashamed of the pleasure I'd felt at watching her squirm.

Baghra's voice echoed in my ears: *You're taking to power well. . . . As it grows, it will hunger for more.* And yet, did I believe Zoya? Was the sheen in her eyes real or pretense? She blinked her tears back and glared at me. "I still don't like you, Starkov. I never will. You're common and clumsy, and I don't know why you were born with such power. But you're the Sun Summoner, and if you can keep Ravka free, then I'll fight for you."

I watched her, considering, noting the two bright spots of colour that flamed high on her cheeks, the trembling of her lip.

"Well?" she said, and I could see how much it cost her to ask. "Are you sending me away?"

I waited a moment longer. "You can stay," I said. "For now."

"Is everything all right?" Mal asked. We hadn't even noticed that he'd left off sparring.

In an instant, Zoya's uncertainty was gone. She gave him a dazzling smile. "I hear you're quite the marvel with a bow and arrow. I thought you might offer me a lesson."

Mal glanced from Zoya back to me. "Maybe later."

"I look forward to it," she said, and swept away in a soft rustle of silk.

"What was that about?" he asked as we began the walk up the hill to the Little Palace.

"I don't trust her."

For a long minute he said nothing. "Alina," Mal began uneasily, "what happened in Kribirsk—"

I cut him off quickly. I didn't want to know what he might have done with Zoya back at the Grisha camp. And that was hardly the point. "She was one of the Darkling's favourites, and she's always hated me."

"She was probably jealous of you."

"She broke two of my ribs."

"She *what*?"

"It was an accident. Sort of." I'd never told Mal exactly how bad it had been for me before I'd learned to use my power, the endless, lonely days of failure. "I just can't be sure where her real allegiance lies." I rubbed the back of my neck where the muscles had started to bunch. "I can't be sure of anyone. Not the Grisha. Not the servants. Any of them could be working for the Darkling."

Mal looked around. For once, nobody seemed to be watching. Impulsively, he seized hold of my hand. "Gritzki's throwing a fortune-telling party in the upper town two days from now. Come with me."

"Gritzki?"

"His father is Stepan Gritzki, the pickle king. New money," Mal said in a very good imitation of a smug noble. "But his family has a palace down by the canal."

"I can't," I said, thinking of the meetings, David's mirrored dishes, the evacuation of the school. It just felt wrong to go to a party when we could be at war in a matter of days or weeks.

"You can," said Mal. "Just for an hour or two."

It was so tempting – to steal a few moments with Mal away from the pressures of the Little Palace.

He must have sensed that I was wavering. "We'll dress you up as one of the performers," he said. "No one will even know the Sun Summoner is there."

A party, late in the evening, after the day's work was done. I'd miss one night of futile searching through the library. What was the harm in that?

"All right," I said. "Let's go."

His face broke into a grin that left me breathless. I didn't know if I'd ever get used to the idea that a smile like that might actually be for me.

"Tolya and Tamar won't like it," he warned.

"They're my guards. They follow my orders."

Mal snapped to attention and swept me an elaborate bow. "*Da, moi soverenyi,*" he pronounced in sombre tones. "We live to serve."

I rolled my eyes, but as I hurried to the Materialki workrooms, I felt lighter than I had in weeks.

CHAPTER 18

The Gritzki mansion was in the canal district, considered the least fashionable part of the upper town because of its proximity to the bridge and the rabble across it. It was a lavish little building, bordered by a war memorial on one side and the gardens of the Convent of Sankta Lizabeta on the other.

Mal had managed to secure a borrowed coach for the evening, and we were tucked inside its narrow confines with a very cranky Tamar. She and Tolya had grumbled long and loudly about the party, but I'd made it clear that I wasn't going to budge. I also swore them to secrecy; I didn't want word of my little excursion beyond the palace gates to reach Nikolai.

We were all dressed in the style of Suli fortune-tellers, in vibrant orange silk cloaks and red lacquered masks carved to resemble jackals. Tolya had remained behind. Even covered head to toe, his size would draw too much attention.

Mal squeezed my hand, and I felt a surge of giddy excitement. My cloak was uncomfortably warm, and my face was already starting to itch beneath the mask, but I didn't care. I felt as if we were back at Keramzin, casting off our chores and braving the threat of the switch just to sneak away to our meadow. We would lie in the cool grass and listen to the hum of the insects, watch the clouds break apart overhead. That kind of peace seemed so far away now.

The street leading to the pickle king's mansion was clogged with carriages. We turned onto an alley near the convent so that we'd be better able to mix in with the performers at the servants' entrance.

Tamar carefully shifted her cloak as we descended from the coach. She and Mal were both carrying hidden pistols, and I knew beneath all the orange silk, she had her twin axes strapped to each thigh.

"What if someone actually wants his fortune told?" I asked, tightening the laces of my mask and pulling my hood up.

"Just feed him the usual drivel," said Mal. "Beautiful women, unexpected wealth. Beware of the number eight."

The servants' entrance led past a steam-filled kitchen and into the house's back rooms. But as soon as we stepped inside, a man dressed in what must have been the Gritzki livery seized my arm.

"Just what do you think you're doing?" he said, giving me a shake. I saw Tamar's hand go to her hip.

"I—"

"You three should already be circulating." He shoved us in the direction of the main rooms of the house. "Don't spend too long with any single guest. And don't let me catch you drinking!"

I nodded, trying to get my heart to stop hammering, and we hurried into the ballroom. The pickle king had spared no expense. The mansion had been decorated to look like the most decadent Suli camp imaginable. The ceiling was hung with a thousand star-shaped lanterns.

Silk-covered wagons were parked around the edges of the room in a glittering caravan, and fake bonfires glowed with dancing coloured light. The terrace doors had been thrown open, and the night air hummed with the rhythmic clang of finger cymbals and the wail of violins.

I saw the real Suli fortune-tellers scattered throughout the crowd and thought what an eerie sight we must make in our jackal masks. The guests didn't seem to mind. Most of them were already well in their cups, laughing and shouting to one another in boisterous groups, gawking at the acrobats twirling from silk swings overhead. Some sat swaying in their chairs, having their fortunes told over golden urns of coffee. Others ate at the long table that had been set up on the terrace, gorging on stuffed figs and bowls of pomegranate seeds, clapping along with the music.

Mal snuck me a little glass of *kvas*, and we found a bench in a shadowy corner of the terrace while Tamar took up her post a discreet distance away. I rested my head against Mal's shoulder, happy just to be sitting beside him, listening to the thump and jangle of the music. The air was heavy with the scent of some night-blooming flower and, beneath that, the tang of lemons. I breathed deeply, feeling some of the exhaustion and fear of the last few weeks ease away. I wriggled my foot from my slipper and let my toes dig into the cool gravel.

Mal adjusted his hood to better hide his face and tipped up his mask, then reached forward and did the same with mine. He leaned in. Our jackal masks bumped snouts.

I started to laugh.

"Next time, different costumes," he grumbled.

"Bigger hats?"

"Maybe we could just wear baskets over our heads."

Two girls came swaying up to us. Tamar was by my side in an instant. We pushed our masks back into place.

"Tell our fortunes!" the taller girl demanded, practically toppling over her friend.

Tamar shook her head, but Mal gestured to one of the little tables laid with blue enamel cups and a golden urn.

The girl squealed and poured out a tiny amount of sludge-like coffee. The Suli told fortunes by reading the dregs at the bottom of the cup. She downed the coffee and grimaced.

I elbowed Mal in the side. *Now what?*

He rose and walked to the table.

"Hmmm," he said, peering into the cup. "Hmmm."

The girl seized his arm. "What is it?"

He waved me over. I gritted my teeth and bent over the cup.

"Is it bad?" the girl moaned.

"Eeet eeees . . . goooood," said Mal in the most outrageous Suli accent I'd ever heard.

The girl sighed in relief.

"You weeel meet a handsome stranger."

The girls giggled and clapped their hands. I couldn't resist.

"He weeel be very wicked man," I interjected. My accent was even worse than Mal's. If any real Suli overheard me, I'd probably end up with a black eye. "You must run from theees man."

"Oh," the girls sighed in disappointment.

"You must marry ugly man," I said. "Very fet." I held my arms out in front of me, indicating a giant belly. "He weeel make you heppy."

I heard Mal snort beneath his mask.

The girl sniffed. "I don't like this fortune," she said. "Let's go and try another one." As they flounced away, two rather tipsy noblemen took their place.

One had a beaky nose and wobbly jowls. The other threw back his coffee like he was gulping *kvas* and slammed the cup down on the table. "Now," he slurred, twitching his bristly red mustache. "What've I got in store? And make it good."

Mal pretended to study the cup. "You weeel come into a great fortune."

"Already have a great fortune. What else?"

"Uh . . ." Mal hedged. "Your wife weel bear you three handsome sons."

His beak-nosed companion burst out laughing. "Well, then you'll *know* they aren't yours!" he bellowed.

I thought the other nobleman would take offence, but instead he just guffawed, his red face turning even redder.

"Have to congratulate the footman!" he roared.

"I hear all the best families have bastards," chortled his friend.

"Well, we all have dogs too. But we don't let them sit at the table!"

I grimaced beneath my mask. I had a sneaking suspicion they were talking about Nikolai.

"Oh dear," I said, yanking the cup from Mal's hand. "Oh dear, so sad."

"What's that?" said the nobleman, still laughing.

"You weel go bald," I said. "Very bald."

He stopped laughing, and his meaty hand strayed to his already thinning red hair.

"And you," I said, pointing at his friend. Mal gave my foot a warning nudge, but I ignored him. "You weel catch the *korpa*."

"The what?"

"The *korpa*!" I declared in dire tones. "Your private parts weel shrink to nothink!"

He paled. His throat worked. "But—"

At that moment there was shouting from inside the ballroom and a loud crash as someone upended a table. I saw two men shoving each other.

"I think it's time to leave," said Tamar, edging us away from the commotion.

I was about to protest when the fight broke out in earnest. People started pushing and shoving, crowding the doors to the terrace. The music had stopped, and it looked like some of the fortune-tellers had been drawn into the scramble too. Over the crowd, I saw one of the silken wagons collapse. Someone came hurtling towards us and crashed into the noblemen. The coffee urn toppled off the table, and the little blue cups followed.

"Let's go," said Mal, reaching for his pistol. "Out the back."

Tamar led the way, axes already in hand. I followed her down the stairs, but as we stepped off the terrace, I heard another horrible crash and a woman screaming. She was pinned beneath the banquet table.

Mal holstered his pistol. "Get her to the carriage," he shouted to Tamar. "I'll catch up."

"Mal—"

"Go! I'll be right behind you." He pushed into the crowd, towards the trapped woman.

Tamar tugged me down the garden stairs and up a path that led back along the side of the mansion to the street. It was dark away from the glowing lanterns of the party. I let a soft light blossom to guide our steps.

"Don't," said Tamar. "This could be a distraction. You'll give away our location."

I let the light fade, and a second later, I heard a scuffle, a loud *oof*, and then – silence.

"Tamar?"

I looked back to the party, hoping I would hear Mal's approach.

My heart started to pound. I raised my hands. Forget giving away our location, I wasn't going to just stand around in the dark. Then I heard a gate creak and strong hands took hold of me. I was yanked through the hedge.

I sent light searing out in a hot flare. I was in a stone courtyard off the main garden, bordered on all sides by yew hedges, and I was not alone.

I smelled him before I saw him – turned earth, incense, mildew. The smell of a grave. I raised my hands as the Apparat stepped out of the shadows. The priest was just as I remembered him, the same wiry black beard and relentless gaze. He still wore the brown robes of his station, but the King's double eagle was gone from his chest, replaced by a sunburst wrought in gold thread.

"Stay where you are," I warned.

He bowed low. "Alina Starkov, Sol Koroleva. I mean you no harm."

"Where's Tamar? If she's been hurt—"

"Your guards will not be harmed, but I beg you to listen."

"What do you want? How did you know I would be here?"

"The faithful are everywhere, Sol Koroleva."

"Don't call me that!"

"Every day your holy army grows, drawn by the promise of your light. They wait only for you to lead them."

"My army? I've seen the pilgrims camped outside the city walls – poor, weak, hungry, all desperate for the scraps of hope you feed them."

"There are others. Soldiers."

"More people who think I'm a Saint because you've sold them a lie?"

"It is no lie, Alina Starkov. You are, Daughter of Keramzin, Reborn of the Fold."

"I didn't die!" I said furiously. "I survived because I escaped the Darkling, and I murdered an entire skiff of soldiers and Grisha to do it. Do you tell your followers that?"

"Your people are suffering. Only you can bring about the dawn of a new age, an age consecrated in holy fire."

His eyes were wild, the black so deep I couldn't see his pupils. Was his madness real or part of some elaborate act?

"Just who will rule this new age?"

"You, of course. Sol Koroleva, Sankta Alina."

"With you at my right hand? I read the book you gave me. Saints don't live long lives."

"Come with me, Alina Starkov."

"I'm not going anywhere with you."

"You are not yet strong enough to face the Darkling. I can change that."

I stilled. "Tell me what you know."

"Join me, and all will be revealed."

I advanced on him, surprised by the throb of hunger and rage that shot through me. "Where is the firebird?" I thought he might respond with confusion, that he might pretend ignorance. Instead, he smiled, his gums black, his teeth a crooked jumble. "Tell me, priest," I ordered, "or I'll cut you open right here and your followers can try to pray you back together." With a start, I realised that I meant it.

For the first time, he looked nervous. *Good.* Had he expected a tame Saint?

He held up his hands placatingly.

"I do not know," he said. "I swear it. But when the Darkling left the Little Palace, he did not realise it would be for the last time. He left many precious things behind, things others believed long since destroyed."

Another surge of hunger crackled through me. "Morozova's journals? You have them?"

"Come with me, Alina Starkov. There are secrets buried deep."

Could he possibly be telling the truth? Or would he just hand me over to the Darkling?

"Alina!" Mal's voice sounded from somewhere on the other side of the hedge.

"I'm here!" I called.

Mal burst into the courtyard, pistol drawn. Tamar was right behind him. She'd lost one of her axes, and there was blood smeared over the front of her cloak.

The Apparat turned in a musty whirl of cloth and slipped between the bushes.

"Wait!" I cried, already moving to follow. Tamar

bolted past me with a furious roar, diving into the hedges to give chase.

"I need him alive!" I shouted at her disappearing back.

"Are you all right?" Mal panted as he came level with me.

I took hold of his sleeve. "Mal, I think he has Morozova's journals."

"Did he hurt you?"

"I can handle an old priest," I said impatiently. "Did you hear what I said?"

He drew back. "Yes, I heard you. I thought you were in danger."

"I wasn't. I—"

But Tamar was already returning, her face a mask of frustration. "I don't understand it," she said, shaking her head. "He was there and then he was just gone."

"Saints," I swore.

She hung her head. "Forgive me."

I'd never seen her look so downcast. "It's all right," I said, my mind still churning. Part of me wanted to go back down that alley and shout for the Apparat, demand that he show himself, hunt him through the city streets until I found him and pried the truth from his lying mouth. I peered down the row of hedges. I could still hear shouting from the party far behind me, and somewhere in the dark, the bells of the convent began to ring. I sighed. "Let's get out of here."

We found our driver waiting on the narrow sidestreet where we'd left him. The ride back to the palace was tense.

"That brawl was no coincidence," said Mal.

"No," agreed Tamar, dabbing at the ugly cut on her chin. "He knew we would be there."

"How?" Mal demanded. "No one else knew we were going. Did you tell Nikolai?"

"Nikolai had nothing to do with this," I said.

"How can you be so sure?"

"Because he has nothing to gain." I pressed my fingers to my temples. "Maybe someone saw us leaving the palace."

"How did the Apparat get into Os Alta without being seen? How did he even know we would be at that party?"

"I don't know," I replied wearily. "He said the faithful are everywhere. Maybe one of the servants overheard."

"We got lucky tonight," said Tamar. "This could have been much worse."

"I was never in any real danger," I insisted. "He just wanted to talk."

"What did he say?"

I gave her the barest description, but I didn't mention Morozova's journals. I hadn't talked to anyone except Mal about them, and Tamar knew too much about the amplifiers already.

"He's raising some kind of army," I finished. "People who believe that I've risen from the dead, who think I have some kind of holy power."

"How many?" Mal asked.

"I don't know. And I don't know what he intends to do with them. March them against the King? Send them to fight the Darkling's horde? I'm already responsible for the Grisha. I don't want the burden of an army of helpless *otkazat'sya*."

"We're not all quite so feeble," said Mal, an edge to his voice.

"I didn't . . . I just meant he's using these people. He's exploiting their hope."

"Is it any different from Nikolai parading you from village to village?"

"Nikolai isn't telling people that I'm immortal or can perform miracles."

"No," Mal said. "He's just letting them believe it."

"Why are you so ready to attack him?"

"Why are you so quick to defend him?"

I turned away, tired, exasperated, unable to think past the whir of thoughts in my head. The lamplit streets of the upper town slid by the coach's window. We passed the rest of the ride in silence.

Back at the Little Palace, I changed clothes while Mal and Tamar filled Tolya in on what had happened.

I was sitting on the bed when Mal knocked. He shut the door behind him and leaned against it, looking around.

"This room is so depressing. I thought you were going to redecorate."

I shrugged. I had too many other things to worry about, and I'd almost got used to the room's quiet gloom.

"Do you believe he has the journals?" Mal asked.

"I was surprised he even knew they existed."

He crossed to the bed, and I bent my knees to make room for him.

"Tamar's right," he said, settling by my feet. "That could have been much worse."

I sighed. "So much for seeing the sights."

"I shouldn't have suggested it."

"I shouldn't have gone along with it."

He nodded, scuffed the toe of his boot along the floor. "I miss you," he said quietly.

Soft words, but they sent a painful, welcome tremor through me. Had a part of me doubted it? He'd been gone so often.

I touched his hand. "I miss you too."

"Come to target practice with me tomorrow," he said. "Down by the lake."

"I can't. Nikolai and I are meeting with a delegation of Kerch bankers. They want to see the Sun Summoner before they guarantee a loan to the Crown."

"Tell him you're sick."

"Grisha don't get sick."

"Well, tell him you're busy," he said.

"I can't."

"Other Grisha take time to—"

"I'm not *other* Grisha," I said more harshly than I intended.

"I know that," he said wearily. He let out a long breath. "Saints, I hate this place."

I blinked, startled by the vehemence in his voice. "You do?"

"I hate the parties. I hate the people. I hate everything about it."

"I thought . . . you seemed . . . not happy exactly, but—"

"I don't belong here, Alina. Don't tell me you haven't noticed."

That I didn't believe. Mal fitted in everywhere. "Nikolai says everyone adores you."

"They're amused by me," Mal said. "That's not the same thing." He turned my hand over, tracing the scar that ran the length of my palm. "Do you know I actually miss being on the run? Even that filthy little boarding house in Cofton and working in the warehouse. At least then I felt like I was doing something, not just wasting time and gathering gossip."

I shifted uncomfortably, feeling suddenly defensive. "You take every chance you get to be away. You don't have to accept every invitation."

He stared at me. "I stay away to protect you, Alina."

"From what?" I asked incredulously.

He stood up, pacing restlessly across the room. "What do you think people asked me on the royal hunt? The first thing? They wanted to know about me and you." He turned on me, and when he spoke his voice was cruel, mocking. "*Is it true that you're tumbling the Sun Summoner? What's it like with a Saint? Does she have a taste for trackers or does she take all of her servants to her bed?*" He crossed his arms. "I stay away to put distance between us, to stop the rumours. I probably shouldn't even be in here now."

I circled my knees with my arms, drawing them more tightly to my chest. My cheeks were burning. "Why didn't you say something?"

"What could I say? And when? I barely see you any more."

"I thought you wanted to go."

"I wanted you to ask me to stay."

My throat felt tight. I opened my mouth, ready to tell him that he wasn't being fair, that I couldn't have known. But was that the truth? Maybe I had really believed Mal was happier away from the Little Palace. Or maybe I'd just told myself that because it was easier with him gone, because it meant one less person watching and wanting something from me.

"I'm sorry," I rasped.

He raised his hands as if to plead his case, then dropped them helplessly. "I feel you slipping away from me, and I don't know how to stop it."

Tears pricked my eyes. "We'll find a way," I said. "We'll make more time—"

"It's not just that. Ever since you put on that second amplifier, you've been different." My hand strayed to the fetter. "When you split the dome, the way you talk about the firebird . . . I heard you speaking to Zoya the other day. She was scared, Alina. And you liked it."

"Maybe I did," I said, my anger rising. It felt so much better than guilt or shame. "So what? You have no idea what she's like, what this place has been like for me. The fear, the responsibility—"

"I know that. I know. And I can see the toll it's taking. But you chose this. You have a purpose. I don't even know what I'm doing here."

"Don't say that." I swung my legs off the bed and stood. "We do have a purpose. We came here for Ravka. We—"

"No, Alina. *You* came here for Ravka. For the firebird. To lead the Second Army." He tapped the sun over his heart. "I came here for you. *You're* my flag. *You're* my nation. But that doesn't seem to matter any more. Do you realise this is the first time we've really been alone in weeks?"

The knowledge of that settled over us. The room seemed unnaturally quiet. Mal took a single tentative step towards me. Then he closed the space between us in two long strides. One hand slid around my waist, the other cupped my face. Gently, he tilted my mouth up to his.

"Come back to me," he said softly. He drew me to him, but as his lips met mine, something flickered in the corner of my eye.

The Darkling was standing behind Mal. I stiffened.

Mal pulled back. "What?" he said.

"Nothing. I just . . ." I trailed off. I didn't know what to say.

The Darkling was still there. "Tell him you see me when he takes you in his arms," he said.

I squeezed my eyes shut.

Mal dropped his hands and stepped away from me, his fingers curling into fists. "I guess that's all I needed to know."

"Mal—"

"You should have stopped me. All the time I was standing there, going on like a fool. If you didn't want me, you should have just said so."

"Don't feel too bad, tracker," said the Darkling. "All men can be made fools."

"That's not it—" I protested.

"Is it Nikolai?"

"What? No!"

"Another *otkazat'sya*, Alina?" the Darkling mocked.

Mal shook his head in disgust. "I let him push me away. The meetings, the council sessions, the dinners. I let him edge me out. Just waiting, hoping that you'd miss me enough to tell them all to go to hell."

I swallowed, trying to block out the vision of the Darkling's cold smile.

"Mal, the Darkling—"

"I don't want to hear about the Darkling! Or Ravka or the amplifiers or any of it." He slashed his hand through the air. "I'm done." He turned on his heel and strode towards the door.

"Wait!" I rushed after him and reached for his arm.

He turned around so fast, I almost careened into him. "Don't, Alina."

"You don't understand—" I said.

"You *flinched*. Tell me you didn't."

"It wasn't because of you!"

Mal laughed harshly. "I know you haven't had much experience. But I've kissed enough girls to know what that means. Don't worry. It won't happen again."

The words hit me like a slap. He slammed the door behind him.

I stood there, staring at the closed doors. I reached out and touched the bone handle.

You can fix this, I told myself. *You can make this right.* But I just stood there, frozen, Mal's words ringing in my ears. I bit down hard on my lip to silence the sob that shook my chest. *That's good*, I thought as the tears spilled over. *That way the servants won't hear.* An ache had started between my ribs, a hard, bright shard of pain that lodged beneath my sternum, pressing tight against my heart.

I didn't hear the Darkling move; I only knew when he was beside me. His long fingers brushed the hair back from my neck and rested on the collar. When he kissed my cheek, his lips were cold.

Chapter 19

Early next morning, I tracked down David on the roof of the Little Palace, where construction had begun on his gigantic mirrored dishes. He'd set up a makeshift workspace in the shade of one of the domes, and it was already covered in bits of shiny detritus and discarded drawings. The barest breeze ruffled their edges. I recognised Nikolai's scrawl in one of the margins.

"How's it going?" I asked.

"Better," he said, studying the slick surface of the nearest dish. "I think I've got the curvature right. We should be ready to try them out soon."

"How soon?" We were still receiving conflicting reports of the Darkling's location, but if he hadn't finished creating his army, it wouldn't be long.

"A couple of weeks," David said.

"That long?"

"You can have it soon, or you can have it right," he grumbled.

"David, I need to know—"

"I told you everything I know about Morozova."

"Not about him," I said. "Not exactly. If . . . if I wanted to remove the collar. How would I do that?"

"You can't."

"Not now. But after we've—"

"No," David said, without looking at me. "It's not like other amplifiers. It can't just be taken off. You'd have to break it, violate its structure. The results would be catastrophic."

"How catastrophic?"

"I can't be certain," he said. "But I'm pretty sure it would make the Fold look like a paper cut."

"Oh," I said softly. Then it would be the same with the fetter. Whatever I was becoming, there was no turning back. I'd hoped the visions were the result of the bite from the *nichevo'ya*, that the effects might somehow diminish as the wound slowly healed. That didn't seem to be happening. And even if it did, I would always be tied to the Darkling through the collar. Again, I wondered why he hadn't chosen to try to kill the sea whip himself and bind us closer still.

David picked up a bottle of ink and began twirling it between his fingers. He looked miserable. *Not just miserable*, I thought. *Guilty.* He had forged this connection, placed this chain around my neck for eternity.

Gently, I took the ink bottle from his hands. "If you hadn't done it, the Darkling would have found someone else."

He twitched, something between a nod and a shrug. I set the ink down at the far edge of the table where his jittery fingers couldn't reach it and turned to go.

"Alina . . . ?"

I stopped and looked back at him. His cheeks had gone bright red. The warm breeze lifted the edges of his shaggy hair. At least that awful haircut was growing out.

"I heard . . . I heard Genya was on the ship. With the Darkling."

I felt a pang of sorrow for Genya. So David hadn't been completely oblivious.

"Yes," I said.

"She's all right?" he asked hopefully.

"I don't know," I admitted. "She was when we escaped." Though if the Darkling knew that she'd as good as let us go, I didn't know how he might have dealt with her. I hesitated. "I begged her to come with us."

His face fell. "But she stayed?"

"I don't think she felt she had a choice," I said. I couldn't believe I was making excuses for Genya. I just didn't like the idea of David thinking less of her.

"I should have . . ." He didn't seem to know how to finish.

I wanted to say something comforting, something reassuring. But there were so many mistakes in my own past that I couldn't think of anything that wouldn't ring false.

"We do the best we can," I offered lamely.

David looked at me then, the regret plain on his face. No matter what I said, we both knew the hard truth. We do our best. We try. And usually, it makes no difference at all.

I carried my black mood with me to the next meeting at the Grand Palace. Nikolai's plan seemed to be working. Though Vasily still dragged himself to the council chamber for our meetings with the ministers, he arrived later and later, and occasionally, I caught him dozing off. The one time he failed to appear, Nikolai hauled him from his bed, cheerfully insisting that he get dressed and that we simply couldn't proceed without him. A clearly hungover Vasily had made it through half of the meeting, swaying at the head of the table, before he bolted into the hallway to vomit noisily into a lacquered vase.

Today, even I was having trouble staying awake. Any bit of breeze had vanished, and despite the open windows, the crowded council chamber was unbearably stuffy. The meeting plodded on until one of the generals announced the dwindling numbers from the First Army's troop rolls. The ranks had been thinned by death, desertion, and years of brutal war, and given that Ravka was about to be fighting on at least one front again, the situation was dire.

Vasily waved a lazy hand and said, "Why all the gnashing of teeth? Just lower the draft age."

I sat up straighter. "To what?" I asked.

"Fourteen? Fifteen?" Vasily offered. "What is it now?"

I thought of all the villages Nikolai and I had passed through, the cemeteries that stretched for miles. "Why not just drop it to twelve?" I snapped.

"One is never too young to serve one's country," Vasily declared.

I don't know if it was exhaustion or anger, but the words were out of my mouth before I thought better of them. "In that case, why stop at twelve? I hear babies make excellent cannon fodder."

A disapproving murmur rose from the King's advisers. Beneath the table, Nikolai reached over and gave my hand a warning squeeze.

"Brother, bringing them in younger won't stop them from deserting," he said to Vasily.

"Then we find some deserters and make an example of them."

Nikolai raised a brow. "Are you sure that death by firing squad is more terrifying than the prospect of being torn apart by *nichevo'ya*?"

"If they even exist," Vasily scoffed.

I couldn't believe what I was hearing.

Nikolai just smiled pleasantly. "I saw them myself aboard the *Volkvolny*. Surely you're not calling me a liar."

"Surely you're not suggesting that treason is preferable to honest service in the King's Army."

"I'm suggesting that maybe these people are just as fond of life as you are. They're ill-equipped, undersupplied and short on hope. If you'd read the reports, you'd know that officers are having trouble keeping order in the ranks."

"Then they should institute harsher punishments," said Vasily. "It's what peasants understand."

I'd already punched one prince. What was one more? I was halfway out of my seat before Nikolai pulled me back down.

"They understand full bellies and clear directives," he said. "If you would let me implement the changes I've suggested and open the coffers for—"

"You cannot always have your way, *little brother*."

Tension crackled through the room.

"The world is changing," said Nikolai, the steel edge emerging in his voice. "We change with it, or there will be nothing left to remember us but the dust."

Vasily laughed. "I can't decide if you're a fearmonger or a coward."

"And I can't decide if you're an idiot or an idiot."

Vasily's face turned purple. He shot to his feet and smacked his hands down on the table. "The Darkling is one man. If you're afraid to face him—"

"I *have* faced him. If you're not afraid – if *any* of you aren't afraid – it's because you lack the sense to understand what we're up against."

Some of the generals nodded. But the King's advisers, Os Alta's noblemen and bureaucrats, looked skeptical and sullen. To them, war was parades, military theory, little figures moved around on a map. If it came to it, these were the men who would ally themselves with Vasily.

Nikolai squared his shoulders, the actor's mask descending over his features once more. "Peace, brother," he said. "We both want what's best for Ravka."

Vasily wasn't interested in being soothed. "What's best for Ravka is a Lantsov on the throne."

I drew in a sharp breath. A deadly stillness descended over the room. Vasily had as good as called Nikolai a bastard.

But Nikolai had regained his composure, and now nothing would shake it. "Then let us all say a prayer for Ravka's rightful King," he said. "Now, shall we finish our business?"

The meeting limped along for a few more minutes and then came to a welcome close. On our walk back to the Little Palace, Nikolai was uncharacteristically silent.

When we reached the gardens by the pillared folly, he paused to pluck a leaf from a hedge and said, "I shouldn't have lost my temper that way. It just pricks his pride, makes him dig in his heels."

"So why did you?" I asked, genuinely curious. It was rare for Nikolai's emotions to get the best of him.

"I don't know," he said, shredding the leaf. "You got angry. I got angry. The room was too damn hot."

"I don't think that's it."

"Indigestion?" he offered.

I wasn't going to be put off by a joke. Despite Vasily's objections and the council's reluctance to do much of anything, through some magical combination of patience and pressure, Nikolai had still managed to push through a few of his plans. He'd got them to approve relief for the refugees fleeing the shores of the Fold, and requisitioned Materialki corecloth to outfit key regiments of the First Army. He'd even got them to divert funds for a plan to modernise farm equipment so that peasants could manage something other than subsistence. Small things, but improvements that might make all the difference in time.

"It's because you actually care about what happens to this country," I said. "The throne is just a prize to Vasily, something he wants to squabble over like a favourite toy. You're not like that. You'll make a good king."

Nikolai froze. "I . . ." For once, words seemed to have deserted him. Then a crooked, embarrassed smile crept across his face. It was a far cry from his usual self-assured grin. "Thank you," he said.

I sighed as we resumed our pace. "You're going to be insufferable now, aren't you?"

Nikolai laughed. "I'm already insufferable."

The days grew longer. The sun stayed close beneath the horizon, and the festival of Belyanoch began in Os Alta.

Even at midnight, the skies were never truly dark, and despite the fear of war and the looming threat of the Fold, the city celebrated the endless hours of twilight. In the upper town, the evenings were crowded with operas, masques, and lavish ballets. Over the bridge, raucous horse races and outdoor dances shook the streets of the lower town. An endless stream of pleasure boats bobbed through the canal, and beneath the glimmering dusk, the slow-moving water circled the capital like a jewelled bangle, alight with lanterns hung from a thousand prows.

The heat had relented slightly. Behind the palace walls, everyone seemed in better spirits. I'd continued to insist that the Grisha mix their Orders, and at some point, I still wasn't sure how, uncomfortable silence had given way to laughter and noisy conversation. There were still cliques and conflicts, but there was also something comfortable and boisterous in the hall that hadn't been there before.

I was glad – maybe even a little proud – to see Fabrikators and Etherealki drinking tea around one of the samovars, or Fedyor arguing a point with Pavel over breakfast, or Nadia's little brother trying to chat up an older and decidedly disinterested Paja. But I felt as if I were watching them from a great distance.

I'd tried to talk to Mal several times since the night of our argument. He always found an excuse to walk away from me. If he wasn't hunting, he was playing cards at the Grand Palace or haunting some tavern in the lower town with his new friends. I could tell he'd been drinking more. Some mornings his eyes looked bleary and he sported bruises and cuts as if he'd been in a brawl, but he was unfailingly punctual, relentlessly polite. He kept to his guard duties, stood silently in doorways, and maintained a respectful distance as he trailed me around the grounds.

The Little Palace had become a very lonely place. Though I was surrounded by people, it was almost as if they couldn't see me, only what they needed from me. I was afraid to show doubt or indecision, and there were days when I felt I was being worn down to nothing by the constant weight of responsibility and expectation.

I went to my meetings. I trained with Botkin. I spent long hours at the lake trying to hone my use of the Cut. I even swallowed my pride and made another attempt to visit Baghra, hoping that, if nothing else, she might help me to develop my power further. She refused to see me.

None of it was enough. The ship that Nikolai was building in the lake was a reminder that everything we were doing was most likely futile. Somewhere out there, the Darkling was gathering his forces, building his army, and when they came, no gun, no bomb, no soldier or Grisha would be able to stop them. Not even me. If the battle went badly, we would retreat to the domed hall to await relief from Poliznaya. The doors were reinforced with Grisha steel, and the Fabrikators had already started sealing up cracks and gaps to prevent entry by the *nichevo'ya*.

I didn't think it would come to that. I'd reached a dead end in my attempts to locate the firebird. If David couldn't get those dishes working, then when the Darkling finally marched on Ravka, we would have no choice but to evacuate. Run and keep running.

Using my power brought me none of the comfort it once had. Every time I summoned light in the Materialki workshops or on the shore of the lake, I felt the bareness of my right wrist like a brand. Even with everything I knew about the amplifiers, the destruction they might bring, the permanence of the way they might change me, I couldn't escape my hunger for the firebird.

Mal was right. It had become an obsession. At night I lay in bed, imagining that the Darkling had already found the final piece of Morozova's puzzle. Maybe he held the firebird captive in a spun gold cage. Would it sing to him? I didn't even know if a firebird could sing at all. Some of the tales said so. One claimed the firebird's song could lull entire armies to sleep. When they heard it, soldiers would cease fighting, lay down their weapons, and nod off peacefully in their enemies' arms.

I knew all the stories by now. The firebird wept diamond tears, its feathers could heal mortal wounds, the future might be seen in the flap of its wings. I'd scoured book after book of folklore, epic poetry, and collections of peasant tales, searching for some pattern or clue. The sea whip's legends centred around the icy waters of the Bone Road, but stories of the firebird came from every part of Ravka and beyond, and none of them connected the creature to a Saint.

Worse, the visions were getting clearer and more frequent. The Darkling appeared to me almost every day, usually in his chambers or the aisles of the library, sometimes in the war room during council meetings or as I walked back from the Grand Palace at dusk.

"Why won't you leave me alone?" I whispered one night as he hovered behind me while I tried to work at my desk.

Long minutes passed. I didn't think he would answer.

I even had time to hope he might have gone, until I felt his hand on my shoulder.

"Then I'd be alone too," he said, and he stayed the whole night through, till the lamps burned down to nothing.

I got used to seeing him waiting for me at the end of corridors, or sitting at the edge of my bed when I fell asleep at night. When he didn't appear, I sometimes found myself looking for him or wondering why he hadn't come, and that frightened me most of all.

The one bright spot was Vasily's decision to abandon Os Alta for the yearling auctions in Caryeva. I nearly crowed with delight when Nikolai gave me the news on one of our walks.

"Packed up in the middle of the night," Nikolai said. "He says he'll be back in time for my birthday, but I wouldn't be surprised if he finds some excuse to stay away."

"You should try not to look so smug," I said. "It's not very regal."

"Surely I'm allowed some small dispensation for gloating," he said with a laugh. He whistled that same off-key tune I remembered from the *Volkvolny* as we walked along. Then he cleared his throat. "Alina, not that you aren't always the picture of loveliness, but . . . are you sleeping?"

"Not much," I admitted.

"Nightmares?"

I did still dream of the broken skiff, of people running from the darkness of the Fold, but that wasn't what kept me up at night. "Not exactly."

"Ah," said Nikolai. He clasped his hands behind his back. "I notice your friend has been throwing himself into his work lately. He's much in demand."

"Well," I said, keeping my voice light, "that's Mal."

"Where did he learn to track? No one seems to be able to decide if it's luck or skill."

"He didn't learn. He's just always been able to do it."

"How nice for him," said Nikolai. "I've never been a natural at anything."

"You're a spectacular actor," I said drily.

"Do you think so?" he asked. Then he leaned in and whispered, "I'm doing 'humble' right now."

I shook my head in exasperation, but I was grateful for Nikolai's cheery babble, and even more thankful when he let the subject drop.

It took David almost two more weeks to get his dishes operational, and when he was finally ready, I had the Grisha gather on the Little Palace roof to watch the demonstration. Tolya and Tamar were there, alert as always, scanning the crowd. Mal was nowhere to be seen. I'd stayed up the previous night in the common room, hoping to catch him and ask him personally to attend. It was long past midnight when I gave up and went to bed.

The two huge dishes were positioned on opposite sides of the roof, on the flat lip that extended between the domes of the eastern and western wings. They could be rotated through a system of pulleys, and each was manned by a Materialnik and a Squaller, outfitted in goggles to protect against the glare. I saw that Zoya and Paja had been teamed up, and Nadia had been paired with a Durast on the second dish.

Well, even if this is a total failure, I thought anxiously, *at least they're working together. Nothing like a fiery explosion to build camaraderie.*

I took my place in the middle of the roof, directly between the dishes.

With a jolt of nervousness, I saw that Nikolai had invited the captain of the palace guard to observe, along with two generals and several of the King's advisers. I hoped they weren't expecting anything too dramatic. My power tended to show best in full darkness, and the long Belyanoch days made that impossible. I'd asked David if we should schedule the demonstration for later in the evening, but he'd just shaken his head.

"If it works, it will be plenty dramatic. And I suppose that if it doesn't work, it will be even more dramatic, what with the blast."

"David, I think you just made a joke."

He frowned, utterly perplexed. "Did I?"

At Nikolai's suggestion, David had chosen to take his cue from the *Volkvolny* and use a whistle to signal us. He gave a shrill blast, and the onlookers backed up against the domes, leaving us plenty of room. I raised my hands. David blew on the whistle again. I called the light.

It entered me in a golden torrent and burst from my hands in two steady beams. They struck the dishes, reflecting off them in a blinding glare. It was impressive, but nothing spectacular.

Then David whistled again, and the dishes rotated slightly. The light bounced off their mirrored surfaces, multiplying upon itself and focusing into two blazing white shafts that pierced the early twilight.

An *ahhhh* went up from the crowd as they shielded their eyes. I guess I didn't have to worry about drama.

The beams sliced through the air, sending off waves of cascading brilliance and radiant heat, as if they were burning through the sky itself. David gave another short blast on the whistle, and the beams fused into a single molten blade of light. It was impossible to look directly at it. If the Cut was a knife in my hand, then this was a broadsword.

The dishes tilted, and the beam descended. The crowd gasped in astonishment as the light slashed through the edge of the woods below, levelling the treetops.

The dishes tilted further. The beam seared into the lakeshore and then into the lake itself. A wave of steam billowed into the air with an audible hiss, and for a moment, the entire surface of the lake seemed to boil.

David gave a panicked blast on the whistle. Hastily, I dropped my hands and the light vanished.

We ran to the edge of the roof and gaped at the sight before us.

It was as if someone had taken a razor and lopped off the top of the woods in a clean diagonal cut from the tip of the tree line to the shore. Where the beam had touched down, the ground was marked by a glowing trench that ran all the way to the waterline.

"It worked," David said in a dazed voice. "It actually worked."

There was a pause and then Zoya burst out laughing. Sergei joined her, then Marie and Nadia. Suddenly, we were all laughing and cheering, even moody Tolya, who swept a befuddled David up on his enormous shoulders. Soldiers were hugging Grisha, the King's advisers were hugging the generals, Nikolai was dancing a begoggled Paja around the roof, and the captain of the guard caught me up in a giddy embrace.

We whooped and screamed and bounced up and down, so that the whole palace seemed to shake. When the Darkling decided to march, the *nichevo'ya* would have quite a surprise waiting for them.

"Let's go see it!" someone shouted, and we raced down the stairs like children at the sound of the school bell, giggling and careening off the walls.

We charged through the Hall of the Golden Dome and flung open the doors, tumbling down the steps and outside. As everyone sprinted down to the lake, I skidded to a halt.

Mal was coming up the path from the wooded tunnel.

"Go on," I said to Nikolai. "I'll catch up."

Mal watched the path as he approached, not meeting my gaze. As he drew closer, I saw that his eyes were bloodshot and there was an ugly bruise on his cheekbone.

"What happened?" I asked, lifting a hand to his face. He ducked away, darting a glance at the servants who stood by the Little Palace doors.

"Ran into a bottle of *kvas*," he said. "Is there something you need?"

"You missed the demonstration."

"I wasn't on duty."

I ignored the painful jab in my chest and pushed on. "We're going down to the lake. Would you like to come?"

For a moment, he seemed to hesitate, then he shook his head. "I just came back to get some coin. There's a card game going at the Grand Palace."

The shard twisted. "You may want to change," I said.

"You look like you slept in your clothes." I was instantly sorry I'd said it, but Mal didn't seem to care.

"Maybe because I did," he said. "Is there anything else?"

"No."

"*Moi soverenyi.*" He executed a sharp bow and vaulted up the steps as if he couldn't wait to be away from me.

I took my time walking down to the lake, hoping that somehow the ache in my heart would ease. My joy at the success on the roof had drained away, leaving me hollow, like a well someone could shout down and hear nothing back but echoes.

By the shore, a group of Grisha were walking the length of the trench, calling out measurements in growing triumph and elation. It was nearly two feet wide and just as deep, a furrow of charred earth that stretched to the water's edge. In the woods, felled treetops lay in a clutter of branches and bark. I reached out and ran my hand over one of the severed trunks. The wood was smooth, sliced cleanly across, and still warm to the touch. Two small fires had started, but the Tidemakers had quickly put them out.

Nikolai ordered food and champagne brought down to the lake, and we all spent the rest of the evening on the shore. The generals and advisers retired early, but the captain and some of his guard remained. They stripped off their jackets and shoes and waded into the lake, and it wasn't long before everyone decided they didn't care about wet clothes and plunged into the water, splashing and dunking each other, then organising swim races to the little island. To no one's surprise, a Tidemaker always won, borne aloft by lucky waves.

Nikolai and his Squallers offered to take people up in the recently completed craft he'd dubbed the *Kingfisher*. At first they were wary, but after the first brave group came back flapping their arms and babbling about actually flying, everyone wanted a turn. I'd sworn my feet would never leave the ground again, but finally I gave in and joined them.

Maybe it was the champagne or just that I knew what to expect, but the *Kingfisher* seemed lighter and more graceful than the *Hummingbird*. Though I still gripped the cockpit with both hands, I felt my spirits lift as we rose smoothly into the air.

I gathered my courage and looked down. The rolling grounds of the Grand Palace stretched out below us, crosscut by white gravel paths. I saw the roof of the Grisha greenhouse, the perfect circle of the double eagle fountain, the golden glint of the palace gates. Then we were soaring over the mansions and long, straight boulevards of the upper town. The streets were full of people celebrating Belyanoch. I saw jugglers and stiltwalkers on Gersky Prospect, dancers twirling on a lit stage in one of the parks. Music floated up from the boats on the canal.

I wanted to stay up there forever, surrounded by the flood of wind, watching the tiny, perfect world beneath us. But eventually Nikolai turned the wheel and brought us back to the lake in a slow, descending arc.

The twilight deepened to a lush purple. The Inferni lit bonfires along the lakeshore, and somewhere in the dusk, someone tuned a balalaika. From the town below, I heard the whistle and clap of fireworks.

Nikolai and I sat at the end of the makeshift pier,

our trousers rolled up, feet dangling over the side. The *Kingfisher* bobbed beside us, its white sails trimmed.

Nikolai kicked his foot through the water, sending up a little splash. "The dishes change everything," he said. "If you can keep the *nichevo'ya* busy long enough, we'll have time to find and target the Darkling."

I flopped back on the dock, stretching my arms overhead and taking in the blooming violet of the night sky. When I turned my head, I could just make out the shape of the now-empty school building, its windows dark. I would have liked the students to see what the dishes could do, to give them that bit of hope. The prospect of a battle was still frightening, especially when I thought of all the lives that might be lost. But at least we weren't just sitting on a hilltop waiting to die.

"We may actually have a fighting chance," I said in amazement.

"Try not to let the excitement overwhelm you, but I have more good news."

I groaned. I knew that tone of voice. "Don't say it."

"Vasily is back from Caryeva."

"You could do the kind thing and drown me now."

"And suffer alone? I think not."

"Maybe for your birthday you can ask that he be fitted with a royal muzzle," I suggested.

"But then we'd miss all his exciting stories about the summer auctions. You're fascinated by the breeding superiority of the Ravkan racehorse, right?"

I let out a whimper. Mal was supposed to be on duty for Nikolai's birthday dinner the following night. Maybe I could get Tolya or Tamar to take his place. Right now, I didn't think I could handle watching him stand stone-faced at attention all night, especially not with Vasily yammering away.

"Be of good cheer," said Nikolai. "Maybe he'll propose again."

I sat up. "How do you know about that?"

"If you recall, I did pretty much the same thing. I'm just surprised he hasn't tried a second time."

"Apparently I'm not easy to get alone."

"I know," said Nikolai. "Why do you think I walk you back from the Grand Palace after every meeting?"

"For my sparkling company?" I said sourly, annoyed by the twitch of disappointment I felt at his words. Nikolai was so good at making me forget that everything he did was calculated.

"That too," he said. He lifted his foot out of the water and scrutinised his wiggling toes. "He'll get around to it again, eventually."

I sighed with exaggerated woe. "How does one say no to a prince?"

"You've managed it before," Nikolai said, still contemplating his foot. "And are you so sure you want to?"

"You can't be serious."

Nikolai shifted uncomfortably. "Well, he is first in line for the throne, of pure royal stock, and all that."

"I wouldn't marry Vasily if he had a pet firebird named Ludmilla, and I couldn't care less about his royal stock." I peered at him. "You said the gossip about your bloodlines didn't bother you."

"I may not have been completely honest about that."

"You? Less than truthful? I'm shocked, Nikolai. Shocked and horrified."

He laughed. "I guess it's easy to say it doesn't matter when I'm away from court. But no one here seems to want to let me forget, especially my brother." He shrugged. "It's always been this way. There were rumours about me even before I was born. It's why my mother never calls me Sobachka. She says it makes me sound like a mongrel."

My heart gave a little pang at that. I'd been called plenty of names growing up.

"I like mongrels," I said. "They have cute floppy ears."

"My ears are very dignified."

I ran my finger over one of the pier's sleek planks. "Is that why you stayed away so long? Why you became Sturmhond?"

"I don't know if there's just one reason. I guess I never felt I belonged here, so I tried to make a place where I could belong."

"I never felt I fitted in anywhere either," I admitted. *Except with Mal.* I pushed the thought away. Then I frowned. "You know what I hate about you?"

He blinked, startled. "No."

"You always say the right thing."

"And you hate that?"

"I've seen the way you change personas, Nikolai. You're always what everyone needs you to be. Maybe you never felt like you belonged, or maybe you're just saying that to make the poor, lonely orphan girl like you more."

"So you do like me?"

I rolled my eyes. "Yes, when I don't want to stab you."

"It's a start."

"No it isn't."

He turned to me. In the half-light, his hazel eyes looked like chips of amber.

"I'm a privateer, Alina," he said quietly. "I'll take whatever I can get."

I was suddenly aware of his shoulder resting against mine, the press of his thigh. The air felt warm and smelled sweet with the scent of summer and woodsmoke.

"I want to kiss you," he said.

"You already kissed me," I replied with a nervous laugh.

A smile tugged at his lips. "I want to kiss you again," he amended.

"Oh," I breathed. His mouth was inches from mine. My heart leapt into a panicked gallop. *This is Nikolai*, I reminded myself. *Pure calculation*. I didn't even think I wanted him to kiss me. But my pride was still smarting from Mal's rejection. Hadn't he said he'd kissed plenty of girls?

"I want to kiss you," Nikolai said. "But I won't. Not until you're thinking of me instead of trying to forget him."

I shoved myself back and lurched awkwardly to my feet, feeling flushed and embarrassed.

"Alina—"

"At least now I know you don't always say the right thing," I muttered.

I snatched up my shoes and escaped down the pier.

Chapter 20

I stayed well clear of the Grisha bonfires as I strode around the lakeshore. I didn't want to see or talk to anyone.

What had I expected from Nikolai? Distraction? Flirtation? Something to shake the ache in my heart free? Maybe I'd just wanted some petty way to get back at Mal. Or maybe I was so desperate to feel connected to anyone that I would settle for a false kiss from an untrustworthy prince.

The idea of tomorrow night's birthday dinner filled me with dread. Perhaps I could make some excuse, I considered as I stomped across the grounds. I could send a nice note to the Grand Palace sealed with wax and emblazoned with the Sun Summoner's official seal:

To Their Most Royal Majesties, the King and Queen of Ravka:

It is with a sad heart that I must proffer my regrets and inform you that I will be unable to attend the festivities celebrating the birth of Prince Nikolai Lantsov, Grand Duke of Udova.

Unfortunate circumstances have arisen, namely that my best friend can't seem to stand the sight of me, and your son didn't kiss me and I wish he had.

Or I wish he hadn't. Or I'm still not sure what I wish, but there's a very good chance that if I'm forced to sit through his stupid birthday dinner, I'll end up sobbing into my cake.

With best wishes on this most happy of occasions,
Alina Starkov, Idiot

When I reached the Darkling's chambers, Tamar was reading in the common room. She looked up as I entered, but my mood must have shown on my face, because she didn't say a word.

I knew I wouldn't be able to sleep, so I propped myself up in bed with one of the books I'd taken from the library, an old travel guide that listed Ravka's famous monuments. I had the barest hope that it would point me towards the arch.

I tried to focus, but I found myself reading the same sentence again and again. My head was muzzy with champagne, and my feet still felt cold and waterlogged from the lake. Mal might be back from his card game. If I knocked on his door and he answered, what would I say?

I tossed the book aside. I didn't know what to say to Mal. I never did these days. Maybe I could just start with the truth: that I was lost and confused, and maybe losing my mind, that I scared myself sometimes, and that I missed him so much it was like physical pain. I needed to at least try to heal the rift between us before it was completely beyond repair. No matter what he thought of me afterwards, it couldn't get much worse. I could survive another rejection, but I couldn't bear the thought that I hadn't even tried to put this right.

I peeked into the common room.

"Is Mal here?" I asked Tamar.

She shook her head.

I swallowed my pride and asked, "Do you know where he went?"

Tamar sighed. "Get your shoes. I'll take you to him."

"Where is he?"

"The stables."

Unsettled, I ducked back into my bedroom and quickly pulled on my shoes. I followed Tamar out of the Little Palace and across the lawns.

"You're sure you want to do this?" Tamar asked.

I didn't reply. Whatever she had to show me, I knew I wasn't going to like it. But I refused to just go back to my room and bury my head under the covers.

We made our way down the gentle slope that led past the *banya*. Horses whinnied in the paddocks. The stables were dark, but the training rooms were ablaze with light. I heard shouting.

The largest training room was little more than a barn with a dirt floor, its walls covered in every weapon imaginable. Usually, it was where Botkin doled out punishment to Grisha students and put them through their drills. But tonight it was crowded with people, mostly soldiers, some Grisha, even a few servants. They were all shouting and cheering, jostling and jockeying to try to get a better look at whatever was happening in the middle of the room.

Unnoticed, Tamar and I worked our way through the crush of bodies. I glimpsed two royal trackers, several members of Nikolai's regiment, a group of Corporalki, and Zoya, who was screaming and clapping with the rest of them.

I'd almost reached the front of the crowd when I caught sight of a Squaller, fists raised, chest bare, stalking his way around the circle the onlookers had formed. *Eskil*, I remembered, one of the Grisha who had been travelling with Fedyor. He was Fjerdan and he looked it – blue eyes, white-blond hair, tall and broad enough that he completely blocked my view.

It's not too late, I thought. *You can still turn round and pretend you were never here.*

I stayed rooted to the spot. I knew what I would see, but it was still a shock when Eskil moved aside and I got my first glimpse of Mal. Like the Squaller, he was stripped to the waist, his muscled torso streaked with dirt and sweat. There were bruises on his knuckles. A trickle of blood coursed down his cheek from a cut below his eye, though he hardly seemed to notice.

The Squaller lunged. Mal blocked the first punch, but the next caught him beneath the kidneys. He grunted, dropped his elbow, and swung hard at the Squaller's jaw.

Eskil bobbed out of Mal's range and scooped his arm through the air in a swooping arc. With a stab of panic, I realised he was summoning. The gust rustled my hair, and in the next second, Mal was blown off his feet by Etherealki wind. Eskil threw out his other arm, and Mal's body shot upwards, slamming into the roof of the barn. He hung there for a moment, pinned to the wooden beams by the Grisha's power. Then Eskil let him drop. He crashed to the dirt floor with bone-rattling force.

I screamed, but the sound was lost in the roar of the crowd. One of the Corporalki bellowed encouragement at Eskil while another was shouting at Mal to get up.

I pushed forward, light already blooming from my hands. Tamar grabbed my sleeve.

"He doesn't want your help," she said.

"I don't care," I yelled. "This isn't a fair fight. That isn't allowed!" Grisha were never permitted to use their powers in the training rooms.

"Botkin's rules don't apply after dark. Mal's in the middle of a fight, not a lesson."

I yanked away from her. Better Mal angry than Mal dead.

He was on his hands and knees, trying to get to his feet. I was amazed he could even move after the Squaller's attack. Eskil raised his hands again. The air billowed up in a flurry of dust. I called the light to me, not caring what Tamar or Mal had to say about it. But this time, Mal rolled, dodging the current and launching to his feet with surprising speed.

Eskil scowled and scanned the perimeter, considering his options. I knew what he was weighing. He couldn't just let loose without risking knocking us all down, and maybe part of the stables too. I waited, keeping a tenuous grasp on the light, unsure of what to do.

Mal was breathing hard, bent at the waist, hands resting on his thighs. He'd probably cracked at least one rib. He was lucky he hadn't broken his spine. I willed him to get back down and stay there. Instead, he forced himself upright, hissing at the pain. He rolled his shoulders, cursed, spat blood. Then, to my horror, he curled his fingers and beckoned the Squaller forward. A cheer went up from the crowd.

"What is he doing?" I moaned. "He's going to get himself killed."

"He'll be fine," Tamar said. "I've seen him take worse."

"*What?*"

"He fights here almost every night when he's sober enough. Sometimes when he's not."

"He fights Grisha?"

Tamar shrugged. "He's actually pretty good."

This was what Mal did with his nights? I remembered all the mornings he'd appeared with bruises and scrapes. What was he trying to prove? I thought of my careless words as we'd returned from the fortune-telling party. *I don't want the burden of an army of helpless* otkazat'sya.

I wished I could take them back.

The Squaller feinted left, then raised his hands for another attack. Wind blew through the circle, and I saw Mal's feet lose contact with the floor. I gritted my teeth, sure I was about to see him tossed against the nearest wall. At the last second, he spun, wrenching away from the blast of air and charging the startled Squaller.

Eskil let out a loud *oof* as Mal clamped his arms around him, keeping the Grisha's limbs pinned so that he couldn't summon his power. The big Fjerdan snarled, muscles straining, teeth bared as he tried to break Mal's hold.

I knew it must have cost him, but Mal tightened his grip. He shifted, then drove his forehead into his opponent's nose with a nauseating *crunch*. Before I could blink, he'd released Eskil and hammered a flurry of punches into the Squaller's gut and sides.

Eskil hunched over, trying to protect himself, struggling for breath as blood gushed over his open mouth. Mal pivoted and delivered a brutal kick to the back of the Squaller's legs. Eskil fell to his knees, swaying, though still somehow upright.

Mal backed away, surveying his work. The crowd was whooping and stomping, their screams rising to a frenzy, but Mal's wary eyes were trained on the kneeling Squaller.

He studied his opponent, then dropped his fists. "Go on," he said to the Grisha. The look on his face sent a chill through me. There was challenge there and a kind of grim satisfaction. What was he seeing when he looked at Eskil on his knees?

Eskil's eyes were glassy. With an effort, the Grisha lifted his palms. The barest breeze fluttered towards Mal. A chorus of boos rose from the crowd.

Mal let it wash over him, then stepped forward. Eskil's weak gust faltered. Mal planted his hand on the Squaller's chest and gave a single, disdainful shove.

Eskil toppled. His big body hit the ground, and he curled in on himself, moaning.

Jeers and elated shrieks erupted all around us. A gleeful soldier grabbed Mal's wrist and lifted it over his head in triumph as money began to change hands.

The crowd surged towards Mal, carrying me with them. Everybody was talking at once. People slapped him on the back, jamming money into his palms. Then Zoya appeared in front of him. She flung her arms around his neck and pressed her lips against his. I saw him go rigid.

A rushing sound filled my ears, drowning out the noise of the crowd.

Push her away, I begged silently. *Push her away.*

And for a moment, I thought he might. But then his arms closed around her, and he kissed her back as the crowd hooted and cheered.

The bottom fell out of my stomach. It was like putting a foot wrong on a frozen creek, the crack of ice, the sudden drop, the knowledge that there was nothing beneath but dark water.

He pulled away from her, grinning, his cheek still bloodied, and that was when his eyes met mine. His face went white.

Zoya followed his gaze and lifted a defiant brow when she saw me.

I turned and began forcing my way back through the crowd. Tamar fell into step beside me.

"Alina," she said.

"Leave me alone."

I broke away from her. I had to get outside, had to get away from everyone. Tears were beginning to blur my vision. I wasn't sure if they were for the kiss or what had gone before it, but I couldn't let them see. The Sun Summoner didn't cry, especially over one of her *otkazat'sya* guards.

And what right did I have? Hadn't I almost kissed Nikolai? Maybe I could find him now, convince him to kiss me no matter who I was thinking of.

I burst from the stables and into the half-light. The air was warm and thick. I felt like I couldn't breathe. I strode away from the well-lit path by the paddocks and made for the shelter of the birchwood grove.

Someone tugged at my arm.

"Alina," Mal said.

I shook him off and hurried my steps, practically running now.

"Alina, stop," he said, easily keeping pace with me, despite the injuries he'd received.

I ignored him and plunged into the woods. I could smell the hot springs that fed the *banya*, the sharp scent of birch leaves beneath my feet. My throat ached. All I wanted was to be left alone to cry or be sick, maybe both.

"Damn it, Alina, would you please stop?"

I couldn't give in to my hurt, so I gave in to my anger.

"You're the captain of my guard," I said, blundering through the trees. "You shouldn't be brawling like some kind of commoner!"

Mal caught hold of my arm and yanked me round. "I *am* a commoner," he growled. "Not one of your pilgrims or your Grisha or some pampered watchdog who sits outside your door all night on the off-chance that you might need me."

"Of course not," I seethed. "You have much better things to do with your time. Like getting drunk and shoving your tongue down Zoya's throat."

"At least she doesn't flinch when I touch her," he spat. "You don't want me, so why do you care if she does?"

"I don't," I said, but the words came out as a sob.

Mal released me so suddenly that I almost fell backwards. He paced away from me, shoving his hands through his hair. The movement made him wince. His fingers tested the flesh at his side. I wanted to yell at him to go find a Healer. I wanted to smash my fist into the break and make it hurt worse.

"Saints," he swore. "I wish we'd never come here."

"Then let's leave," I said wildly. I knew I wasn't making any sense, but I didn't much care. "Let's run away, tonight, and forget we ever saw this place."

He let out a bitter bark of laughter. "Do you know how much I want that? To be with you without rank or walls or anything between us? Just to be *common* again together?" He shook his head. "But you won't do it, Alina."

"I will," I said, tears spilling over my cheeks.

"Don't kid yourself. You'd just find a way back."

"I don't know how to fix this," I said desperately.

"You can't fix it!" he shouted. "This is the way it is. Did it ever occur to you that maybe you were meant to be a queen and I'm not meant to be anything at all?"

"That isn't true."

He stalked towards me, the boughs of the trees making strange shifting shadows across his face in the twilight.

"I'm not a soldier any more," he said. "I'm not a prince, and I'm sure as hell not a Saint. So what am I, Alina?"

"I—"

"What am I?" he whispered.

He was close to me now. The scent I knew so well, that dark green scent of the meadow, was lost beneath the smell of sweat and blood.

"Am I your guardian?" he asked.

He ran his hand slowly down my arm, from shoulder to fingertips.

"Your friend?"

His left hand skimmed down my other arm.

"Your servant?"

I could feel his breath on my lips. My heart thundered in my ears.

"Tell me what I am." He pulled me against his body, his hand circling my wrist.

When his fingers closed, a sharp jolt rocked through me, buckling my knees. The world tilted, and I gasped. Mal dropped my hand as if he'd been burned.

He backed away from me, stunned. "What was that?"

I tried to blink away the dizziness.

"What the hell was that?" he said again.

"I don't know." My fingers still tingled.

A humourless smile twisted his lips. "It's never easy with us, is it?"

I shoved to my feet, suddenly angry. "No, Mal, it isn't. It's never going to be easy or sweet or comfortable with me. I can't just leave the Little Palace. I can't run away or pretend that this isn't who I am, because if I do, more people will die. I can't ever just be Alina again. That girl is gone."

"I want her back," he said roughly.

"I can't go back!" I screamed, not caring who heard me. "Even if you take away this collar and the sea whip's scales, you can't carve this power out of me."

"And what if I could? Would you let it go? Would you give it up?"

"Never."

The truth of that word hung between us. We stood there, in the darkness of the woods, and I felt the shard in my heart shift. I knew what it would leave behind when the pain was gone: loneliness, nothingness, a deep fissure that would not mend, the desperate edge of the abyss I had once glimpsed in the Darkling's eyes.

"Let's go," Mal said at last.

"Where?"

"Back to the Little Palace. I'm not going to just leave you in the woods."

We walked up the hill in silence and entered the palace through the Darkling's chambers. The common room was blessedly empty.

At the door to my room, I turned to Mal.

"I see him," I said. "I see the Darkling. In the library. In the chapel. That time on the Fold when the *Hummingbird* nearly crashed. In my room, the night you tried to kiss me."

He stared at me.

"I don't know if they're visions or visitations. I didn't tell you because I think I might be going mad. And because I think you're already a little afraid of me."

Mal opened his mouth, closed it, tried again. Even then, I hoped he might deny it. Instead, he turned his back on me. He crossed to the guards' quarters, stopping only to snatch a bottle of *kvas* from the table, and softly shut the door behind him.

I got ready for bed and eased between the sheets, but the night was too warm. I kicked them into a tangle at my feet. I lay on my back gazing up at the obsidian dome marked by constellations. I wanted to bang on Mal's door, tell him I was sorry, that I'd made a terrible mess of things, that we should have marched into Os Alta that first day hand in hand. But would it have mattered in the end?

There is no ordinary life for people like you and me.

No ordinary life. Just battle and fear and mysterious crackling jolts that rocked us back on our heels. I'd spent so many years wishing to be the kind of girl that Mal could want. Maybe that wasn't possible any more.

There are no others like us, Alina. And there never will be.

When the tears came, they burned hot and angry. I turned my face into my pillow so that no one would hear me cry. I wept, and when there was nothing left, I fell into a troubled sleep.

"Alina."

I woke to the soft brush of Mal's lips on mine, the barest touch to my temple, my eyelids, my brow. The light from the guttering flame on my bedside table glinted off his brown hair as he bent to kiss the curve of my throat.

For a moment, I hesitated, confused, not quite awake, then I wrapped my arms around him and pulled him closer. I didn't care that we'd fought, that he'd kissed Zoya, that he'd walked away from me, that everything felt so impossible. The only thing that mattered was that he'd changed his mind. He'd come back, and I wasn't alone.

"I missed you, Mal," I murmured against his ear. "I missed you so much."

My arms glided up his back and twined around his neck. He kissed me again, and I sighed into the welcome press of his mouth. I felt his weight slide over me and ran my hands over the hard muscles of his arms. If Mal was still with me, if he could still love me, then there was hope. My heart was pounding in my chest as warmth spread through me. There was no sound but our breathing and the shift of our bodies together. He was kissing my throat, my collarbone, drinking my skin. I shivered and pressed closer to him.

This was what I wanted, wasn't it? To find some way to heal the breach between us? Still, a sliver of panic cut through me. I needed to see his face, to know we were all right. I cupped his head with my hands, tilting his chin, and as my gaze met his, I shrank back in terror.

I looked into Mal's eyes – his familiar blue eyes that I knew even better than my own. Except they weren't blue. In the dying lamplight, they glimmered quartz grey.

He smiled then, a cold, clever smile like none I'd ever seen on his lips.

"I missed you too, Alina." That voice. Cool and smooth as glass.

Mal's features melted into shadow and then formed again like a face from the mist. Pale, beautiful, that thick shock of black hair, the perfect sweep of jaw.

The Darkling rested one gentle hand on my cheek. "Soon," he whispered.

I screamed. He broke into shadows and vanished.

I scrambled out of bed, clutching my arms around myself. My skin was crawling, my body quaking with terror and the memory of desire. I expected Tamar or Tolya to come bursting through the door. Already, I had a lie on my lips.

"Nightmare," I would say. And the word would come out steady, convincing, despite the rattling of my heart in my chest and the new scream I felt building in my throat.

But the room stayed silent. No one came. I stood shaking in the near dark.

I took a shallow, trembling breath. Then another.

When my legs felt steady enough, I pulled on my robe and peeked into the common room. It was empty.

I closed my door and pressed my back against it, staring at the rumpled covers of the bed. I was not going back to sleep. I might never sleep again. I glanced at the clock on the mantel. Sunrise came early during Belyanoch, but it would be hours before the palace woke.

I dug through the pile of clothes that I'd kept from our journey on the *Volkvolny* and pulled out a drab brown coat and a long scarf. It was too hot for either, but I didn't care. I drew the coat on over my nightshift, wrapped the scarf around my head and neck, and tugged on my shoes.

As I crept through the common room, I saw the door to the guards' quarters was closed. If Mal or the twins were inside, they must be sleeping deeply. Or maybe Mal was somewhere else beneath the domes of the Little Palace, tangled in Zoya's arms. My heart gave a sick twist. I took the doors to the left and hurried through the darkened halls, into the silent grounds.

CHAPTER 21

I drifted through the half-light, past the silent lawns covered in mist, the clouded windows of the greenhouse. The only sound was the soft crunch of my shoes on the gravel path. The morning deliveries of bread and produce were being made at the Grand Palace, and I followed the caravan of wagons straight out of the gates and through the cobblestone streets of the upper town. There were still a few revellers about, enjoying the twilight. I saw two people in party dress snoozing on a park bench. A group of girls laughed and splashed in a fountain, their skirts hiked up to their knees. A man wearing a wreath of poppies sat on a kerb with his head in his hands while a girl in a paper crown patted his shoulder. I passed them all unseen and unremarked upon, an invisible girl in a drab brown coat.

I knew I was being foolish. The Apparat's spies might be watching, or the Darkling's. I might be seized and hauled away at any moment. I wasn't sure it mattered to me any more. I needed to keep walking, to fill my lungs with clean air, to shake the feeling of the Darkling's hands on my skin.

I touched the scar at my shoulder. Even through the fabric of my coat, I could feel its raised edges. Aboard the whaler, I'd asked the Darkling why he'd let his monster bite me. I'd thought it was out of spite, so I would always wear his mark. Maybe there had been more to it than that.

Had the vision been real? Was he there, or was he something my mind had conjured? What sickness was inside of me that I would dream such a thing?

I didn't want to think. I just wanted to walk.

I crossed the canal, the little boats bobbing in the water below. From somewhere beneath the bridge, I heard the wheeze of an accordion.

I floated past the guard gate and into the narrow streets and clutter of the market town. It seemed even more crowded than it had before. People hung off stoops and overflowed from porches. Some played cards on makeshift tables made of boxes. Others slept propped up against each other. A couple swayed slowly on a tavern porch to music only they could hear.

When I came to the city walls, I told myself to stop, to turn round and go home. I almost laughed. The Little Palace wasn't really home.

There is no ordinary life for people like you and me.

My life would be allegiance instead of love, fealty instead of friendship. I would weigh each decision, consider every action, trust no one. It would be life observed from a distance.

I knew I should go back, but I kept on, and a moment later, I was on the other side of the wall. Just like that, I'd left Os Alta.

The tent city had grown. There were hundreds of people camped outside the walls, maybe thousands. The pilgrims weren't hard to find – I was surprised to see how their numbers had increased. They crowded near a large white tent, all facing east, awaiting the early sunrise.

The sound began as a swell of rustling whispers that fluttered on the air like the wings of birds and grew to a low hum as the sun peered over the horizon and lit the sky pale blue. Only then did I begin to make out the words.

Sankta. Sankta Alina. Sankta. Sankta Alina.

The pilgrims watched the growing dawn, and I watched them, unable to look away from their hope, their expectation. Their faces were exultant, and as the first rays of sun broke over them, some began to weep.

The hum rose and multiplied, cresting and falling, building to a wail that raised the hair on my arms. It was a creek overflowing its banks, a hive of bees shaken from a tree.

Sankta. Sankta Alina. Daughter of Ravka.

I closed my eyes as the sun played over my skin, praying I would feel something, anything.

Sankta Alina. Daughter of Keramzin.

Their hands lifted heavenward, their voices rose to a frenzy, shouting now, crying out. Old faces, young ones, the sick and the frail, the healthy and the strong. Strangers every one.

I looked around me. *This isn't hope*, I thought. *It's madness. It's hunger, need, desperation.* I felt as if I were waking from a trance. Why had I come here? I was more alone among these people than behind the palace walls. They had nothing to give me, and I had nothing to offer them.

My feet ached and I realised just how tired I was. I turned and began pushing my way back through the crowd, towards the city gates, as the chanting reached a roaring clamour.

Sankta, they shouted. *Sol Koroleva. Rebe Dva Stolba.*

Daughter of Two Mills. I'd heard that before, on the journey to Os Alta, a valley named after some ancient ruin, home to a sprawl of tiny, unimportant settlements on the southern border. Mal had been born near there too, but we'd never had a chance to go back. And what would have been the point? Any bit of family we might have had was long buried or burned.

Sankta Alina.

I thought again of my few memories from before Keramzin, of the dish of sliced beets, my fingers stained red with them. I remembered the dusty road, seen from someone's broad shoulders, the sway of ox tails, our shadows on the ground. Someone's hand pointing out the ruins of the mills, two narrow fingers of rock, worn down to bare spindles by wind, rain, and time. That was all that remained in my memory. The rest was Keramzin. The rest was Mal.

Sankta Alina.

I shoved my way through the mass of bodies, pulling my scarf tighter around my ears to try to block out the noise. An old pilgrim woman stepped into my path, and I nearly knocked her over. I reached out to steady her, and she latched on to me, barely keeping her balance.

"Forgive me, *babya*," I said formally. Never let it be said that Ana Kuya hadn't taught us manners. I gently set the woman back on her feet. "Are you all right?"

But she wasn't looking at my face – she was staring at my throat. My hand flew up to my neck. It was too late. The scarf had slipped free.

"Sankta," the woman moaned. "Sankta!" She fell to her knees and seized my hand, pressing it to her wrinkled cheek. "Sankta Alina!"

Suddenly there were hands all around me, grasping at my sleeves, the hem of my coat.

"Please," I said, trying to push away from them.

Sankta Alina. Muttered, whispered, wailed, shouted. My name was strange to me, spoken like a prayer, a foreign incantation to keep away the dark.

They crowded around me, closer and closer, jostling to get near, reaching out to feel my hair, my skin. I heard something rip and realised it was the fabric of my coat.

Sankta. Sankta Alina.

The bodies pressed tighter, pushing and shoving, shouting at each other, each wanting to get nearer. My feet lost contact with the ground. I cried out as a chunk of my hair was ripped from my scalp. They were going to tear me apart.

Let them do it, I thought with sudden clarity. It could be over that easily. No more fear, no more responsibility, no more nightmares of broken skiffs or children devoured by the Fold, no more visions. I could be free from the collar, from the fetter, from the crushing weight of their hope. *Let them do it.*

I closed my eyes. This would be my ending. They could give me a page in the *Istorii Sankt'ya* and put a gold halo around my head. Alina the Heartsick, Alina the Petty, Alina the Mad, Daughter of Dva Stolba, torn to pieces one morning in the shadow of the city walls. They could sell my bones by the side of the road.

Someone screamed. I heard an angry shout. Massive hands took hold of me, and I was lifted into the air.

I opened my eyes and saw Tolya's grim face. He had me in his arms.

Tamar was beside him, palms up, turning in a slow arc.

"Stay back," she warned the crowd. I saw some of the pilgrims blink sleepily, a few simply sat down. She was slowing their heart rates, trying to calm them, but there were just too many. A man dove forward. Like a flash, Tamar had drawn her axes. The man bellowed as a red streak bloomed on his arm.

"Come closer, and you'll lose it," she snapped.

The pilgrims' faces were wild.

"Let me help," I protested.

Tolya ignored me, pushing his way through the crowd; Tamar circled around him, blades in motion, widening the path. The pilgrims groaned and wailed, their arms outstretched, straining to get to me.

"Now," Tolya said. Then louder, "Now!"

He bolted. My head banged against his chest as we plunged towards the safety of the city walls, Tamar at our heels. The guards had already seen the turmoil erupting and had started to close the gates.

Tolya bulled forward, knocking people from his path, charging through the narrowing gap between the iron doors. Tamar slipped in after us, seconds before the gates clanged shut. On the other side, I heard the thump of bodies pounding against the doors, hands clawing, voices raised in hunger. Still I heard my name. *Sankta Alina*.

"What the hell were you thinking?" Tolya bellowed as he set me down.

"Later," Tamar said curtly.

The city guards were glaring at me. "Get her out of here," one of them yelled angrily. "We'll be lucky if we don't have a full-fledged riot on our hands."

The twins had horses waiting. Tamar yanked a blanket from a market stall and threw it around my shoulders. I clutched it to my neck, hiding the collar. She leapt into her saddle, and Tolya tossed me up unceremoniously behind her.

We rode in harried silence all the way to the palace gates. The unrest outside the city walls had not yet spread within, and all we garnered were a few questioning looks.

The twins didn't say a word, but I could tell they were furious. They had every right to be. I'd behaved like an idiot, and now I could only hope that the guards below could restore order without resorting to violence.

Yet beneath the panic and regret, an idea had entered my mind. I told myself it was nonsense, wishful thinking, but I could not shake it.

When we arrived back at the Little Palace, the twins wanted to escort me straight to the Darkling's rooms, but I refused.

"I'm safe now," I said. "There's something I need to do."

They insisted on trailing me to the library.

It didn't take me long to find what I wanted. I'd been a mapmaker, after all. I tucked the book under my arm and returned to my room with my scowling guards in tow.

To my surprise, Mal was waiting in the common room. He was seated at the table, nursing a glass of tea.

"Where were—" Mal began, but Tolya had him out of his chair and slammed against the wall before I could even blink.

"Where were *you*?" he snarled into Mal's face.

"Tolya!" I shouted in alarm. I tried to pull his hand from around Mal's throat, but it was like trying to bend a steel bar. I turned to Tamar for help, but she stood back, arms crossed, looking just as angry as her brother.

Mal made a choking sound. He hadn't changed his clothes from last night. There was stubble on his chin, and the smell of blood and *kvas* hung on him like a dirty coat.

"Saints, Tolya! Would you just put him down?"

For a moment, Tolya looked like he had every intention of crushing the life out of him, but then he relaxed his fingers and Mal slid down the wall, coughing and gulping air.

"It was your shift," Tolya rumbled, jabbing a finger at Mal's chest. "You should have been with her."

"I'm sorry," Mal rasped, rubbing at his throat. "I must have fallen asleep. I was right next—"

"You were at the bottom of a bottle," Tolya seethed. "I can smell it on you."

"I'm sorry," Mal said again, miserably.

"*Sorry?*" Tolya's fists flexed. "I ought to tear you apart."

"You can dismember him later," I said. "Right now I need you to find Nikolai and tell him to meet me in the war room. I'm going to go change."

I crossed to my room and closed the doors behind me, trying to pull myself together. So far today, I'd nearly died and possibly started a riot. Maybe I could set fire to something before breakfast.

I washed my face and changed into my *kefta*, then hurried to the war room. Mal was waiting there, slumped in a chair, though I hadn't invited him. He'd changed clothes, but he still looked rumpled and red-eyed. There were fresh bruises on his face from the previous night. He glanced up at me as I entered, saying nothing. Would there ever be a time when it didn't hurt to look at him?

I set the atlas on the long table and crossed to the ancient map of Ravka that ran the length of the far wall. Of all the maps in the war room, this one was by far the oldest and most beautiful. I trailed my fingers over the raised ridges of the Sikurzoi, the mountains that marked Ravka's southernmost border with the Shu, then followed them down into the western foothills. The valley of Dva Stolba was too small to be marked on this map.

"Do you remember anything?" I asked Mal without looking at him. "From before Keramzin?"

Mal hadn't been much older than I was when he came to the orphanage. I still remembered the day he'd arrived. I'd heard another refugee was coming, and I'd hoped it would be a girl for me to play with. Instead I'd got a pudgy, blue-eyed boy who would do anything on a dare.

"No." His voice still sounded rough from the near choking he'd received at Tolya's hands.

"Nothing?"

"I used to have dreams about a woman with long gold hair in a braid. She would dangle it in front of me like a toy."

"Your mother?"

"Mother, aunt, neighbour. How should I know? Alina, about what happened—"

"Anything else?"

He contemplated me for a long moment, then sighed and said, "Every time I smell liquorice, I remember sitting on a porch with a red painted chair in front of me. That's it. Everything else . . ." He trailed off with a shrug.

He didn't have to explain. Memories were a luxury meant for other children, not the Keramzin orphans. *Be grateful. Be grateful.*

"Alina," Mal tried again, "what you said about the Darkling—"

At that moment, Nikolai entered. Despite the early hour, he looked every inch the prince, blond hair gleaming, boots polished to a high shine. He took in Mal's bruises and stubble, then raised his brows and said, "Don't suppose anyone's rung for tea?"

He sat down and stretched his long legs out before him. Tolya and Tamar had taken up their posts, but I asked them to close the door and join us.

When they were assembled around the table, I said, "I went among the pilgrims this morning."

Nikolai's head snapped up. In an instant, the easygoing prince had vanished. "I think I must have misheard you."

"I'm fine."

"She was almost killed," said Tamar.

"But I wasn't," I added.

"Are you completely out of your mind?" Nikolai asked. "Those people are fanatics." He turned on Tamar. "How could you let her do something like that?"

"I didn't," said Tamar.

"Tell me you didn't go alone," he said to me.

"I didn't go alone."

"She went alone."

"Tamar, shut up. Nikolai, I told you, I'm fine."

"Only because we got there in time," said Tamar.

"How did you get there?" Mal asked quietly. "How did you find her?"

Tolya's face went dark, and he pounded one of his giant fists down on the table. "We shouldn't have had to find her," he said. "You had the watch."

"Leave it alone, Tolya," I said sharply. "Mal wasn't

where he should have been, and I'm perfectly capable of being stupid on my own."

I took a breath. Mal looked desolate. Tolya looked as if he was about to smash several pieces of furniture. Tamar's face was stony, and Nikolai was about as angry as I'd ever seen him. But at least I had their attention.

I pushed the atlas to the middle of the table. "There's a name the pilgrims use for me sometimes," I said. "Daughter of Dva Stolba."

"Two Mills?" said Nikolai.

"A valley, named after the ruins at its mouth."

I opened the atlas to the page I had marked. There was a detailed map of the southwestern border. "Mal and I are from somewhere around here," I said, running my finger along the edge of the map. "The settlements stretch all along this area."

I turned the page to an illustration of a road leading into a valley studded with towns. On either side of the road stood a slender spindle of rock.

"They don't look like much," grumbled Tolya.

"Exactly," I said. "Those ruins are ancient. Who knows how long they've been there or what they might have been? The valley is called Two Mills, but maybe they were part of a gatehouse or an aqueduct." I curved my finger across the spindles. "Or an arch."

A sudden silence descended over the room. With the arch in the foreground and the mountains in the distance, the ruins looked exactly like the view behind Sankt Ilya in the *Istorii Sankt'ya*. The only thing missing was the firebird.

Nikolai pulled the atlas towards him. "Are we just seeing what we want to see?"

"Maybe," I admitted. "But it's hard to believe it's a coincidence."

"We'll send scouts," he suggested.

"No," I said. "I want to go."

"If you leave now, everything you've accomplished with the Second Army will be undone. I'll go. If Vasily can run off to Caryeva to buy ponies, then no one will mind if I take a little hunting trip."

I shook my head. "I have to be the one to kill the firebird."

"We don't even know it's there."

"Why are we even discussing it?" asked Mal. "We all know it's going to be me."

Tamar and Tolya exchanged an uneasy glance.

Nikolai cleared his throat. "With all due respect, Oretsev, you don't quite seem at your best."

"I'm fine."

"Have you looked in a mirror lately?"

"I think you do that enough for the both of us," Mal shot back. Then he scrubbed a hand over his face, looking more weary than ever. "I'm too tired and too hungover to argue this. I'm the only one who can find the firebird. It has to be me."

"I'm going with you," I said.

"No," he said with surprising force. "I'll hunt it. I'll capture it. I'll bring it back to you. But you're not coming with me."

"It's too risky," I protested. "Even if you caught it, how would you get it back here?"

"Get one of your Fabrikators to rig something up for me," he said. "This is best for everyone. You get the firebird, and I get free of this saintsforsaken place."

"You can't travel by yourself. You—"

"Then give me Tolya or Tamar. We'll travel faster and draw less attention on our own." Mal pushed his chair back and stood. "You figure it out. Make whatever arrangements you want." He didn't look at me when he said, "Just tell me when I can leave."

Before I could raise another objection, he was gone.

I turned away, fighting to hold back the tears that threatened. Behind me, I heard Nikolai murmuring instructions to the twins as they departed.

I studied the map. Poliznaya, where we'd done our military service. Ryevost, where we'd begun our journey into the Petrazoi. Tsibeya, where he'd kissed me for the first time.

Nikolai laid his hand on my shoulder. I didn't know whether I wanted to swat it away or turn and fall into his arms. What would he do if I did? Pat my back? Kiss me? Propose?

"It's for the best, Alina."

I laughed bitterly. "Have you ever noticed people only say that when it isn't true?"

He dropped his hand. "He doesn't belong here."

He belongs with me, I wanted to shout. But I knew it wasn't true. I thought of Mal's bruised face, of him pacing back and forth like a caged animal, of him spitting blood and beckoning to Eskil for more. *Go on.* I thought of him holding me in his arms as we crossed the True Sea. The map blurred as my eyes filled with tears.

"Let him go," said Nikolai.

"Go where? Chasing after some mythical creature that may not even exist? On some impossible quest into mountains crawling with Shu?"

"Alina," Nikolai said softly, "that's what heroes do."

"I don't want him to be a hero!"

"He can't change who he is any more than you can stop being Grisha."

It was an echo of what I'd said only hours ago, but I didn't want to hear it.

"You don't care what happens to Mal," I said angrily. "You just want to get rid of him."

"If I wanted you to fall out of love with Mal, I'd make him stay here. I'd let him keep soaking his troubles in *kvas* and acting like a wounded ass. Is this really the life you want for him?"

I took a shaky breath. It wasn't. I knew that. Mal was miserable here. He'd been suffering since the moment we arrived, but I had refused to see it. I'd railed at him for wanting me to be something I couldn't, and all the while, I'd demanded the same thing from him. I brushed the tears from my cheeks. There was no point arguing with Nikolai. Mal had been a soldier. He wanted purpose. Here it was, if I would just let him take it.

And why not admit it? Even as I protested, there was another voice inside me, a greedy, shameful hunger that demanded completion, that clamoured for Mal to go out and find the firebird, that insisted he bring it back to me, no matter the cost. I'd told Mal that the girl he knew was gone. Better for him to leave before he saw just how true that was.

I let my fingers drift over the illustration of Dva Stolba. Two mills, or something more? Who could say when there was nothing left but ruins?

"You know the problem with heroes and saints, Nikolai?" I asked as I closed the book's cover and headed for the door. "They always end up dead."

CHAPTER 22

M al avoided me all afternoon, so I was surprised when he showed up with Tamar to escort me to Nikolai's birthday dinner. I'd assumed he'd get Tolya to take his place. Maybe he was making amends for missing his previous shift.

I'd given serious thought to not attending the dinner myself, but there didn't seem to be much point. I couldn't think of a likely excuse, and my absence would just offend the King and Queen.

I'd dressed in a light *kefta* made of shimmering panels of sheer gold silk. The bodice was set with sapphires of deep Summoner's blue that matched the jewels in my hair.

Mal's eyes flickered over me as I entered the common room and it occurred to me that the colours would have suited Zoya better. Then I had to wonder at myself. Gorgeous as she might be, Zoya wasn't the problem. Mal was leaving. I was letting him go. There was no one else to blame for the rift between us.

Dinner was held in one of the sumptuous dining rooms of the Grand Palace, a chamber known as the Eagle's Nest for the massive frieze on its ceiling depicting the crowned double eagle, a sceptre in one talon and a cluster of black arrows bound by red, blue, and purple ribbons in the other. Its feathers had been wrought in real gold and I couldn't help but think of the firebird.

The table was crowded with the highest-ranking generals of the First Army and their wives, as well as all the most prominent Lantsov uncles, aunts, and cousins. The Queen sat at one end of the table looking like a crumpled flower in pale rose silk. At the opposite end, Vasily sat next to the King, pretending not to notice as his father ogled an officer's young wife. Nikolai held court at the centre table, with me beside him, his charm sparkling as always.

He'd asked that no ball be thrown in his honour. It didn't seem fitting with so many refugees going hungry outside the city walls. But it was Belyanoch, and the King and Queen didn't seem able to restrain themselves. The meal consisted of thirteen courses, including a whole suckling pig and a life-size gelatine mould cast in the shape of a fawn.

When the time came for gifts, Nikolai's father presented him with an enormous egg glazed in pale blue. It opened to reveal an exquisite miniature ship set on a lapis sea. Sturmhond's red dog banner flew from the ship's mast and its little cannon fired with a *pop* that released the tiniest puff of white smoke.

Throughout the meal, I listened to the conversation with one ear while I studied Mal. The King's guards were placed at intervals along each wall. I knew Tamar stood somewhere behind me, but Mal was directly across from me, standing at rigid attention, hands behind his back, eyes straight ahead in the blank focus of all anonymous servants. It was like some kind of torture, watching him this way. We were just a few feet apart, but it felt like miles. And hadn't that been the way of it since we'd come to Os Alta? There was a knot in my chest that seemed to grow tighter every time I glanced at him. He'd shaved and had his hair trimmed. His uniform was neatly pressed. He looked weary and distant, but he looked like Mal again.

The nobles raised toasts to Nikolai's health. The generals praised his military leadership and courage. I expected to see Vasily sneer at all the praise being heaped onto his brother, but he looked positively cheery. His face was rosy with wine, and there was what could only be described as a smug smile on his lips. His trip to Caryeva seemed to have left him in a good mood.

My eyes flitted back to Mal. I didn't know whether I wanted to cry or stand up and start hurling dishes against the wall. The room felt too warm, and the wound at my shoulder had started to itch and pull again. I had to resist the urge to reach up and scratch it.

Great, I thought dismally. *Maybe I'll have another hallucination in the middle of the dining room, and the Darkling will climb out of the soup tureen.*

Nikolai bent his head and whispered, "I know my company doesn't count for much, but could you at least try? You look as if you're about to burst into tears."

"Sorry," I murmured. "I'm just . . ."

"I know," he said, and gave my hand a squeeze beneath the table. "But that gelatine deer gave its life for your entertainment."

I tried to smile, and I did make an effort. I laughed and chatted with the round, red-faced general on my right and pretended to care as the freckled Lantsov boy across from me rambled on about repairs to the dacha he'd inherited.

When the flavoured ices had been served, Vasily rose to his feet and lifted a glass of champagne.

"Brother," he said, "it is good to be able to toast your birth this day and to celebrate with you when you have spent so long on other shores. I salute you and drink to your honour. To your health, little brother!"

"*Ne zalost!*" chorused the guests, drinking deeply from their glasses and resuming their conversations.

But Vasily hadn't finished. He tapped the side of his glass with his fork, producing a loud *clink clink clink* that regained the party's attention.

"Today," he said, "we have more to celebrate than my brother's *noble* birth."

If the emphasis weren't enough, Vasily's smirk would have been. Nikolai continued to smile pleasantly.

"As you all know," Vasily continued, "I have been travelling these last weeks."

"And no doubt spending," chortled the red-faced general. "Have to build yourself a new stable soon, I suspect."

Vasily's glare was icy. "I did not go to Caryeva. Instead, I journeyed north on a mission sanctioned by our dear father."

Beside me, Nikolai went very still.

"After long and arduous negotiations, I am pleased to announce that Fjerda has agreed to join us in our fight against the Darkling. They have pledged both troops and resources to our cause."

"Can this be?" asked one of the noblemen.

Vasily's chest swelled with pride. "It can. At long last and through no small effort, our fiercest enemy has become our most powerful ally."

The guests broke out into excited conversation. The

King beamed and embraced his eldest son. "*Ne Ravka!*" he shouted, lifting his champagne.

"*Ne Ravka!*" sang the guests.

I was surprised to see Nikolai frowning. He'd said his brother liked shortcuts, and it seemed Vasily had found one. But it wasn't like Nikolai to let his disappointment or frustration show.

"An extraordinary achievement, brother. I salute you," Nikolai said, lifting his glass. "Dare I ask what they wanted in return for this support?"

"They do drive a hard bargain," Vasily said with an indulgent laugh. "But nothing too onerous. They sought access to our ports in West Ravka and requested our help policing the southern trade routes against Zemeni pirates. I imagine you'll be of some assistance with that, brother," he said with another warm chuckle. "They wanted a few of the northern logging roads reopened, and once the Darkling is defeated, they expect the cooperation of the Sun Summoner in our joint efforts to push back the Fold."

He grinned broadly at me. I bridled a little at his presumption, but it was an obvious and reasonable request, and even the leader of the Second Army was a subject of the King. I gave what I hoped was a dignified nod.

"Which roads?" asked Nikolai.

Vasily waved his hand dismissively. "They're somewhere south of Halmhend, west of the permafrost. They're sufficiently defended by the fort at Ulensk if the Fjerdans get any ideas."

Nikolai stood up, his chair scraping loudly against the parquet floor. "When did you lift the blockades? How long have the roads been open?"

Vasily shrugged. "What difference—"

"How long?"

The wound at my shoulder throbbed.

"A little over a week," Vasily said. "Surely you're not concerned that the Fjerdans intend to march on us from Ulensk? The rivers won't freeze for months, and until then—"

"Did you ever stop to consider why they might concern themselves with a logging route?"

Vasily gave a disinterested wave. "I assume because they're in need of timber," he said. "Or maybe it's sacred to one of their ridiculous woodsprites."

There was nervous laughter around the table.

"It's defended by a single fort," Nikolai growled.

"Because the passage is too narrow to accommodate any real force."

"You are waging an old war, brother. The Darkling doesn't need a battalion of foot soldiers or heavy guns. All he needs are his Grisha and the *nichevo'ya*. We have to evacuate the palace immediately."

"Don't be absurd!"

"Our one advantage was early warning, and the scouts at those blockades were our first defence. They were our eyes and you blinded us. The Darkling could be mere miles from us by now."

Vasily shook his head sadly. "You make yourself ridiculous."

Nikolai slammed his hands down on the table. The dishes jumped with a loud rattle. "Why isn't the Fjerdan delegation here to share in your glory? To toast this unprecedented alliance?"

"They sent their regrets. They were not able to travel immediately, due—"

"They're not here because there's about to be a massacre. Their pact is with the Darkling."

"All of our intelligence puts him in the south with the Shu."

"You think he doesn't have spies? That he doesn't have his own operatives within our network? He laid a trap that any child could recognise and you walked right into it."

Vasily's face turned purple.

"Nikolai, surely—" his mother objected.

"The fort at Ulensk is manned by a full regiment," put in one of the generals.

"You see?" said Vasily. "This is fearmongering of the worst kind, and I will not stand for it."

"A regiment against an army of *nichevo'ya*? Everyone at that fort is already dead," said Nikolai, "sacrificed to your pride and stupidity."

Vasily's hand went to his sword hilt. "You overreach, you little bastard."

The Queen gasped.

Nikolai released a harsh laugh. "Yes, call me out, brother. A lot of good it will do. Look around this table," he said. "Every general, every nobleman of high rank, most of the Lantsov line, *and* the Sun Summoner. All in one place, on one night."

A number of faces at the table went suddenly pale.

"Perhaps," said the freckle-faced boy across from me, "we should consider—"

"No!" said Vasily, his lip trembling. "This is his own petty jealousy! He cannot stand to see me succeed. He—"

The warning bells began to ring, distant at first, down near the city walls, one and then another, joining each other in a rising chorus of alarm that echoed up the streets of Os Alta, through the upper town, and over the walls of the Grand Palace.

"You've handed him Ravka," said Nikolai.

The guests rose, pushing back from the table in a gabble of panic.

Mal was at my side immediately, his sabre already drawn.

"We have to get to the Little Palace," I said, thinking of the mirrored dishes mounted on the roof. "Where's Tamar?"

The windows exploded.

Glass rained down on us. I threw up my arms to shield my face and the guests screamed, huddling against each other.

The *nichevo'ya* swarmed into the room on wings of molten shadow, filling the air with the whirring buzz of insects.

"Get the King to safety!" Nikolai cried, unsheathing his sword and running to his mother's side.

The palace guards stood paralysed, frozen in terror.

A shadow lifted the freckled boy from his feet and threw him against the wall. He slid to the ground, his neck broken.

I raised my hands, but the room was too crowded for me to risk using the Cut.

Vasily still stood at the table, the King cowering beside him.

"You did this!" he screamed at Nikolai. "You and the witch!"

He lifted his sabre high and charged, bellowing with rage. Mal stepped in front of me, raising his sword to block the blow. But before Vasily could bring down his weapon, a *nichevo'ya* grabbed hold of him and tore his arm from its socket, sword and all. He stood for a moment, swaying, blood pumping from his wound, then dropped to the floor in a lifeless heap.

The Queen began to shriek hysterically. She shoved forward, trying to reach her son's body, feet slipping in his blood as Nikolai held her back.

"Don't," he pleaded, wrapping his arms around her. "He's gone, *Madraya*. He's gone."

Another pack of *nichevo'ya* descended from the windows, clawing their way towards Nikolai and his mother.

I had to take a chance. I brought the light down in two blazing arcs, cutting through one monster after another, barely missing one of the generals who crouched cowering on the floor. People were screaming and weeping as the *nichevo'ya* fell upon them.

"To me!" Nikolai shouted, herding his mother and father to the door. We followed with the guards, backing our way into the hall, and ran.

The Grand Palace had erupted into chaos. Panicked servants and footmen crowded the corridors, some scrambling for the entrance, others barricading themselves into rooms. I heard wailing, the sound of breaking glass. A *boom* sounded from somewhere outside.

Let it be the Fabrikators, I thought desperately.

Mal and I burst from the palace and careened down the marble steps. A screech of twisting metal rent the air. I looked down the white gravel path in time to see the golden gates of the Grand Palace blown off their hinges by a wall of Etherealki wind. The Darkling's Grisha streamed onto the grounds in their brightly coloured *kefta*.

We pelted down the path to the Little Palace. Nikolai and the royal guards trailed behind us, slowed by his frail father.

At the entrance to the wooded tunnel, the King bent double, wheezing badly as the Queen wept and held tight to his arm.

"I have to get them to the *Kingfisher*," said Nikolai.

"Take the long way around," I said. "The Darkling will be headed to the Little Palace first. He'll be coming for me."

"Alina, if he captures you—"

"Go," I said. "Save them, save Baghra. I won't leave the Grisha."

"I'll get them out and come back. I promise."

"On your word as a cutthroat and a pirate?"

He touched my cheek once, briefly. "Privateer."

Another explosion rocked the grounds.

"Let's go!" shouted Mal.

As we sprinted into the tunnel, I glanced back and saw Nikolai silhouetted against the purple twilight. I wondered if I'd ever see him again.

The wound at my shoulder burned and throbbed, driving me faster as we raced along the path. My mind was reeling – *if they had a chance to seal themselves in the main hall, if they had time to man the guns on the roof, if I can just reach the dishes*. All of our plans, undone by Vasily's arrogance.

I burst into the open, and my slippered feet sent gravel flying as I skidded to a halt. I don't know if it was momentum or the sight before me that drove me to my knees.

The Little Palace was wreathed in seething shadows. They clicked and whirred as they skittered over the walls and swooped down on the roof. There were bodies lying on the steps, bodies crumpled on the ground. The front doors were wide open.

The path in front of the steps was littered with shards of broken mirror. Lying on its side was the shattered hulk of one of David's dishes, a girl's body crushed beneath it, her goggles askew. Paja. Two *nichevo'ya* crouched before the dish, gazing at their broken reflections.

I released a howl of pure rage and sent a fiery swathe of light burning through both of them. It fractured along the edges of the dish as the *nichevo'ya* disappeared.

I heard the rattle of gunfire from up on the roof. Someone was still alive. Someone was still fighting. And there was one dish left. It wasn't much, but it was all we had.

"This way," said Mal.

We tore across the lawn and in through the door that led to the Darkling's chambers. At the base of the stairs, a *nichevo'ya* came shrieking at us from a doorway, knocking me off my feet. Mal slashed at it with his sabre. It wavered, then re-formed.

"Get back!" I yelled. He ducked, and I sent the Cut slicing through the shadow soldier. I took the stairs two at a time, my heart pounding, Mal close on my heels. The air was thick with the smell of blood and the bone-shaking clatter of gunfire.

As we emerged onto the roof, I heard someone shout. "Away!"

We just had time to duck before the *grenatki* exploded high above us, searing our eyelids with light and leaving our ears ringing. Corporalki manned Nikolai's guns, sending torrents of bullets into the mass of shadows as Fabrikators fed them ammunition. The remaining dish was surrounded by armed Grisha, struggling to keep the *nichevo'ya* at bay. David was there, clinging awkwardly to a rifle and trying to hold his ground. I threw the light high in a blazing whipcrack that split the sky overhead and bought us a few precious seconds.

"David!"

David gave two hard blasts on the whistle around his neck. Nadia dropped her goggles, and the Durast manning the dish moved into position. I didn't wait – I lifted my hands and sent light streaming at the dish. The whistle blew. The dish tilted. A single pure beam of light blasted from the mirrored surface. Even without the second dish, it skewered the sky, slashing through the *nichevo'ya* as they burned away to nothing.

The beam swept the air in a gleaming arc, dissolving black bodies before it, thinning the horde until we could see the deep Belyanoch twilight. A cheer went up from the Grisha at the first sight of stars and a thin sliver of hope pierced my terror.

Then a *nichevo'ya* broke through. It dodged the beam and hurled itself at the dish, rocking it on its moorings.

Mal was on the creature in an instant, slashing and cutting. A group of Grisha tried to seize its muscled legs, but the thing shifted and skittered away from them. Then the *nichevo'ya* were descending from all sides. I saw one slip past the beam and dive straight into the back of the dish. The mirror rocked forward. The light faltered, then winked out.

"Nadia!" I screamed. She and the Durast leapt from

the dish just in time. It toppled on its side in a tremendous crash of breaking glass as the *nichevo'ya* renewed their attack.

I threw out arc after arc of light.

"Get to the hall!" I cried. "Seal the doors!"

The Grisha ran, but they were not fast enough. I heard a shout and saw the brief flash of Fedyor's face as he was lifted from his feet and tossed from the roof. I lay down a bright shower of cover, but the *nichevo'ya* just kept coming. If only we'd had both dishes. If only we'd had a little more time.

Mal was suddenly beside me again, rifle in hand. "It's no good," he said. "We have to get out of here."

I nodded, and we backed towards the stairs as the sky grew dense with writhing shapes. My foot connected with something soft behind me, and I stumbled.

Sergei was huddled against the dome. He held Marie in his arms. She'd been torn open from neck to navel.

"There's no one left," he sobbed, tears running down his cheeks. "There's no one left." He rocked back and forth, holding Marie tighter. I couldn't bear to look at her. Silly, giggling Marie with her lovely brown curls.

The *nichevo'ya* were skittering over the roof, rushing towards us in a black tide.

"Mal, get him up!" I shouted. I slashed out at the throng of shadows.

Mal grabbed Sergei and pulled him away from Marie. He flailed and struggled, but we got him inside and banged the door shut behind us. We half carried, half shoved him down the stairs. On the second flight, we heard the roof door blow open above us. I threw a slicing cut of light high, hoping to hit something other than the staircase, and we tumbled down the final flight.

We threw ourselves into the main hall, and the doors crashed closed behind us as the Grisha rammed the lock into place. There was a loud *thud* and then another as the *nichevo'ya* tried to break through the door.

"Alina!" Mal shouted. I turned and saw that the other doors were sealed, but there were still *nichevo'ya* inside. Zoya and Nadia's brother were backed against a wall, using Squaller winds to heave tables and chairs and broken bits of furniture at an oncoming pack of shadow soldiers.

I raised my hands, and the light swept forward in sizzling cords, tearing through the *nichevo'ya* one by one, until they were gone. Zoya dropped her hands, and a samovar fell with a loud clang.

At every door we heard thumping and scraping. The *nichevo'ya* were clawing at the wood, trying to get in, searching for a crack or gap to seep through. The buzzing and clicking seemed to come from all sides. But the Fabrikators had done their work well. The seals would hold, at least for a little while.

Then I looked around the room. The hall was bathed in blood. The walls were smeared with it, the stone floor was wet with it. There were bodies everywhere, little heaps of purple, red, and blue.

"Are there any others?" I asked. I couldn't keep the tremor from my voice.

Zoya gave a single, dazed shake of her head. A spatter of blood covered one of her cheeks. "We were at dinner," she said. "We heard the bells. We didn't have time to seal the doors. They were just . . . everywhere."

Sergei was sobbing quietly. David looked pale, but calm. Nadia had made it down to the hall. She had her arm around Adrik, and he still had that stubborn tilt to his chin, though he was shaking. There were three Inferni and two more Corporalki – one Healer and one Heartrender. They were all that remained of the Second Army.

"Did anyone see Tolya and Tamar?" I asked. No one had. They might be dead. Or maybe they'd played some part in this disaster. Tamar had disappeared from the dining room. For all I knew, they'd been working with the Darkling all along.

"Nikolai might not have left yet," Mal said. "We could try to make it to the *Kingfisher*."

I shook my head. If Nikolai wasn't gone, then he and the rest of his family were dead, and possibly Baghra too. I had a sudden image of Nikolai's body floating facedown in the lake beside the splintered pieces of the *Kingfisher*.

No. I would not think that way. I remembered what I'd thought of Nikolai the first time I'd met him. I had to believe the clever fox would escape this trap too.

"The Darkling concentrated his forces here," I said. "We can make a run for the upper town and try to fight our way out from there."

"We'll never make it," said Sergei hopelessly. "There are too many of them." It was true. We'd known it might come to this, but we'd assumed we'd have greater numbers, and the hope of reinforcements from Poliznaya.

From somewhere in the distance, we heard a rolling crack of thunder.

"He's coming," moaned one of the Inferni. "Oh, Saints, he's coming."

"He'll kill us all," whispered Sergei.

"If we're lucky," replied Zoya.

It wasn't the most helpful thing to say, but she was right. I'd seen the truth of how the Darkling dealt with traitors in the shadowy depths of his own mother's eyes, and I suspected Zoya and the others would be treated far more harshly.

Zoya tried to wipe the blood from her face, but only succeeded in leaving a smear across her cheek. "I say we try to get to the upper town. I'd rather take my chances with the monsters outside than sit here waiting for the Darkling."

"The odds aren't good," I warned, hating that I had no hope to offer. "I'm not strong enough to stop them all."

"At least with the *nichevo'ya* it will be relatively quick," David said. "I say we go down fighting." We all turned to look at him. He seemed a little surprised himself. Then he shrugged. He met my eyes and said, "We do the best we can."

I looked around the circle. One by one they nodded.

I took a breath. "David, do you have any *grenatki* left?"

He pulled two iron cylinders from his *kefta*. "These are the last."

"Use one, keep the other in reserve. I'll give the signal. When I open the doors, run for the palace gates."

"I'm staying with you," Mal said.

I opened my mouth to argue, but one look told me there would be no point.

"Don't wait for us," I said to the others. "I'll give you as much cover as I can."

Another clap of thunder split the air.

The Grisha plucked rifles from the arms of the dead and gathered around me at the door.

"All right," I said. I turned and laid my hands on the

carved handles. Through my palms, I felt the thump of *nichevo'ya* bodies as they heaved themselves against the wood. My wound gave a searing throb.

I nodded to Zoya. The lock snicked back.

I threw the door open and shouted, "Now!"

David lobbed the flash bomb into the twilight as Zoya swooped her arms through the air, lofting the cylinder higher on a Squaller draft.

"Get down!" David yelled. We turned towards the shelter of the hall, eyes squeezed shut, hands thrown over our heads, bracing for the explosion.

The blast shook the stone floor beneath our feet, and the glare burned red across my closed lids.

We ran. The *nichevo'ya* had scattered, startled by the burst of light and sound, but only seconds later, they were whirling back to us.

"Run!" I shouted. I raised my arms and brought the light down in fiery scythes, cutting through the violet sky, carving through one *nichevo'ya* after the next as Mal opened fire. The Grisha ran for the wooded tunnel.

I called on every bit of the stag's power, the sea whip's strength, every trick Baghra had ever taught me. I pulled the light to me and honed it into searing arcs that cut luminous trails through the shadow army.

But there were just too many of them. What had it cost the Darkling to raise such a multitude? They surged forward, bodies shifting and whirling like a glittering cloud of beetles, arms stretched forward, sharp talons bared. They pushed the Grisha back from the tunnel, black wings beating the air, the wide, twisted holes of their mouths already yawning open.

Then the air came alive with the rattle of gunfire.

There were soldiers pouring out of the woods to my left, shooting as they ran. The war cry that issued from their lips raised the hair on my arms. *Sankta Alina.*

They hurtled towards the *nichevo'ya*, drawing swords and sabres, slashing out at the monsters with terrifying ferocity. Some were dressed as farmers, some wore ragged First Army uniforms, but each of them bore identical tattoos: my sunburst, wrought in ink over the sides of their faces.

Only two were unmarked. Tolya and Tamar led the charge, eyes wild, blades flashing, roaring my name.

CHAPTER 23

The sun soldiers plunged into the shadow horde, cutting and thrusting, pushing the *nichevo'ya* back as the riflemen fired again and again. But despite their ferocity, they were only human, flesh and steel pitted against living shadow. One by one, the *nichevo'ya* began to pick them off.

"Make for the chapel!" Tamar shouted.

The chapel? Did she plan to throw hymnals at the Darkling?

"We'll be trapped!" cried Sergei, running toward me.

"We're already trapped," Mal replied, slinging his rifle onto his back and grabbing my arm. "Let's go!"

I didn't know what to think, but we were out of options.

"David!" I yelled. "The second bomb!"

He flung it at the *nichevo'ya*. His aim was wild, but Zoya was there to help it along.

We dove into the woods, the sun soldiers bringing up the rear. The blast tore through the trees in a gust of white light.

Lamps had been lit in the chapel and the door stood open. We burst inside, the echoes from our footfalls bouncing up over the pews and off the glazed blue dome.

"Where do we go?" Sergei cried in panic.

Already we could hear the whirring, clicking hum from outside. Tolya slammed the chapel door shut, dropping a heavy wooden bolt into place. The sun soldiers took up positions by the windows, rifles in hand.

Tamar hurdled over a pew and shot past me up the aisle. "Come on!"

I watched her in confusion. Just where were we supposed to go?

She tore past the altar and grasped one gilded wood corner of the triptych. I gaped as the water-damaged panel swung open, revealing the dark mouth of a passageway. This was how the sun soldiers had got into the grounds. And how the Apparat had escaped from the Grand Palace.

"Where does it go?" asked David.

"Does it matter?" Zoya shot back.

The building shook as a loud crack of thunder split the air. The chapel door blew to pieces. Tolya was thrown backwards, and darkness flooded through.

The Darkling came borne on a tide of shadow, held aloft by monsters who set his feet upon the chapel floor with infinite care.

"Fire!" Tamar shouted.

Shots rang out. The *nichevo'ya* writhed and whirled around the Darkling, shifting and re-forming as the bullets struck their bodies, one taking the place of another in a seamless tide of shadow. He didn't even break stride.

Nichevo'ya were streaming through the chapel door. Tolya was already on his feet and rushing to my side with pistols drawn. Tamar and Mal flanked me, the Grisha arrayed behind us. I raised my hands, summoning the light, bracing for the onslaught.

"Stand down, Alina," said the Darkling. His cool voice echoed through the chapel, cutting through the noise and chaos. "Stand down and I will spare them."

In answer, Tamar scraped one axe blade over the other, raising a horrible shriek of metal on metal. The sun soldiers lifted their rifles, and I heard the sound of Inferni flint being struck.

"Look around, Alina," the Darkling said. "You cannot win. You can only watch them die. Come to me now, and I will do them no harm – not your zealot soldiers, not even the Grisha traitors."

I took in the nightmare of the chapel. The *nichevo'ya* swarmed above us, crowding up against the inside of the dome. They clustered around the Darkling in a dense cloud of bodies and wings. Through the windows I could see more, hovering in the twilight sky.

The sun soldiers' faces were determined, but their ranks had been badly thinned. One of them had pimples on his chin. Beneath his tattoo, he didn't look much older than twelve. They needed a miracle from their Saint, one I couldn't perform.

Tolya cocked the triggers on his pistols.

"Hold," I said.

"Alina," Tamar whispered, "we can still get you out."

"*Hold*," I repeated.

The sun soldiers lowered their rifles. Tamar brought her axes to her hips but kept her grip tight.

"What are your terms?" I asked.

Mal frowned. Tolya shook his head. I didn't care. I knew it might be a ploy, but if there was even a chance of saving their lives, I had to take it.

"Give yourself up," said the Darkling. "And they all go

free. They can climb down that rabbit hole and disappear forever."

"Free?" Sergei whispered.

"He's lying," said Mal. "It's what he does."

"I don't need to lie," said the Darkling. "Alina wants to come with me."

"She doesn't want any part of you," Mal spat.

"No?" the Darkling asked. His dark hair gleamed in the lamplight of the chapel. Summoning his shadow army had taken its toll. He was thinner, paler, but somehow the sharp angles of his face had only become more beautiful. "I warned you that your *otkazat'sya* could never understand you, Alina. I told you that he would only come to fear you and resent your power. Tell me I was wrong."

"You were wrong." My voice was steady, but doubt rustled in my heart.

The Darkling shook his head. "You cannot lie to me. Do you think I could have come to you again and again, if you had been less alone? You called to me and I answered."

I couldn't quite believe what I was hearing. "You . . . you were there?"

"On the Fold. In the palace. Last night."

I flushed as I remembered his body on top of mine. Shame washed through me, but with it came overwhelming relief. I hadn't imagined it all.

"That isn't possible," Mal bit out.

"You have no idea what I can make possible, tracker."

I shut my eyes.

"Alina—"

"I've seen what you truly are," said the Darkling, "and I've never turned away. I never will. Can he say the same?"

"You don't know anything about her," Mal said fiercely.

"Come with me now, and it all stops – the fear, the uncertainty, the bloodshed. Let him go, Alina. Let them all go."

"No," I said. But even as I shook my head, something in me cried out, *Yes*.

The Darkling sighed and glanced back over his shoulder. "Bring her," he said.

A figure shuffled forward, draped in a heavy shawl, hunched and slow-moving, as if every step brought pain. *Baghra*.

My stomach twisted sickly. *Why did she have to be so stubborn? Why couldn't she have gone with Nikolai?* Unless Nikolai had never made it out.

The Darkling laid a hand on Baghra's shoulder. She flinched.

"Leave her alone," I said angrily.

"Show them," he said.

She unwound her shawl. I drew in a sharp breath. I heard someone behind me moan.

It was not Baghra. I didn't know what it was. The bites were everywhere, raised black ridges of flesh, twisting lumps of tissue that could never be healed, not by Grisha hand or by any other, the unmistakable marks of the *nichevo'ya*. Then I saw the faded flame of her hair, the lovely amber hue of her one remaining eye.

"Genya," I gasped.

We stood in terrible silence. I took a step towards her. Then David pushed past me down the altar steps. Genya cringed away from him, pulling up her shawl, and turned to hide her face.

David slowed. He hesitated. Gently, he reached out to touch her shoulder. I saw the rise and fall of her back, and knew she was crying.

I covered my mouth as a sob tore free from my throat.

I'd seen a thousand horrors on this long day, but this was the one that broke me, Genya cringing away from David like a frightened animal. Luminous Genya, with her alabaster skin and graceful hands. Resilient Genya, who had endured countless indignities and insults, but who had always held her lovely chin high. Foolish Genya, who had tried to be my friend, who had dared to show me mercy.

David drew his arm around Genya's shoulders and slowly led her back up the aisle. The Darkling didn't stop them.

"I've waged the war you forced me to, Alina," said the Darkling. "If you hadn't run from me, the Second Army would still be intact. All those Grisha would still be alive. Your tracker would be safe and happy with his regiment. When will it be enough? When will you let me stop?"

You cannot be helped. Your only hope was to run. Baghra was right. I'd been a fool to think I could fight him. I'd tried, and countless people had lost their lives for it.

"You mourn the people killed in Novokribirsk," the Darkling continued, "the people lost to the Fold. But what of the thousands that came before them, given over to endless wars? What of the others dying now on distant shores? Together, we can put an end to all of it."

Reasonable. Logical. For once, I let the words in. An end to all of it.

It's over.

I should have felt beaten down by the thought,

defeated, but instead it filled me with a curious lightness. Hadn't some part of me known it would end this way all along?

The moment the Darkling had slipped his hand over my arm in the Grisha pavilion so long ago, he'd taken possession of me. I just hadn't realised it.

"All right," I whispered.

"Alina, no!" Mal said furiously.

"You'll let them go?" I asked. "All of them?"

"We need the tracker," said the Darkling. "For the firebird."

"He goes free. You can't have both of us."

The Darkling paused, then nodded once. I knew he thought he would find a way to claim Mal. Let him believe it. I would never let it happen.

"I'm not going anywhere," Mal said through clenched teeth.

I turned to Tolya and Tamar. "Take him from here. Even if you have to carry him."

"Alina—"

"We won't go," said Tamar. "We are sworn."

"You will."

Tolya shook his huge head. "We pledged our lives to you. All of us."

I turned to face them. "Then do as I command," I said. "Tolya Yul-Baatar, Tamar Kir-Baatar, you will take these people from here to safety." I summoned the light, letting it blaze in a glorious halo around me. A cheap trick, but a good one. Nikolai would have been proud. "*Do not fail me.*"

Tamar had tears in her eyes, but she and her brother bowed their heads.

Mal hooked my arm and turned me round roughly. "What are you doing?"

"I want this." *I need it.* Sacrifice or selfishness, it didn't matter any more.

"I don't believe you."

"I can't run from what I am, Mal, from what I'm becoming. I can't bring the Alina you knew back, but I can set you free."

"You can't . . . you *can't* choose him."

"There isn't any choice to make. This is what was meant to be." It was true. I felt it in the collar, in the weight of the fetter. For the first time in weeks, I felt strong.

He shook his head. "This is all wrong." The look on his face almost undid me. It was lost, startled, like a little boy standing alone in the ruin of a burning village. "Please, Alina," he said softly. "Please. This can't be how it ends."

I rested my hand on his cheek, hoping that there was still enough between us that he would understand. I stood on my toes and kissed the scar on his jaw.

"I have loved you all my life, Mal," I whispered through my tears. "There is no end to our story."

I stepped back, memorising every line of his beloved face. Then I turned and walked up the aisle. My steps were sure. Mal would have a life. He'd find his purpose. I had to seek mine. Nikolai had promised me a chance to save Ravka, to make amends for all I'd done. He'd tried, but it was the Darkling's gift to give.

"Alina!" Mal shouted. I heard scuffling behind me and knew Tolya had taken hold of him. "Alina!" His voice was raw white wood, torn from the heart of a tree. I did not turn.

The Darkling stood waiting, his shadow guard hovering and shifting around him.

I was afraid, but beneath the fear, I was eager.

"We are alike," he said, "as no one else is, as no one else will ever be."

The truth of it rang through me. *Like calls to like.*

He held out his hand, and I stepped into his arms.

I cupped the back of his neck, feeling the silken brush of his hair on my fingertips. I knew Mal was watching. I needed him to turn away. I needed him to go. I tilted my face up to the Darkling's.

"My power is yours," I whispered.

I saw the elation and triumph in his eyes as he lowered his mouth to mine. Our lips met, and the connection between us opened. This was not the way he'd touched me in my visions, when he'd come to me as shadow. This was real and I could drown in it.

Power flowed through me – the power of the stag, its strong heart beating in both our bodies, the life he'd taken, the life I'd tried to save. But I also felt the Darkling's power, the power of the Black Heretic, the power of the Fold.

Like calls to like. I'd sensed it when the *Hummingbird* entered the Unsea, but I'd been too afraid to embrace it. This time, I didn't fight. I let go of my fear, my guilt, my shame. There was darkness inside me. He had put it there, and I would no longer deny it. The volcra, the *nichevo'ya*, they were my monsters, all of them. And he was my monster, too.

"My power is yours," I repeated. His arms tightened around me. "And yours is mine," I whispered against his lips.

Mine. The word reverberated through me, through both of us.

The shadow soldiers shifted and whirred.

I remembered the way it had felt in that snowy glade, when the Darkling had placed the collar around my neck and seized control of my power. I reached across the connection between us.

He reared back. "What are you doing?"

I knew why he had never intended to kill the sea whip himself, why he hadn't wanted to form that second connection. He was afraid.

Mine.

I forced my way across the bond forged by Morozova's collar and grabbed hold of the Darkling's power.

Darkness spilled from him, black ink from his palms, billowing and skittering, blooming into the shape of a *nichevo'ya*, forming hands, head, claws, wings. The first of my abominations.

The Darkling tried to pull away from me, but I clutched him tighter, calling his power, calling the darkness as he had once used the collar to summon my light.

Another creature burst forth, and then another. The Darkling cried out as it was wrenched from him. I felt it too, felt my heart constrict as each shadow soldier tore a little bit of me away, exacting the price of its creation.

"Stop," the Darkling rasped.

The *nichevo'ya* whirred nervously around us, clicking and humming, faster and faster. One after another, I pulled my dark soldiers into being, and my army rose up around us.

The Darkling moaned, and so did I. We fell against each other, but still I did not relent.

"You'll kill us both!" he cried.

"Yes," I said.

The Darkling's legs buckled, and we collapsed to our knees.

This was not the Small Science. This was magic, something ancient, the making at the heart of the world. It was terrifying, limitless. No wonder the Darkling hungered for more.

The darkness buzzed and clattered, a thousand locusts, beetles, hungry flies, clicking their legs, beating their wings. The *nichevo'ya* wavered and re-formed, whirring in a frenzy, driven on by his rage and my exultation.

Another monster. Another. Blood was pouring from the Darkling's nose. The room seemed to rock, and I realised I was convulsing. I was dying, bit by bit, with every monster that wrenched itself free.

Just a little longer, I thought. *Just a few more. Just enough so I know that I've sent him to the next world before I follow.*

"Alina!" I heard Mal calling as if from a great distance. He was tugging at me, pulling me away.

"No!" I shouted. "Let me end this."

"Alina!"

Mal seized my wrist, and a shock passed through me. Through the haze of blood and shadow, I glimpsed something beautiful, as if through a golden door.

He wrenched me away from the Darkling, but not before I called out to my children in one final exhortation: *Bring it down.*

The Darkling slumped to the ground. The monsters rose in a whirling black column around him, then crashed against the walls of the chapel, shaking the little building to its very foundations.

Mal had me in his arms and was running up the aisle. The *nichevo'ya* were hurling themselves against the chapel walls. Slabs of plaster crashed to the floor. The blue dome swayed as its supports began to give way.

Mal leapt past the altar and plunged into the passage. The smell of wet earth and mould filled my nostrils, mingling with the sweet incense scent of the chapel. He ran, racing against the disaster I'd unleashed.

A *boom* sounded from somewhere far behind us as the chapel collapsed. The impact roared through the passageway. A cloud of dirt and debris struck us with the force of an oncoming wave. Mal flew forward. I tumbled from his arms, and the world came down around us.

The first thing I heard was the low rumble of Tolya's voice. I couldn't speak, couldn't scream. All I knew was pain and the relentless weight of the earth. Later I would find out that they'd laboured over me for hours, breathing air back into my lungs, staunching the flow of blood, trying to mend the worst breaks in my bones.

I drifted in and out of consciousness. My mouth felt dry and swollen shut. I was pretty sure I'd bitten my tongue. I heard Tamar giving orders.

"Bring the rest of the tunnel down. We need to get as far from here as we possibly can."

Mal.

Was he here? Buried beneath the rubble? I could not let them leave him. I forced my lips to form his name.

"Mal." Could they even hear me? My voice sounded muffled and wrong to my ears.

"She's hurting. Should we put her under?" Tamar asked.

"I don't want to risk her heart stopping again," replied Tolya.

"Mal," I repeated.

"Leave the passage to the convent open," Tamar said to someone. "Hopefully, he'll think we went out there."

The convent. Sankta Lizabeta. The gardens next to the Gritzki mansion. I couldn't order my thoughts. I tried to speak Mal's name again, but I couldn't make my mouth work. The pain was crowding in on me. What if I'd lost him? If I'd had the strength, I would have screamed. I would have railed. Instead, I sank into darkness.

When I came to, the world was swaying beneath me. I remembered waking aboard the whaler, and for a terrifying moment, I thought I might be on a ship. I opened my eyes, saw earth and rock high above me. We were moving through a massive cavern. I was on my back on some kind of litter, borne between the shoulders of two men.

It was a struggle to stay conscious. I'd spent most of my life feeling sick and weak, but I'd never known fatigue like this. I was a husk, hollowed out, scraped clean. If any breeze could have reached us so far below the earth, I would have blown away to nothing.

Though every bone and muscle in my body shrieked in protest, I managed to turn my head.

Mal was there, lying on another litter, carried along just a few feet beside me. He was watching me, as if he'd been waiting for me to wake. He reached out.

I found some reservoir of strength and stretched my

hand over the litter's edge. When our fingers met, I heard a sob and realised I was crying. I wept with relief that I would not have to live with the burden of his death. But lodged in my gratitude, I felt a bright thorn of resentment. I wept with rage that I would have to live at all.

We travelled for miles, through passages so tight that they had to lower my litter to the ground and slide me along the rock, through tunnels high and wide enough for ten haycarts. I don't know how long we went on that way. There were no nights and days below ground.

Mal recovered before I did and limped along beside the litter. He'd been injured when the tunnel collapsed, but the Grisha had restored him. What I had endured, what I had embraced, they had no power to heal.

At some point, we stopped at a cave dripping with rows of stalactites. I'd heard one of my carriers call it the Worm's Mouth. When they set me down, Mal was there, and with his help, I managed to get into a sitting position, propped against the cave wall. Even that effort left me dizzy, and when he dabbed his sleeve to my nose, I saw that I was bleeding.

"How bad is it?" I asked.

"You've looked better," he admitted. "The pilgrims mentioned something called the White Cathedral. I think that's where we're headed."

"They're taking me to the Apparat."

He glanced around the cavern. "This is how he escaped the Grand Palace after the coup. How he managed to evade capture for so long."

"It's also how he appeared and disappeared at the fortune-telling party. The mansion was next to the Convent of Sankta Lizabeta, remember? Tamar led me straight to him, and then she let him get away." I heard the bitterness in my weak voice.

Slowly, my addled mind had pieced it all together. Only Tolya and Tamar had known about the party, and they'd arranged for the Apparat to meet me. They'd already been among the pilgrims that morning when I'd nearly started the riot, there to watch the sunrise with the faithful. That was how they'd got to me so quickly. And Tamar had vanished from the Eagle's Nest as soon as she'd begun to suspect danger. I knew that the twins and their sun soldiers were the only reason any of the Grisha had survived, but their lies still stung.

"How are the others?"

Mal looked over to where the ragged group of Grisha huddled in the shadows.

"They know about the fetter," he said. "They're frightened."

"And the firebird?"

He shook his head. "I don't think so."

"I'll tell them soon enough."

"Sergei isn't doing well," Mal continued. "I think he's still in shock. The rest seem to be holding up."

"Genya?"

"She and David stay behind the group. She can't move very quickly." He paused. "The pilgrims call her *Razrusha'ya*."

The Ruined.

"I need to see Tolya and Tamar."

"You need to rest."

"Now," I said. "Please."

He stood, but hesitated. When he spoke again, his voice was raw. "You should have told me what you intended to do."

I looked away. The distance between us felt even deeper than it had before. *I tried to free you, Mal. From the Darkling. From me.*

"You should have let me finish him," I said. "You should have let me die."

When I heard his footsteps fade, I let my chin droop. I could hear my breath coming in shallow pants. When I worked up the strength to lift my eyes, Tolya and Tamar were kneeling before me, their heads bowed.

"Look at me," I said.

They obeyed. Tolya's sleeves were rolled up, and I saw that his massive forearms were emblazoned with suns.

"Why not just tell me?"

"You never would have let us stay so close," replied Tamar.

That was true. Even now I wasn't sure what to make of them.

"If you believe I'm a Saint, why not let me die in the chapel? What if that was meant to be my martyrdom?"

"Then you would have died," said Tolya without hesitation. "We wouldn't have found you in the rubble in time or been able to revive you."

"You let Mal come back for me. After you gave me your vow."

"He broke away," said Tamar.

I lifted a brow. The day Mal could break Tolya's hold was indeed a day of miracles.

Tolya hung his head and heaved his huge shoulders.

"Forgive me," he said. "I couldn't be the one to keep him from you."

I sighed. Some holy warrior.

"Do you serve me?"

"Yes," they said in unison.

"Not the priest?"

"We serve you," said Tolya, his voice a fierce rumble.

"We'll see," I murmured, and waved them away. They rose to go, but I called them back. "Some of the pilgrims have taken to calling Genya *Razrusha'ya*. Warn them once. If they speak that word again, cut out their tongues."

They didn't blink, didn't flinch. They made their bows and were gone.

The White Cathedral was a cavern of alabaster quartz, so vast it might have held a city in its glowing ivory depths. Its walls were damp and bloomed with mushrooms, salt lilies, toadstools shaped like stars. It was buried deep beneath Ravka, somewhere north of the capital.

I wanted to meet the priest standing, so I held tight to Mal's arm as we were brought before him, trying to hide the effort it took just to stay upright and the way my body shook.

"Sankta Alina," the Apparat said, "you are come to us at last."

Then he fell to his knees in his tattered brown robes. He kissed my hand, my hem. He called out to the faithful, thousands of them gathered in the belly of the cavern. When he spoke, the very air seemed to tremble. "We will rise to make a new Ravka," he roared. "A country free from tyrants and kings! We will spill from the earth and drive the shadows back in a tide of righteousness!"

Below us, the pilgrims chanted. *Sankta Alina.*

There were rooms carved into the rock, chambers that glowed ivory and glittered with thin veins of silver. Mal helped me to my quarters, made me eat a few bites of sweet pea porridge, and brought me a pitcher of fresh water to fill the basin. A mirror had been set directly into the stone, and when I glimpsed myself, I let out a little cry. The heavy pitcher shattered on the floor. My skin was pale, stretched tight over jutting bones. My eyes were bruised hollows. My hair had gone completely white, a fall of brittle snow.

I touched my fingertips to the glass. Mal's gaze met mine in the reflection.

"I should have warned you," he said.

"I look like a monster."

"More like a *khitka.*"

"Woodsprites eat children."

"Only when they're hungry," he said.

I tried to smile, to hold tight to this glimmer of warmth between us. But I noticed how far from me he stood, arms at his back, like a guard at attention. He mistook the sheen of tears in my eyes.

"It will get better," he said. "Once you use your power."

"Of course," I replied, turning away from the mirror, feeling exhaustion and pain settle into my bones.

I hesitated, then cast a meaningful glance at the men the Apparat had stationed at the door to the chamber. Mal stepped closer. I wanted to press my cheek to his chest, feel his arms around me, listen to the steady, human beat of his heart. I didn't.

Instead, I spoke low, barely moving my lips. "I've tried," I whispered. "Something's wrong."

He frowned. "You can't summon?" he asked hesitantly. Was there fear in his voice? Hope? Concern? I couldn't tell. All I could sense in him was caution.

"I'm too weak. We're too far below ground. I don't know."

I watched his face, remembering the argument we'd had in the birchwood grove, when he'd asked if I would give up being Grisha. *Never*, I'd said. Never.

Hopelessness crowded in on me, dense and black, heavy like the press of soil. I didn't want to say the words, didn't want to give voice to the fear I'd carried with me through the long, dark miles beneath the earth, but I forced myself to speak it. "The light won't come, Mal. My power is gone."

After

Again, the girl dreamed of ships, but this time, they flew. They had white wings made of canvas, and a clever-eyed fox stood behind the wheel. Sometimes the fox became a prince who kissed her lips and offered her a jewelled crown. Sometimes he was a red hellhound, foam on his muzzle, snapping at her heels as she ran.

Every so often, she dreamed of the firebird. It caught her up in wings of flame and held her as she burned.

Long before word came, she knew the Darkling had survived and that she had failed once more. He had been rescued by his Grisha and now ruled Ravka from a throne wreathed in shadows, surrounded by his monstrous horde. Whether he'd been weakened by what she'd done in the chapel, she didn't know. He was ancient, and power was familiar to him as it had never been to her.

His *oprichniki* guards marched into monasteries and churches, tore up tiles and dug down through floors, seeking the Sun Summoner. Rewards were offered, threats were made, and once again the girl was hunted.

The priest swore that she was safe in the sprawling web of passages that crisscrossed Ravka like a secret map. There were those who claimed the tunnels had been made by armies of the faithful, that it had taken hundreds of years with picks and axes to carve them. Others said they were the work of a monster, a great worm who swallowed soil, rock, root, and gravel, who hollowed out the underground roads that led to the old holy places, where half-remembered prayers were still said. The girl only knew that no place would keep them safe for long.

She looked into the faces of her followers: old men, young women, children, soldiers, farmers, convicts. All she saw were corpses, more bodies for the Darkling to lay at her feet.

The Apparat wept, shouting his gratitude that the Sun Saint still lived, that she had once again been spared. In his wild black gaze, the girl saw a different truth: a dead martyr was less trouble than a living Saint.

The prayers of the faithful rose around the boy and the girl, echoing and multiplying beneath the earth, bouncing off the soaring stone walls of the White Cathedral. The Apparat said it was a holy place, their haven, their sanctuary, their home.

The boy shook his head. He knew a cell when he saw one.

He was wrong, of course. The girl could tell from the way the Apparat watched her struggle to her feet. She heard it in each fragile thump of her heart. This place was no prison. It was a tomb.

But the girl had spent long years being invisible. She'd already had a ghost's life, hidden from the world and from herself. Better than anyone, she knew the power of things long buried.

At night, she heard the boy pacing outside her room, keeping watch with the golden-eyed twins. She lay quiet in her bed, counting her breaths, stretching towards the surface, seeking the light. She thought of the broken skiff, of Novokribirsk, of red names crowding a crooked church wall. She remembered little human heaps slumped beneath the golden dome; Marie's butchered body; Fedyor, who had once saved her life. She heard the pilgrims' songs and exhortations. She thought of the volcra and of Genya huddled in the dark.

The girl touched the collar at her neck, the fetter at her wrist. So many men had tried to make her a queen. Now she understood that she was meant for something more.

The Darkling had told her he was destined to rule. He had claimed his throne and a part of her too. He was welcome to it. For the living and the dead, she would make herself a reckoning.

She would rise.

Acknowledgments

The problem with acknowledgements is that they quickly devolve into long lists of names suitable for skimming. But many people are required to make a book happen, and they deserve recognition, so please bear with me. (If it gets boring, I recommend singing aloud. Get a friend to beatbox for you. I'll wait.)

As a new author, you quickly learn how much you're going to ask of your agent: You need her to be a diplomat, a therapist, an advocate, and occasionally, a brawler. How lucky for me that I found all of these things in the remarkable Joanna Volpe. Many thanks to the entire team at New Leaf Literary and Media, including Pouya Shahbazian, Kathleen Ortiz, and Danielle Barthel.

My editor, Noa Wheeler, is clearly a master of the Small Science. She pushes here, prods there, asks the questions you don't want to hear, and at the end of it all, you see your story transformed into something so much better. It's almost like magic.

I want to thank everyone at Macmillan/Holt Children's. I love this venerable, badass, brilliant house, and I'm so proud to be a part of it. Special thanks to Jean Feiwel and Laura Godwin, who have gone out of their way for this series again and again, the fierce Angus Killick, the glamorous Elizabeth Fithian, the ever on-point

Allison Verost, the magnificent Molly Brouillette, and Jon Yaged, who is still punk rock. Ksenia Winnicki, my fellow fangirl, worked tirelessly to reach out to bloggers. Kate Lied got the Fierce Reads tour on the road. Karen Frangipane and Kathryn Bhirud made the beautiful trailer for *Shadow and Bone* (that's how epic's done, son). I'm grateful to Rich Deas, April Ward, Ashley Halsey, Jen Wang, and Keith Thompson, who make books into art. Also Mark von Bargen, Vannessa Cronin, and all the wonderful people in sales who help put my books into people's hands.

Now let's talk about my army: the brave and beautiful Michelle Chihara of thisblueangel.com; Joshua Joy Kamensky, who sustains me with music, wit, and kindness; Morgan Fahey, a bold woman who makes bold claims – also a generous reader and a great wartime consigliere; Sarah Mesle of sunsetandecho.com, who understands structure and story and heart, and all of the ways they fit together; and Liz Hamilton (aka Zenith Nadir of Darlings Are Dying), who can work copy and a cocktail like nobody's business. Gamynne Guillote brought Grisha swag to life with patience and an unerring eye. Love also to Peter Bibring, Brandon Harvey, Dan Braun, Jon Zerolnik, Michael Pessah, Heather Repenning, Kurt Mattilan, Rico Gagliano, Corey Ellis, William Lexner and the Brotherhood Without Banners (particularly Andi and Ben Galusha, Lady Narcissa, Katie Rask, Lee and Rachel Greenberg, Xray the Enforcer, Blackfyre, Adam Tesh, and the Mountain Goat), Ann Kingman of Books on the Nightstand, E. Aaron Wilson and Laura Recchi, Laurie Wheeler, Viviane Hebel of HebelDesign. com, David Peterson, Aman Chaudhary, Tracey Taylor, and Romi Cortier. These people supported me and the Grisha Trilogy at every step, and I can't tell you how much I value and adore them. I want to give a special shout to Rachel Tejada, Austin Wilkin, and Ray Tejada, who helped me expand the Grishaverse with infinite creativity and support.

Certain supergeniuses helped to make the impossible improbable: the lovely Heather Joy Kamensky talked me through the logistics of David's mirrored dishes; John Williams helped me to build the *Hummingbird*; and Davey Krieger advised me on the boarding and building of ships and other things nautical (though he will most likely be horrified by the liberties I've taken).

Many thanks to the inspiring women of Pub(lishing) Crawl – particularly Amie Kaufman, Susan Dennard, and Sarah J. Maas. Also, Jacob Clifton, Jenn Rush, Erica O'Rourke, Lia Keyes, Claire Legrand, Anna Banks (how *dare* you), Emmy Laybourne, and the Apocalypsies. Several extraordinary writers supported this trilogy early and loudly: Veronica Roth, Cinda Williams Chima, Seanan McGuire, Alyssa Rosenberg, and the inimitable Laini Taylor. Finally, my LA crew, especially Jenn Bosworth, Abby McDonald, Gretchen McNeil, Jessica Brody, Jessica Morgan, Julia Collard, Sarah Wilson Etienne, Jenn Reese, and Kristen Kittscher. Ladies, without you, I'd get right stabby. Thanks for keeping me (mostly) sane.

I dedicated this book to my mother, but she also deserves extra thanks here. I couldn't have made it through the first draft of *Siege and Storm* without her there to read pages, offer encouragement, and keep me in seaweed snacks. She is a marvellous mom and an even better friend. Irritable. Cantankerous. Defiant. These are our words.

I am forever indebted to the incredible booksellers, librarians, and bloggers who talked up *Shadow and Bone* and foisted it on friends, customers, and hapless passersby

And finally, to my marvellous readers: Thank you for every email, every tweet, every gif. You make me grateful each day.

Turn the page for

SIEGE AND STORM

bonus materials

SHADOW AND BONE TRILOGY

CHARACTER ART

One of the most surprising and inspiring perks of becoming a published author has been seeing my characters brought to life by talented artists.

I'm delighted to introduce a stunning new portrait of Nikolai Lantsov – prince, privateer and star of my forthcoming duology, King of Scars – drawn by the always brilliant Kevin Wada.

—LEIGH BARDUGO

Nikolai Lantsov

LEIGH BARDUGO

talks about *Siege and Storm*

As the second book in a trilogy, how was writing *Siege and Storm* different from writing *Shadow and Bone*?

It was so much more intense. I'd never written under a deadline before, and I was terrified that I wouldn't be able to deliver or that my editor would take one look at the new manuscript and scream in horror. (For all I know, she did.) *Siege and Storm* also felt more complicated than *Shadow and Bone*. The book is longer, I go more deeply into the politics and power dynamics of the world, and there are simply more characters on the page. Still, I'll never forget the feeling of accomplishment I had when I turned in my first draft. It was proof that *Shadow and Bone* wasn't a fluke, that I had a process, that I could actually do this job.

Die-hard fans often write about the Shadow and Bone Trilogy's genre. Do you agree when readers identify it as high fantasy or dark fantasy?
What do you call it?

I like "dark fantasy," though I'm not totally sure what it means. Personally, I'm fond of the term "tsarpunk." My editor and I coined it as a joke, but it really does seem to say the most about the series. When people hear "high fantasy" or "epic fantasy," they tend to think of worlds based on medieval Europe. But the world of the Grisha Trilogy was inspired by tsarist Russia of the early 1800s— think sabers, muskets, and samovars instead of broadswords, crossbows, and tankards. So for now, I'm sticking with tsarpunk. Or just waggling my fingers and saying "Faaaantasy!"

You have done an amazing job of building this world, basing it on Russia but making it something all its own. Do your readers recognize the Russian themes and imagery? Why did you choose to infuse hints of this culture into Ravka?

Thank you! I wanted to take readers someplace a little different but still grounded in reality. Even people who know nothing about Russia have very strong images associated with its culture. I felt it was a good point of departure for a fantasy world. Some people haven't liked the choices I made with regard to the world, and I have to respect that, but at the same time, it's incredible to get e-mail from fans in Russia and Ukraine who are excited about the book. I've also had readers tell me that *Shadow and Bone* got them going on a Russian culture binge. I've seen posts from them on Russian folklore and received requests for recommendations on Russian authors. One girl on tumblr reached out to tell me she petitioned her school for a Russian language elective. It's nice to know that Ravka led them there.

What was the most difficult scene to write in *Siege and Storm*? What was your favorite scene to write?

Writing the final battle scene almost killed me. It was originally nearly one hundred pages long, and I had to rewrite it several times before I realized that there was simply too much happening. I ended up moving two really big moments into the third book, *Ruin and Rising*, and suddenly the pacing made sense.

As for favorite scenes, I loved writing the argument between Sturmhond, Mal, and Alina when Sturmhond proposes. If I could spend all my days writing emotionally weighted banter, I'd be pretty content.

First Mal, then the Darkling, and now Sturmhond—you've given readers quite the lineup of great male characters. What is your favorite defining characteristic about these men? And who is your favorite to write?

Competence! They're all very good at what they do. But of course, they all falter, too, and that's what makes their journeys interesting to me. Sturmhond is definitely the most fun to write. Most of my characters grapple with who they are and whether they're up to the task at hand, but Sturmhond is pure confidence, total clarity of intent.

The Darkling is an especially complex character—he brings out both the best and the worst in Alina. Do you think Mal does the same to her?

Interesting question. I guess I'd say that the Darkling and Mal challenge Alina in different ways—and vice versa.

Both of them force her to question who she wants to be, and as her circumstances change, her answer to that question changes as well. But she has a powerful effect on them, too. Not getting what you want can be quite an education.

Mal is Alina's best friend and love interest. Do you think it's possible to be friends with someone you are attracted to and not be linked romantically? Inquiring minds want to know!
Ha! Really, I think it just depends on the depth of the attraction. I mean, I have friends who are easy on the eyes, and I can appreciate that without getting goofy about it. But there's a big difference between that and really falling for someone. When your heart gets involved, all bets are off. I've been there, too, and I can't say I'd ever want to go back again.

Which order do you relate to best—Corporalki, Etherealki, or Materialki?
I'd love to be a Corporalnik because I'm a belligerent and bloodthirsty sort. But at heart, I'm probably a Materialnik. I'm happiest working away in solitude, and I'm way too lazy to go charging into battle.

The True Sea is a key setting in *Siege and Storm*. Did you research seafaring travel before you began to write this book? If so, how?
Confession: I do not like nautical research. But the story needed to go to sea, so I had to go there, too. I love reading about the American Revolution, so I began with books like *Patriot Pirates* and *George Washington's Secret Navy*. I

found *Pirates & Patriots of the Revolution: An Illustrated Encyclopedia of Colonial Seamanship* invaluable because of the clear diagrams of sails and knots and the illustrations of everything from a ditty bag to a battle whistle. I was also lucky enough to have friends I could call on, like Davey Krieger, who is a legitimate pirate expert.

When discussing *Siege and Storm*, it is often said, "Darkness never dies." This is pretty terrifying! How does this idea play out in the book?

The line refers to the Darkling's return and to the new way he's found to use his power. But it's also about what Alina is dealing with as she comes to grips with her own strength, what it means to be the Sun Summoner, and the choices she made at the end of *Shadow and Bone*. I'm not interested in characters who are just one thing, who are wholly evil or wholly good. People aren't like that. We all have our own darkness to contend with, and that isn't necessarily a bad thing.

We get to see more of the volcra, the man-eating beasts who live in the Fold, in *Siege and Storm*. Do any of your characters or monsters haunt your dreams? Do any of them come from your dreams?

Not my dreams, exactly. I was raised by my grandparents, and one end of their house was separated from the other by this long, dark hallway. Every time I had to go there, I would psyche myself up, then bolt to the other end. I was always sure something was right behind me, ready to snag me by the ankle or catch the back of my nightgown. I'd completely forgotten about it until recently, but now I wonder if that wasn't my own little Shadow Fold.

I'd love to dream about my world—even the scary parts—but I've only dreamed of Ravka once. An episode of the Food Network's *Chopped* was taking place in the Shadow Fold, and I was competing against the Darkling. I woke up right when Ted told us to open our baskets.

Alina is a strong, brave character, though her flaws keep her human and make her easy to identify with. What heroines in literature have you admired?

I love Tamora Pierce's Alanna. I love George R. R. Martin's Arya Stark and Brienne of Tarth. Veronica Roth and I were talking about this recently, and it was funny because when she mentioned Jane Eyre, I only partially jokingly shouted out "Bertha Rochester!" It's not that I admire Bertha—actually, no, maybe I do. She's crazy, but she also refuses to be invisible. "You want to put me in this attic? You want to nab yourself some unsullied child bride? Fine, Imma burn this place *down*." So often in the classics, women who are difficult or demanding or who want something other than what the world offers end up committing suicide in ennobling, picturesque fashion. At least Bertha does some damage on the way out.

Costumes and cosmetics can be powerful devices, as we see when Alina lets Genya change her appearance to fit in with the Grisha. In addition to being a writer, you have also been a makeup artist. Does the experience of creating

visual art extend to your writing?

I think makeup is really just another way of creating illusion. When I was a makeup artist, whether I was building something glamorous or grotesque, the challenge was to bring a little bit of fantasy to life, and to do it in a way that felt seamless to the audience. Some days I got it right. Some days I failed in spectacular fashion.

Second books can often be more difficult to write than the first. Of the series you've read and movies you've seen, what are your favorite sequels?

Anne Rice's *The Vampire Lestat* comes to mind. Also, George R. R. Martin's A Song of Ice and Fire is probably my favorite series, but I can never decide if I prefer *A Clash of Kings* or *A Storm of Swords*. When it comes to movies, is there any question? Best sequel of all time is easily *The Empire Strikes Back*. It set the standard for great action, crushing heartbreak, and killer cliffhangers.

If you could write anywhere, where would it be?

Sometimes I imagine a little cabin on the coast, someplace gray and rainy and lashed by waves. But I also daydream about Venice, Italy. It's my favorite city. I like to fantasize about staying in a loft or a palazzo, preferably somewhere near the Accademia or the Peggy Guggenheim Collection. I'd write in the morning, then go to the museums or explore in the afternoon. While we're at it, Henry Cavill happens to be staying next door, and he likes to drop by to discuss *Game of Thrones*.

What would fans be surprised to learn about you?

I think I've blown any sense of mystery to pieces by now. I don't know. I think with social media the way it is, people get only the best of you. They don't get you on your dark days or your petty days. I think readers would be surprised to learn that I'm quite shy and grumpy. I am many dwarves.

Did you set out to write one book or a trilogy when you started _Shadow and Bone_?

Shadow and Bone was my first book, and when I sat down to write it, my only goal was to complete it. I had no thoughts of a series in my head. But about halfway through, I realized the story was bigger than I'd initially intended. I scrapped the original ending and started making notes for a second and a third book. Still, I didn't know if anyone would want the first book, let alone a trilogy, so I tried to give _Shadow and Bone_ an ending that would satisfy even if the rest of the story never got told.

What can we expect from the third book in the series, _Ruin and Rising_? No spoilers, please!

It's almost impossible to talk about this book without revealing spoilers, but here's what you need to know:

1. Not everyone is going to survive.
2. Those who do will be much changed.
3. Yes, you will learn the Darkling's true name. Despite the Internet rumors, it is not Hubert.

ENTER THE
GRISHAVERSE

THE SHADOW AND BONE TRILOGY

THE SIX OF CROWS DUOLOGY

THE WANDERING ISLE

◉ LEFLII

NOVYI ZEM

● WEDDLE

REB HARBOR

EAMES HARBOR

SHRIFTPORT

EAMES CHIN

◉ COFTON

SOUTHERN COLONIES

JELKA

VILKI

THE BONE ROAD

THE TRUE SEA

KETTERDAM

KERCH

LAND BRIDGE

Map illustration by Keith Thompson

THE GRISHA

SOLDIERS OF THE SECOND ARMY
MASTERS OF THE SMALL SCIENCE

CORPORALKI
(The Order of the Living and the Dead)

Heartrenders
Healers

ETHEREALKI
(The Order of Summoners)

Squallers
Inferni
Tidemakers

MATERIALKI
(The Order of Fabrikators)

Durasts
Alkemi

For my mother,
who believed even when I didn't.

ORION CHILDREN'S BOOKS

First published in Great Britain in 2013 by Indigo
This edition published in Great Britain in 2018 by Hodder and Stoughton

3 5 7 9 10 8 6 4

ISBN 978-1-51010-526-3

Typeset by Input Data Services Ltd, Somerset

Printed and bound in Great Britain by CPI Group (UK) Ltd, Croydon CRO 4YY

The paper and board used in this book are made
from wood from responsible sources.

MIX
Paper from
responsible sources
FSC® C104740
www.fsc.org

Orion Children's Books
An imprint of
Hachette Children's Group
Part of Hodder and Stoughton
Carmelite House
50 Victoria Embankment
London EC4Y 0DZ

An Hachette UK Company
www.hachette.co.uk

www.hachettechildrens.co.uk

SIEGE
AND
STORM

LEIGH BARDUGO

Orion